The Man
I Never Met

A Novel

Elle Cook

DELL BOOKS
New York

A Dell Trade Paperback Original

Copyright © 2022 by Elle Cook

Published in the United States by Dell, an imprint of Random House, a division of Penguin Random House LLC, New York.

DELL is a registered trademark and the D colophon is a trademark of Penguin Random House LLC.

Library of Congress Cataloging-in-Publication Data
Names: Cook, Elle, author.
Title: The man I never met: a novel / Elle Cook.
Description: New York: Dell Books, [2022]
Identifiers: LCCN 2022019427 (print) | LCCN 2022019428 (ebook) |
ISBN 9780593500859 (trade paperback; acid-free paper) |
ISBN 9780593500866 (ebook)
Subjects: LCGFT: Romance fiction. | Novels.
Classification: LCC PR6103.O6624 M36 2022 (print) |
LCC PR6103.O6624 (ebook) | DDC 823/.92—dc23/eng/20220422
LC record available at https://lccn.loc.gov/2022019427
LC ebook record available at https://lccn.loc.gov/2022019428

Printed in the United States of America on acid-free paper

randomhousebooks.com

2 4 6 8 9 7 5 3 1

Book design by Fritz Metsch

For Steve,
the man I almost lost.

And for Mr. Henry Lewi,
the man who saved him.

The Man
I Never Met

Chapter 1

Hannah, December

DO YOU REMEMBER where you were and what you were doing the moment your life changed forever? I do. I was standing outside the gym, hair in a bit of a tangle, in need of a shower after a grueling spin class, rifling in my bag for my gloves while my mobile buzzed away. But of course I didn't know it at the time. That's always how it is, though, isn't it? You never realize the true significance of a moment until later.

I grab my phone, still unable to find the gloves that have disappeared into the depths of my bag. The December weather is biting cold, and although it's only early evening the sky is already a shade of ink, strewn with gray clouds that look as if they've been painted on and dragged gently from one side of the canvas to the other.

The dialing code says +1 and so I pause momentarily as my phone continues to vibrate in my hand. Where on earth is +1? Call centers start with a random assortment of codes and this doesn't look like any of those.

"Hello?" I ask.

"Hello," a man, with an American accent, replies. And then in a deeper, friendlier tone, "Jonathan White?"

I laugh. "Do I sound like a Jonathan White?"

"Oh, no. I'm sorry. I mean, is he there?"

"No. Sorry, you've got the wrong number."

A pause, a rustle of papers. "OK. Sorry. Bye."

"Bye," I say, but he's already gone. And then barely ten seconds pass before my phone rings again.

I draw out the word "Hello" as I answer—the same +1 number shining on my screen.

"Oh, not again," he says in exasperation. "How have I dialed it wrong a second time? I can't be that stupid." Which makes me laugh again, although not unkindly.

"I think you have."

Silence and then, "Hold on."

I wait, smiling with amusement. The cold weather is seemingly not as cold now as it was before.

"Is this plus-four-four . . ." and he reels out a list of digits that are most certainly mine.

"It is. What number were you looking for?"

"This one."

I try not to laugh.

"Shit," he replies. "I wrote it down wrong. I'm supposed to call this number at four P.M. UK time, for a job interview."

"Not this number, I'm afraid. Maybe try switching one of the digits?"

"Yeah," he says uncertainly. "But which one? There's about a billion possible combinations."

"I have no idea. Where are you ringing from?"

"Texas."

"And you have a job interview with someone on a UK number? Are you getting a job over here?" I'm so nosy.

"Hopefully . . ."

"Unlikely, given you're on the phone to me and you should be answering questions about . . . whatever it is you're interviewing for."

"Buildings. I should be answering questions about buildings right about now. Shit."

"Buildings?"

"Architecture, specifically." He has a really nice voice. Deep, but not too deep.

"Try and google the office number," I suggest, in case he really is that stupid and hasn't thought of it.

"I'm already on it." He's speaking quickly, both of us aware that he should be minutes into an interview by now.

"Well, good luck. I hope you get it."

"The right number or the job?"

"Both. Starting with the right number," I say, with a smile.

"Thanks. Sorry for bothering you. Twice."

"It's fine. I'm keen to know now if you get the job."

"Thanks again," he says. "Bye."

"Bye," I reply as the line goes dead. I stare at the phone for a few seconds, hoping he isn't silly enough to ring the same number a third time . . . just to be sure. It wouldn't be a terrible thing if he rings again, but now I want this man with the lovely voice to actually call the correct number, answer questions about buildings, and get the job. Whomever he might be.

It's not really the done thing to come home from an hour's spin class and crack open both a microwave meal and a large glass of wine, but given it's Friday night, that's what I do. And anyway I wouldn't have been at the gym if I hadn't been canceled by a flaky man, with whom I'd already decided I would categorically *not* reschedule. He's done this twice now and we still haven't actually had a first date yet. My best friend, Miranda, calls it Cancel-itis. So this glass of wine was the one that I would have had if I had been out. There, I have justified that, if not the hideous microwave curry.

Hours later I flick through the various options on TV and wonder how it is that I've managed to watch everything decent on Netflix when I really don't spend that much time at home. Perhaps, for once, I should watch the news and at least try to be as informed as my co-workers about the daily goings-on in the world. I really need to work with people who watch more trashy dramas than *Question Time*.

Next to me my phone dings, telling me I have a message. I read it. It's from a number I don't recognize, until I look closer and see it's the American's. The message contains three words. I got it.

I mute the TV and let it continue showing me a background of filler news pieces that I haven't been paying attention to.

Does he want a reply? Does he expect one? I'm glad, I type, followed by, Congratulations. I'm guessing you found the right number in the end.

I didn't pose it as a question. I didn't expect a reply, but one comes moments later.

Yeah. I apologized for being a few minutes late and told him what I'd done. He was cool about it.

I'm glad, I type. And then I delete it because it is exactly what I've written a moment ago. I replace it with, Always best to be honest.

Definitely.

I watch the screen. He isn't typing. It's my turn to reply, but I can't think of anything else to say and so, after a moment, he resumes.

So, England in January. Cold?

A smile finds the corners of my mouth. Very. Sorry about that. Is that when you arrive?

Exactly one month from now. Yeah.

Where are you in Texas?

Austin, he replies.

No, I have no idea where that is. I leave the chat, google Austin, Texas, and then open the chat window back up, ready to display my newfound knowledge. Warm this time of year.

Warm all times of year.

I googled, I confess. Capital city of Texas, so Wikipedia tells me. I've just discovered Houston is also in Texas. So there you go.

He replies with a laughter emoji and then, Where are you?

London.

Great. Now I'll know another person when I get there.

I look at his message, unsure what to think. Is he suggesting we meet up? Become friends? I look at the message so long that the screen goes black and I have to key in my code to unlock it again. It shows his number and, underneath, that he's still online. What's your name? I ask.

Davey. Yours?

Hannah.

Nice to meet you, Hannah.

I smile again. It is nice to meet him. Albeit, this is the strangest way I've ever "met" anyone. How old are you? I ask.

Twenty-nine. And then another message. I've been told it's not OK to ask a woman her age, so . . .

I'm twenty-seven, I reply to his leading prompt. I'm enjoying this and wonder now for the first time what he looks like, this twenty-nine-year-old man from Texas. His WhatsApp profile picture is blank, the circle at the top of the chat displaying the standard gray-and-white icon. Who does that? Mind you, mine is a picture of our family dog wearing sunglasses, so I'm not exactly one to talk.

What time is it there? he asks.

Almost 11 P.M.

It was nice talking to you, Hannah.

Oh. That's a blunt ending to the conversation, and disappointment that he's signing off makes me pause before replying, **Like-wise.**

I'd like to talk again. If you'd like to, that is, he suggests.

I let that message display on the screen for a moment as I think about it. How to reply without sounding eager or utterly disinterested?

I opt for a casual, **Sure.**

OK, he says.

And then he's gone.

Chapter 2

I WAKE WITH sweet relief that it's not a work day. I only get to enjoy that feeling twice a week and I revel in it. I don't hate my job. I work in marketing, and it pays the bills and means I can afford a couple of decent holidays a year. It'll do for now, although I know I should probably have my eye on the next career horizon, but I haven't quite worked out what that might be yet. I get up, slowly, and only after I've had the most amazing lie-in. I toy with the idea of making something creative for brunch. But avocado on toast is about as creative as I ever get. For a reason that I can't pinpoint, today I fancy pancakes and maple syrup, but I'm not going to make them. Not when there's a great brunch spot down the road that will make them better than I can. But that involves getting dressed and heading out. And if I do that, it means I miss one of my favorite weekend mid-morning rituals, talking to my neighbor Joan over the fence. And I couldn't miss that. I couldn't do that to her.

I live in a ground-floor flat, which I've already sworn to myself I will never, ever leave. If I do, it's because I've died and they've had to take me out in a box. Nowhere will I get a ground-floor two-bed flat with a garden at this price ever again. I know this because I have a Rightmove alert set up, which I salivate over whenever it arrives in my inbox. I used to share my flat with Miranda, but when she moved out to live with her boyfriend,

Paul, I dug deep and decided to cover the cost of the entire rent myself, instead of looking for a one-bed somewhere else. I can afford it, just. Mainly because Joan next door owns both her building and mine and might not be quite up to date with current rental prices. She shrugs it off, saying that I and the never-there cabin-crew girl from upstairs take such good care of our flats that she wouldn't drive us out with rent increases.

I pull my dressing gown around me and put on my Ugg boots. None of that attire is going to stop the crispness of the winter day penetrating my skin, but it's bright outside, which is something.

Joan and I have a little weekend ritual. I text her when I'm awake, and she cranks up her Nespresso machine. Five minutes later we meet in our back gardens by the fence. She hands me one of her posh coffees and I bring out a plate of supermarket biscuits. It's not really a fair trade, but Joan balked when I suggested that I might buy myself a proper coffee machine. I think she thought I was going to abandon our chats, so I conceded that I wouldn't and she promised to keep me in a vibrant array of colorful coffee capsules every weekend.

I can already smell the coffee as I open the back door, slip out, and close it behind me to keep the warmth in. "What's this one today?" I call as I stand by the fence, resting my elbows on it and looking into her perfectly cultivated garden. Her back door is open and she can hear me while she's inside her kitchen, with the whoosh of the final cup being made by the machine. Even in the depths of winter her garden looks lush and green, as if part of a National Trust garden had upped and brought itself straight to Wanstead.

Joan appears on cue, with a cup in each hand and a coffee leaflet in her teeth. She leans toward me and I take the leaflet from her, as well as the cup she offers.

"I thought we'd try Firenze Arpeggio today," she declares.

I read the leaflet. "Intense and creamy. Aren't they all?"

I sip. It tastes exactly the same as the one from last week. It's delicious and does exactly what I want it to do, hitting my taste-buds with a caffeinated heat that I need in this cold weather.

Joan nods and says, "Definitely a four out of five." She's lived here since she inherited the house from her mum about thirty years ago. I've never asked how old she is, but I've pieced together a gradual timeline from her stories and have decided she's probably in her seventies, at a push. Her husband died twenty years ago or so, but she's not lonely, as far as I can tell. She's out and about at all hours of the day, driving fiercely in her battered old Citroën Saxo as if she's an eighteen-year-old boy high on life and the success of a freshly passed driving test. I used to think these coffee mornings were for her. But now I think they actually hold her up from her life. I'm sobered by this as I tuck into a chocolate biscuit and offer the plate to her.

"So, what's the latest news from the young, free, and single?" she asks, dipping a biscuit into her cup and leaving it there to soak for far too long. I watch, waiting for it to fall into her cup with a dissatisfying floop noise. Joan is no amateur and saves it at the final second. "Last night's date?" she prompts. "Not still in there, is he?"

"No!" I exclaim, horrified. "I don't sleep with men on the first date."

"Anymore," Joan points out.

"Anymore," I confirm sheepishly. "I didn't go."

"We've talked about this," Joan chastises. "You only live once. How will you know if he's the one, if you don't even go on a date with him?"

"I didn't go," I say, nibbling another biscuit—this will be my brunch, I decide—"because he stood me up. Or, rather, he can-celed. Again. And so that's it."

"Are we swearing off men again?"

I shake my head. "No. That way lies madness. But I'm swearing off him."

"Good girl. On to the next."

I look at Joan. Does she imagine I have a conveyor belt of men that I'm working my way through? I offer a nod rather than a comment. "What are you doing today?" I ask, happy to change the subject.

"Lunch at my friend Sheila's, drinks with a lovely man named Geoff this evening."

"Really? Who's Geoff?" I dip my biscuit into my coffee, daring to hold it in for a fraction longer than I should. Unsurprisingly, it disappears into the depths of the dark liquid and I'm left deciding whether to drink/eat it or fish it out with my fingers. I do neither.

Joan doesn't answer. She's looking into my cup and then raises an eyebrow at me. "Do you want a new coffee?"

I laugh at myself. "No, this one's still good."

She hides a snigger. "Geoff's a lovely man I've been introduced to by my daughter. Thinks I'm lonely."

"Are you?"

"Not really, but no man is an island, and all that."

A date will be a good thing for Joan. "And what's he like—this Geoff?"

"He's very nice. Good-looking. A bit younger than me."

"Joan," I joke. "You minx!"

She laughs, enjoying the limelight focusing on her love life for once. Not that I have a love life. Just the distant thought that there might be one. I date. But it's a string of first dates and I'm exhausted. Every now and again they progress to a second date. Sometimes even a third. And then it all fizzles out. The lure of dating apps and the ease with which we can swipe someone into our lives, then swipe someone out of our lives, means that now we're forever chasing something else, someone else. It's making us lazy.

I long for those magic days Joan talks about when she met her husband as they both tried to rent the last deck chair on Southend seafront, both finding the other attractive and neither of them deciding to rent the chair. Instead her future husband bought them both an ice cream, and they sat on the sand under the pier to escape the heat of the midday summer sun. Why don't people meet like that now? I drink my coffee, forgetting there's a clump of soggy biscuit lurking within its depths, which hits me in the mouth as Joan continues to tell me about Geoff, whose picture she's seen, but whom she's never actually spoken to. At my suggestion, Joan fetches her mobile and proudly displays a photo of Geoff.

"Is he wearing a leather jacket?" I ask admiringly. This seventy-something man is trendier than I am.

"He is," Joan says, then takes the phone back and looks at Geoff's image. "I do hope he's not a complete bastard," she goes on, and I cough out the last of my biscuit-laced coffee.

Even Joan's love life is more exciting than mine, I reflect as I go about the worst part of my weekend—the ritual of cleaning my flat from top to bottom. I save it for Saturday so that it's out of the way, leaving Sunday blissfully free.

I don't know why, but I think about Davey, a man I've never met or seen a photograph of, but to whom I have spoken. In stark contrast to Joan, who hasn't spoken to Geoff but who she has seen in a photograph.

If Davey messages me again, as he says he would, I'm going to get brave and ask for a photograph. Would that come across as strange? I just want to know what he looks like now. Maybe I won't ask next time. I'll ask the time after that. If he messages, that is.

* * *

We're sitting in the pub that evening surrounded by Christmas decorations. It's the only "old man" pub, as Miranda and I affectionately name it, that's near us. Brown bar, brown tables, brown chairs, cheap chrysanthemums in dusty jars. But on Saturdays the owner's Thai wife takes over the kitchen and the food offering moves up a few notches. Paul, Miranda, and I used to eat here every Saturday night before she moved in with him, and it's a tradition we're loath to stop, now that the food's got so good.

"I swear this is cheaper than a takeaway," Paul says, tucking into his pad thai. Every week he says he's going to try something different from the menu. Every week he doesn't. He and Miranda have been together for five years and are annoyingly perfect for each other, but they don't rub it in, which I appreciate. I'm not lonely. But there are some couples who make you realize you've been alone for quite some time. My last proper boyfriend was two years ago, give or take. And it wasn't even that proper. Does seven and a half months count? I like to think it does or it's even sadder than I thought.

The waitress brings us our second carafe of house red, and Wham!'s "Last Christmas" plays on a never-ending rotation of festive music as fairy lights twinkle on and off behind the bar. Outside it's dark and bitterly cold—a stark contrast to in here, and to our Thai food, which is so entirely warming it makes me want to book a holiday to distant shores. I've not been to Thailand and I make a note to look at prices for a break sometime next year. Which begs the question of whom I would go with.

Miranda no longer goes on holidays without Paul, which is fair enough when you only get twenty-one paid days per year. I get twenty-five, but I don't remind Miranda of this when we chat about how I've managed to save up a few days to go home and see my parents and stay with them in between Christmas and New

Year's. I save up those days every year. I'm meticulous about it. I pull out my phone to set myself a reminder to ask a few old uni friends if they'd be up for a chilled Thailand trip next year, and find a message on my phone. While I'm opening it up, a third carafe arrives, and Miranda and Paul look at it and then at me in confusion. None of us ordered this, and none of us are volunteering to tell the waitress.

"Things are going to get messy," Miranda declares in a sing-song voice, before giving me a wicked look and spooning some of her yellow curry into her mouth.

Davey has messaged a simple Hi, twenty-five minutes ago. I look at the message and bite my lip to prevent a smile from forming. It will lead to questions from my best friends, which will suddenly turn into an inquisition.

The reason I pulled my phone from my bag is entirely forgotten and I message back an equally simple Hi.

He's online and replying. Is it weird I'm messaging you again? After I sent it, I thought this might come across as weird.

It takes me a moment to think and I reply honestly, This is kind of weird. But good weird.

Yeah, that's what I was hoping for. How's your day going?

Miranda coughs pointedly and then says, "Excuse me. Phones? At the table? Didn't we agree we wouldn't be those friends who Instagram their nights away while out with each other?"

I look up and apologize, while making no effort to put my phone down. I reply to Davey quickly, It's still going actually. Can I message you later?

Sure, he says and signs off.

It's Paul who knows something's amiss. "You're smiling. She's smiling," he says to Miranda, handing her the invisible baton to investigate further.

"Ye-e-es," Miranda says slowly. "Thank you for the subtitles."

Oh no, she has that schoolmarm voice that says I'm not getting out of here alive. Only there's nothing to tell, so this should be easy. I wait for the questions to begin.

"Who is he?" Miranda cuts to the chase and tops up my wineglass. She nudges it toward me as if it's truth serum.

"No one," I say far too casually and then regret it immediately. I try a better tone. "I mean . . . actually he really is no one. He rang me by mistake yesterday afternoon and we got chatting. He's nice. He lives in the US and he's moving here in a month. That's it. The whole story."

Miranda's mouth drops open and, in a very quiet voice, she asks, "You spoke to a man who rang you by mistake and you've managed to get him to move continents for you, in under twenty-four hours?"

I laugh so hard I spit wine, which is so incredibly unattractive, but my friends have never cared about that kind of thing. "Of course not," I say and then explain the situation, with a bit more detail thrown in. At the end they both hurl questions at me.

"Will I like him?" Paul asks.

"Is he fit?" Miranda asks.

Paul gives her such a look.

"I think you're both jumping the gun a bit here. Nothing's happening. And, Miranda," I say, "I don't know what he looks like. He hasn't added a profile picture." Although I do really hope he's fit. But I don't know why. What does it matter, really? Let's say we do get along and become friends when he moves here, then who cares what he looks like? What kind of shallow people care what friends look like?

"Have you looked up his social-media accounts?" Miranda says, and immediately grabs her phone and opens Instagram.

"No," I reply. "I don't know his last name. And I don't immediately stalk social media for guys I'm"—what am I doing with

Davey?—"messaging," I finish. This is a lie. I do absolutely always stalk social media for guys I'm messaging. But I'm enjoying not having been able to do this, so far.

"Hannah Gallagher," Miranda chastises. "Why don't you know his last name?"

"It's not come up in conversation."

"How old is he?" Paul cuts in.

"Twenty-nine."

Miranda folds her arms. "*That* came up in conversation then."

There's silence all around, and I take a sip of wine so that I'm not expected to speak.

"OK, we'll leave this there. For now," Paul suggests, as if he's in a police drama and is preparing to switch off the interview tape.

"Are you going to talk to him later?" Miranda asks. But I don't even get the chance to reply as she continues, "Find out his last name. And get a picture."

"Oh my God," I mutter as I drink more wine. I wonder if Joan's getting this much flak about Geoff from *her* friends.

I don't text Davey back that night, as I said I would, because I'm a terribly drunk human being by the end of the evening. By the time we've settled the bill, we've finished all the wine and have finally moved on to Singha beers, which I don't even like that much, but "one for the road" is hard to argue with.

Paul and Miranda walk me back to my place, which is on the way to theirs. The night is full of Christmas parties chucking out of restaurants and moving from bar to bar. We run the gauntlet of revelers with a smile on our faces that we might not have at any other time of year. Christmas does that to people. It's that special time of the year when anything goes. Even snogging someone at an office Christmas party becomes the norm, when you wouldn't snog them in the middle of October.

Miranda trips in her heels and we grab hold of her, laughing.

She insists on wearing them, even though she's incredibly tall. She owns her height. I own my medium stature by only ever wearing flats. I've never gotten the hang of wearing proper high heels. I'm like a baby giraffe that's just been born when I try to wear them. So I don't bother. But Miranda is a thing of wonder. Men stop and stare, but she has no space for that in her life. Totally oblivious. She has a height criteria that any man she dates has to fulfill, and she and Paul met because they were quite literally the only two people queuing at a bar who were head and shoulders above everyone else around them.

I often wonder what it would be like to meet someone who simply . . . fits. I'm ready to do that, I think. Even though my life is full of friends, work, family, fun things. Wouldn't it be nice to share that with someone? To have a cheerleader. To cheerlead with someone. I'm tipsy. I need to go to sleep.

I wake on Sunday knowing that the gym is going to be a hard place to drag myself to. But at least my friend George will be working there. He's a personal trainer and will only rib me if I don't go, so I'll dig deep into my energy reserves.

George and I met in the gym a few months ago when they'd installed a new set of power-plates and I clambered aboard and stood there, looking lost. He showed me how to use them and we ended up laughing, as I was shaken around on what has to be the most unflattering gym equipment ever invented. Never again. Most weeks, when I've finished working out, and if he doesn't have a client to train, we hang out in the café, sinking whatever the latest flavor of smoothie is.

But before I head out to the gym, a coffee with Joan will start me off well, so I message her, gather biscuits, and unlock the back door into my wasteland of a garden. I scout around. I really do need to get hold of some pots, or maybe even a veg trug. I realize I've been waiting for ages, and there's no sign of Joan pulling up her roller blind and unlocking her door. I message her again.

Another few minutes go by and I start on the biscuits, toying with nipping back inside, now that my hangover has taken hold, and putting at least three slices of thick white bread into the toaster. I dream of slathering them in salted butter. Still no Joan. I go back inside, heading directly toward the white bread, and pause as I start to push the toast lever down. Joan had her date with Geoff last night. And now Joan is not at home. That's interesting and also mildly disconcerting. I smile to myself. Surely not?

In the gym I'm trying so hard to concentrate on the running machine, but am distracted by a true-crime podcast, so that I'm practically walking as I wait with bated breath to discover who the presenters think the killer is. I should listen to music, so I up my pace, but my head still hurts and I've drunk all my water. I need to refill from the water station, but the moment I climb off here, someone will leap on, so I stick it out for the next twenty minutes until George swaggers over. He's beautiful to look at. Some men are handsome, manly. George looks like a Burberry model. He sees my desperate fitness condition week in, week out and knows that if he keeps staring at me with his baby-blue eyes I might cave in and ask him to be my personal trainer. He keeps talking about long-haul holidays, and I suspect he sees me and my dubious fitness goals as a way toward funding that.

"Hey, gorgeous," he starts. He's so ridiculously flirty and actually, shamefully, I quite like it. I am sweating. I am red. I am definitely not gorgeous right now, but I've stopped correcting him.

We chat for a while about my fitness regimen. George enthuses about a "wonderful" vegan protein powder that he's just found, and I nod along as we walk to the water station. Obviously I neglect to mention my white-toast-and-butter frenzy this morning.

My phone dings in my hand and, while George talks about the various flavors, I steal a glance at it. For some reason I expect it to be Davey, but it's only 6 A.M. where he is right now (I've looked up the time difference) and, actually, it was my turn to respond. I must do that.

It's Joan. I'm desperate to know where she was, and what she was doing. I think I know. It didn't even occur to me that Geoff might have been an axe murderer and Joan was lying dead in a ditch all this time (why always a ditch—they're actually really hard to find in London).

I don't swipe to read her message because George is looking at me, that deadly smile that would melt a lesser woman. I've obviously missed something he's said and have to apologize and ask him to repeat it.

"I just asked you out for a drink," he explains.

"A smoothie in the café?"

"No. I mean a proper one in a bar."

"Oh, really?"

I'm too confused and he laughs. "Yeah, you don't fancy it?"

It's the strangest reply. How do I answer that? "Er, yeah, OK." Have I just agreed to a date with George? No, this isn't what he's asking, surely.

"Tonight?" he prompts.

"Crikey, you work fast."

He laughs again. "Not really; we've been hanging out for a few months. If anything, this is slow for me."

Oh. Does he like me? That was . . . unexpected.

He mentions a bar in the Square Mile. "Meet you at eight?"

"Sure."

It's only later, as I'm working out what to wear for our "date," that I remember it's a Sunday. Tomorrow is a "school day." Every day's a school day for George. I think he's in that gym seven days a week.

I spend the rest of the day in town, doing the food shop and feeling righteous that I worked out while in the midst of a crashing hangover. I'll pay for that later, I'm sure. I respond to Joan and find out that she did indeed spend the night with Geoff. My heart does a little leap for her. She's still there in the afternoon when she replies to me. They're going out for tapas in the evening.

I thought we didn't sleep with people on the first date. Anymore, I tease her.

You might not was her simple response, which made me laugh out loud in the supermarket.

I look at the time and realize Davey will definitely be awake now and well into his day. He's six hours behind. I look at the weather app to see what temperature it is there. It's thirty-five degrees here. Thirty-five—that's ridiculous. It's sixty-two degrees in Austin. I'm instantly picturing this man I don't know in sunglasses. If only his WhatsApp profile picture wasn't the standard gray icon. What kind of person doesn't update that? I think I will ask him for a photo.

I'm in the bread aisle, trying to be holier than I was this morning, and am looking at the whole-grain options and at loaves covered in seeds. But I pause and finally respond to Davey.

Hello, long-distance friend, I type, choosing the word "friend" very carefully.

He's not online, and it's only when I make it into the wine aisle that my phone dings and I see he's replied.

Hey, yourself, he writes, and I watch as he types. Good weekend?

Very, I reply. Dinner and a LOT of drinks with friends, which is why I didn't reply yesterday. Sorry. Gym today. And . . . I pause before finishing my sentence, but I've got nothing to hide by telling him, so I carry on typing, I'm going on a date tonight, which is a bit unexpected actually.

Why unexpected?

I didn't realize he liked me. How's your weekend? I ask.

Good. Admin mainly. Prepping to leave for the UK.

His response makes me smile, thinking of him working out travel plans. What date do you arrive? I ask.

January 10.

When you're settled, shall we meet? I dare, and hope the platonic nature of my message is obvious.

That's a given, he says and then puts a smiley face, which does what it was intended to do and makes me smile. **At some point, if you don't mind, I'd love to ask you about the best areas in London to stay, and where to rent and that kinda thing. I don't know anyone else there to ask. That OK?**

Of course, I type.

Great. I've got lots of things to get through, but can I call you later? he continues.

I stop as I approach the wine I usually buy. I stare at the phone. An actual phone call? No. Who does that? Text only, surely. Isn't that how we all communicate now? I can't actually *say* no to him, though, can I?

Sure, I type while I think. I reckon I'll finish with George after about three hours. Even sooner, if it goes badly. **11 P.M. my time?** I suggest. Then I add, **Which in your time is—**

But he replies before I can hit send. **5 P.M. my time. Sounds good.**

OK. It's a date, I reply.

George and I are sitting incredibly close to each other at the bar. He's not in gym gear—of course he's not. I don't know why I expected him to be in gym gear: a bit like that time I dated a British Airways pilot and he actually turned up in his first officer's uniform. He said it was because he'd just flown in, but I had serious doubts. And yes, he was the one I slept with on the first date. It was inevitable.

I'm wearing a pink leopard-print dress and ballet flats, with my hair scooped up into a messy bun. I thought lipstick might be a bit too much, so I've opted not to overdo it on the makeup. I'm still not entirely sure why I'm doing this. I'm not sure this is going to go anywhere. But then you need to take a chance every now and again, don't you? So I'm here, feeling quite flattered actually. George is in suit trousers and an open-necked shirt and he does look good, I'll give him that. Heads have turned to stare at him. Even the men.

"You know all the guys here are looking at you," George surprises me by saying.

I spin my head around to check, as I was sure they were staring at him, and my neck clicks audibly.

"You need a neck massage," he laughs. "I'll do it later for you, if you like?"

"Are you a masseur as well as a personal trainer?" I ask.

"Sports massage, yeah." He nods and orders us a round of cocktails.

"Man of many talents."

He orders the same drink for both of us. He didn't ask what I wanted, and in a way I like his assertive confidence. But I didn't actually want a Negroni. I really wanted a piña colada. I know that's terribly unsophisticated, but I want to go on holiday and everyone knows coconut cocktails ooze holiday vibes.

We get talking about vacations, and I suggest Thailand as my next point of call. We sit together looking at prices to Thailand on his phone. Actually, this Negroni isn't bad. He sounds quite up for a holiday and I think to myself: If George and I just stay friends, instead of doing something silly and sleeping with each other . . . we could actually go away together. We've known each other awhile and he's nice, easy to get on with. All my uni friends have either already booked their summer jaunts with their husbands and boyfriends or are saving to buy their own flats and can't afford a holiday. But is it a strange thing to suggest? It probably is, but I like the idea. I ask George how he feels about a holiday together, as friends—in case there is any doubt—and he nods along.

"Yeah . . . why not? I'm self-employed and can take some time away for a proper break."

"Great," I say with genuine enthusiasm. Although I've known George for a few months, I feel like I've properly made two new male friends this week, and it's all platonic and easy. Who says sex gets in the way of friendship between men and women?

We agree we might just do this trip. It's not as reckless as it sounds. I went backpacking with a colleague I'd only known a fortnight, when we were sent to a work conference together and decided to cram in a quick trip the week before it. George and I plan to get away in February. George is actually incredibly easy-going in the gym, and right now on this date/non-date, so I hope he'll be easygoing on a long-haul break too. He's courteous and, hurrah, actually asks me questions about myself. Believe me, I've dated enough men who don't. But this isn't a date really. At least I don't think it is. It's a friend-date. We have genuine conversations about life and food. We order more cocktails and then some picky bits from behind the bar. He orders us some handmade Scotch eggs and black-pudding bites as well as some triple-cooked chips, throwing out the idea that he might be vegan.

"Are you going to have to self-flagellate later about all of this?" I say, gesturing to the snacks.

"Yeah," he grins. "Why do you think I'm in the gym all day long?" The question is rhetorical, but he leans in a bit closer and continues: "I'll let you in on a little secret. I used to be fat. Like . . . really fat."

I stare at this incredibly good-looking man, who I am determined will remain only a friend, and immediately don't believe him. I've seen the tight shirts he wears in the gym. "Really?"

"Truly. I love food. Food doesn't love me."

"Interesting," I say, popping a black-pudding bite into my mouth.

He grins and puts one in his own mouth. I decide I really like George. This could be the start of a wonderful friendship.

At 11 P.M. I'm walking home from the bus stop. George didn't offer to walk me home after we said goodbye. And I take this as quite a positive sign. Often men only walk me home so they get invited in and, unless they're British Airways pilots in full kit, that won't be happening. Anymore. Assuming that George didn't want to be invited in makes me quite happy—more invested in our friendship. We kissed on the cheek as we said goodbye, and that was enough. I'm glowing, despite the cold, because I had a great evening. I pull my coat around me, tightening my scarf, and look inside sitting-room windows where curtains have been left open. It means I see various Christmas trees with their fairy lights still glowing brightly, although some are already switched off for the night. I breathe deeply, the cold air entering my lungs. This time of year is glorious.

My phone rings and it's a WhatsApp call from Davey. I still haven't saved his number in my phone. It felt premature, but now I realize I should, probably. This is so weird, but good weird.

"Hi," I say and watch the warm air smoke and swirl from my breath as I walk through the night.

"Hi," he replies. "Still OK to talk?"

His voice is warm and comforting. "Definitely. I'm just walking home from my date."

"Are you still with him—do you want to talk some other time?"

"No, now's good. I'm alone."

He's silent and then, "How was it?"

"It was fun, actually. I've known him a little while. He's a personal trainer. We had cocktails and planned to go on holiday together." Now I say it out loud, it sounds like the most bonkers thing ever. I clarify, "I mean, it was a friend-date more than anything. It's not going to turn into anything, and we both fancy a trip to Thailand. It's a bit random really, now that I think about it," I say, laughing.

Davey laughs along with me. "It is, yeah. But it's good to make plans."

"It is," I agree. "So how are you getting on with your life-admin and sorting out moving here?" I fumble in my bag for my keys. I'm approaching my flat. The lights are on in Joan's house next door, and I remember I need to catch up with her on how her date went. I want all the sordid details. I'm going to have to live vicariously, through her, for a while.

"Good. Getting the ball rolling on leaving. Flight booked."

"That can't be it?" I say.

"Well, no. But I have a British passport."

"Really? How?"

"My family left England when I was five months old. I've never known anything but Texas, but my family's from Cornwall. So it's easier for me to move."

"You're English then?" I say in surprise, slotting my key in the door and letting myself in. My heating is on and I'm immediately warmed as I flick on the lamp in the hallway and throw my keys onto the side table, among the detritus of receipts and emptied-out coat pockets.

"Don't let my dad hear you say that. He takes great pains to tell me he's Cornish first, British second."

It's so nice hearing Davey's voice.

"Why did your family move from Cornwall to Texas?" I inquire as I kick off my ballet flats and take off my coat. I put my bag under the hallway table and discard everything else in random positions. I'll pick it up later.

"My dad works for an oil company and put in for a transfer," Davey says. "He and my mom got settled here, and that was it. The Great American Dream . . . perfect life for a Cornishman."

"I can see the lure," I say. "I used to love our family holidays to the US. Everything's better, bigger, cheaper."

"And I've always secretly been an Anglophile," Davey laughs. "Biding my time, waiting to return to my roots."

I flick on the fairy lights I put up last Christmas and refused to take down. I flop onto the sofa, shrouded in a flickering glow from the lights, and tuck my feet underneath me. "I like your style, by the way—calling a girl, not messaging."

"You don't talk on the phone?" he asks.

"It's quite rare these days. In fact I was so surprised when my phone rang, the first time you called me, that I only answered out of curiosity."

"Isn't that why most people answer?" he laughs.

"I guess. But no one talks anymore. No one calls."

"My new boss wanted me to call in. I don't think he knew how much a call like that was gonna cost me. He's not one for Skype or WhatsApp calls, apparently."

"Old-school," I say.

"Yeah. I like old-school, though. Don't you?"

I tuck my feet further underneath me. "I do. Ironically, it's refreshing."

"I like to call rather than message. You and I talked on Friday. We were pretty good at it, as I recall. Besides, it's what will define us against the generation after us: being able to still talk on a phone."

"True," I say and a comfortable silence grows in the five thousand miles of distance between us. "Davey?" I ask.

"Hannah," he says in a mock-serious tone.

"What do you look like?" Now that I've asked it, I feel like a fool. The Negronis have clearly taken hold.

He pauses. "How do I answer this honestly, without making myself sound like either a Hemsworth brother or Gollum?"

I splutter with laughter, get up, and fetch a glass of water from the kitchen tap.

"Honesty is one thing," Davey says, "but if I'm self-deprecating, that could lead you to imagine all kinds of things about how I look. What do you look like?" he asks, when we've both finished laughing.

I glimpse myself in the reflection of the kitchen window as I run the tap. "I've dressed up for a date and so, right now, I look better than I've looked all week," I say, realizing that neither of us has really answered the question.

"I'll show you what I look like. Hang on." Davey goes silent and I hear the dull thud of him tapping his finger against his phone. My WhatsApp dings and he says, "Go ahead. I'll wait while you look."

I'm so intrigued that I almost drop the phone as I move away from the call and open my message from Davey. My mouth drops open. It's a selfie of a man without a shirt on. His skin on his tanned chest is covered in droplets of water, as if he's just got out of a pool or a shower. His blond cropped hair is damp and he's smiling—a hint of white, but not blindingly white teeth. Behind him college football flags are on his wall. I'm not sure what to do with this image. This man is . . . gorgeous, all-American. I briefly compare him to George's English-and-looks-it pale skin and high cheekbones. It's an unfair comparison. I click on "save to photos." I'm going to look at this again later. I return to our call.

"Yep, got it," I reply, all too casually. "One question: I asked what you look like, so . . . is this what you look like or is this *actually* you?"

"It's me," he says as if I'm completely stupid.

I click back to the picture and look again. Christ! He really does look like a Hemsworth brother.

"Definitely not Gollum," I reply and then swallow, as I process how attractive the man at the other end of the line has turned out to be. "Did you just take that? Are you shirtless?"

He laughs. "I didn't really have time to scroll for an old picture and I just got out of the shower, so I took it right now. Your turn."

I don't do selfies. In fact I hate them. I've never got my head around them. All those pouting images. Why do people pout when they do it? I've un-followed all my friends who regularly pout in selfies. Brutal, but the truth. Here goes.

"Hold on," I say. I realize I also haven't got time to scroll through and find a picture of me, so I switch on the camera, take a picture, and look at it. No, that's awful. I try again quickly. Better. But still no. Third time lucky: I look at my hair, my smile, my eyes elongated with a brand-new Benefit mascara, and realize this is as good as it's going to get. Thank God I dressed up tonight. I forward it to Davey. "Incoming," I announce and then bite my lip. Please be kind, I think.

He grows silent and then, "Well, *hi* there," he says.

He makes me laugh all too easily.

"You don't look like how I imagined," he continues. "In a really good way."

"Likewise," I reply. I'm still aiming for casual. I'm not sure if I'm hitting it or not. Is it my imagination or has sending photographs switched this chat up a bit?

"So," he says, changing the subject. "We were going to talk about places to live. Where do you recommend?"

"Depends on your budget," I say, sounding like an estate agent and hating that we've flicked onto practical subjects. "You're an architect, you said, so you must be rolling in it." In the background Davey chuckles. "That means you can probably rent in any of the locations starting with B."

He laughs. "B?"

"All the best locations start with B: Battersea, Belgravia; Blackheath is cute—very villagey; Bermondsey's quite cool; Brixton, too."

"I'll keep B in mind. And where do you suggest I look to find a place to rent somewhere beginning with B? Like, what kind of websites?"

"I use Rightmove, and there's a couple of others. Do you want to flat-share, though?"

He thinks. "No, I don't think so. I can probably afford to rent a small place by myself."

"One bed or two?" I ask. And then horror strikes me. Why haven't I asked the obvious? "Are you moving here alone? Or . . . with a girlfriend?"

"Alone," he says and I can hear the curious humor in his voice as he says it.

I decline to respond, but inwardly I'm buoyed. When I next look at the time, it's because hours have passed while we've been talking. It's one o'clock in the morning and my phone battery is on its way out.

"Hang on, I need to find a charger."

"Me too. And some clothes. I've been in this towel for hours."

I think I audibly gulp as he says that, but move on quickly, plugging in my phone. I also need to pee, but don't quite know how to broach that subject. I try, "Could you just hold on for one second, I need to . . . um—"

"Sure," he says, cutting in. "I'll wait."

I put the phone down on my bed as it charges and run to the bathroom, pee so quickly I can practically hear my mum fifty miles away muttering the phrase "like a racehorse." I wash my hands and dry them on my dress as I go back to the bedroom, flump down on the bed, and set myself against the pillows.

"It's really late for you now," he says when I've announced I'm back. "What is it—like midnight?"

He's an hour out, but I don't tell him that. "Do you want to hang up?" I offer. He's quiet and I prompt, "Davey?"

"Sorry, I just shook my head as if you could see me. What an idiot."

"Ha," I reply and settle back.

"Do you have to get up for work early?" he asks.

I nod my head and then realize what I've done and reply in the affirmative.

"What do you do?" he asks. I can hear the rustle of fabric and assume he's putting on clothes while we talk.

"Marketing."

"Enjoy it?"

"Yea-a-ah," I say slowly.

"You sound unconvinced."

"Yea-a-ah," I say slowly again and he laughs. "It's an agency, so we've got quite a lot of different clients, which I thought would mean the work was varied. And it is," I'm quick to say. "But I've been there a few years now, and part of me thinks that's not enough of a reason to leave."

"But the other part of you . . . ?"

I shrug. "I think maybe it's gone a bit stale. But it's OK—pays for all the things I need it to."

"Which is maybe all we can really hope for, in this day and age," he responds.

"Words of wisdom."

"What kind of marketing is it?" he asks.

I tell him about the brochures I'm in charge of creating for the agency I work for; the website I manage for our investors; the customer-services messages I put together for the end user. I'm trying so hard to make it sound snazzy and glitzy, but am missing by a mile. We talk about his job, about the buildings he's helped design. Most recently a school nursery, and now he's ready for something bigger—something to get his teeth into, as he says.

"Jonathan White's a really good firm," he says. "Skyscrapers, you know, big offices in London and all around the world."

I love the word "skyscrapers." We don't use it enough in England. But instead I say with a laugh, "Big extensions of some corporate God's dick?" and then wish I hadn't, but Davey doesn't reply because he's laughing too.

"Exactly," he says. "Actually, we could really use that for our marketing. When I pitch my designs, I'm goin' in with that phrase. 'It's a big extension of your dick. You will get laid forever if you commission this.' And we'll watch the madness as they try to secure our services."

I love laughing with him. And then, when we both fall silent, I yawn and realize I've heralded the end of our phone call.

"You need some sleep," he says. And then he's quiet again. I can tell he's thinking. "Can I call you again?" he asks.

"Yes," I say, all too quickly.

"OK, during the week?"

"I'd like that," I say.

"Me too," he says. "Good night, Hannah. Sleep well."

"Good night, Davey."

He's still on the line and so I say it again, softer than before. And then so does he. And then we hang up.

Chapter 3

I'M IN THE pub nearest work on Thursday evening. One more day to go and then it's the weekend, but tonight some colleagues have made up a pub-quiz team for charity. I'm crap at pub quizzes. Our team crashes out of every round, and I catch Clare from HR giving me a look that says, "We are shit at this."

I nod. We really are.

During the quiz my phone dings on the seat next to me, and Clare points to it. I shake my head as I listen to the next question. I don't know the answer to this one, either. God, this is embarrassing. We're definitely coming in last. If I'm caught using my phone in the midst of a quiz, the whole team gets disqualified—a fact I remind Clare of.

"Do it," she hisses. "Save us all from this."

I decide to save myself by getting up to buy a round of drinks instead. I'm not sure it's my turn but, regardless, I need to take a break without doing something that looks as if I'm cheating. I wonder who has just messaged me. Davey said he'd call me this week, but so far it hasn't happened. I'm trying not to read too much into it. We're simply friends. Long-distance friends. Who haven't met. Clare joins me at the bar, having unceremoniously ditched our teammates during the sport round.

"This is awful," she says. "Why did we agree to this?"

I smile and then pay for our drinks, and she offers to help me carry them back to the table.

When they announce the results, none of us are surprised when we come in last. We chat for a bit at the end before dispersing, and Clare says, "Did Kevin tell you your holiday form got approved?" before she takes a sip of the dregs of her wine.

"Really? Thanks."

"Thank *you*," she says, "for not choosing a holiday during half-term week, which is when every other bugger here puts their forms in for. Where are you going?"

I tell her about George and Thailand.

Her eyes glaze over in wistfulness. "Christ, I could do with getting shagged in a super-king bed by a fit personal trainer in Thailand. I will need all the details when you return, please."

"As an HR professional, Clare, are you actually allowed to make sexual assumptions about me—out loud?" I watch her turn white. Then I can't suppress my laughter any longer and put her out of her misery.

"Fucking hell," she says as she exhales. "Don't scare me like that. The last thing this company needs is another tribunal."

I give her a kiss on the cheek and wave goodbye to everyone else. I can't be bothered to explain that George and I are just friends, so now seems like a good time to leave, simply to put an end to the conversation rather than start a whole new volcano of questions erupting. Also, I'm tired. As I leave, I pull my coat around me and watch as office Christmas parties pile out into the street. There's a couple standing under a streetlamp, kissing— office workers, I'm guessing—and I make up a story about them: of secret love undeclared until the night of their Christmas party. And now they're going to have to hide it from the rest of their office until the end of time. My phone rings and I laugh at myself.

Davey is WhatsApp-calling me, and I realize how much I've been willing him to get in touch again.

"Hi," I say.

"Hi, yourself. Good night?"

"Yeah. Pub quiz."

"How did you—"

"Last," I admit, almost with pride.

"Ah, you can't win 'em all. Besides, I still think you're great."

I see the green man flash on the crossing up ahead and make a dash for it.

"Was that too much?" Davey asks. "Me saying you're great. It feels like too much. Sorry."

"No, sorry, I was just running for the green man."

"Green man?"

"The light crossing," I clarify.

"OK," he replies. "I don't wanna be creepy."

"You are not creepy," I reply, thinking again of that image of him: shirtless, droplets of water on his chest. "I'm glad you rang, even though this is all completely out of the ordinary."

"Me too. And who wants ordinary anyway?" he asks.

We talk as I walk toward Liverpool Street Station. He's on a late lunch break and tells me he's sitting in a park with the sun beating down on him, eating a "sub."

"I need to know what that is," I say.

"What my dad always calls a 'roll'—pretty much. A big sandwich thing."

"Is it nice?" I ask as a filler question to nowhere.

"Uh-huh," he says and I can tell he's chewing.

The lights of the pubs and offices shine out at me as I walk. London is never dark. It's comforting. Oversized Christmas trees adorn the foyers of offices. "Is it Christmassy where you are?" I ask.

"You bet. I mean, not in the park. But I can't turn around in a coffee shop without seeing red cups everywhere, and there are flavors of coffee you'd never drink at any other time of year."

I tell him about Joan and our quest to get through all the Nespresso flavors. "We were almost there, only they keep introducing these limited-edition ones and Joan does get lured into a flavor parade."

"And what's your favorite?" he asks and I hear him take a bite again. If it was anyone else, I might be a bit grossed out by that, but with Davey I feel flattered, realizing he's squeezing into his lunch break calling some random girl he misdialed a week or so ago, when he could be doing anything else he wanted.

"I think I like the plain old blue Lungo ones. I'm a girl with simple tastes." I shrug but he can't see me.

"I'm a double-espresso kinda guy," he says as if it's a big secret. "Straight up."

We talk about his life in Austin. How he's a member of a local soccer team. "It's my dad's fault. I could never get into football"— and by this I assume he means American football. "Dad loves his soccer"—and by this I'm assuming the British version, football, but I don't query it. "And so I joined the soccer team in high school and never really stopped playing," he says. "I play twice a week here. I'd like to keep it up when I get to England. I run and play soccer because I don't like the gym," he confesses.

"Oh, I do," I say, settling into my walk and watching London go by in a daze until I get to another crossing. "I love the gym."

"Is that because you're dating your personal trainer? Or for other reasons?"

"I'm not dating George," I say after a beat.

"George," Davey repeats his name. "Why aren't you dating him?" The question is curious, not catty.

"I just think he's going to be a better friend," I say diplomatically. In truth, I'm not sure why I'm not interested in George. He's certainly attractive, and funny, but deep down I suspect he *may* be a Lothario. Perhaps that's unfair of me. Anyway we're going to

Thailand together simply as friends, so I'm categorically not going to go there.

"When was the last time you dated someone?" Davey asks and I hear him sip something through a straw.

"Properly?"

"Uh-huh."

I think. "A couple of years ago. Guy called Phil. Nice. Just . . . you know . . ."

"Not nice enough?" Davey queries.

"Yeah, maybe that," I say. And then, "Definitely that, actually. You?"

"A woman named Charlotte. Also nice, but not nice enough."

"Poor Charlotte," I say.

"Poor Phil," he chuckles.

"So what will you do between now and your arrival?" I ask, changing tack.

"I finish my job here in a couple of weeks. And Mom and Dad are already planning a going-away party for some friends and family."

"Are you sad to be leaving them all behind?" I ask as I pass the ornately Gothic Bank of England building.

"Hardly," he says. "My best friend, Grant, has already booked a ticket to come over in March. He's also English, moved out here when he was a kid, and he can't wait to visit. And my parents have suggested they fly out in April, so I'm going to be all set for company for a while."

"That's so lovely," I say.

"Where do you live?" he asks. "I mean, which part of town?"

"East London. Wanstead, near the park. It's nice. You should look at it. Have you looked at places to live yet?"

"I have. I'll look at Wanstead later, but from the list you gave me I'm almost settled on Brixton. It looks kinda cool, based on the Google images I've seen of it. I'll try it for six months and take it from there."

"Didn't fancy the dizzying heights of Belgravia?" I suggest.

"I looked at it, but my checking account curled up and died when I saw the rents for a studio apartment there."

"It is pricey. Also a bit wanky," I say.

"Wanky?" he laughs.

"You know," I giggle.

"I know," he says. And then, "I gotta run back to work. What are you doing later?"

"Not too much," I tell him as I turn the corner toward Liverpool Street Station. "Bed for me."

"Then good night," he says.

"What are *you* doing later?" I don't want this conversation to end, despite the fact that I'm nearing the station and the signal will cut out as I enter the Underground.

"Netflix," he says. "A rare night in for me. Since I started telling people I'm leaving, suddenly I'm Mr. Popular and am booked up for drinks most nights for the foreseeable future."

"What do you watch on Netflix?" I pause by the escalator, trying to hear our conversation over the multitude of tired-looking commuters.

"Documentaries, mostly. Some unexpected. Some interesting. Some both."

I take a deep breath, inhale the cold night air. "Enjoy your documentaries."

"I will. Enjoy your sleep," he says.

"I will."

Chapter 4

MIRANDA IS OPEN-MOUTHED in the pub at our usual table as I show her the picture of Davey. It's Saturday night and we're waiting for our food to arrive.

"Oh my God," she says for the second time. "Is this actually him?"

Paul sips his beer and is done with waiting patiently. He's given up craning his neck to see, but now he's had enough and snatches the phone with the words "Fuck's sake." He takes a look, then raises his eyebrows. "He looks like he should be in a superhero film. Even I want to shag him now." He laughs at his own joke and tries to hand the phone back to me, but Miranda pulls it from him, scanning the picture.

"How can you be sure it's actually him?"

I laugh. "I can't be sure, obviously, but—"

"What's his last name? Let's google him."

"I . . . I've never asked him, actually."

Miranda thuds her beer bottle down on the mat. "Still? You've still not asked him? You had one job to do."

I had two jobs, and one was to extract a picture, which I did. Besides, I'm not doing this for her. This is for me. I do actually enjoy hanging out with Davey, even though it's only on a phone line.

"Anyway, obviously you are now pursuing this man as a potential life partner?" she asks, and after a few seconds I realize she's deadly serious.

"What? No."

She points at his picture. "Why not?"

"He's nice. We talk. But he's thousands of miles away."

"But not for long. Get in quick. Now! Before he arrives and someone else snaps him up. They'll be like bees around a honeypot."

Paul narrows his eyes. "Don't bees *make* honey? Why would they crowd around a honeypot? Do you mean flowerpot?"

I stifle a laugh and Miranda just ignores him. "Don't let him get away," she says. "Really. I mean it. If he's as nice as you say . . ."

"He is." The pressure of this conversation is stifling.

"And he calls you when he says he will?" she prompts.

I nod and look to Paul for assistance, but he sips his beer quietly, clearly still considering the flowerpot/honeypot debate.

In the end I'm saved by the waitress who brings our starters. I dip a chicken skewer into satay sauce and try not to spear my mouth on the end of the stick.

"He's fit," Miranda says once again. "He's nice. He's moving here. Declare undying love for this man immediately and snare him quickly. Quickly," she reiterates.

I decide she's mad or she's already had too much to drink. But I still love her, despite her overeager nature. Obviously I'm not going to do any of what she's suggested. I barely know Davey. Although that now feels slightly less true since we've spent hours talking so easily.

I look to Paul, who leans forward as if he's preparing to say something insightful. He opens his mouth and looks right at me. "I'm sure she means flowerpot."

I can't believe you made me wait all week to tell me what's happened with you and Geoff, I message Joan as I'm pulling on my dressing gown on Sunday. I dig out my battered Ugg boots from where I've hastily thrown them at the back door last week, and tuck my pajama bottoms into them, which flare out like harem pants. The effect is less Kate Moss at Glastonbury and more MC Hammer. **I'm ready!** I text and I lay out this week's selection of biscuits— Hobnobs—and make my way into the garden.

"Good morning," a male voice says over the fence. I stop and stare at this man in Joan's garden. He's late sixties/early seventies, and he's smiling kindly at me. "I'm Geoff," he says with a little wave.

My mouth drops open. Geoff is hot, for an older chap, and he's clearly been at Joan's for what Joan and I sometimes describe as an adult sleepover. "Hi . . . Geoff." I make my way over and offer a biscuit. "I'm Hannah."

"Nice to meet you, finally. I've heard lots of lovely things."

"Likewise," I offer, but actually I could really have done with hearing more.

"Joan says I have to tell you it's Esperanza de Colombia this morning. If that means anything to you?"

I laugh. "Not yet. But I'm sure there'll be a leaflet."

Geoff laughs. "Yes, she's fumbling around for it now."

I immediately like Geoff. And I try to stop a wide smile spreading over my face. I'm so happy for Joan. After all these years, romance at last. But it does mean I can't get the gossip about him, with him standing right there.

Joan arrives, clutching a tray of mugs, and we make small talk about the cold weather and how much colder it's going to get. "Snow, apparently," says Geoff, which I'm always happy to hear. Christmas is only two weeks away. Then we get on to the coffee chat while we give it our star rating out of five. Geoff is kinder about it than we are, but asks why we aren't rating out of ten. Joan and I look at each other as if that's an incomprehensible suggestion and then he excuses himself, to get ready.

I give Joan a look and she laughs.

"Joan! You naughty girl."

"It's not only you young people getting all the fun," she declares, eyeing the plate of biscuits I've put down by my feet.

I lift them up and hand her back my empty coffee cup as she selects a biscuit. "I'm not getting any fun at all actually," I sigh.

She asks about my recent escapades and I tell her about my non-date with George. Then I tell her about Davey and her eyes glisten. She practically explodes with questions, which seems to happen with anyone I tell about Davey, and I'm forced to show her his picture. She takes an audible breath.

"You wouldn't kick him out of bed on a Monday, would you?"

Which is a phrase I don't quite understand, but I think I get the point. "I suppose not, no."

"I do love that he telephones you. When are you talking to him next?"

"I'm not sure—it's all very easy and fluid." I don't worry about when he'll call next because I know he will. "Every few days, usually."

"You lucky sausage," Joan says.

"I think we're just friends, really."

"Do you miss not speaking to him on the days when he doesn't call?" she asks.

"Yes and no," I say, working it out as I talk. "I kind of live off the conversations for a little while—does that make sense? And when that well empties out a bit, he calls again or he messages me and it kind of . . ."

"Lifts you up?" Joan volunteers.

I nod and smile. "Yes, I think that's a nice way of putting it."

"And so he arrives in . . . when is it?"

"Roughly four weeks."

"It's so romantic," Joan says with a sigh.

"Oh, I'm not sure about that," I reply. "Nothing's happened. It's just . . . nice."

"It's how it should be," Joan says, resting her arms on the fence. "It's how all romances start: with something nice, something easy that brings two people together."

This embarrasses me and I shuffle in my boots. "Oh well, we'll see."

I'm reluctant to make anything of her comment. I've lost track of the number of men who started as friends and ended up being deleted from my social-media contacts. I don't want that with Davey. Our friendship—our connection—is, I know, quite strange in terms of how it's happened, but it's lovely. And something that starts so well like this *can't* end up with us blocking each other on chat platforms.

"OK." I bring this talk to a close. "The gym beckons. Got to work off those Hobnobs."

"See you next weekend?" Joan asks.

"If you're here, and not having an adult sleepover at Geoff's, then sure." I wave and head toward my back door. "I really like him, by the way."

"Davey?" she questions.

I give her a look. "Geoff," I clarify.

"So do I."

The gym is packed. They've run a special offer in the local paper and it really grates when they do this, because it's always packed out for at least a fortnight afterward, before people lose motivation and let their fresh memberships languish. I queue politely at a distance for the cross-trainer and select my playlist. I might as well start listening to it and, just as I'm putting my headphones in, George strides across the floor with a wave.

"Hey, gorgeous," he starts and every female turns to look at him, hoping beyond hope that he's addressing them.

"I've got my holiday form approved," I say and he gives the widest grin.

"Fantastic," George whoops, picking me up and spinning me around. He is so acutely at ease with himself that he doesn't care people are watching. "Thailand is on! Let's meet in the café downstairs and look at flight times after we've finished up here. Actually"—he glances at his watch—"want a free training session? I've got time to kill."

"Oooh, yes, please," I enthuse. I've never had a proper personal-training session before. That time on the power-plates doesn't count. And half an hour later I know why. It is brutal. George is a taskmaster, throwing phrases at me like, "Come on, Hannah, you're capable of so much more than this."

"I no longer find you attractive," I tell him as we sit in the café. I can feel the burn in my thighs. I buy our coffees—it's the very least I could do, for the torture he just inflicted without charging me.

He looks at me with those blue eyes. "You find me attractive?"

Oh no, what have I done? "A bit. Not today, though. Now I actively dislike you," I joke.

"You find me attractive," he says knowingly. "I find you attractive as well," he says, as if it's a huge secret, which I suppose it is.

"Well, stop," I say. "I'm not booking a holiday with you if you think there's nookie on the cards."

"Nookie?" he laughs. "Who even says that anymore?"

It's a word I've picked up from Joan, and I tell him all about her. "Although she's progressed to calling it 'adult sleepovers' now."

"She sounds fun. I'd like to meet her. And I promise in Thailand I will not try to initiate an adult sleepover. This is strictly friendship."

"Good man," I say, pulling out my phone. George is not fussy about where we go. He's just excited to be going. We decide to make it an easy ten days and go for a two-part stay in Bangkok and

Phuket. Neither of us fancies backpacking, and we simply want a bit of culture and then to finish it off with some kind of cheesy, all-inclusive beach break. We find a boutique hotel in Bangkok and a four-star all-inclusive place in Phuket that looks fantastic.

"Great fitness program," George says and I resist saying, "Great bars."

"Two rooms, right?" he says.

"Obviously."

"Good, because I'll be bringing girls back probably and I don't want you getting annoyed."

"George, for God's sake." And then, "Girls, plural?"

"Not at the same time," he chuckles and then thinks. "Maybe at the same time? Who knows. Holiday, baby!"

I laugh but roll my eyes.

"So we're booking this now?" he asks, pulling out his wallet.

"Yes!" I practically squeal. "I'm so excited."

"Me too. I want to be there now." George books and pays for it with his credit card and I transfer him the money. As he concentrates on paying, I look out of the window and wonder what Davey's doing right now. Out toward the car park it's started snowing.

I'm shopping for holiday clothes. In the middle of December this is incredibly difficult, and I decide now's as good a time as any to start buying Christmas presents for friends and family.

I'm excited to see Mum and Dad at Christmas. Despite the fact that they only live in Kent, I rarely make it home. But we chat a lot and text a lot, and they both work, so we're all as busy as each other. Dad's a GP and Mum's a receptionist at a hotel. She gets special staff discounts in the spa and spends a lot of time test-driving the treatments. I head to Waterstones to stockpile books for both of them. They're book fiends and it's become our ritual that we buy each other a grab bag selection for Christmas.

I end up in the travel section and find a book about London. I put it in my basket and decide to gift wrap it for Davey and hand it to him when he arrives. There's no point sending him something he'll have to pack.

When I eventually tick everyone off my list, I move on to finding holiday clothes in the other shops. The snow's falling fast now and my Uggs are getting soaked through, but eventually I catch the bus home and sit clutching my shopping bags, watching the edges of London blur into East London. At the park I get off and walk home, settling into the sofa with a book and a cup of tea. I've already strung fairy lights around my flat; they live there all year, but I always leave the tree until last because it's such an effort. The decorations are from John Lewis—intricate, ornate baubles, which cost a complete fortune, but they look good now, twinkling delicately as I switch on the new fairy lights I bought to wind around the tree.

My phone dings and I wonder if it's Davey. It's not. It's a rare Rightmove alert about a two-bed flat in Wanstead with a garden. I'm horrified to see the cost per month is at least £300 more than I'm currently paying. I love Joan for not upping the rent. I click onto flats in Brixton and look at the kind of properties Davey might rent. I look at places similar to my own, cute Victorian terraces with high ceilings, and some distinctly different, cool new-builds with open-plan spaces and small kitchen areas. I wonder what he'll go for and message him to ask. Who says I always have to wait for him to contact me?

He messages back almost immediately. I love that about him. I've found a place, he confirms. I'm putting down a security deposit.

But you've not even seen it. You're going to rent a flat you've not even looked at?

Uh, yeah? How else was I going to do it? he writes and puts a little laughing face.

Send me, I volunteer. I'll go look for you. Choose your top three and I'll view them for you after work, or on the weekend or something.

Can I call you? he asks and I reply happily with a thumbs-up emoji.

"Hi," he says when we connect.

"Hi," I say, warmed by hearing his voice.

"Are you sure you don't mind going to see them? Is it far from you? I don't want to put you out."

"No trouble. I love looking in people's houses. I'm nosy like that."

"Good to know."

We talk about the kind of times I can do, and he tells me about the flat he really liked the look of. "I spent hours clicking and dragging on Street View to figure out what the local area around it was like. How far it was from Tube stations and whatever. Brixton looks fun. Thanks for the suggestion."

He's looking at one-bed flats and sends me the links to both his favorite choices. I look through the pictures eagerly, and we discuss the high ceilings and cornicing. I watch a lot of Channel 4 property programs in my spare time, and Davey's entranced by the idea of Kirstie and Phil's *Location, Location, Location*. "There's like thirty-five seasons!" he declares excitedly. "Man alive, I'm here for this. Move over, Netflix."

"Where are you?" I ask, wanting to picture him.

"Lying on my bed. You?"

"Sofa."

"Send me a picture," he says, which makes me sit up immediately.

"Of . . . my sofa?" I try.

"Ha, no. Of you."

"You've already seen one. Plus, I'm in weekend mode," I say by way of an exit from this idea.

"What does that mean?"

"You know, jeans with a rip in them, T-shirt that looks a bit slubby, hair *might* need a little wash."

"Send me a picture," he repeats.

"Ugh, no! I'm going to have to go and put on a lot of makeup if you pursue this idea."

"I'll bet you don't need it."

I really do. It takes a lot of makeup to look as if I'm wearing no makeup. "You send me a picture first. How do I know that initial one you sent was really you?"

He's silent. "Why wouldn't it be me?" he asks eventually, curiously.

Because you're so flipping gorgeous it must have been stolen from the internet. "Just because," I say instead.

"How do I prove to you the next one I send is me?" he says.

I think. Davey has a point.

"Hang on. I have an idea how I can prove it," he suggests.

He takes a selfie and sends it. In it he's holding up his iPad and is staring longingly at a picture of Kirstie and Phil.

I feel my shoulders shake with laughter and I come back to the phone. "Clever. Also funny." I'm so relieved. It really is him. He genuinely is as handsome as his first photo. And I like his silly sense of humor.

"Now it's your turn," he says.

"Hmm," I say reluctantly. "Fair's fair, I suppose." I turn the phone around and take a picture. I'm grateful I've only got the table lamps on, and the twinkling fairy lights shine softly behind me. I hit send. It's not perfect. But then I'm not perfect.

I go back to the phone and wait.

"You look nice," he says. "I like weekend you."

"And weekend me likes weekend you," I say. I'm sure I can actually hear him smiling. "Davey?"

"Mmm?"

"What's your last name?"

"Carew. What's yours?"

"Gallagher. Carew isn't a very American name."

"It's Cornish," he reminds me.

"I'd forgotten about that. I love Cornwall," I say. "Those clear blue seas and cliffs, white sand and fishing boats." I'm dreaming of holidays again.

"I've only been a few times," Davey says. "Mom and Dad took me to see my grandparents when I was a kid. But then they started to come here for visits, since Dad could barely ever get away from his job. The only other times I've been back were for their funerals."

"I'm so sorry."

"Ah, don't be. The last one to pass away was when I was eighteen, so it was a while ago."

"So you've not been to England since you were eighteen?" I ask.

"No. But I went over to Europe as part of a study-abroad program in college. It's not the same, but y'know."

In the background to his phone call I can hear the hissing of a can of fizzy drink opening and then he takes a sip. The sound of him going about his day is comforting.

"Where in Europe did you go?" I unfurl my legs and go to the kitchen, flicking on the kettle. Outside the snow is falling more heavily than before and the afternoon has grown dark. The world outside my kitchen window is shrouded in an artificial bright-white gauze.

"I went to Paris and then to Rome."

"Sounds heavenly. I've never been to Rome."

"Oh, you've missed out," he says. "Top of my bucket list is to learn how to make pizza and pasta in Rome. I can make both, kinda, but I want a real Italian in some tiny culinary school to show me properly. I'm even learning Italian in preparation for a trip I haven't yet booked."

"Are you using London as a gateway drug to get to Italy?"

"Yes. Tea and biscuits until I can hit the hard stuff."

I like this. I like him. I look toward Joan's back fence and curse her and Miranda for putting that suggestion in my head.

"What time is it there?" he asks.

I pull my phone away and look at it. "Six P.M. It's snowing, by the way."

"Is it? We don't get too much of that here. And by 'too much,' I really mean any."

"Get ready for a million different weather outcomes every day when you come here. I carry a cardigan and umbrella around with me every single day. Even in the middle of August."

"I'm looking forward to it. Not the cardigan part, but I'll bring a sweater. You should go outside when you get off this call. You should go make snow angels. I'm jealous at the thought of you doing that."

"Snow angels? What am I? Five?"

"Do it. You'll have fun."

"OK. Send me the details of those flats and I'll schedule tours and look one night after work this week."

"Thanks, Hannah. I'm really glad I found you."

"Have a good afternoon," I say.

"Have a good evening," he replies.

When I'm off the call I sip my tea and move into the sitting room to start wrapping Christmas presents. Then I turn around, open the back door, lie in the snow, and make snow angels.

Chapter 5

I LEAVE WORK bang-on 5 P.M. on Thursday night. I'm usually very diligent and almost never leave on time, making sure all my emails are answered and my to-do list is done. It's been a long week, but I've made time pass with lunches with friends and colleagues and a bit more—probably unnecessary—Christmas shopping. I've even packed a suitcase for Thailand, checking how much all my planned clothes and shoes weigh, so I know how many bottles of sun lotion I can feasibly get in. Why does everything weigh so much? I'm ready for a holiday that I'm not even going on for well over a month.

Tonight I'm heading to Brixton. I've got two flat viewings for Davey, one straight after the other, and only a few roads apart. Thankfully both are unlived in. There's nothing worse than looking around a flat when tenants are still in situ. It's so awkward. Although I will miss out on looking at stocked bookshelves and seeing what kind of stuff people have. The first flat Davey's chosen is a new-build in a brand-new development. Very snazzy, close to all the amenities. The second is in one of Brixton's many Victorian terraces, very similar to mine. It's first-floor, so it's without a garden, but the light is amazing and the rooms are huge. He hasn't told me which is his favorite, but I suspect it's this one. I hope it's this one. I've taken pictures of both and hit send on the stream of images, so he can see it without the lie that is the estate agent's fish-eye camera.

I have thoughts, I message him. I'll write them down for you when I'm home.

But when I return, having trudged back through the snow, my feet damp on the way back from the Underground station, I find a message on my phone from Davey. Don't spend time writing it all out. Call me?

I've never called him before. It's always been him calling me. But I assemble myself some dinner and look out at the fresh snow in my garden. My snow angels from days ago have been blanketed in a fresh coat of powder. I pick up my phone while my pasta bubbles away gently on the stove and call Davey, who picks up immediately.

"Hey," he says and I smile. I always smile at his voice. He asks about my day and I ask about his. He's been enjoying his last few weeks in Austin, taking in the botanical gardens one final time today, before he leaves. "I realize I've been a terrible tourist in my own hometown, so I'm adventuring," he tells me.

There are so many places I want to take him—if he would like me to, that is—and we talk about the National Portrait Gallery, my favorite of all London's galleries. There are so many sites he wants to visit, and we make plans to be tourists together. I'm excited to see the city I call home through his eyes. I long to go on a big red bus tour of London, hop off at the Tower of London, and take a picture of us with a Beefeater. I never even did that as a child.

"A picture of us," he echoes. "I'm looking forward to that. It'll be so strange to actually see you—for real—after all these times we've messaged and talked."

I stir my pasta and switch off the stove, nodding in agreement. "I can't wait."

"Really?" he questions. "Me neither."

We go quiet and contemplative, and finally he says in mock-seriousness, "Hannah, I think we need to move to the next level of our friendship."

Although it's a semi-joke, it's as if he's fired a starting pistol and I blink. "What do you mean?"

"I think we need to progress from calls to video calls."

"Now?" I catch a glimpse of myself in the reflection of the kitchen window. I've done a full day at work. And then two flat viewings. I'm a wreck.

"Yeah, why not? You OK with that?"

My stomach tightens, but I think it's in a good way. I nod my silent answer, realizing he can't see me. "OK," I say and then he's gone. The call has ended. "Oh."

Seconds later he's video-calling and I brace myself, swiping to answer. I hold my phone out at arm's length and watch as his eyes crinkle and he smiles at me.

"Oh my God," I say, wishing my stomach would untighten. "This is so weird."

"It's great," he says. "It's long overdue."

He looks terrific on video. I'm in a small square in the corner of my phone screen and I try so hard not to look at myself on it, judge myself and my lack of makeup, which has long since slipped from my face.

"You're even prettier in motion than you are in your photos," he says.

I don't blush, as far as I'm aware, but in the corner of the screen I can see my face smile and I have to look away in happy embarrassment. "Thank you," I whisper. I am not going to tell him how good-looking he is. There is no way on God's green earth he doesn't already know this. In his flat I see him lean back against his gray sofa. "Do you live by yourself?" I ask.

"Yeah."

"I had this feeling you lived with your parents," I say and then realize how offensive that might seem, although plenty of twenty-nine-year-olds still live at home.

He looks confused. "Why?"

"College football flags in your bedroom. In the picture you sent."

"Oh. No. My mom and dad use my old bedroom at their place as an office now, and so all my stuff got sent to me. I just hung them in there, as a reminder, I guess. Although most of that stuff's going back to them when I move to England. Little do they know," he says darkly.

"I have to confess I'm ridiculously nosy when it comes to property, so I'm going to need you to take me on a tour of your flat," I command.

"It's never gonna get old, you calling an apartment a flat." But Davey stands up, obliges me. I feel dizzy all of a sudden as I whizz up into the air with him as he stands. I ask him a question it has never occurred to me to ask. "Davey? How tall are you?"

"Six two."

"Six foot two? Cripes. I'm five foot five. You're going to tower over me."

I can't see or hear his reaction, as he's slowly moving the video around his flat. He shows me his simple, mostly gray sitting room: arty black-and-white photos of landmark buildings from years gone by litter the walls. He takes me into each room slowly and talks in the background about some of the architectural drawings he's got laid out on his desk—about the kind of projects he's been working on, the kind of projects he'll be doing at his new job. It sounds so varied it's dizzying. Schools and nurseries, huge offices, hotels, shopping centers.

"What's your favorite?" I ask.

"I love the power and the beauty of watching a magnificent skyscraper go up, from a drawing I've helped with. But there's something so warm and simple about watching a new school being built, knowing so many kids are going through those doors for the next hundred—two hundred—years maybe."

I could listen to him talk like this for hours. I prop the phone against the toaster and start mixing my pasta and sauce together as he finishes the tour of his flat. I make a green salad, grab a fork and then carry him to my little two-person kitchen table that I almost never eat at. I push a lot of paperwork out of the way and prop him against it. "I'm going to have to eat my dinner, if that's OK?"

"I don't mind." He walks around his kitchen and I see his face light up from the bulb within the fridge as he opens it. He grabs a can and walks back to his sofa, clicks it open, and I eat and he drinks as we talk about the flats I went to see.

"Can I guess which one's your favorite?" I ask.

He smiles. "Sure."

"Well," I say, in between mouthfuls of pasta and salad, "I feel that given you're an architect and love clean lines and new things, it should be the new-build. But I actually think it's the Victorian terrace."

He smiles again. "Busted. How did you know?"

"It's bright, light. High ceilings. Beautiful detail. Decent-size kitchen. It was my favorite."

"Was it? Well, I look forward to cooking for you one night in the decent-size kitchen," he teases. "I'll go ahead and put my deposit down, if you didn't find anything to worry about. No rats in the halls? No corpse in the bathtub?"

"None of that. It was perfect."

"How far is it from where you live?" he asks.

"About an hour."

"OK," he says and I can't tell what he thinks about that.

I give him a tour of my flat, eventually ending up in the sitting room, where I plug my phone in and we talk about Christmas. I talk about my hometown, Whitstable, where I'm going to be in a week or so's time. He talks about the family dinner he'll have with his parents. He goes first thing in the morning, helps cook dinner, and they start drinking champagne and orange juice from the get-go. I tell him about my mum flapping around the kitchen, determined to take charge, and my dad who storms in like the cavalry and helps cook the only meal he cooks all year and then takes all the credit. Mum doesn't mind. It's sort of a tradition now. We talk about walks on Whitstable seafront to blow away the cobwebs after a day spent mostly eating and reading, and playing silly board games that we'll never play the rest of the year.

"Sounds like heaven."

"It is. I finish work in a few days. I've saved up so much of this year's holiday allowance so that I can go home, and I'm there all the way through until after New Year."

"I have to work," he says. "But I don't mind. I'm actually working from home this afternoon, so I should probably get back to it. But . . . can I call you this weekend?"

"Yes, please," I say. I'd be disappointed if he didn't want to talk to me. Whatever is happening between us is so delicate, so early, that I'm afraid we might overdo it. I've never had anything like this with anyone: this complete openness, friends who might be something else, forced into a slowness that I like because we physically can't be anything else. Because now this feels like it might be something else; something amazing. And it is turning into something with possibilities, and it's moving there so incredibly slowly that I'm not sure I even noticed when it happened.

Chapter 6

"YOU CAN'T REMEMBER Davey's last name?" Miranda asks as Paul tries to flag a waitress down during our Thai night out. She's new, she's ignoring us, and Paul declares he's going to give her the largest tip at the end of the night.

Miranda and I balk at this idea.

"It's so she remembers us for next week." Paul shrugs. "Then we get good service. It's all about playing the long game," he says, offering the waitress a winning smile, which she ignores as she rushes past us once again.

Miranda and I look back at each other, leaving Paul to his task. I try to remember. "I'm sorry," I say. "Callow or Carrow—it was something like that. I've genuinely forgotten. It didn't seem important after I asked it. And after I'd established he was who he said he was via a second photo . . . I was happy."

"Christ, have I taught you nothing?" Miranda asks. She's holding her mobile phone, stalking Davey's social-media accounts. Only she can't find him. She was reliant on his last name. "It was Cornish," I volunteer and she begins researching Cornish last names.

The waitress suddenly arrives at our side and we begin a frenzy of ordering absolutely everything in one go—starters, mains, sides, more drinks than we'll need—as we're now in fear we won't ever see her again. She looks flustered and we know we've bombarded the poor woman. We also know half our order is coming out of that kitchen incorrect. We'll eat it anyway.

Miranda puts her phone away, annoyed, and mutters, "You're useless."

It's our last night out for a while, as I'm heading back home in a few days for Christmas, and we swap gifts tonight with strict instructions not to open them until Christmas Day. I'll pack their gifts to me and take them with me to Whitstable.

I've put their presents in a huge box and everything is gift-wrapped individually. Paul holds the box up, shakes it fiercely, and then says, "What is it?"

"A puppy," I reply with a wicked look, as he stops shaking it violently and stares at me.

"So when are you talking to Davey next?" Miranda asks.

"Not sure. Maybe later today?"

"How can you be so cool about it?" she asks.

"It's easy," I say truthfully. "I know he'll ring and when we speak . . ." I don't want to say "it's wonderful," so I don't. But it is.

The waitress arrives next to us, carrying a tray with a jug of water, various small picky bits to keep us going until our mains arrive and three carafes of red wine.

Paul's eyes light up. "Now we're talking."

I'm at home later that evening and decide I'm going to call Davey. I'm not brave enough to risk a video call. I feel that trying to Face-Time or WhatsApp video-call someone, unannounced, is a bit rude. It gives them no time to prep. What if they're on the loo? I'm tired, ready to sleep, but instead of heading to bed I'd rather talk to Davey. This is how I know that I like him. Has that feeling crept up on me or did I have it from the start? I call and he picks up immediately. I knew he would.

"Hey, you beat me to it," he declares.

"I'm sure my turn to call was overdue," I state.

"It was, but I didn't want to push it."

He asks after my night, and I ask after his day. We've both been busy with the minutiae of life and the magnificence of friends, and then he asks if he can video-call me. I'm ready this time. I'm wearing more makeup than usual. Just in case.

We reconnect and I hold my phone out in front of me, hoping I'm at a flattering angle. I'm probably not. I'll never get the hang of this.

A message dings audibly and I see George's name flash up, before I swipe it away.

I watch Davey settle back against the pillows on his bed as I do this.

"Sorry," I say. "Only George." Davey smiles and doesn't ask, but I feel the need to explain anyway. "My friend I'm going on holiday with."

Recognition sweeps over his face. "Are you friends with him the way you and I are friends?"

I sit back on the sofa. "No." And it could be the three carafes of wine I shared, alongside the few beers I've once again downed in the pub even though I don't like them, but I become brave. "*Are* you and I just friends?"

"No," he says and lifts one corner of his mouth in a half-smile I find adorable. "No, I don't think so." Everything in my torso tightens expectantly as he continues, "I don't know what this is, Hannah. But it's cool and easy and . . . nice, and I really like it."

"Me too," I say in joint recognition that what started so platonically is moving so very gently toward something else. It's moving toward the *potential* to be something else. But it really isn't there yet. Would I allow myself to think all this if Davey wasn't about to move here? I have no idea. My mouth chooses the worst time to yawn.

He looks at his watch and I see him do some simple maths. "It's really late for you."

I nod.

"You want me to go, so you can sleep?"

I shake my head. I really don't want him to go yet. "I might get into my pajamas and climb into bed for a bit, though. Is that weird?"

It's his turn to shake his head. "No. You can turn me around to face the wall, if you want to change, or leave me here or . . . something."

"I'll take you with me," I say, but I have no intention of letting him see me change. Whatever this is between us, we are not *there* yet. I turn off the lights as I go and check that the front door is locked as we talk, and then I apologize as I put him facedown on the bed. When I'm in my pajamas I pick the phone back up again, pull up the duvet, and lie on my side, propping the phone against the pillow next to me so we can see each other. He's lying on his bed, the light from his window letting in the bright Texan sun and, as we talk, my night rolls gently into the next day and his midafternoon turns subtly toward early evening.

I yawn. I'm in serious danger of falling asleep. Yawning is infectious, and I watch him stifle one from the other side of the world. We're in a comfortable silence that I've never had with anyone else I was dating. Although this isn't dating. These accidental weeks we've had, getting to know each other from thousands of miles away . . . this will never happen again. Soon he'll be here. I should enjoy whatever magic this is, while it lasts.

I've turned the brightness down on my phone so it's not so blinding, and the dim glow from it is the only light in my room. Davey's so at ease with himself, just being there on his bed. And lying in bed on a video call with someone I've never actually met is possibly the weirdest thing I've done in quite a while. I find my eyes closing and blink them rapidly awake as Davey starts saying something.

I try to focus on his mouth as he talks, in order to stay awake.

I wonder what it would be like to kiss him. Would he be a good kisser? What else would be good with him? God, I bet everything would be. I do my best to banish from my mind unladylike thoughts about Davey in bed. I close my eyes. I really am tired. Behind my curtains, dawn is breaking and my eyes are already stinging from tiredness. I open them quickly as I feel myself drift off. He looks tired too. I think I really like him. And then I can't help it, but slowly, and without realizing it, I fall asleep.

Chapter 7

WHITSTABLE AT CHRISTMAS is heaven. The high street is lit up with shooting-star Christmas lights and I've spent the last couple of days shopping in the independent boutiques for things I don't need but love, and catching up with a couple of old school friends over coffee in the Whitstable Coffee Company or quiet drinks in the Old Neptune, a Dickensian-looking clapboard pub that stands all alone across the end of the pebble beach toward the Thames Estuary, to which the river falls widely into the North Sea. I never realize how much I miss it here until I'm actually home again.

By Christmas Eve I've only been here a few days, but I've already drunk more Baileys with Mum and Dad in that short space of time than I've drunk in my entire life. It goes down like nectar, and Mum and I are dancing around the kitchen as Dad wanders in and inquires if we should move on to Mint Baileys. The answer is a unanimous yes.

I really love my parents and miss them both in equal measure. Dad's busy all year round as a GP and hardly ever ventures into the city, but Mum comes in a bit, although not as regularly as I'd like. I could come home more often, but for some reason I don't. Life is busy.

Our house is in a postwar terrace a few streets away from the main drag and, other than parking being a complete nightmare, returning here is my solace. It's where I grew up. Mum and Dad have never felt that urge to move around. They've stayed settled together and, in some small way—no, in some large way—I think that's what I want eventually. I've never had a big family. Mum's and Dad's parents are long gone and I've no siblings. Apparently they tried to have me for nearly ten years and, after I arrived, Mum spares no pain in telling me I was a handful of a baby and it put them off having any more. She always makes up for it by saying I was an easy child, though. I doubt this very much.

Mum's sister Karen is coming around on Boxing Day with her new husband, but on Christmas Day it's just us: cooking, playing games, eating and then eating some more, and drinking more units than Dad would ever confess to his patients. By early evening we've all slumped into a food-and-drink coma and as Mum flicks through the channels, looking for the *Doctor Who* Christmas special, which is not my cup of tea at all, I make an exit, offering to take the dog for a scamper on the beach.

I wrap up warmly and head through the narrow streets toward the seafront, which is quiet—everyone's indoors, napping off their Christmas lunch. Curtains are open and I can see through table lamp–lit windows that children are running around sitting rooms, playing with oversized cardboard boxes from which their presents emerged; and Christmas-tree lights twinkle determinedly behind adults who are fast asleep in front of the television. I do a quick calculation while I walk. In sixteen days Davey arrives in London. I feel warmed by this, even as the cold coastal air winds itself up from the sea, wrapping itself around the streets and around me.

Next to me the dog trots along, stopping to sniff every now and again. Our dog is called Andrex. He's a beautiful pale Labrador, and I was in charge of naming him ten years ago when we got him. I thought Andrex was a hilarious name, given that he looked like the dog from the toilet-roll commercial. But when I took him to parks and he got off his leash and I had to call him back . . . it grew a little embarrassing. Andrex and I sit on the pebbles on the beach and I throw his ball. The lights from across the estuary twinkle festively for us. I should probably move more, as I've eaten so much, but the fresh air is invigorating enough and Andrex is running around happily for both of us, so I continue sitting.

I text **Happy Christmas** to Davey and he calls me. I'm starting to feel so incredibly guilty that it's always him calling me, but I still feel strange about ringing him out of the blue. I always feel I should issue a little notice first, which in part is what my text was. But he always, mostly, beats me to the actual call.

The signal is hazy out here, but he asks where I am and I tell him what I can see. Darkness is descending and the lights over in Essex are switching on and flickering so very gently, all those miles away across the water. I can only just make out the wind farm in the distance and the red rusting forts out to sea. A view that I recognize and love so well.

"I would love to see that," he says. "I don't think I've ever been to a pebble beach. How's your Christmas been?"

I tell him about my day, about how wonderful it is to be home. "How's yours been?" I ask.

"Great. We're about to sit down to eat. I feel really lucky. I love my folks. I'm gonna miss them so much. But I'm excited that I'm going to be in England soon. New job. New life—not that my current life is bad. But I'm so ready, so excited for all of it. And seeing you, in real life."

I breathe in the cold air happily. "I can't wait to see you," I say. While we've messaged each other inane texts and frequent "Hello, how's your day?" comments over the past week or so, I know it was that night I accidentally fell asleep with him that changed everything. It was personal. I let him in. I let him watch me sleep. In the morning I woke up and found he'd gone, quietly hung up and continued with his evening without disturbing me while I slept. And in place of a video version of him, I woke to a message telling me how adorable I was when I slept, how much he liked me and how he'd never liked anyone this much, which he knew was strange because we'd never actually met.

"And what about New Year's?" he asks, and I'm immediately overwhelmed, because I've never quite got the point of New Year's. There's such pressure around *having a good time* and, in the end, the pressure overshadows the entire event.

For me, I say, New Year's Eve is "feet up, TV remote in hand, glass of champagne, and maybe heading right back down to the beach to stand in this very spot and watch the fireworks over on the other side of the Thames Estuary."

"It actually sounds perfect," he says. And then he sighs. "And, ordinarily, I'd be so up for that. But this year New Year's Eve has kinda turned into my leaving party."

He tells me he's heading down to somewhere called Sixth Street to see some live blues, and then a gang of them are going to a rooftop club called Summit to dance the night away under the city's skyline. I listen to this man tell me about his life in one of the hottest cities in the world, as I sit on a cold beach in Kent in December. How did any of this happen?

By the time New Year's Eve comes I am so ready just to relax in front of the TV, watch Jools Holland and his varying array of guests and then, with Mum and Dad, head down to the pebbles at ten to midnight, leaving Andrex at home with some classical music playing loudly so he can't hear the fireworks.

I digest the year I've had and, really, I couldn't be happier. But doesn't everyone get to New Year's and feel a little bit as if they're ready for the past year to end? Resolutions are made, ready to be broken. I think last year I vaguely said I'd try to read every novel Charles Dickens ever wrote. Instead I think I mainlined all my back issues of *Grazia* until I caught up, exhausted, and started on the new ones.

But this year will be different. In February I'm going on a blow-out holiday, though I think a bit of regret slowly creeps in that I'm going with George. He's lovely. But he's going to spend the entire time trying to get laid. Hopefully, not with me.

And before that there's Davey. I'm not usually the kind of girl who pins all her hopes on a man. Actually I'm never that girl. But I do feel January is going to be different. I like Davey, and I know that he likes me. We've just never—actually—pinned down or said what it is that is happening between us. What we're doing can't be categorized yet. And I think we're both OK with that. Either way, it's only for the next week and a half and then . . . he's here. I can't actually believe Davey will be here. What will it be like to stand in front of him? What will it be like to kiss him?

We're on the beach and midnight strikes. Over the water the fireworks sparkle: effervescent lights. Tiny dots of different-colored gunpowder wow silently from all those miles away in Essex, a different county, divided by the ebb and flow of the Thames. Behind us, in Whitstable, the town lights up in various shades of gilt pyrotechnics from houses and beach parties.

Mum puts her arm around me. Dad, on the other side, does the same and I'm sandwiched between the two of them: safe, which I've always felt, even though I'm not always with them. And then, because it's midnight, they dip behind me and kiss each other. I smile and then feel them both kiss me quickly—one on each of my cheeks. We say "Cheers" with the champagne glasses we've brought down to the beach with us, and "Happy New Year" to each other. The beach isn't deserted. Others have had the same idea. But we're spaced so far apart from the other revelers it's almost as if we're alone.

As we turn to head back home, a few minutes after twelve, my phone rings. It's Davey, and I tell my parents to go on and I'll be home in a while. My dad agrees, because they have to get back to Andrex, and I settle myself on one of the wooden groins that divide the beach every now and again and swipe to answer the call. The tide is out, and if I wanted I could walk so far out that I could turn around and see most of my town from a distance.

"Happy New Year, Hannah," he tells me, timing it perfectly.

"Happy New Year, Davey," I say and then realize he's got hours to go. He's made the effort to call me at my midnight, when it isn't even his yet. "How long until you head out for your leaving party/New Year's blowout?"

I can picture him checking his watch.

"Not long," he says a bit vaguely.

"Are you OK?" I ask.

"I have been drinking *all* day."

I laugh. "I wasn't expecting Drunk Davey."

"Neither was Sober Davey. Drunk Davey just kinda showed up."

"The power of New Year's." I take a sip from my champagne flute.

"Maybe it's because I'm *trashed*," he says, and I laugh; there are some words he says that make me remember he's American, "but I wanted to tell you that I really, really like you, Hannah."

I smile. This is going to be a fun conversation that I'm going to rib him about for weeks. Months. Although I worry how he's going to get through the next however many hours until midnight if he's already this drunk, and I tell him.

"Ah, I'll be fine. Actually, I'll let you in on a little secret," he says and I picture him swaying as he says it. "In about ten minutes I'm going to throw up and pass out. And *then* I'm going to be fine."

"Oh my God!" I exclaim. "Where are you now?"

"I'm at my friend Grant's house."

"Hi, Hannah!" I hear in the background of Davey's call.

"That's Grant," Davey says and I'm smiling, even though I'm actually quite worried for Drunk Davey.

"Hi, Grant!" I say, and Davey relays my message to yet another man I've never met.

"OK," Davey says. "We are going out now." He sounds almost robotic. "I am going out now. We are going out now."

I can't stop laughing. "With a bang?" I suggest.

"With a *bang*," he says.

"Davey?" I ask. I'm genuinely worried, although I'm still laughing.

"H-Hannah," he says and I wish I could stop laughing.

"Can you message me when you get home? Or maybe earlier than that?" I ask.

"Yes. Do you like me?"

"What?" I ask, staring out to sea.

"I mean, do you like me?" He repeats the same question with no further explanation.

"Yes, Drunk Davey, do you like me?"

"You bet. OK," says the man who looks like he should be in a superhero film, "I'm going to go throw up and then I'm going out."

I laugh again. "Happy New Year, Davey."

"Happy New Year, Hannah."

Chapter 8

January

NEW YEAR'S DAY with old school friends always makes me feel as if I'm being visited by ghosts of New Year's yet to come. We spend it in a little restaurant called Samphire and every year a friend has either found a new boyfriend or had another baby.

I never think, "When will it be my turn?" These things are just organic. One day this will be my life, I think, as I look around at friends juggling breastfeeding with counting down the weeks left on their maternity leave. I'm not ready for that yet. I get sent a picture from George. In it he's wearing sunglasses, even though it's a cold and dreary New Year's Day. He's clearly hungover, and I send him back a photograph of my brunch with the glass of Buck's Fizz in shot.

He responds with the vomit emoji.

When the conversation around me turns to me and my "love life," I feel like Bridget Jones around the dinner-party table. Smug marrieds everywhere. I don't tell them about Davey. How do I even begin to explain that, without sounding like a lunatic? I won't show them the pictures Davey's sent me. That will send them falling from their chairs. Instead I remain enigmatic. Mostly.

The snow never even touched Whitstable, and even though London received a flurry in my absence, it's cleared by the time I get back to Wanstead. Out with the old and in with the new.

Davey texted in the early hours of this morning, with a photograph of him smiling and clearly totally wasted. Next to him is a man I'm assuming is his best friend, Grant. I'll be surprised if I hear from Davey again today—I hope he's had such a wonderful time that I don't hear from him. I message him telling him as much, and that I hope he's getting some rest. Ten days, and counting, until he arrives.

I don't hear back from Davey for two days, which isn't totally unusual, but I start to worry. I've messaged him a few times, but in the interim I've taken this time to clean my flat and start running daily, for the month of January. This is partly in preparation for my holiday and partly in prep for Davey's arrival. Christmas has not been kind to me. But it's also because George has confessed that the gym is already heaving and it's only the third of January. "So many people wanting a personal trainer. I've got loads of new clients." I'm happy for him and his finances, but I also know that I'll never get anywhere near my beloved cross-trainer now.

My Christmas break at home has reset me. I feel invigorated by life, excited for what the new year will bring. Perhaps this will be a different year. I daren't imagine what might happen between Davey and me. We have a genuine connection. I tried not to feel it at first. When Miranda kept banging on about it, I think I was purposefully vague, not wanting to attach too much meaning to our conversations. But I've started to get that feeling—you know, the one where you look at your phone and you *will* it to ring and wait expectantly for the vibrant sound of a new message stream. Is it because I've never met him? It's the allure of the unknown and the known, all at the same time.

Davey calls me that evening and the rush of joy is palpable. I'm almost breathless as I answer. He asks me how I am, and how the rest of my break was. He's got such lovely manners and I'm drawn to that dangerous place of wondering if my mum and dad will like him. They'll love him. I don't even get a chance to ask how his party was, because he launches straight in with a graphic description of how ill he's been and how shocked with himself he was. I tell him about our conversation when I was on the beach and he was already halfway between the gutter and the stars.

"Damn," he laughs. "I don't even remember calling you. Did I say anything stupid?"

"Such as?" I tease.

"Oh, shit, now I'm really worried."

I laugh. "Don't be. You were your usual charming self—just a very merry version."

"Phew. Did you tell me to stop drinking?"

"No," I laugh.

"You should have."

"Would you have listened to me?"

"I always listen to you," he says. "Grant had to practically carry me home. I've *never* had a hangover like that in my life. I slept all of New Year's Day and all of yesterday. Thank God it was the weekend. Back to work tomorrow. Man, that's gonna be *hard*. I can't believe how tired I still am."

"You clearly need more rest. Maybe you've been overdoing it— trying to get too much done before you leave."

"Maybe," he says. "Listen, I gotta go, but I just wanted to say a quick hi."

"Can I video-call you tomorrow?" I ask, and he makes a silly noise like a child who's been handed a balloon. "You want to video-call *me*? Have I converted you?"

"Maybe," I say. "Perhaps I miss your face."

"Perhaps I miss yours too."

This is nice, this easiness. I hope it's this easy when he arrives. I hope we don't need the physical distance to remain wide in order to make this work.

The next day I go back to work and it's better than I remember.

I forgot how merry everyone is the first few days back after New Year's and the Christmas break. I make good on my plan to video-call later and time it at what has now become our usual time: II P.M. for me, 5 P.M. for him. I've overcome any embarrassment about being in my pajamas and, because of these video chats, I wisely invested in some nice new nightwear when I was home in Whitstable. The pajamas have tapered legs, so they don't ride up while I'm sleeping. They're a total game-changer.

We talk for hours face-to-face. I've grown so used to it now that I have to remember to put him down when I go to pee. I'm in total danger of simply taking him everywhere, as the conversation flows from one topic to another.

We're back on our bucket lists again. Like me, Davey's already planning holidays, loving how every country he's ever really wanted to visit is now on his doorstep—or will be in a few days' time. He tells me how his long-term dream is to take a sabbatical, hire a camper van on the far side of Europe and travel to as many countries as possible.

I tell him, honestly, how I've always hated camping, but I think I could just about muster time in a camper van.

"You'll have to come with me," he suggests.

And I nod, thinking to myself how lovely that would be. But is it actually likely to happen? Pipe dreams and big plans with a man I've never met are perhaps a tad silly, but I think about it all the same.

"It won't happen for a good few years, though," he says, as if sensing what I'm thinking. "They don't hand out sabbaticals the moment you start at a new company, sadly."

"Which countries would you go to?" I ask.

"All of them. I'll drive fast." He gets up to make himself a drink and I can see packing boxes and suitcases lined up. He's ready to leave, and my stomach tightens again as I know this is real. Davey being here is actually going to happen.

"And then," he continues, "we'll end up in Rome for a long weekend and we'll treat ourselves to a few nights in a hotel that overlooks the dome of St. Peter's Basilica."

"That sounds like heaven," I say, and then I ask if we can take in Tuscany. I tell him about my favorite film, the Merchant Ivory adaptation of *A Room with a View,* and how a young Helena Bonham Carter wafts around in floaty Edwardian dresses, being seduced by a shy young Englishman, and how he swoops in out of nowhere into a field and gives her the snogging of her life. "And after that, I suppose, I've always wanted to at least see Tuscany, although I've never been. Perhaps it's because I'm scared I'll go and it won't live up to how I picture it in my head."

"We'll go together," he says. "I'll drive us in the van, and you can put on a floaty dress and we'll go stand in a field together and look at the view."

"That sounds wonderful," I agree. My mind travels to Tuscany and I have to push aside all sorts of thoughts of Davey and me in a sun-drenched field.

"Davey?" I ask and he looks at me with that smile. "Are you having phone calls like this with anyone else?"

He shakes his head. "No, just you."

Thank God. I inhale and exhale.

But it's Davey who opens the conversation up. "I really like you, Hannah."

My stomach does that tightening thing again, but in such a good way. I'm going to get abs without even trying. Saying it when drunk is one thing, but he's sober now. "I really like you too," I say, "I can't wait to see you."

"I can't wait, either. I picture you a lot, y'know? I wonder what you're doing when I wake up and you've already begun your day. I think about you long after you've gone to sleep. Is that crazy?"

I exhale a long, happy sigh. "No."

The light from his fridge shines in his face and he fumbles

around, the camera briefly showing me that the contents within are dwindling. He's winding down his life there, piece by piece, getting ready to start over here.

"We've already had this time," I say, "and I feel we know each other quite well."

He cuts in: "I think we know each other really well."

I nod. "We do. But I'm curious about so much."

"Such as?"

"What you look like in the flesh?"

He holds the phone out at arm's length and says, "Like this."

"I know, but it's the little things. For instance," I say and then prop my head up on my elbow, "I have a little scar by my eyebrow, where I fell over when I was five on a marble step. It could have been so much worse, but there's a little reminder on my face forever of what happens when you run around hotel stairs with too many Barbies in your arms and don't hold on to the banisters."

I show him up close and he nods. "I can't wait to discover all these things about you," he says. And then, "My right arm—a bone sticks out a little further than it should, by my wrist. It got set a bit strange when I broke my arm when I was eleven."

It's these little things I want to know. "I can't wait to find out the rest—all the things that make you *you*—when you get here. I want to know what it's like to walk alongside you. I want to know how many steps I have to take to keep up with your giant stride."

"My giant stride?" His six-foot-two frame shakes with laughter. "I promise to go slow or I'll just hold your hand and pull you alongside me."

I don't tell him I want to know what it's like to kiss him, whether I'll have to get on tiptoes to reach him or whether he'll lean down toward me. Maybe a mixture of both. I look at his mouth, his lips, and want to kiss him now. Will we kiss when we meet?

He must be thinking the same thing as he asks, "Will you meet me at the airport?"

"Yes," I say instantly. "Would you like me to?"

"Yes," he says.

By the time we've talked about his flight times and he's promised to send me his flight number for me to track his landing, it's about three in the morning for me, and I need to get up for work in a little under four hours. We hang up in our usual way, a simple but emotive good night that seems to be laced with so much from each of us—so much hope, so much of everything.

Chapter 9

DAVEY AND I hardly speak over the following days and instead send an array of poorly timed texts that neither of us manages to answer in any semblance of time. I have two lots of birthday drinks to go to this week, and work is so crazy I barely get out on time, but I don't mind. All this only makes time pass more quickly, and the countdown speeds up to his arrival.

He messages that he's sorry he keeps putting his phone down and finding my messages hours later. He's in a frenzy of finishing work, packing boxes that are going to his parents' garage for now, and struggling to work out those final few items he wants to bring with him and those that he's going to donate to charity. He says he's only bringing two rucksacks of clothes and it's too expensive to ship all his furniture over, so he's going to leave it all; that he's not looking forward to going shopping for kitchen items and furniture. I tell him about the equal joy and pain of shopping in Ikea, and he replies that they have those in Texas too. I had no idea.

He messages me early one morning, and I know it's the middle of the night when he's sent it. **Do you want to have a date night?** he asks and I inhale slowly and exhale even more slowly, merely reading the word "date." He seems to be tentatively putting a name to what we're doing. And I, equally tentatively, agree.

He asks what I'm doing tonight, and although Miranda has

suggested that we meet for drinks—just her and me, for a change—I blow her off, which I hate myself for. But when a fit, kind man asks you on a video date (which I know is not a thing), you simply have to go for it. At least I don't lie to her. I tell her what I'm doing, and Miranda tells me to "crack on" and that drinks will keep for another time. I'm so grateful. Davey arranges to ring me much earlier than usual. He's suggested that we watch a movie together, and I've no idea how that's going to work, but he told me it was "ladies' choice," so I selected my favorite film and then worried about my choice. All. Day. Long.

I've dressed up, because it's a date and I'm always either in pajamas or my weekend "bumming around" clothes, or even my office wear, when we speak. I rush home from work, put on lip gloss and a navy jumpsuit with spaghetti straps. I don't bother with shoes because I'm indoors, but I do bother with perfume, even though Davey can't smell it.

He calls at the time he says he will. We ease in with our respective updates on how our days have been and what we've been doing. Davey says he's on the "homestretch"—mentally in London, but physically still present in the US. Somehow we end up on the subject of our future selves: where we see ourselves settling down. I still have no idea who asked this question first. I think it was him, because he waits for me to answer.

"Kent," I say. "It doesn't have to be Whitstable, but around that way. It's easy to commute to London for work, but I suppose it really depends on who I end up with and where they want to be."

"You'd relocate for a man?" he questions with a look of surprise.

"Yes. I think so. As long as I was happy to. Not to sound trite, but home is where the heart is. Home is where you're happy. That doesn't have to be a place. It can be a person."

He nods. "Yeah," he says slowly. "I never really thought of it that way. I guess I'm busy designing homes for people, so I think of homes as . . . homes. I like how you think."

I smile.

"I want to know so much more about you, Hannah."

"Such as?" I settle onto the sofa and sip the wine I've brought to our date night.

He drinks his glass of wine and then looks awkward.

I wait.

"I want to know what you look like under those pajamas you're always wearing." He's so serious, almost seductive, but suddenly he laughs because he can see my eyes open wide, startled like a rabbit.

"Wow, OK," I say.

"You don't want to know what I look like under . . . ?" He gestures toward his clothes, which today involve dark-blue jeans and a tight button-down shirt.

Instantly I feel flustered, because . . . how the hell do I answer this? I simply nod the truth.

And then he's serious again and it's as if all the cold January air, tempered by my radiator, has been sucked entirely from the room, leaving me in a vacuum of my own self-consciousness.

"It's not enough," he says. "This."

I nod again, knowing what he means but unable to voice it.

"Just seeing each other on these calls," he says. "It's not enough. It's why long-distance relationships don't work, in my opinion. Because everyone I've ever known that's tried a long-distance relationship . . . they've all broken up. Is it enough for you?"

"No," I say, watching him and his quiet energy, his openness.

"We've been doing this for a month. It's exciting and fun. But if I weren't coming there to live in a few days, I'd have been on a plane to you already by now."

My mouth falls open and I ask, "Really?"

"Sure. The only thing stopping me is counting down the days until I get there."

"Oh," I say, while inwardly my heart gallops along and I know my smile has widened. We sit in quiet contemplation, our eyes on each other until our smiles grow so wide we're in danger of looking unstable.

"Hannah?"

"Yes?"

"You wanna watch this movie?"

I nod, but I can't think about the film now. I can only think about what it will be like to see him, to meet this man I am 99 percent certain I am falling for. How can this be? How can this have happened over such a short period of time? It's hard to believe. But it's incredible and it's happening.

We start our films at the same time. He says he's had to really dig around the outer corners of every streaming service under the sun to find it, and I am full of dread. What if he really hates what has always been my favorite film? This is a bit like letting someone inside your soul.

He positions the phone on the table in front of him, so I can face him, so I can see his reactions to every part of *A Room with a View*. We'd agreed to get popcorn and we sit and eat. Separately but together. It's almost, but not quite, a real date. But this—this is the kind of thing people do when they're dating, letting the other person in. He says nothing for such a long time until he announces, "I gotta pause."

I hit pause on my TV and watch him on my phone for a reaction. But Davey looks thoughtful and I prompt, nervously, "Are you enjoying it?"

"Yeah," he says with certainty, picking me up and taking me with him to the fridge to top up his wineglass. "Different. And now I really want to go to Tuscany." I don't expect him to continue, but he does as he moves back to the sofa, positioning me back on the table so that I can see him. "I like the hero. Sensitive. Maybe a bit too sensitive, y'know, but the girl"—he points to his screen—"Lucy, is clearly falling for him. That deep, caring side."

I nod.

"OK," he says, "I'm pushing play."

I push play too and watch my TV.

A while later he announces he's pushing pause again and I do the same. He looks at me knowingly, both our screens silent. "Is this the kissing-in-the-field scene?" he asks with a grin.

"Maybe."

"He's on his own. She's coming in. I see where this is going. Is this where I pick up tips on how to seduce a girl in a field? Is there gonna be striding?" he laughs.

"Yes and yes," and I actually giggle.

"OK, I'm pushing play," he says and I do the same. And then shortly after, without even pausing, he just shouts, "No! She cannot go home and marry that other dude. That other dude's a *dick*."

And I laugh so happily, because he gets it. Davey gets my favorite film. "Next time we'll watch your favorite film," I suggest as I dig deep into my popcorn bag for the final crunchy kernels.

"Next time we do this, we can do it for real. Next to each other, on your couch, or mine if I've bought one in time—you and me . . . in real life."

I can't process how wonderful it is to think of Davey and me, in real life.

And then it's the day before his arrival and I've done the silliest thing. I've liberated a big ream of poster-sized paper from the office printer. It wasn't easy to sneak it out, but I'm at home, sprawled on the floor watching a Louis Theroux documentary on Netflix that Davey recommended and scrawling, "Welcome to London, Davey" on the paper in bubble-writing. When I'm done I stare at the sign. Will he think this is cute or weird? Do I think it's cute or weird? I was going for silly. Tomorrow I'm actually going to see him.

I message Davey telling him how excited I am. And because I don't want him to look shocked at my stupid poster when he actually walks into the terminal, I send a picture of it, accompanied by the words, I'll be the girl holding this in the Arrivals area.

He gives me a huge thumbs-up and, for the first time ever, a big red-heart emoji that I try not to read too much into. I feel like another line is about to be crossed between us and I am so happy I could burst. He messages that he's finished work and has crammed in leaving drinks with all his friends and that on his final day—today—he's spending it with his mum and dad. His best friend, Grant, is driving him to the airport and then, before I know it, he must be in the air and on his way here.

Davey said he'd send me a message when he was on his flight, but I don't get one. He must be too busy. If I were packing up, decanting my life from one continent to another, by the time I got on board the flight I'd probably mentally decompress and forget to text too. But I look at the airline website and it shows that his flight is in the air. He took off an hour ago. "Oh my God," I breathe. "This is actually happening."

In around nine hours he'll be here.

My heart beats so fast that I can barely hear myself think over the sound of it thudding in my ears. I'm at the airport in a chain coffee shop, fielding messages from Miranda.

Is he here yet? she asks.

No, I reply. One hour to go, as I look at the board.

She's been messaging me all morning, telling me how romantic it all is, how jealous she is that this is a story we'll be able to tell our children. My eyes widen at that one. Who else gets a story like this? she asks. Who else meets The One because he misdials?

Suddenly the pressure mounts and I turn the phone facedown

on the table I'm sitting at as I sip my second coffee. I am buzzing and I pass the time wondering if I should buy Davey a coffee, remembering that he drinks double espresso, when the screen shows that he should be collecting his luggage. No, I won't do that, because how am I going to hold up my poster, with a coffee in one of my hands? Perhaps I should ditch my poster and buy the coffee . . . Maybe he'll appreciate that gesture more, after a near ten-hour flight. But if I'm holding a coffee, how am I going to throw my arms around him and hold him for the first time ever?

I look at my hands, clasped around my cup for warmth, and they're shaking. I'm genuinely nervous. My leg is twitching up and down under the table. I can see the large automatic doors that mark the transition of worlds between passengers just arriving and those who've made it through those doors, unscathed by lost baggage or enthusiastic customs officials. People move out through the doors, looking tired but relieved, with blow-up pillows hanging around their necks.

I stand up. This is it. I move closer to the barrier and unfurl my poster. Yeah, I'm doing it. It's cute. It is. It really is. I hope Davey can tell that. Even if he doesn't think it's cute, he's not going to judge me and my newfound silliness. It's amazing what really liking someone will do to a person, because I realize now that might actually be what has happened to me. Seeing him will simply cement that I am falling, just a little bit.

When he walks through those doors, will we kiss? I think I'm going to have to kiss him. Not to kiss—after all this time—would seem even stranger. Or maybe we'll wait until we get in the taxi? I'm not navigating the Tube system with Davey and his suitcases, after that length of flight. That would be cruel. We've already decided he'll come back to my place for the first couple of nights while he furnishes his flat, but whether we'll share a bed is unspoken. I assume we will, even if he—being a gentleman—doesn't. Plus, I really, really want to. I am going to explode if Davey doesn't kiss me, if we don't get through the front door and kiss as we walk toward the bedroom. Now I don't need this second coffee I'm holding. Now I need a cold shower.

The initial stream of travelers through the doors dwindles and I wonder if that was even his flight. I steal a look at the monitor and have no real way of telling. Two flights have landed around the same time and both have now gone through the baggage-reclaim area, but there's no Davey. He's probably freshening up. He also said he'd text when he landed, but I don't have a text yet. My leg is still twitching nervously, which is hard to do when I'm standing up, but somehow I achieve it. And then the board shows that more flights have landed, and a while later they too go through baggage reclaim and their numbers dwindle. And now I'm simply confused. I pull out my phone. There's a message, but it's from Miranda, with a GIF of a couple kissing at an airport. I smile, but it's thin. The joy has been swept from me, momentarily. I dismiss her message and call Davey. It doesn't even ring. It merely goes to voicemail. I hang up and send a message instead: Are you here?

I wait. Nothing. Where is he? Is he lost? Has he come out and gone past me, and is he out here looking for me? I start walking around the Arrivals area, looking for a glimpse of a tall blond man lugging at least two bags, one in each hand. There are plenty of people who look like that from the back, but from the front . . . none of them are him.

It's been an hour, and I sit back in the coffee shop. I can't buy another coffee, so I select two mineral waters. One for me and one for Davey, because he's going to be thirsty after a flight. And I wait. I think it's been two hours at least now and there's been no word from him. I get up from the coffee shop. Nervous energy has engulfed me and I walk around the terminal again. Just to be sure. My phone rings and I leap on it. It's George and I've swiped too soon, to accept the call, because I don't actually want to talk to anyone who isn't Davey at the moment. I can't compute what's happened. I hang up immediately. It's rude, but I can't deal with George right now, for all his fun chat and good intentions. I'll call back tomorrow, when Davey's settled in.

I text Davey again: Where are you? Do I have the wrong terminal? Do I have the wrong airport? I'm not that stupid. Christ, I hope he's not at Heathrow wondering where in God's name I am. But his flight numbers line up. He should be here.

I have no idea what to do now. He's not online. He's not responding. I realize I've left the poster I made in the coffee shop and glance over. A waitress is clearing up the detritus of my purchases, which I should have cleared myself, but my mind was elsewhere. She's scrunching up my poster and pushing it deep into the black sack that she's moving around with. My heart sinks even further at this.

Davey, it's been almost three hours. I don't want to leave but I don't think you're here, so I'm going to start making my way home. I'll keep watching my phone. Call me and I'll come back. Did you miss your flight?

He's obviously missed it. Hope sinks at how strange all of this is. I don't know what to think. So instead I head toward the train station and prepare to step back out into the January cold and, in a daze, reluctantly I go home.

It takes me an hour and a half to get to my flat, and my phone dings intermittently as I fall in and out of signal.

Miranda cannot stop asking for information. Ordinarily I'd find this cute, encouraging—the stuff of which good best friends are made—but now I wish she'd stop. She doesn't know what's happened and I need her to stop the romantic GIFs of couples kissing. I tell her, His flight was delayed. I'll call with news tomorrow. I hope this isn't a lie. I hope when I message her back tomorrow I do have actual news of Davey. Or that he's arrived, is with me, asleep, his long legs draped over the side of my small two-person sofa while he gives in to his jet lag.

The rest of the day passes in a haze. My flat is spotless already and so, instead of cleaning for something to do, I sit there nursing a cup of tea, reluctant to reply to messages, reluctant to do anything. I don't even turn on the TV to look out for dreadful news of mid-air collisions. His plane didn't crash. It landed. Only Davey wasn't on it.

I message him again. I am 99.9 percent sure there is going to be a solid reason why he wasn't on that flight. I just need to know what it is. There's no point sugar-coating my desperation to find out what's happened, so I go in with, **Please tell me what's going on. Please tell me where you are.**

He doesn't ever update his social media, but I go and take a look anyway at his near-dormant accounts across the various platforms, to see if he's posted anything. He hasn't. But he's been tagged in a few images of leaving drinks and New Year's Eve. And that's it. In these scant pictures he looks happy, smiling, holding a drink in one photo and not in the other—his arm around someone, who I guess must be Grant, although Grant's not been tagged. I click off. There are no answers to be found here.

I lie in bed and at 11 P.M. I video-call him. It's a last-ditch effort. He doesn't pick up. I lie awake for hours in a stunned daze until finally, as the birds begin their effortless song outside my window, I fall asleep.

My phone alarm is still set for work. I forgot to turn it off. I've had about three hours' sleep and my eyes are tinged red and stinging. I always leave my phone on, so my parents can get hold of me if anything drastic happens overnight; and I would, normally, wake up if it rang, so I know . . . I just know there's nothing on there. I've taken the day off work today so that I could spend it with

Davey. I toy with the idea of getting dressed, going to work any-way, clawing back this day that was supposed to be so precious. Clare will amend my HR file easily enough so that I can use the holiday another time. I have nothing else to do, so I go through the rigmarole of putting on work clothes, brushing my teeth; I put makeup on my face, automatically applying each item. I don't buy a coffee on the way to the station. I don't have it in me to go through every single part of my day the way I normally would, and when I'm on the train I regret this bitterly. I'm exhausted, drained, a mix of totally emotional and utterly emotionless.

As I emerge from the station I can't wait any longer. If Davey's still in Texas, which is what I assume, then it will be the middle of the night for him. He didn't answer me yesterday. Why would he now, in the middle of the night? A thought enters my head. If I've been stood up, then this is a nasty way of doing it. What if he saw me at the airport and then dodged me—decided I wasn't what I appeared from the safety of video calls, exited, and is now in his flat in Brixton?

As a form of restrained anger, I send him: I am now a mixture of pissed off and worried about you. Please put me out of my misery. If you're not coming, could you just say. There's really nothing I can add to this and so I hit send, go to work, and prepare to stare at my screen for most of the day, fielding questions about why I'm there when I said I was taking a day off. None of them know about Davey. I'm certainly not telling them now.

Clare knows something's amiss and her eyes search my very red, bloodshot ones, looking for the words I'm not saying. But with so many people in the office to overhear our every word if they want to, she accepts that I'm here and that I'm working, sort of, and because she knows something's out of the ordinary, she doesn't try to drum into me whatever the strange HR rules are that say you can't mess around with your holiday dates once the form has been processed. It's only Clare who processes them and, in the state I'm in, I think she's decided to give that chat a miss.

My mobile dings with a text message five minutes later when I'm at my desk and I fall on it. It's Clare, which makes me laugh a strange, shocked, hollow kind of noise.

What's happened? she demands. **You look like shit. You sound like shit. Are you sure you wouldn't rather be at home? Just sneak out—I won't tell anyone. As long as you delete this message.**

I tell her thanks, but no. I'm staying. I can't sit in my flat staring at the walls. He's not coming. I know that now. But I don't know why.

At home at the end of the day I finally eat something. I didn't realize how hungry I was. I butter two slices of bread and devour them, ravenously, standing up in my kitchen.

And then my phone rings and I look at it, expecting it to be Miranda yet again or any number of people, but not the one I want it to be. But it is the one I want it to be. It is Davey. I drop the plate I'm holding onto the counter so hard it clatters, and I swipe.

"Davey," I announce into the phone. "Where are you?"

It's quiet at the other end and I wait, the sound of my breath and his converging into one.

"It's so good to hear your voice," he says. He sounds down, and my stomach twists and turns the bread I've just eaten.

"Davey," I say again. "Where are you? Where have you been?"

He gives a sad, short sigh. "Hannah . . ."

"Yes, what? What is it?"

"I'm at the hospital."

"What? Why?"

"I don't even know how to tell you," he begins. And I pull out my kitchen chair. I feel weak, I need to sit.

"Tell me," I prompt.

And he does. He tells me how he woke up feeling awful, the worst he'd ever felt in his life. He thought he had some kind of bug or infection, as he could barely walk. "And I hadn't even been drinking," he says, trying for humor. "And so my mom drove me to the hospital and I've been here ever since. I've had some blood tests and a scan, and they won't discharge me. Now I'm waiting to see a doctor. I don't know what's wrong with me, Hannah."

He sounds choked.

"The doctors will know. They'll tell you and then it will be OK," I suggest.

"Yeah, I guess. I'm so sorry I didn't call. I wasn't able to and—"

"It's fine." I now hate myself for being so pissed off. "I'm only glad you called now. I was so worried about you."

"Thanks. I just woke up, and in the middle of all this shit I've missed my flight. I'm gonna have to rebook."

I nod, but he can't see me. "Just find out what's wrong."

"Hannah, I have to go, the doctor just came in."

I start to say goodbye, but he's already hung up.

I stare at the phone and then put it down on the kitchen table. My mouth is open and I close it, then look blankly at the wall. Everything will be OK. Everything will be fine. They'll let him out with a pack of pills, order him to rest for a bit and then, in a few days, he'll be on a plane. But somehow I know—I simply know, I feel—that isn't going to happen any time soon.

Chapter 10

I DON'T WANT to bother him, so I don't. I just wait. And I wait and wait and he doesn't call me back. My rib cage aches with anxiety. I can't think, sleep, or eat, and it's only when a courier comes later that evening and rings the doorbell that I'm startled from a daze in which I find myself sitting entirely in the dark. I move through the flat, switching on lights, and take the parcel in. I can't even remember what I ordered, what this might be. I don't open it. Instead I sling it under the hall table and vow to look at it later. I go through the rigmarole of switching off the lights, when only a minute ago I switched them all on, and I automatically begin the process of going to bed. My body takes me physically toward sleep, but my mind won't follow and I watch my phone, ready to take hold of it and swipe to answer. Only he doesn't ring.

At work I watch my phone all day and if anyone calls me, I converse fast and furiously, ready to end the call should my mobile ring. But it's not until I get home that I see a message from Davey has come in while I've been commuting. Can I call you? he asks.

I beat him to it, WhatsApp-calling him so fast I drop the phone in the process.

"Tell me," I say immediately.

"Oh God, Hannah," he says. And he tells me what's happened

to him. What the tests show, what the scan identifies. And what his diagnosis is.

"Testicular cancer," he says. "I'm still . . . in shock."

"Fuck" is all I can say as I feel the bottom fall out of his world. "Fuck."

"Yep," he agrees. "Fuck."

"What does that mean? What . . ." But I don't know what other questions to ask. "What does that mean?" I ask again. "How did this happen?"

"The way it always happens," he says. "It just starts."

"Fucking hell." My breath has quickened and I'm hyperventilating so much I turn the phone away from my mouth, so he can't tell what's happening to me. I don't want Davey comforting me. This isn't about me.

He tells me he woke up feeling like death, his groin was uncomfortable and he thought it felt odd, but didn't think much more about it than that until he started sweating and getting chills. His mum thought he had mumps, although he was sure he'd been vaccinated. She rushed him to the hospital.

"Mumps can cause infertility in men," he says. "It never crossed my mind it would be worse than that."

"Oh my God, Davey, I'm so sorry. Will you . . . be OK?" I dare.

"I guess. I think. I'm not sure, actually. I've had it explained to me, but I'm in a state of . . . oh, man."

My hyperventilation crosses over into panic and I start crying, although I hide it for a minute or two while he explains that the tumor is too big to use radiotherapy on. It needs to be removed. "The whole testicle needs to go. I'm going in for surgery in three days."

"That soon?" I ask.

"They need to get it out before I can start chemotherapy."

At that word I feel bile rise in my throat—an involuntary reaction I can't control, and I run to the bathroom and throw up in the toilet. He hears and tries soothing me. "Hannah, are you OK?"

"No," I say as if he's crazy. "Of course not."

"I'm sorry," he says. "I shouldn't put this on you."

"I want to know. I want to . . . help," I say stupidly as I slump to the bathroom floor.

"Thanks," he says.

A moment of quiet passes and I put my hand into my hair and pull at my scalp and then release it.

"Three days," I say. "And then when will they start the—" I can't even say the word.

"Chemo," he says. "A few weeks after. I have to recover from the surgery and then I have to go bank some sperm."

I frown, blink a few times. "Bank sperm?" a voice that doesn't sound like mine asks.

He laughs, "Yeah, I know. It's a precaution but . . . I might need it, should I ever want to—y'know—have kids."

"Fucking hell," I say again. I can't stop swearing. I feel sick and I'm trying to keep the tears at bay. I'd expected this man to be here, in my sitting room. And he's still in Texas, in a hospital, sick. I try to take a deep breath, approach this pragmatically. "I'm going to ask you what I can do. But I know I can't do anything from here."

"You can just be you. Just . . . be you."

"I can be that."

"I'm sorry," he says quietly.

The tears fall freshly down my face. "What for?"

"For this. For what was supposed to be the start of us . . . not being the start of us."

"Davey," I say with a sigh and I can't see anything because my eyes are full of tears.

"I gotta go. If I call you later . . ." he says.

"I'll pick up."

"Thanks," he says. "Bye, Hannah."

"Bye, Davey."

When he hangs up, I pull great heaving, racking breaths in and out of my body and realize that not knowing what had happened to him was far better than knowing.

I spend all night on the internet. At first I use my phone, but the small oblong screen isn't moving fast enough between pages and I move to my laptop, opening up Macmillan Cancer Support and Cancer Research UK, the NHS pages and forums of men discussing their diagnoses. I read stories similar to Davey's of fit young men who suddenly get struck down by this shock. They make light of so many things, but it feels like false bravado. Between the lines I can see they're scared. Davey must be scared. He said shocked, but now I think it has to be fear.

I feel so useless here, when he's there. I can't do anything. I can't be anything more to him than I already am. My job is to wait, to encourage, to talk when he wants to talk. I send him a message telling him this, and Davey sends back a note telling me not to worry, that he's sure he'll be fine.

I look at the stages of cancer and am reassured that the prognosis in this case is generally good, when caught early. I put a lot of stock in that. But the next day I'm floored when Davey calls again and tells me he has something called a non-seminoma—I write it down, I'll look it up later—and that "it's spread. It's in my lymph nodes."

Inside I'm crumbling. But outwardly, for him, I say "OK," aiming for pragmatic. "What does that mean?"

"It's in my chest. But not in my organs. So I'm Stage Three."

I feel bile rise again. "OK," I say.

"So . . . not Stage Four," he says positively.

"What's Stage Four?" I ask and wish I hadn't.

"In my upper organs. It's not there yet. That's why I need to start chemo quickly before the stage moves on."

"What's Stage Five?" I ask.

He pauses and then says, 'There is no Stage Five."

"Oh my God, Davey," I cry again.

"So I've had a couple of days to try and wrap my head around this now. I'm not quite out of shock yet, but they say it's going to be a long time in and out of the hospital. On a very aggressive chemo regime. Apparently."

"OK," I repeat, but it's not OK and I can't stop saying it. I wait for him to say more, but no more comes.

I give up on all plans for the weekend. I text Joan and tell her I'm going home to my parents, so I can't pop out for coffee. I can't contemplate socializing. I can't contemplate anything. While I'm on the train home to Kent, Miranda calls me—something she never does—and asks me flat out what's wrong. I have to tell her and I cry almost the whole way through it, so she has to ask me to repeat details. Passengers on the train stop reading their magazines. I watch one pull an earbud out of his ear, as those surrounding me listen intently to words I never thought I'd hear myself say, with feelings I never thought I'd have, about someone I've never met.

She's silent. Frightened for me. Frightened for him. Frightened that this could happen to Paul. And then she asks how someone so young could get cancer. "How does it happen? Did he get a sports injury? Is that what started it off?"

"I don't know," I say. "I don't think that's how it works." But I have no idea. Despite my internet searches, which last all night until the sun rises in the winter skies, I still have no idea. She tells me to keep her posted and that she loves me, and I tell her the same as I walk through town carrying my overnight bag.

My parents are shocked to see me and I realize that, in my

haste to get away from the confines of my flat, I never even told them I was coming home for the weekend. They stare at me as if I were a ghost and then smile as if nothing could ever be wrong, and that's when I crumble and words flood out of me. I'd never even told them about Davey, and now I try to explain to them everything that's happened between us. They look scared for me, because I've hurtled through the front door on the brink of tears and they can see that throughout the tale of growing affection between me and a man so far away, this story that I'm telling them isn't going to end well.

An hour later my dad has made me more than one stiff drink and we're seated at the dining table. He's pulled out his laptop and we're looking through websites, so that he can reassure me, from official sources, that if Davey is as fit and healthy as I say he is, if they caught it early, if they remove the tumor, and if the treatment regime works, Davey will be fine. "In the end."

If. If. If, I think. But I repeat his words, "In the end?" and I can see him trying not to go into GP mode, but to act as a father. I scrutinize his eyes as he ponders how to phrase it. I watch him for any telltale sign that he's lying, glossing over how awful this is.

"He needs to be positive," my dad says.

"Why?"

"He just does, sweetheart. The chemo will do its bit. Davey has to do the rest."

"That doesn't sound like a GP talking," I sniffle. "That's a bit woo-woo for you, actually, Dad."

He smiles and reaches for my hand.

Throughout the week I return to work, message Davey, message Joan, whom I haven't told about Davey's news yet, and who makes me smile every now and again with salacious updates about her and Geoff. If I thought Davey and I were moving fast, she encourages me into feeling more relaxed about it. Geoff's taking Joan on a month-long cruise. Part of me wants to be retired, so that I can go on month-long cruises. The other part of me doesn't even know how I'm going to get through the week. The gravity of Davey's situation has shocked me into a numb, dazed silence.

The day of his surgery comes and Davey calls me moments before, joking, "Just in case it's the last time I get to talk to you, y'know."

"Don't say that. It's going to be fine."

"I know. My surgeon does, like, fifty of these a week."

"Good. He's a pro."

Three hours later I get a text from a US number I don't recognize: Hi, Hannah, this is Grant, Davey's friend. I wanted to let you know Davey's out of surgery, he's come around and is a bit groggy. The surgeon told us they got everything out they wanted to, and they're happy with how it went. Davey wanted me to message you. Feel free to message me back if you want. I think he'll try to talk to you later. Grant x.

I message him back, immediately noticing the stumpy nails of my fingers as I type. Somehow throughout all this I've developed a new habit of biting my nails. I thank Grant so much for telling me and say that I'm so relieved. I don't tell him anything else. I'm in danger of over-sharing, so I cut myself off at the pass.

Davey doesn't ring me, so I wait until it's a suitable time the following day and I call him. He doesn't pick up and I assume he's still resting, sleeping. I call him much later on and, when he picks up, I can hear that he's down. Who wouldn't be, given what he's going through? I knew the perpetual upbeat nature was going to make way for the inevitable depression. I can feel it. I want to take the cancer that remains in his lymph nodes from him, make it mine, so he doesn't have to go through this anymore.

He's sharp. "Don't ever say that again. You don't want this. Trust me."

"I'm sorry," I say. "I'm so sorry for everything."

"It's not your fault." It's a default answer and he says no more.

"Would you like me to come and see you?" I ask, before I realize I've asked it.

He's silent and then, "No. Thank you. But no."

"Are you sure?"

"I don't want you to see me like this," he says.

"Really? Like what, I can't—"

"I'm going to look very different throughout this—not like the me you've gotten to know," he says simply, and I push him because I can't comprehend how. Davey takes a deep breath. "I've seen guys in here around my age. I know what's coming," he says. "I'm going to be put on a whole bunch of steroids. I'm going to lose my hair. So Grant's shaving my head for me tomorrow. I need to get used to it."

I inhale sharply.

"It's the only thing I can control," he says. "I'm taking my hair off before the chemo does."

I nod and then I try for a sexy lightheartedness, but in my eagerness to make everything OK I misfire. "I love a bad-boy look. Send me a picture."

"No," he says solemnly. "No more pictures. No more video calls."

I close my eyes at the sharpness of his reaction. "I understand," I say quietly.

"Thank you," he says. "But you can't possibly understand, and that's not your fault. Listen, Hannah, I need some sleep. I have a big day tomorrow."

"What are you—"

"Sperm bank. Tomorrow I have to go look at porn and finish into a jar," he says with an absurd laugh. I put my hand over my mouth at this sudden, unexpected turn in the conversation.

"You know where I am if you . . ." I trail off. I have nothing to add that's ladylike.

"If I need a hand?" he questions darkly and I start laughing, slowly and quietly, for fear of upsetting him. But at the other end of the phone I can hear him chuckling away until the two of us are laughing together. It's nice. It's how it was before. And then I remember it's not. We say goodbye and that we're going to talk again soon, but the sands have already shifted beneath us.

His chemo regime begins at the end of the month and we talk the night before Davey's due to arrive at the hospital. He's going to stay as an in-patient for at least three days, and then he's moving back home with his parents. The lease on his apartment has ended and he's living out of the two oversized rucksacks he packed for London, only he's still in Texas. We're struggling to find times to talk when we can be alone, given that his mum won't stop fussing around him. He's taking his dad with him tomorrow. "He's made of sterner stuff," Davey says simply. "And to be honest, I can't handle all the crying from my mom anymore."

I make a mental note not to cry again during our phone calls. I will be buoyant and upbeat, but hopefully not annoyingly so. But I'm stunned when he tells me he's going to need months of treatment and, as he runs through the cycle, my heart hurts for him. I feel so stupidly helpless, and so much further away now than I was before. I need to stop saying "OK." I need to find other words, but I have none.

"You'll be fine" has become my new go-to phrase. But I can tell that's starting to get on his nerves. He goes quiet every time I say it. During his first long, awful treatment cycle we hardly talk. I message him words of encouragement, and because I want him to know normality awaits him when this is all over, I send him pictures of early snowdrops that have grown in the park, pictures of me every now and again with a smile on my face. I wait for what feels like forever for him to reply and I carry on: buoyant, encouraging, silently frightened.

When he's home from the first three-day stint in the hospital we finally talk. He sounds awful, groggy, and the tiredness in his voice never leaves him throughout our call. And so I'm left filling silences with chatter about my day, about how I've finally gone back to the gym, about how Miranda is coming over later for the first time in ages. He listens and in the background I hear the tide turn, as it's he who starts crying. I stop talking and say, "Davey?"

"I'm sorry," he says.

"Please don't be."

He goes quiet. He won't say what he's feeling and I don't want to prompt, but I don't want him to feel lost, alone.

"Tell me," I say.

"I can't. It's so fucked up. I'm fucked up now."

"You aren't," I say. "It's scary. It's all so scary, but things are happening fast."

"I just lie here," he says. "While chemicals try to chase the cancer away."

"I know. But it will be over one day, and when it is . . . I've read the statistics. You have an eighty percent chance of a full recovery. That's so high. You have to keep going. Just . . . keep going."

"Yeah," he agrees. "Twenty percent chance I'm going to die. Not the odds I would choose. You know, there's a part of me that always thought I was invincible. That nothing would ever really take me down. But I think this might."

"No," I say. "Don't think like that. Don't say that."

"It's the small things—as well as this humongous thing. The nurse gave me anti-sickness pills to come home with. I didn't think I was gonna need them. I thought, 'I don't get sick,' so I didn't take them. Of course I get sick. I got fucking cancer. I spent all night throwing up. My mom didn't know what was wrong. I couldn't even stop long enough to tell her I didn't take the pills, so she could understand why I was throwing up so violently. I couldn't even breathe through the vomiting."

I close my eyes, a tear falls out and I can't tell him what's happening to me. What's happening to him is the worst thing imaginable.

"Hannah," he says softly. "This isn't the way it was supposed to be between us."

I slump into my bed, squish myself in against my pillows. "I know."

"This isn't how you and I are supposed to start. And I've thought a lot about that. I've had a lot of time to think, while I've been lying here doing nothing. It's not fair," he continues. "None of this is fair. Cancer coming for me at twenty-nine years old is not fair. The surgery, the chemo, the sickness, the steroids—none of this is fair. And I'm forced to take people through this with me. I can't help it. My mom and dad. Grant. You."

I tell him I'm happy to be with them on this. Well, not happy but here, very much here the whole way through this bloody awful journey.

"I'm not," he says. "And so because it's not fair and this isn't what either of us signed up for . . . I'm ending it."

My entire body goes cold, the edges of my face feel as if chill fingers have scraped down both sides.

"I'm ending it," he says again when I don't reply. "You're not coming any further on this . . . this piece of shit roller coaster. This is where I keep going. This is where you get off."

Oh my God. Tears prick at the back of my eyes, but I can't speak.

"You still there?" he asks. I nod mutely and then realize I need to speak.

"Yes," I say, and it comes out as an exhale. I haven't breathed for the last few seconds. He can't be serious.

"Are you OK?" he asks and it's a genuine question, I can tell.

"No. Of course not. I don't want that. Do you really, actually want that?"

"Yes," he says and it couldn't sound less truthful.

"Don't," I say. "Don't do this. You and I have barely even got off the ground, and this is how you end it?" He starts to talk, but I cut in. "This will end. The chemo will end. You'll recover and then you'll come here and—"

"No," he says. "I don't think I will."

I stare, shocked, straight ahead into my mirror and see the wideness of my eyes. "You're not coming here? After . . . ?"

"I don't think so. I can't tell right now. I can't see anything past this."

"Oh," I say, thinking fast. I like him. I am not prepared to let go of this as easily as he is. "Then . . . I'll come out to see you."

"No," Davey says again. "No, thank you," he says far more politely than I can tell he feels. "I don't want that. I don't want to meet you."

It cuts into my stomach. "Oh God, I see."

"Not like this," he clarifies.

"Then after . . . after all this is over."

"No," he says again and the sternness is back in his voice. "Because if I say that to you—if I say, hang on for me—it won't be fair. You're putting your life on hold, for some guy who's hooked up to drips and monitors. Hannah?" he asks.

"Yes?"

"You, hitting pause on your life . . . that stops today."

I fight off the fear that he actually means this. I vow to give him time to think about it. "I'm not putting my life on hold for you," I counter. Is he right? Have I done that? Not while everything was normal—or as normal as it ever was between us. But these last few weeks since he was diagnosed, since he was supposed to walk through the automatic doors of the airport terminal and didn't . . . yes, since then, yes I have, but of course I have. What else was I going to do?

"I really like you," I tell him. "Please don't do this. Think about it."

"I really like you too, and I have done nothing *but* think about it. It's the right decision. It's the best decision for both of us. Being in this long-distance relationship with you doesn't work like this. It's not fair on me. I'm too sick right now to cope with it. And it's not fair on you, because you could be with someone else."

"I don't want that," I tell him, but Davey's quiet and I wonder if I might be turning him back toward me. "I'll wait. Let's pause . . . us—this—and then in six months when your chemo is over—"

"No," he says with a sigh. "No. Hannah, I'm in a kind of prison and I didn't do anything to get here. You can't be part of this, now or later. I've made up my mind."

"I know. But this . . . I feel like I'm in the first real relationship I've ever had and—"

"And it's not real, Hannah," he says, and if his earlier words cut me, this completely guts me. I've resisted falling into something that neither of us could manage while we were apart. And now that we're not going to meet, he's not going to let us take this further. How do I fight that?

"I'm going to let you go now," he says.

And I can't tell if he means conversationally, so I can sleep, which of course I won't do, or actually let me go, let me disappear back into the world I inhabited before him? I don't want either of those things.

"Can I . . . can I call you?" I ask.

"Hannah," he says and he's pleading, begging me not to pursue this.

"In a week or . . . This can't be it? We started as friends. Can't we still be that?"

"We never really started as friends, did we? There was always something more to this. You must have felt it too."

He's not helping and I tell him as much, but in doing so, it's the death knell for our conversation, for the fledgling particles of our relationship, which are fragmenting, falling away, and it's out of my power to reach out and put it all back together.

"I'm going to go now. I don't mean this disrespectfully, but . . . Hannah, please don't call me again."

I suck in so much air I'm in danger of choking. What can I do to make this continue, to stop Davey from ending it, or at least to stop him from ending the call?

"Bye, Hannah."

"Davey?"

"You have to say goodbye," he instructs. "I can't just hang up on you. We have to say goodbye."

I count to three, lingering because this really isn't how this ends. But on three, because I have nothing else to say—no fight remains within me—I whisper, "Goodbye."

And he's gone.

Chapter 11

February

I WATCH THE world go by. People laugh and smile, joke with friends, jog past me as I sit in Wanstead Flats in the fierce, cold winter near the overgrown grassland. Happy walkers, eager and pleased to be enjoying their weekend, whistle and hum to themselves, and I want to scream at them: How can you do that? Don't you know what's happening to the man I . . . don't you know? But I don't. I watch as fathers push buggies, as the red light of Canary Wharf in the distance flashes on . . . off . . . on . . . off, over and over again in the wintry sky. I'm done. Mentally, I'm done. This is a strange kind of grief, one where no one's died. And over the past few days since Davey finished things between us, put forward the idea that we'll never meet, I've fallen into a rabbit hole of self-loathing and of staring at my phone, *willing* him to ring.

He's as good as his word and he doesn't call. But that can't be it. For all these weeks—for all the nuanced conversation, the plans we'd made, the moments we'd shared—that cannot be it. But I fear it is.

And the hardest part is that I know he's going to be enduring the worst thing he has ever been through and he doesn't want me to be a part of it in any way. He doesn't want to call me. He doesn't want me to call him, to support him. I've listened to tales of woe and heartbreak when some of my girlfriends have been dumped, and I've always wondered—never understood—how any woman can be so into a man that she turns into a gibbering wreck the moment that man exits her life. Now I get it, and I apologize mentally to all my friends I've comforted while they cried heaving, racking sobs in and out of their chests after having been dumped. Because that's what this is. I've been dumped, by a man going through something so terrible I can't do anything. I just have to accept it. For him. And it's so fucking hard.

I stand with Joan in the garden as the February sleet gathers in the clouds above. My phone told me it was Valentine's Day this morning. I'm ashamed to admit I stuck my middle finger up at it. I'd been seeing red crap in the shops for weeks, so I assumed it had been and gone by now. We both look up; the hoods on our winter coats are up and our dressing gowns are underneath, layered up. We should move this chat indoors, but we've trained ourselves to be hardy in all these talks over the past few years and never once have we moved inside. Sure, we'll skip some weeks, as has been the case recently, and I apologize to Joan that I've missed so much of her life. I've missed so much of my own too.

She tells me about Geoff. About their upcoming cruise. We score our coffee out of five and I stare through the tasting notes she gives me. It should feel normal, but I struggle to smile when she tells me how she's met Geoff's family. How they've planned Sunday lunches together. Joan's a sensible woman. She won't even consider moving in with Geoff; not this early on. But I can see it on the horizon for them, and that's what finally makes me smile while she's talking about something else entirely.

It's she who mentions Davey to me—who asks me how he is, how I am. Although we've spent time commiserating about Davey's situation recently, things have moved on since we last spoke and I'm forced to confess that we aren't together. We were never together. Only now we really aren't.

"Cancer is a bitch," Joan says and it makes me smile, wryly.

"Yeah, it really is."

"And so . . . that's it? He's not coming here? After everything?"

I shake my head.

"And you're not going there?" she probes.

I shake my head again. "I'm not allowed. I want to be that girl who gets on a plane, who simply turns up. But I genuinely think that would be a mistake. I think he'd be horrified."

Joan sucks cold air in through her teeth. Just nods her head slowly. "Perhaps give it some time. Give him some time."

I make a noncommittal noise. "I'm not sure. As much as I hate to say it, I think that was it for us. Davey sounded so sure. Like it was too much effort, and if he's not coming to England even after he recovers—*if* he recovers . . ." I trail off and fight the tears, pull myself together, and say, "Then, I guess, that's it. What can I do? Nothing."

She reaches over the fence and puts her hand on mine, where it's resting on top of the coarse panel.

"Joan?" I ask as we're preparing to wrap up for the morning. What Davey and I had, no matter how fleeting, can in no way be compared to a life together, a marriage like Joan had, but I ask this question nonetheless. "Do you ever think about your late husband?"

"Yes, all the time," she says.

"Do you ever feel strange, being with another man, but sometimes your mind drifts back to . . . him?"

"I've had a long time to come to terms with Richard's passing, and life is for living. No point living in the past. What we had was ours—special—and it's not gone. It's always there. Only now, after all this time, I have room for someone else in my heart."

I try to take from that something that's relevant to me. Eventually I'll let go. Eventually. But not yet. And that's OK.

I've avoided George these past few weeks as I've not felt up to the gym. A hurried reply to a message here, a quick thumbs-up emoji there. I've given myself permission to be a shit friend, but in the middle of my lunch break, while I'm queuing for a soup pot and a salad at Pret, that permission gets revoked because he finally gives in and phones me. Even after Davey's insistence on phoning, I'm still thrown when anyone else I've got stored in my phone book actually rings me.

I give it a few rings in case it's a mistake. "Hello?" I ask eventually, cradling my phone against my ear while I tap my card to pay and take my purchases.

"Oh, good, you're still alive. OK, cool, I can go now. Bye." George hangs on, no intention of hanging up.

"Hi," I say guiltily and then immediately apologize for being a terrible friend as I work my way out into the bitter streets of the city.

"Holiday!" He yells down the phone in place of a proper answer. "So I need to talk to you about Thailand," he goes on, and I'm jolted into the realization that our holiday is only days away. "Shall we go to the airport together or shall I meet you there?"

"Um." I don't know the answer to this. *I'm not going.* That's the answer I want to say but, for the moment, I don't.

"It's not a trick question," he replies. "I can come by, pick you up. Shall we get an Uber to the airport, do it in style? Can't be buggered to haul suitcases on the Underground, can you?"

"No."

"No to what? No to the Uber or no to the Underground?"

"Either. Whatever you want."

"Uber then. I'll book it."

I'm not going, I think. I'll tell him in a second. But George chatters on and I'm powerless to stop the flow of excited boyish chat that continues. He lists a whole bunch of places he wants to go in Bangkok. How he's bought a travel guide, has dog-eared almost every page. I nod along in silence. I can't do any of this. I only have the ability to get up, go to work, come home. I'm on autopilot and I can't factor in a plane ride, a holiday where George takes on the persona of Tour Guide Barbie. I'm exhausted already. I need a break. I know I need a break and it will be good to stop thinking about Davey for a few minutes, but maybe I can do that just by staying at home, watching TV, reading a book. And then I won't have to be with George. I hate how cruel I'm being and I listen back in to the call. He's gone silent and it's obviously my turn to talk.

"Something's happened?" he says. "What? What's happened?"

His intuitiveness stuns me. "What do you mean?"

"What's the deal? Why are you all weird?"

"I'm not being weird. Am I?"

"Yeah," he says. "Your enthusiasm is . . . nil."

"Sorry. I'm . . ." And then for reasons unbeknownst to me, I tell him in the most basic way possible. "I've been dumped."

"By who?" he asks immediately. And I tell him, in the shadow of the Gothic architecture and the modern glass buildings that surround me in the City, I tell him everything. He's quiet. I'm not pouring out my soul—not to George. I'm working up to something. I'm giving him everything from start to finish, so that when I end and tell him I'm in no mood for a holiday, that I'm going to write the cost off and that I hope he has a nice time, because I'll be the worst travel companion ever . . . he'll understand, thanking God that I'm not going with him.

But he says, "Oh, Hannah. That's bloody awful. The poor guy."

"So you see why I can't come? Why I can't force myself to have a good time? You are, honestly, better off without me. I might even go back to my parents for a little bit of it. But I can't face going to Thailand."

He's quiet and I wait for a contemplative response, but George merely says, "Don't be a dick."

I widen my eyes in shock. "I'm not being a dick."

"You really are. You've been dumped. Happens to everyone. If everybody stuck a pin in their lives just because they'd had a rough ride, most planes would be traveling around the world half-empty." I try to interject, but he continues, "Dig out your passport, blow the dust off your sunglasses and I'll see you at yours in an Uber the day after tomorrow."

How has the time gone by so fast that it's the day after tomorrow? He doesn't even say goodbye. He simply hangs up, like some kind of dramatic, impressive exit. I realize now that George always has to have the last word. I eat my soup at my desk with one hand, typing with another: **I'm not coming, George.** I hit send.

I see he's online and then he's offline. He doesn't even respond. I am being a dick. I know I am. I'm losing a friend over this, but I mean it. I can't go. Maybe if I wasn't going with George, it would be easy. Maybe I could happily—and I use the term "happily" loosely—holiday on my own. But I can't handle George and his Duracell-bunny outlook on life. Not now. Not the day after tomorrow. And not for ten days in Thailand, with his "every page is dog-eared" travel guide. Although, actually, I'd be free most evenings to wallow in my own self-pity because he'll be out chasing girls for one-night stands.

I want to message Davey. I want to say something heartbreakingly cruel, such as, "Remember that fit personal trainer I went on a date with, when you and I were getting to know each other? Remember I was going on holiday with him? Well, I still am. Enjoy being alone."

But I don't send it.

Instead I type a different message to him. He's told me not to contact him and it's so raw, so fresh—this strange relationship that never was, this ending—but I type it all the same: I miss you. I wish you hadn't ended us. How are you? Are you coping? Call me. I'm here.

I don't know what else to write, so I just look at the cursor blinking at the end of my sentence. I hold it in my hand for a moment and then I hit backspace until the whole message has gone. I look up at the top of the screen. He's offline: *Davey, last seen today at 12:01 p.m.* Only an hour ago. Who did he message at that time? What is he doing now? Is it one of his chemo days? I have no idea. The cycle sounded grueling, and far too sporadic for me to keep up with from afar. I miss our chats, our laughter, our being together while being apart. I miss everything and I have to go to the toilet, lock myself in a cubicle, and cry as silently as possible so that no one hears me.

My doorbell rings in the middle of the next night and I lurch awake. I have woken from a dream. One in which I was halfway through a video call with Davey. I don't know what we were talking about, but I was laughing. I wake with a smile on my face at something so wonderful—not even a memory, but a wish of what there might still have been. But then as the doorbell sounds again, I blink in shock, climb out of bed, pull the front door open a smidge, with the chain still on for safety, and look into the face of George.

"Watcha," he says, looking me up and down, taking in me, my pajamas, my scruffy bed-hair. "Do you need a few minutes?" he asks.

"What for? What are you doing here?"

"It's taxi time, baby. Have you overslept? I didn't even bother going to bed. No point."

I stare blankly at him. "I'm not coming," I say.

"What the fuck?" he replies.

I close the door, slip off the chain, open it up wide. His face is total confusion. He looks me up and down again, realizing that I'm not dressed for a reason. "I didn't think you were serious," he cries. "Hannah . . . you have to come."

"I don't want to."

"I don't care," he says. "Get dressed. Let's go."

"George," I plead.

"No," he says, almost barging his way into my flat. "You have two options. You get dressed, grab your bag, and bring it out to the car, where I'll be waiting. You have ten minutes max. Or you get dressed, grab your bag, and *I'll* take it out to the car, and I sit here in your flat to make sure you do it."

"George!"

"Get dressed, Hannah," he barks at me. "Fucking hell. Chop-chop."

He pushes me in the direction of the shower. "I don't even think we've got time for you to shower, but it's a bloody long flight, so get a move on. Where's your stuff?"

He spies my suitcase in the corner of my bedroom and makes a beeline for it. "This it? You packed? You'd better be bloody packed, woman."

"I . . . I am . . . but I'm not—"

"If you say you're not coming one more time, I swear to God I'm going to lose my mind. Shower, now! Passport?"

"In that drawer," I reply, because I can't do anything else. He's not going to let me. He grabs my passport and puts it with his, in his jeans pocket.

Ten minutes later I've done my teeth and washed, and dressed in leggings and a baggy T-shirt and a sweater for a flight that I can't believe I'm getting on. George looks me up and down. "Fucksake, are you back in your pajamas again?"

"No," I cry, pulling on my trainers. "I'm dressed."

"You look exactly the same as you did ten minutes ago," he says incredulously. "Right, let's go."

"Hang on," I reply, running around and grabbing last-minute essentials: my phone charger, wallet, a book for the flight. If there's anything else I've missed, I'll have to buy it at the airport. As with the rest of my moments over the past few weeks, I'm operating without a manual.

It's strange to be back at the airport again. I try with all my might not to let it overwhelm me. Only a month ago I was here, waiting for a man who never showed up. George leads me like a lost child, handles our baggage and check-in, has already printed off a boarding pass for me, as if he knew I was going to be trouble from the start.

The sun is rising outside the terminal as we sit facing the runway, watching the skids on the tarmac as planes land, wheels bouncing gently; watching planes take off at almost impossible angles, wheels folding in on themselves, tucking invisibly inside the plane as they soar into the sky. I wish I could do that. Tuck myself up, become invisible.

I close my eyes and try to sleep. I've become a child. George will tell me when it's time to get up and go. And he does. Somewhere in between sitting and getting up an hour or so later, he went shopping when I just couldn't face it. He's bought us each one of those squishy pillows, and I look at him thankfully. He puts his hand on my back, steering me toward the plane. On board he looks toward our seats, checking them against the boarding pass, and then angles me toward the window seat, letting me slump in, nestle into the corner, putting my head against my new squishy cushion and sleeping away the initial hours of our flight.

By the time we land, George is asleep and I'm wide awake, watching him look so incredibly peaceful, so at ease with himself. I wonder what that's like. I'm sure that's once how I was, and not even that long ago. The heavenly sunshine awaits us and, as we step into the searing heat outside the terminal, the humidity and the sunshine hitting me by surprise, my phone tells me it's a glorious eighty-four degrees.

Our hotel is on the Khao San Road and I can't help but be distracted by the buzz of backpackers and tourists, the flurry of humans, the heat, the smells of sweat and spice. As early evening draws in, we check in. I want nothing more than to sleep the night away but after we've showered, George drags me out for street food and we eat it walking through the musky streets, with George always at my side, steering me through the melee of traffic and pedestrians. Tuk-tuks whizz by us and George asks if we should get one tomorrow. I decide I need to start showing enthusiasm on this holiday. George is the only thing keeping me from descending into some kind of depressed byway out of my own life, and so I nod, agree, smile, and somewhere deep within I do feel quite excited to get on a tuk-tuk. And although we've only been here a matter of hours, I know that if I was here without George I would probably sit in my room or venture as far as the rooftop pool and that would be it.

George's enthusiasm, his tour-guide routine, could drive me mad, but actually I need this, I need him now, and I'm pleased beyond belief that he's here; that I'm here. We finish our food, bin the remnants, and I buy us some sickly-sweet bottled beers that we drink on the way back to our hotel. We've blown away the cobwebs of our flight. Because I've shown enthusiasm for the first time since he rang the other day, I've perked George up. Poor man. What's possessed him to come here with me, knowing that I'm such a misery at the moment? I smile at him. He smiles back at me, grinning his easy charm. He's surprisingly tanned, given that it's February. Has he been applying fake tan? He drapes his arm over my shoulders as we enter the fray of the Khao San Road, and I put mine around his waist as we head back to the hotel.

Chapter 12

THE NEXT FEW days are a surprising frenzy of joy and heat, beers and good food—some of it nourishing, some of it not. But I hear nothing from my personal-trainer friend about the number of calories we're both packing away. We hit the tourism trail hard by day, taking in ornate gold, impressive temple after ornate gold, impressive temple until my enthusiasm wanes again, and it's absolutely nothing to do with my thoughts of Davey wangling their way back in again. I take George by the collar as he turns the page of his book and reads, "The Wat Saket temple has—"

"No," I say, holding his collar tight and shaking him, his head jostling around comically. He laughs. "No more temples, George. A museum now. A gallery. Anything. Anything at all, but no more temples."

"Got it," he says. "What do you want to do?" he offers.

I think. "I know we've got a week of vegging next week in Phuket, but could we just hit the rooftop pool today, do you think? Cocktails, sticky mango drinks, club sandwiches, reading our books . . . y'know?"

He closes his travel book and looks at me. "Yeah, go on then." We hail a tuk-tuk, which has become our preferred method of transport, and head back to the hotel, where we sleep in the sun, drink far more than we should, and doze next to each other on sun loungers.

After we've been in Bangkok for almost a week and it's time for us to move on, I realize George hasn't ditched me once, in favor of finding women to get laid with. We've had a really casual break, gotten to know each other better, our quirks and differences. He's a really easy travel buddy.

I've not been in the mood for watching idle backpackers get fresh out of their minds, climbing over heaving bodies gyrating together, and so we've eschewed the idea of clubbing, but on our last night we decide we're going for an expensive dinner, and George surprises me by having pre-booked a restaurant called Sirocco. He doesn't tell me anything about it. Only that I'm to "dress posh. The sexiest of all those sexy dresses you've got."

And so I do. George promises me no walking. Only taxis or tuk-tuks, so I risk the only pair of little heels I've got. As I emerge from the lift of our hotel, meeting George in the lobby, he wolf-whistles at me and then says, "Wit-woo."

"What are you, an owl?" I chuckle and he laughs back, but only for a second as he looks me up and down.

"Well, don't you scrub up all right, Gallagher?"

"So do you," I tell George as I look him up and down. He's leaning against the lobby's cool marble wall in a dark-blue suit, although he's carrying his jacket over his shoulder in the night's heat. I sense he won't put that jacket on—that it's for effect. He looks posed, staged, as if he's waiting for his photograph to be taken. And so I tell him to hang on, as I fish my phone from my bag and take a picture of him. I think of the man whose presence lingers in my phone; of the two picture messages Davey sent of himself, which I've not looked at since we stopped talking to each other. I notice how my anger at him breaking up with me is diminishing over time. That's what people mean by "give it time." It's only been a few weeks since he called it off. But I still miss him. I miss dissecting our days together, the tentative plans we almost made. My regret is that I didn't push hard enough to remain friends, and I ponder this on the way over to Sirocco. George is shocked that I've not heard of this restaurant and recites—word-for-word, I'm sure—the entry in his travel guide about it. Blessedly, he's left his guidebook in his room.

It's on the sixty-third floor of the State Tower and we ride the lift up, with George suddenly pulling my hand toward him and clutching it tightly.

"I'm OK," I tell him suddenly.

"I'm not," he mutters. "I don't really like heights."

"Oh, George, why are we here then?"

"Because it's meant to be magnificent, and I felt we deserved a really decent night out."

I hold his hand tighter, squeezing it gently over and over as the lift rockets us skyward.

"Oh my God," I say as we step out of the air-conditioned lift and out toward a warm breeze and a rooftop bar that's a mix of ornate gilt and glass. I look behind, at the commanding gold dome from which we've emerged, and mutter, "Wow."

Out in the distance and far below, the twinkling lights of Bangkok herald another opportunity-filled night. And then a live jazz band begins and I'm overwhelmed, looking toward George for his reaction in the warm night. He's still holding my hand, his mouth parted as if he wants to comment but can't find the words, and I suddenly like the feel of his hand in mine; now it's not for comfort, more for . . . I'm not sure what for, but he's not letting go and neither am I. Of all the places I've been, I'm going to remember this moment forever. We're led down a huge column of lit stairs and I'm grateful George is holding my hand, because heels and I are not the best of friends, especially when stairs are concerned. As we reach our table, the night surrounds us, and the candle on the table flickers gently in its tea-light holder.

We sit in happy silence, both of us looking out at the horizon and the buildings, all of which are lower than us, as we listen to the jazz and allow our water glasses to be filled. The waiter tells us about the restaurant and the array of menus, and then leaves us with drinks choices to make.

"I'm going to eat everything," George says, and I laugh as his eyes twinkle merrily in the candlelight. We peruse options, showing each other dishes we like the look of and making comments as if we suddenly know what we're talking about when it comes to food. We land on the tasting menu and decide to throw caution to the wind, allow the chef to plan our dining, the sommelier to execute his own wine pairings for the meal. Five courses, five glasses of wine each, not to mention the cocktails George has just called the waiter back to add to our order. He has such enthusiasm for . . . everything, and his zest for life is infectious. With George I feel picked up, carried along on his river of boyish charm. I love the ease of our conversations, how we flit easily from topic to topic.

"Worst date?" he throws at me after one of our courses arrives: a delicate crab and cucumber dish. The sommelier walks over with two glasses of delicious white wine, the condensation running down the sides in the evening heat. I eat, drink, and become merry almost immediately. A part of me never wants this evening to end. It's perfect.

"Worst date . . ." I ponder. "Oh, I know," I say, holding in a laugh, and I tell him how I was taken to the cinema by a guy who was so seriously into his musicals that he sang along out loud to every single song during *La La Land*. "I think he thought it was cute. I wanted to die of embarrassment. It was clear I wasn't the first girl he'd taken to see that particular film. So many people told him to shut up."

"Cringey," George offers, shuddering appropriately, and I ask him about his worst date.

"Ah, I think it was my fault it was my worst date," he confesses.

I inch forward in my chair, put my fingers on the stem of my wineglass. This is my third, as we finish our third course. I'm steadily getting tipsy on wine, full of food, but not tiring of the good company. "Go on," I prompt nosily.

"Took a girl on a picnic. Found this beauty spot. Ginormous hamper full of posh food—y'know, strawberries and champagne, all those picky bits people usually can't get enough of, gourmet pork pies and . . . oh, I don't know—can't remember now. We thought we were on our own and started kissing before we'd even eaten."

"Smooth operator," I comment.

"I try," he says with a grin. "And then, while we aren't looking, a huge dog comes over."

"Oh, don't tell me," I say, "it eats your entire picnic."

"I wish. He took a huge dump on our picnic mat."

This has caught me entirely off guard and I snort wine.

"We try to see the funny side, but she's not really laughing. We bin the picnic mat, take the food, pack it up, move further up the hill. The view's better. I get the food out and go to uncork the champagne and she peers in the hamper, asks what I've bought that's not *meat-based*. I point at the strawberries and she asks about salad and the like, and I have to confess, 'Blokes don't really do salad.' Well, I didn't do salad back then. Then she tells me, in a really huffy voice, that she's a vegetarian and I should have known that. After that, I'll admit the afternoon was pretty much done."

"Eek," I say. "That would do it, yes." As our next course arrives I ask, "Best date?"

He looks around at our surroundings. "This is pretty decent," and I wonder if he's making a casual comment or answering my question.

"Is this a date?" I ask him teasingly.

"If it is, it's up there in my top . . . one."

I smile and he winks, dismissing any awkwardness that might have submerged us. But I find feelings of awkwardness don't come. He lifts his glass and we say "Cheers" in unison.

"Go on then," I say after a while, "tell me why fit, personal-trainer George, who takes girls on amazing dates to rooftop restaurants, is still single?"

It's his turn to think and after a while he says, "I think I just struggle with compatibility. It's not them," he says without a hint of a smile. "It's definitely me."

I wait for more.

"I'm good for a shag, I think," he continues.

I raise my eyebrow. "Is this you telling me you're good in bed?"

"No," he says and the smile returns. "This is me telling you I'm *epic* in bed. Mind-blowing."

I laugh, but something deep within tingles.

He sighs. "But relationships—I seem to fail at that part."

"I hear you," I say, taking a long gulp of wine to finish my glass. The waiter is arriving with our next course—thank God the dishes are small—and the sommelier is hot on his heels with our accompanying glass of wine. "I'm getting sloshed," I say, but I have no intention of refusing the wine. After our food and wine are presented with a flourish, I go on, "Well, you have good chat, and good date quality. This *is* pretty decent. Also picnics on hills with champagne and meat-based products sound flipping awesome. Dog shit aside."

He laughs and so do I.

"So I don't know what you're doing wrong."

"I'm a good-time guy. I look great on a girl's arm. I am *the* perfect plus one for a wedding. But relationships . . . Ah, girls want more than I can offer. I'm not exactly rolling in cash, I work odd hours, sometimes I'm training clients until eleven P.M., and girls want a guy to 'be there' more than I am. I think if I was a heart surgeon, they'd cope all right with my mad schedule, but eventually it all wears a bit thin and off they run."

"Into the arms of a heart surgeon?" I ask.

"Ha, yes, the life-saving fuckers. Your turn," he says. "Best date."

I remember my date with Davey, the film night where he totally understood my strange fascination with *A Room with a View*. But this is personal, something I don't want to share. It's hard to describe how a video date was the best date I've actually had. It was Davey; it wasn't necessarily what we were doing. Instead I look around and echo George's words. "This is pretty decent."

He smiles, raises his glass to me.

"To dog-poo-free dining," I say and he laughs out loud and then repeats, "Dog-poo-free dining."

The couple at the next table look over at us in horror.

I sleep so soundly that night, full of good food and more wine than I think I've ever had in my life, but the moment we're on the plane to Phuket early the next morning I miraculously fall back asleep again. I feel like I only closed my eyes five minutes ago when the wheels hit the runway. George is asleep next to me or, rather, almost *on* me, as our dividing armrest is up and we've managed to curl ourselves into each other. Ordinarily this should feel embarrassing, but it doesn't. I give him a little nudge and watch him swallow in his sleep, give a deep breath, and his eyes open ever so slightly. He's not shaved and the stubble on his chin gives him that rugged look I've not seen on him before. He's usually so clean-cut. I quite like it.

In the taxi to our beach hotel I look over at George, who's studying the guidebook with concentration. I watch him as he scans, and I wait for it. "After we've checked in, do you want to—"

"No," I cut in, lifting my sunglasses. "I don't."

"You don't know what I'm going to say," he exclaims.

"I do," I reply. "And no. We aren't doing tourist things today. Today is about sun loungers and all-inclusive cocktails," I command.

He laughs, closes his book. "Whatever you say, Gallagher."

When we've checked in and I've appreciated the towels on my bed having been folded into elephant shapes, taken a picture, and sent it to Miranda, I go downstairs in my new neon-pink bikini and a kaftan. I've probably eaten far too much last night to make this bikini work, but I stroll down to the beach where George is waiting, having already sourced us sunbeds, towels, and drinks.

"A piña colada?" I query George's drink choice as I slump onto my sun lounger, put down my book, and prepare to stay here all day. "But it's only eleven A.M."

"I'm following your all-inclusive holiday rules," he says, "and giving your favorite drink a shot." He sips, "Jesus, this is sweet. How can you drink it?"

"Too easily." I've already drunk about half of it in one gulp, which is doing my faint hangover no good at all.

George takes another sip of his. "Yeah, it's a grower. I'll persevere."

"Brave man," I tease.

"We just going to do this all day?" he asks. "Lie here? Get brown? Eat? Drink? Swim?"

"Punishing, isn't it?" I tease again and then stifle a scream as George throws a lump of ice from his drink onto my stomach, leaving sticky pineapple juice on my skin.

I throw the ice back at him, close my eyes, prepare to sleep again. I open my eyes, glance over at George, who's still looking at me.

"You look good in that bikini, by the way," he says casually.

"Thanks." I look him up and down. He suits his muscles. Some men look too veiny and as if they've been blown up and stretched, but George looks hard in all the right places. What's happening to me? I look away. "You look good too."

"Have you put sun lotion on?" he asks as my eyes drift closed again.

"No, Dad. Not yet."

Another lump of ice hits me and, with my eyes still closed, I smile as genuine happiness and the sunshine warm me in equal measure.

I can feel something landing on me gently, a sort of strange, warm feeling, and I gradually wake on my lounger awhile later to find George hovering over me, spraying me with sun lotion. I blink slowly, stare up at him.

"You were starting to burn," he says, "and I didn't want to wake you."

I nod, a bit confused and sleepy, as George is still kneeling at the side of my lounger. "OK," I say slowly.

"And now," George says, "I realize I probably should have woken you, because I thought this spray would just sink in, but it's sitting on your skin and needs rubbing in and . . ." He is rambling, and I'm still looking at him. "If I'd rubbed it in while you were sleeping, wouldn't that be . . ." he asks. I narrow my eyes behind my sunglasses. He looks at me; a worried expression has taken over his face and he finishes, quietly, ". . . assault?"

I can't help but laugh at the unexpectedness of what he's said. He's still kneeling.

"Do you want me to rub the lotion in?" he asks slowly.

A huge part of me wants to say yes, but I'm worried about what might happen if he does. I don't answer immediately, but instead I sit up and reach for the bottle still in his grasp. "No, I'll do it."

"Sure," he says, moving back to his lounger.

I'm still hazy from my nap and am putting my confusion down to that. I steal glances at George every now and again. His eyes are open behind his sunglasses, but he's not looking at anything in particular, just straight up to the sky. What's he thinking? He's such an open book that if I ask him, he'll tell me. I'm not going to ask him. That way leads to danger—I can sense it.

I spray lotion onto my hands and try the inelegant task of rubbing it into my back. Why have humans still not developed a magic way of applying lotion to our own backs?

George turns his head and then gestures to the bottle. "Want me to do it?"

No. But I really need to do it. Unless I don't turn over all day and simply bronze my front, like an egg that's sunny side up. Oh, that's going to look weird. "OK," I say reluctantly and pass George the bottle. I move on the lounger, turning so that George resumes his kneeling position. I enjoy the feel of his hands moving slowly over my back far more than I should. He's meticulous, slow and I am clearly sex-starved without realizing it until this moment, because this is the most sensual way anyone has applied sun lotion to me, ever. And now I just want it to be over, but his hands keep moving over my shoulders and neck and I stiffen. This is so innocent, isn't it? Ahead of us another couple are rubbing sun lotion into each other's backs, but it's vigorous, purposeful. I realize that's what George should be doing. But he's not. OK, he needs to stop now. And, mercifully, he does, but his hands remain on me.

"Hannah," he starts from behind me and I stare straight ahead.

"Yep," I say in a clipped voice.

But he doesn't continue and so I turn to look at him, which is a huge mistake, because he's right there, all blue eyes and tanned skin. There's a look in his eyes that I recognize, because I'm sure it's what my own are doing to him. I know what's about to occur next and I know it's going to be a huge mistake, but I don't care because it's happening.

I am too chicken to make the first move, even though I want to. I look at George's mouth and he looks at mine, but only for a second, because then his mouth is on mine and he's kissing me so fiercely that I'm temporarily stunned at what he's doing, at what I'm doing. But I let it happen, I encourage it by kissing him back and I turn fully into the kiss. Our bodies are pressing into each other and after a moment it's George who pulls back, looking at me with an expression that says everything.

"Jesus Christ, we can't do this here," he says throatily. He's breathing fast and so am I.

I move almost immediately, gathering my book and lotion, putting on my sandals and my wrap, which I tie around my waist quickly. George stands up, looks down at his swim shorts and laughs, saying, "I'm going to need a minute." He smiles at me and then changes his mind. "Fuck it, let's go."

We walk back in the direction of our rooms, George holding me almost in front of him as we walk. We've automatically chosen his room and he spins me by the door, pressing my back against it before he inserts the key card. His mouth is on mine, his tongue pushing into mine over and over again, and I'm aware that I sigh deeply as his mouth moves to my neck. I can't concentrate as my hands find his hair and his face moves to mine again, as he both manages to kiss me and unlock the door and we both fall into the room. He kicks the door shut and immediately we're pulling at each other's meager clothes. My hand reaches the waistband of his swim shorts, teasing the line of it as he pulls at my bikini ties, untying them deftly. He picks me up, takes me over to his bed. I briefly note that George has equally natty towel-art, as he swipes his towel-swan to the floor and lowers me onto the bed. And then my bikini briefs are being pulled from me and I'm pulling George's swim shorts off him and he's over me, nudging my legs apart.

God, I'm so ready and he pauses as he hovers over me. I glance down at him. He's as ready as I am, but he says from his position above me, "What are we doing about contraception?"

I am a bad person. In the haste of all of this, contraception has completely gone from my mind. It's been so long since I've had sex or been in a relationship. I came off the pill ages ago.

"Condoms," I say. This is George. He must have brought a million out here with him.

"OK," he nods, getting up and going to his wallet. He puts on a condom and I'm entranced by the action, which only serves to turn me on even more, and then he comes toward me, nudges my legs open again and sinks inside me, making me moan. All that chat about him being epic in bed was categorically not just chat. He really, really knows what he's doing and we move so rhythmically, so in tune together, that he brings me to orgasm within minutes, following me over the edge seconds later. We lie there, covered in sweat because neither of us thought to turn on the air-con. I turn toward him, trace the line of his abdominal muscles with my fingertips.

"That was . . ." I start, because I feel I have to say something but I don't know what. *That was great* is surely the most clichéd thing you could say to someone after you've had sex with them.

But George speaks. "That was . . . a long time coming, Gallagher."

I laugh. "Was it?"

"You don't think? I'm usually better than that. That was a good few months of foreplay and then about five minutes of actual sex."

"Good sex," I say, a little wide-eyed. "Great sex. A shame it's a once-only event, really."

He starts, turns toward me, his skin glistening with perspiration, his chest rising and falling heavily. "Once only?" he questions.

I nod and then, uncertainly, "Isn't it?"

"Why would it be?"

"Why wouldn't it be?" I counter.

His brow furrows. "You don't want sex like that, with me, ever again?" He is genuinely confused.

"I . . . I don't know. I just thought: this is obviously a holiday thing."

He puts his elbow on the bed, props his head up, traces a line up and down my inner thigh with his finger, turning me back on immediately. "Why don't we see how we go?" he says. "Take it one day at a time?" He leans toward me, his fingers roaming gently, teasing as they move up and down my inner thigh, higher and then lower and then even higher again, until I groan in anticipation as his fingers nearly, nearly reach where I want them to.

"OK," I breathe, but I've forgotten what the question was.

His mouth touches mine and he kisses me again, his hands still brushing my skin. I can feel the hardness of him pressing against me again and he whispers, "Shall I get another condom?"

"Yes," I breathe.

We sleep, basking in the glow of fantastic sex, and then later, when thirst and hunger drive us as crazy as we were a few hours ago, we head into his walk-in shower together. George has had the foresight to bring another condom with him and it's definitely the holiday mood we're in, because sex like this doesn't happen in real life, but he lifts me up, my legs hooking around his waist and, with the warm water raining down around us, we have sex against the tiled shower wall. I can barely walk as we head down to take in a late lunch, but George holds my hand as we stand, waiting to be seated, his thumb rubbing my hand.

"Are you on the pill?" he asks before the waiter approaches to seat us for lunch. "Because if you are, we don't have to use condoms. I'm not sleeping with anyone else. Are you?"

"What? No." I whisper in shock as we're seated and are told the kitchen closes in ten minutes. We both order club sandwiches and mango smoothies. When the waiter disappears I say, "I'm not on the pill, no."

He nods. "Do you think you might want to go on it at some point?"

"Um," I say, glancing around to check no one's listening, but there's hardly anyone else left in the restaurant. "I've never really found one that didn't either make me ravenous and fat or kill my libido entirely. But I could try and find another one, if this continues when we get home."

He smiles. "Why do you keep insinuating that it won't?"

I shrug. "I don't know. Playing it safe, I guess." Davey made me really like him and then dumped me. It's not happening again.

"Hannah, I'm not here to hurt you."

"I know," I say, thinking that's a strange conclusion to jump to.

"I do, however, need to buy more condoms if we're going to carry on like this for the rest of the week."

I must look like a rabbit caught in headlights. "I can't have sex three times a day for a week, George. I'll be dead by the end of it."

The waiter appears behind me, placing our mango smoothies down and giving George a knowing look before departing.

George explodes with laughter, sits back and smiles. "Shame."

We spend the rest of the afternoon blissfully sleeping in the sun. This time I feel the sun lotion land on my skin and George begins rubbing it in. I am very aware that if I open my eyes, I'll sit up, kiss him, and we'll be right back where we were earlier. I am determined to ignore it, mutter, "Thanks" and leave it there, but I whisper, "Sexual assault" and then pretend to sleep again as I hear him chuckle in the background.

We skip dinner, still feeling full from the late-afternoon club sandwiches, but we sit in the beach bar, surrounded by other like-minded souls who have decamped from the beach the few paces it takes to find a bar stool.

"I am really glad I came. I'm really glad you burst through my door and dragged me to Thailand."

"Kicking and screaming," he says as we sip the sweetest cocktails on the menu. George winces, then drinks it like a champion.

"Yeah, I'm having a terrible time," I tell him. "It's really shit."

He leans forward, kisses me, brushes sandy hair from my face and it's not sexual at all. It's something else. He looks away, smiling. "I think this is the most perfect day I've ever had," he says as we watch the large orange sun dip so slowly into the horizon.

"Is it because you had sex three times?"

He looks at me. "No. It's you. And the sex. But it's mainly you. I really like spending time with you."

"Thank you," I say. But there's something holding me back from saying anything more.

After another day of sleeping in the sun and then sleeping together after lunch, I suggest we get the tour book out. I can see George itching to get out of what he calls the compound. We take a taxi and then walk up Monkey Hill, buying bunches of bananas for a few baht. We climb up, hand in hand. If there's a moment when we're walking, we're never not hand in hand. Even when it's almost eighty-six degrees and my hand is warm, George is so tactile that it's nice to be wanted and touched. He's chivalrous and kind. My mum will love him. I glance up at him, his Ray-Bans glinting in the sun, his shirt unbuttoned a little further than usual, showing off his tanned chest. I'm not sure my dad will love him.

"What are your parents like?" I ask him, curiously.

He gives me a look. "They're all right."

"Are you close?" I ask.

"No. Are you with yours?"

I nod. "Yeah. I was thinking my mum would love you."

He beams a white smile. "Mums always love me."

"What about dads?" I inquire.

"Not at first. I'm a grower."

"Like a piña colada?"

He laughs. "Yeah, exactly like a piña colada. First taste is always a bit *what the hell?* And then . . . everyone's all right with it."

I squeeze his hand. By the time we arrive at the monkeys, which are scampering across the road at quite a lick, I'm hot and tired but exhilarated. "There are monkeys everywhere," I cry. "This is so mental!"

"I know. Hold out the bananas," he says and hands me a bunch. I hold it out and a monkey darts at me, grabs it, and runs off. I watch it go, heading toward the trees, the simple act of lifting bananas from a tourist accomplished within a second. I look at my empty hand. "Well, that was that then." But George is kneeling, holding out bananas one by one, as smaller monkeys approach him tentatively and then become braver as he pushes the fruit toward them. I watch him through all of this—watch how he just *is*. I take a picture of him, kneeling, feeding the monkeys. This is so surreal. And brilliant. And to think I didn't even want to come on holiday.

I look away, toward the trees where monkeys are devouring bananas. Around us tourists depart or arrive and continue feeding them. Hundreds of monkeys dart around us and when we've finished we begin our stroll back down toward our waiting taxi. George holds my hand again and I feel I'm only really giving this 50 percent of my attention. I'm not devoting any part of my heart to it. Not yet. I will do as George says. I will take it one day at a time and see how it goes. We may get back to England in a few days and he might lose interest. I might lose interest. I'm not sure we're right for each other, but we certainly fit together well. Here. Now. And I do like him.

We sleep together in my room. It's the first night we've spent together. And when I wake up, his eyes flicker open and he smiles at me. We talk about where we see ourselves in a few years, which is heady conversation before coffee, and George makes us some in the room. I still see myself at the same company, if not in the same job. Fingers crossed, some kind of promotion creeps its way into my CV. George is content being a personal trainer, loves the job, can't see himself doing anything else. He's just so . . . easy. This is easy. Through no fault of his own, Davey was complicated. George is easy. I get it now.

We sit on my balcony, George in his boxers and me in my pajama shorts and tank top, my hair in a mess in a topknot. He leans forward to tuck a piece of hair behind my ear and I think I'm genuinely quite happy at the moment. I can just about hear the waves lapping at the sand on the distant shore and the sun is high, bright. George goes to take a shower, but before he does, he flicks the kettle back on, makes me another coffee and brings it out to me.

"Wow, aren't you the gentleman?" I say, before he nuzzles my ear and strolls toward the shower.

"This gentleman needs to buy more condoms," he says over his shoulder as he walks toward the bathroom.

"I'm surprised you bought so few on holiday. I thought the main objective of this trip was for you to get laid many times."

"Mission accomplished."

"George!" I cry.

He laughs, turns back to me, leans against the doorway. "I'm only joking. I didn't honestly expect that to happen. I mean, I'm bloody glad it did. But I'm as shocked as you."

I suspect he's fibbing, but I appreciate it nonetheless. There is a huge part of me that worries we really have ruined our friendship. I hope not. I also hope we've not ruined our holiday. But George is incredibly attractive, good in bed, and quite fun to be with. He turns, heads to the bathroom once again.

I reach for my phone. Miranda and I have been texting each other since I arrived in Thailand, but I've upped the ante, sending pictures of all the little towel-art I've found in my room and George's each day. Yesterday's was a baby elephant with huge ears. It went straight to Miranda, but she's only just replied. I haven't told her about George and me. It's so casual between us that I'm deluding myself there's nothing to tell.

I've zoomed in on this picture, Miranda says and she's sent the image back to me, with red circles drawn around two items on the bedside table.

My face reddens, though there's no one to see me. She's drawn a circle around a box of condoms and George's Ray-Bans. "Oh shit," I say out loud.

Busted, she's written underneath the picture. I need all the gossip. I'm assuming you and George are returning as more than good friends.

It's not phrased as a question.

I put my phone down and think while I drink my coffee and look at the view. The beach isn't busy, but guests are already heading toward the loungers, having had breakfast. George and I should get a move on soon. I look at the sea, glimpsed behind tall trees, swaying gently in the breeze.

I pick up my phone again. I have an unstoppable urge to text Davey, which has come from nowhere. I don't know what possesses me to do this. It's not to rub it in. Not at all. It's something else that motivates me to text him. I feel only good things toward him. I always have. But all this time later, I'm in a different place mentally now. And, I hope, so is he. I think I want Davey to know that. And I want him to know I am here for him, if he ever wants to talk.

He must be approaching his second chemo cycle by now. I actually have no idea. I've lost track of time, stopped wallowing. It's what I needed to do. I realize I have George to thank for that. I'd have got there myself, eventually, but George has sped up the process of whatever the strange grief was that I felt when Davey ended things.

I smile as I think about my message. This comes only from a good place. I click online, open up our dormant chat and see that Davey is online too. But not only is he online, he's typing a message to me. I uncurl myself from my chair, sit up straight, stare at it. "Oh my God," I mutter, waiting—painfully waiting. I'd long since stopped waiting for messages from Davey to magically appear in my inbox. I'd known he was serious when he ended things. I'd known it was in the cards that I'd never hear from him again. But he's still typing. Whatever this message is that he's writing to me, it's lengthy. I scratch my neck in nervous anticipation.

Behind me, the bathroom door opens and I turn. George emerges, wet, naked, giving me a look that's unmistakable, and when I don't immediately move he asks, "Everything OK?" as he sees me stare back down at my phone.

"Yes," I say. "I'll hop in the shower in a sec. You get dressed. Grab a table for us."

"Sure. Want me to raid the buffet for you?"

"Hmm? Oh . . . . yeah, I'll have pancakes," I mutter halfheartedly.

"You had them yesterday," he says and I look back up again.

"Fruit then."

"You can eat what you like, Hannah," he laughs. "I wasn't commenting on the fact they're covered in sugar and you douse them in syrup."

I stare at him, totally unable to comprehend what he's saying. Davey is still typing. Any second now he's going to hit send and I don't know what that's going to do to me. I actually now think this is incredibly cruel. It's making me pathetic. Look what I'm doing: sitting here staring at my phone, waiting for a man I've never met to throw me a bone. And yet . . . it's Davey. I need to know what he wants to say.

"Hannah?" George asks.

"Yeah?"

"Never mind. See you down there." He's already thrown on his T-shirt and shorts, his hair ruffled, cute. He puts it in place in the mirror by the door and leaves.

I look down at my phone again. Davey's offline. And whatever he was typing . . . he's not sent it. Is he mid-flow and come to a natural pause? Has he changed his mind entirely? I want to throw my phone in anger. But I'm angry with myself, not with Davey. Whatever innocuous message I was going to send, would it have done that to him? No. I'll bet it wouldn't. That's why I'm angry. If only Davey had been a complete shit, it would have made these feelings easier to bear. Only he wasn't. Isn't. He's a good man who is going through the unthinkable.

He didn't send the message. He's offline. As if he was never there. Only he *was* there. And so I'm going to be the brave one. I send exactly what I wanted to send him: Davey, I know we said we wouldn't speak anymore. Well, you said it. I agreed. But I'm going back on it. Just this once. Because I want you to know that I'm here for you, if you ever need me. I don't know where you're at with your treatment, but if you want to talk . . . you know where I am. I don't say this to rub anything in, but to let you know that although I miss you, I'm happy. I'm with someone. And he's kind. So please don't feel that by getting in contact with me, it would lead to anything complicated. We started as friends. If you want to be that again, we can be. Hannah xxx

I don't even hesitate. I just hit send.

Chapter 13

Davey

I STARE AT my cellphone—Hannah's words cut like a knife. But honestly, what did I expect? That she would join a convent just because what we had was over? I could see her online as I was typing, and I'll admit it scared me. Not much scares me in this life. Turns out my two current things are the chemo not working and Hannah being online at the same time as I am. I liked to think that she'd taken me seriously not to contact me. That she had to go live her life, not wait for some dude she'd never met. But I was wrong. She was online. I was online. She messaged me. I chickened out.

I do that a lot. Chicken out. I miss Hannah. But I know that what I did—bringing what we had to a close—was for the best. How can I get through each day here knowing I've made some girl on the other side of the Atlantic wait for me? What's that saying, *man makes plans and God laughs*. God must be laughing real hard. My plans are all kinds of messy right now. But that doesn't mean Hannah's have to be. I think of what should be happening right now. It's the end of February, and somewhere along the line I missed Valentine's Day, swept up in my own drama, pulled from appointment to appointment by sheer force of will. I'm glad I missed it. Guilt might have overtaken me, forced me into messaging her. It's for the best that I don't. I pull up the picture of her that she sent me, way back when. I touch her face and my touch-screen cell does all kinds of crazy shit, so I pull my hand away.

The oncologist enters my room. "Hello again, Mr. Carew," he says, fumbling with the notes on his clipboard. I put my cell-phone down on the bed, tell myself to stop being such an idiot, and to get on with the job in hand.

Chapter 14

Hannah

ELEVEN TIMES. GEORGE and I have had sex eleven times during our stay in Phuket. It turns out that if I bribe George with sex, he doesn't insist we visit more temples and Buddhas. I love the temples and I love Buddhas even more, especially when they're bright gold, but I just couldn't see any more. And besides, sex with George is as consistently mind-blowing as he initially led me to believe. And now we're on the plane, working our way back to England. He's asleep and I'm nestled against his biceps, staring out of the window, my breathing in tune to the rise and fall of his chest. This was good. This *is* good, because after dinner last night George made it abundantly clear he wants this to continue when we're home. We walked down to the water's edge, both of us shedding our shoes at the shoreline, carrying them in our arms as we walked alongside each other, our toes getting wet.

"If you can put up with my strange working hours . . . I think we're good together, Gallagher. I like you. I think you like me."

"I do."

"Then let's do it. See where it goes?"

I nodded, held his gaze, smiled.

We sipped our final piña coladas. He looked at his drink. "I quite like these now. If I order one in a bar when we're home, will you judge me?"

I laughed, stood on tiptoes and kissed him, dropping my sandals into the water and calling George "my hero" when he quickly galloped, sloshing his drink everywhere, to retrieve my shoes, which wanted so eagerly to be carried out to sea on the crest of a wave.

We land with a thud. The wheels bounce, sending the plane lurching into the air before it comes back down to earth again, securing its spot on the runway. George's eyes open and he looks at me in bafflement.

"You OK?" I ask.

He blinks. "Yeah, I was having the best dream."

"Which supermodel were you having sex with?" I prompt.

He leans over, whispers in my ear, "Don't be a dick, Gallagher." And then retreats to his seat with a smile.

"So what happens now?" I ask as we head through passport control and wait for our luggage. It's early evening and I don't want to be the one to suggest that we see each other tonight. We've spent ten whole days together. He must need his space. I'm sure I do. Only I'm not sure I want it just yet.

"Back to yours?" he suggests. "I'm not going to lie to you, Gallagher—your flat's nicer than mine. Takeout and flake out?"

"Sounds lovely."

We shower back at mine, freshen up, order take-out pizza to counteract all the wonderful Thai curries we've eaten over the last ten days. Tuck ourselves into a blanket on the sofa, eat, watch TV, and go to bed far too late, wrapping ourselves in each other as we sleep.

George is up before I have a chance to wake. It's only just past 6 A.M. and he's already gone. I assume he's taken his gym kit out of his suitcase, pulled it on, and gone to work. His case is still here and it's nice—a little part of George in my flat, in my life. I'm not sure how this is going to work now we're home, back in reality and not basking in the glory of good sex and sunshine in a make-believe holiday land. I'm keeping an open mind.

I pull my jet-lagged body from my bed and begin getting ready for work. I could feel down about it, but there's always something so reviving about returning to the office after a good holiday. As if my reset button has been pushed and I'm more alive. I am also tanned and my hair is lighter from the sunshine. I'm feeling quite good about it all now and I practically bounce into the office. Midmorning, Clare and I head to our local Italian café bar for some strong coffee and, even though I'm sure I've put weight on while away, I order white toast and Marmite, paying and waiting while they assemble our order.

Clare tells me about her new man, the two dates she's been on with him and how he's already bought her flowers and planned a night out with some of his friends.

I look up. "Meeting the friends?" I question.

"That's the next step, isn't it?" Clare suggests. "Meeting friends. That's date four. We've got date three to get through yet."

"And what's that?" I'm handed my toast in a paper bag and I tuck in immediately, waving goodbye to the owner as we leave.

"He's booked dinner at SushiSamba."

"I've always wanted to go there," I say. "They never have Groupon deals, so alas . . ."

"I will report back. What about you and your holiday with the man you said was only a friend?" she asks.

I look away guiltily.

"I knew it!" Clare says. "Seeing each other?"

"Yeah," I say.

"It was inevitable," she replies knowledgeably.

"Hmm, I'm not sure. But it did happen. And it is good."

"Great," Clare says as we sip our coffee. "Check us out: both of us with new men in the same month. Where's your next date then?"

"Well, I want to go to SushiSamba now," I tease. "Maybe a museum or a gallery would be nice. I have no idea what George is into."

"It's fun to find out, though," Clare says as we step back into the office.

I message George. **Hey, hot stuff. Do you want to go on a date?** I ask him.

I watch the screen, but he's obviously with a client or not near his phone. Last seen at 2:51 A.M. That's a strange time to be online. I thought we were asleep in bed together then, but maybe his jet lag took hold of him. It occurs to me that I have no idea who George's friends are. Actually, despite talking about life and love so much over our holiday, I have very little clue about what goes on in George's life outside the realm of the gym. He's thoughtful, we're like-minded. That's enough for me.

Do you have a best friend? I text George suddenly, which is random, but now I'm curious.

I scroll up to reply to Miranda, who keeps sending me emojis of eggplants with question marks next to them over and over again, prompting me to respond about George, which as yet I've refused to do. Whatever I say to her now will be dissected in great detail at our next night at the pub. I might as well save it until then.

And I look down at my WhatsApp message to Davey, which shows two ticks. He's read it. But it's been a couple of days since I sent it and I've had no response. I could delete it, but I'm assuming it's too late if he's seen it. The damage is done. I leave it there, taunting me. And then above our message stream I see Davey's status suddenly switch from "last seen . . ." to "online." Then he goes offline, just as fast. And then he's back, and my mouth opens in shock as the status next to his name reads: *typing.*

Finally I'm about to get a reply. I watch, intrigued. What can he have to tell me? I want to know about his chemo regime, but maybe that's the last thing on earth he wants to talk about. I miss his face, but I know he doesn't want me to see it. I need to know everything. But most of all I need to know if he's all right, mentally. If he's staying positive, carrying on. He has his mum, his dad, Grant. But does he *feel* alone? I long to know. I'm desperate to tell him again that I care too. But I won't. I've told him already, my message the only static thing on the screen, and I wait as his typing continues.

And then the typing stops and exactly the same thing happens as before—he goes offline. Nothing. No message. Just . . . nothing. Davey's gone, taking his thoughts with him, his message either hanging in midair, waiting to be sent—the same as the last one he wrote—or he's changed his mind and deleted it entirely. What is he doing?

I'm at home and still waiting for a response from George at 10 P.M. His case is still here and he isn't. I'm not expecting him to walk through the door, hollering, "Honey, I'm home," but I was hoping for some sort of "Hi" today, especially after the amazing holiday we've had. But it's clear that's not happening.

This is a message to me not to revolve my life around men. I've always been very good at resisting that, but I could feel, after the past ten days, that I might have very easily slipped. George not replying to me has alerted me to that, and I very smugly decide that I'm going to make myself a cup of tea, take myself to bed, and catch up with some reading. I really need to hit the gym, but it's late, so I get real about that.

I stay awake, reading my book to the bitter end. I've been desperate to finish it since Thailand. I pick up my phone. Nothing from George. I switch off my bedside light, curl up under the duvet—a blessed relief, even now in these first spring-scented days—and go to sleep.

I'm woken by a persistent knock at my door. Am I being robbed? No, robbers don't knock first, and so I go to the door, yell, "Who is it?"

And when George tells me it's him, I open the door in surprise.

"What are you doing here?" I ask, bleary-eyed, blinking myself fully awake.

"What do you mean?" he asks.

I look at my watch, only it's not on my wrist. I've taken it off for the night. "What time is it?" I ask.

"Almost midnight."

I nod. "I hope you're not after sex. Or dinner?"

"Neither of those things, Gallagher." He swoops low, kisses me, and stands upright. "Thought I'd crash with you. Is that OK?"

"Um, yeah—sure." I stand aside and he takes up all the space in the hall, switches on all the lights on his way to the kitchen, pulls a glass out of the cupboard and fills it with water. He's sweaty, in his gym kit, as I expected, and he turns and looks at me.

"You all right?" he asks.

"Yeah. I was asleep. Did I miss a message from you that you were coming here?"

He downs his water. "No."

"I wasn't expecting you."

"Is . . . that a problem?"

"No." I shake my head. "I just had no idea you were coming." I can see we're not going to make headway on this, so I merely say, "I'm going to sleep. Are you coming?"

"Yeah. Shower first, though, and then into bed with the most gorgeous woman on the planet."

I inch forward, kiss him on the lips. "She's not here, I'm afraid. You'll have to make do with me."

By the time George steps into the shower I'm already falling asleep, but he nudges me awake as he climbs into bed, pulls me into his arms, and nuzzles me, until sleepiness is replaced by something else entirely.

George is looking at his phone while raiding the cupboards for coffee the next morning. "Do you only have instant?" he asks.

"Yes," I say, putting on my makeup. "Special coffee comes from the café near the station, or from Joan on Saturdays and some Sundays."

He sniffs. "Fair enough." He resumes looking at his phone, narrows his eyes, and looks at me. "He's called Dex, although we call him Dog. I honestly, hand on heart, cannot remember why now."

I stare at him as I'm applying mascara in my little hand-mirror. "What?"

He waves his phone at me. "You asked me who my best friend is."

I blink. "Yes. Yes, I did. Are you only just reading that message now?"

He nods. "I've got so many to catch up on."

"Mr. Popular."

"Sort of."

He must be reading his other messages, as he laughs out loud at some and replies to very few. He pockets his phone in his sports jacket, zips it up. "Coffee at the station, did you say?"

"Mmm."

"Come on then." He starts jogging on the spot. "When are you going back to the gym, by the way?"

I watch him jogging up and down on the already painfully worn lino. "I'm thinking of starting spin on Fridays and—" I start.

But he cuts back in. "Come to me. I'll train you for free. If you like?"

"Right. Yeah." I look down at my stomach.

"I don't think you're fat, by the way. In case that's where your mind had gone."

I smile. It had. Hotel pancakes, and all that.

"There's got to be some perks to shagging a personal trainer," he jokes. "Make use of me."

"OK, thanks." And then, "George, do you want to go on a date?"

He looks confused. As if I'm speaking a foreign language. He's obviously not read that text I sent, then.

"We went on a date. Remember Sirocco?" he asks.

"I do," I say, thinking of that memorable rooftop experience in Bangkok. "Amazing," I offer. "Shall we, perhaps, try another one? Perhaps rooftop dining can be our *thing*? There's this great restaurant in the City—" I stop talking because George's eyes have narrowed.

"Uppity?" he says, without hearing what I had to say.

"I thought we liked uppity?" I suggest. "I thought we took the epic piss out of pretentious while secretly enjoying it, all the same."

"I've not got much money, Hannah."

"No, well, I'm not exactly a millionaire," I say. "But I'll pay if it's—"

"Whoa!" George says. He stops jogging. "Did you just hear yourself?"

"What?" I ask. "Is it not OK to reciprocate? You treated me so well in Thailand."

He shrugs, resumes jogging on the spot. "Can you get a shift on? Listen." He changes his mind. "I'm going to be late, so don't worry. I'll see you later."

"Sure," I say as he plants a kiss on my cheek. "Er, George?"

"Yeah?"

"You're not going to turn up again at midnight, are you? I do love my sleep," I say, trying to make light of it.

He pauses jogging. "You don't want me here? Booty-calling you something rotten?"

"I do," I say, genuinely meaning it. "But not at midnight."

He looks at me.

"OK, I'll take my case. Crash at mine. I'll see you . . . Saturday? I can do Saturday."

"Night or day?" I ask.

"Night, obviously," he says.

"Teensy problem. I usually see Miranda and Paul on Saturday nights."

"Every single Saturday?" he asks.

"Usually, unless one of us is at a party or a wedding, or home for the weekend or something." And I realize how silly I sound now. "But it's not a problem. I'll cancel if it's the only time we're going to see each other."

"Don't cancel," he says. "I'll come along too."

"Really?" I ask. "You want to come for a night out with my friends?"

"Yeah," he says.

"When can I come for a night out with your friends?" I ask.

"Whenever you want."

"When do you guys normally hang out?" I'm curious.

"Whenever their girlfriends say they can."

I laugh. "Fair enough. So Saturday then?"

"Saturday," he says, pulling his suitcase out as he heads to the door. "Text me the details."

"I will."

He comes back. Kisses me goodbye and then leaves. I'm only minutes behind him, but I see him flag down a black cab. I feel guilty. I've made him get a taxi, all because he's lugging his suitcase around. Although I didn't tell him to take it. But still.

* * *

On Saturday morning I message Joan, tell her I'm ready, then plate up some biscuits and head into the garden. Joan's roller blind is up and I can see her pottering, lifting her cups from the cupboard, loading pods into the Nespresso machine. I pull my dressing gown tighter around me, although March is mild and I'm glad now the weather's turning from winter to spring, so that I don't have to wear my winter coat in the garden. I've still got my battered Uggs on, though, to protect my feet from the cold concrete on my side of the fence. I'm not suicidal.

"Vanilla Éclair," Joan says.

"Vanilla Éclair to you too." I laugh at my own tragic retort.

Joan reads from her coffee leaflet. "If we dare the decadence, we should try it as a cappuccino and find sweet almond notes through the taste of creamy custard."

"Let's dare the decadence then," I say and we take a sip.

I wince. Joan winces.

"Do you think our taste-testing might have run its course?" I suggest.

"Never," Joan battle cries. "We'll go back to the normal flavors when I'm home from my adventure."

"OK." I sip again. It's not so bad, second time around.

We discuss Geoff and Joan's next trip; they are packed and ready for their month-long cruise-ship adventure. Joan produces another leaflet, wowing me with all the stops on the route, and then shows me pictures of the ship, which stun me. There are waterslides and ice rinks. I can't speak, and so Joan speaks for me.

"Yeah," she says, nodding. "We don't tell all you young lot how exciting cruising is, for fear you'll all start doing it too, driving the prices up. It's expensive enough as it is. Although Geoff is treating me. I do think he might be a secret millionaire," she muses.

I laugh and then Joan asks me about my holiday. "Nice tan, young lady. You look vibrant, healthy."

"Thanks. I feel it."

"Did you have adult sleepovers with that young man?"

"Eleven," I boast with a smile.

"Well, I say!" Joan chuckles. "I think that deserves a biscuit."

We each take one from the plate and nibble.

"I take it everything came to a head with Davey then?"

I nod, thinking of him typing to me but never quite managing to hit send. I haven't told anyone this is what Davey's done. Twice. And I don't want to attach any significance to it. But I look Joan in the eye and instead of saying, *Yes. All over,* I say, "He's been messaging me but not sending them."

Joan stares at me. She has no clue, so I explain. "I can see him typing. He doesn't hit send. He's done it twice. That I've witnessed."

And it occurs to me that he might be doing it at other times also. I frown as I realize that. It would be too coincidental that he'd choose those two times I was online and watching to be the only two times he wrote something but didn't send it.

Joan's saying something and I tune back in. "Have you thought to ring him? How long's it been?"

"Almost two months. And no. I'm a coward. I messaged him. He's not replied. I'm not going to phone him. I've already made the first move to be friends. It's his turn now."

"Even if he's unwell? You'll still leave the ball in his court?"

I nod. "It's because he's unwell that I'm leaving the ball in his court. He asked me not to contact him. I didn't adhere to his request. I can't keep going. I can't keep hassling. It really has to be his turn next."

"I understand," Joan says, looking on my side of the garden for the biscuit plate. I pick it up and, after she takes a biscuit, I put it back down.

"You not having one?" she asks.

I shake my head. "I think George thinks I've gotten fat over the holiday."

Joan looks appalled. "George of the eleven adult sleepovers?"

"Yes."

"Hannah," Joan warns.

"No, no. It's not like that. He's just really into health and fitness, and he wants me to mirror that. He took great pains to say he categorically *didn't* think I'd gotten fat, but I reckon he does really. He loves his five a day. And I like pancakes in a breakfast buffet, especially when someone else is going to the hassle of making them."

"Oh yes," Joan says. "I think I'll be piling on the pounds on the cruise if there's daily pancakes."

"You only live once, though, don't you?" I suggest.

"And then a coronary comes for you," Joan warns sagely.

Paul and Miranda and I are waiting patiently for George in the pub. We're on our second round of drinks and Miranda has quick-fired questions at me mercilessly. Paul has cringed as Miranda drags out of me details about the holiday and about George. Miranda and I are loving every second of it.

"How big?" she asks, gesturing to Paul's pint glass. "Here?" she puts her hand somewhere near the top and I shake my head, raising her hand higher.

"You lucky devil," Miranda squawks and offers me a high five, which I accept.

Paul looks at his pint glass with disgust. "For fuck's sake," he says as he pushes the glass further away from him. "You can't ask her stuff like that," he chastises Miranda. "And you've broken every code there is by answering," he moans at me.

"What?" Miranda turns to Paul. "I have to ask her this sort of thing now, because when she's all in love and loyal in about a month's time, I'll not get any details from her." She turns back to me. "Tell me everything."

"Oh, please don't," Paul says and looks out the window into the darkness of the offices nearby.

"Eleven times," Miranda says a moment later. "Eleven. Times. How did you not get a UTI?"

"I don't know," I laugh. "Luck."

"I think the most Paul and I have managed was five times in a week. We were in Scarborough, do you remember?"

Paul looks horrified. "Miranda!"

I'm chuckling and then looking at my watch. Where is he?

"So," Paul chimes in. "Other than the sex, which is *epic*, blah-blah-blah . . . is he nice? Do you like him?"

"Yeah," I say, thinking. Although tired, work-hard George in London is a smidge different from relaxed holiday George in Thailand, but I don't say that.

"I cannot wait to meet him," Miranda says. "I'm going to fancy him immediately, get flirty and silly, and so I apologize to you right now."

"Which one of us are you apologizing to?" Paul asks, folding his arms.

"Both of you, obviously," she says, giving me a wink.

"Good-o," Paul replies. "Just checking." He mutters something under his breath and both Miranda and I look at each other and stifle a giggle.

"You did tell him where we meet and at what time?" Miranda asks.

"I did. It was he who suggested he meet you, so I know he's up for it. He's just late."

"I'm starving," Paul declares and flags the waitress down so we can get some nibbles.

When George walks through the door half an hour later he casts around for us, sees me, gives me a broad grin, and walks over. Although he's late, that smile diffuses any pretend tension

Miranda had conjured up and nearly diffuses any actual tension Paul had allowed to rumble to the surface. George kisses me as I stand, mumbles, "Sorry," and then Paul stands, smiles in return, and offers George his hand. The two men nearly shake each other's hands off, it looks so vigorous. Then George breaks off, kisses the cheek Miranda offers and apologizes to them for his lateness. I notice that he offers no explanation, and I think it's clear we're all waiting for one but he goes straight in with, "What's everyone drinking, can I get a round in?"

"Nah, it's table service," Paul offers. "Thanks, though."

"Excellent," George says and slides into the empty seat.

It's clear George is riding the *Never explain, never complain* mantra to the end, as we're not finding out why he's late.

"You OK?" I probe.

"Sure. You?" he asks and sidles in to kiss me quickly.

"I am now," I say as the waitress moves in to take our order, even though George hasn't had a chance to look at the menu.

"It's cool," George says. "Got plenty of experience with Thai food lately, so I'll just have . . ." He reels off a couple of easy dishes, and the waitress nods and scribbles before turning to the rest of us.

George is on form. He has Miranda in fits of giggles. Every now and again Paul casts me looks, the meaning of which I can't work out. George is fun, friendly, asks questions about Paul and what he does when he's not working. Not once does he ask either of them what they do for a living, which I once read in a women's magazine was the most boring question you could ever ask at a dinner party. We talk about holidays, life and fitness schedules, which I'm impressed we venture onto organically, because George doesn't even mention it. I squeeze his leg under the table and he casts me a contented look, leans over and kisses me quickly before answering Miranda's question about how long he's fancied me.

"Oh, ages. I mean . . . look at her," George riffs.

"You two are so cute," she says.

Later, George and I are curled up in bed and, as I'm drifting off to sleep, Miranda sends me a message: Paul and I LOVE him, she enthuses. He's so great.

I smile at that.

And then she sends a follow-up text: The perfect rebound to take your mind off Davey.

The message strikes a sudden hit of nausea into my stomach and I frown at it. Why would she say that? Why would she suddenly bring that up now? I text her back, to ask her in the least passive-aggressive way possible.

Oh, I didn't mean it! she texts back, lightning fast. I was joking. I'm so sorry. I don't know why I said that. He does seem perfect and . . . Shit, can I call you? I'm so sorry.

No, I text back. I'm in bed. Don't worry about it. No big deal.

I put my phone down. Beside me, George has drifted off to sleep, his breathing heavy, his chest rising and falling to a slow beat. I blow air out of my cheeks. Now I can't sleep. I get out of bed slowly, not wanting to wake George, not wanting to have to get into a discussion about why I can't sleep. What can I tell him? I've not mentioned anything about Davey since the day I told George I wasn't coming on holiday because I'd been dumped.

I'm propelled back toward my phone and I take it from the bedside table into the sitting room, where I scroll down my messages, past the one that Miranda just sent, past messages to and from Mum and Dad, George, Clare, Joan, an ongoing thread with my old uni friends and toward the last communication I had with Davey. He still hasn't replied to the message I sent in Thailand.

I take the phone with me into the kitchen, turning on the little table lamp in the hall as I go, which casts a faint light into my small kitchen. I roll up the blind and look out into my garden. I've never done much with the square of concrete, but I decide when the weather's a bit warmer I might buy some benches, garden cushions, actual pots. I don't like change for change's sake, but I think I could bring myself to admit that I've been here a few years and I'm not leaving any time soon. I should make this place look nicer; invest a bit of myself into this garden. Summer's only around the corner. Mad, really, when I think how quickly time has flown since Christmas, since the start of December when Davey misdialed me.

I have this sudden urge to watch *A Room with a View* again— more for comfort. Maybe I'll drift off to it. Maybe I won't. Watching it with Davey might have ruined it for me, actually. I need to find out. My cup of tea in one hand, I turn on the TV with the other, quickly whip the volume down so I don't wake George, and locate the film, letting it start in the background. I'm restless, so I unlock my phone, intending to look at the news, but it opens on the last screen I was on. The one where I sent a message to Davey telling him I'm with someone, that I'm happy, that I hope he is too, and that I'm still here if he wants to be friends with me. I intend to click off it, open the news, but the message shows Davey is online and he's typing a message to me. I act on impulse. No time to think. Only to type. I dive straight in: I can see you typing. Whatever it is you write, please hit send this time.

Chapter 15

Davey

I DROP MY cellphone as though it's on fire. Shit! She's been watching me type. For how long? And then I reread her message: *please hit send this time.* She's seen me do this before. How many times has Hannah seen me do this? Every time? More than once, that's for sure. Oh God, I'm mortified. I can't risk continuing to type. I can't risk deleting everything I've just written, either. Does it say the word "typing" even if all you're doing is deleting? And I'm sure as hell not hitting send on that outpouring. My phone is still lit up, staring at me from its position on the couch. It'll lock any second. It'll show me as being offline. I'll look like a coward, like I've seen her message and chickened out from replying. Which is exactly what I've done. Predictably the screen locks. Problem solved. I'll log back in later and delete that rambling stream of consciousness.

Since Hannah sent me that message I haven't been able to stop thinking about it. I've compiled reply after reply, and they go on and on. I tell her everything that's been happening to me because I want to tell her. And yet I said I'd let her go, and so I don't hit send. But it feels good. It feels good to let it out, and the more I *know* I'm not going to send it to her, the more I type; the more I tell.

I speak to Grant daily. And then there's Mom and Dad. Dad

clenches his jaw, looks like he wants to cry but can't. Mom does cry. A lot. And then there's Hannah . . . so far away and feeling even further each time I think about her. But this way I can tell her how much it hurts, how horrific I look, how the skin on my head is now so smooth it's softer than my ass, how my eyebrows have almost disappeared, which I did not see coming. And then, because it sounds like I'm a total freak, I delete all of it . . . every time.

Hannah and I parted as friends. So I should be able to tell her this stuff. But now it all feels so much worse than before. I feel so much worse than before. And I'm angry. I'm kind of angry with her that she's seen me type and that she's called me on it. This was really all I had. Writing to her, not sending it, logging in later to stream out yet more crap. And now I can't. Now I have to stop. Thanks, Hannah. I pick up my phone and throw it, watch as it smashes. The relief I felt as it flew through the air, the satisfaction of watching it fragment from something strong to nothing—like me.

They call testicular cancer, cancer with a little "c," because the survival rate is pretty high since they finally nailed the dosage of drugs during trials about fifteen years ago. But it's Chemo with a capital "C." It's not the cancer making me feel like this, it's the chemo. This is why I can't hit send on those messages. They all contain the story of a healthy, strong man who is being taken down, day by day, and this isn't the version of me I want Hannah to see.

I don't even bother to get up and pick up the expensive pieces of my phone. I don't have the energy. I stare out the window of the living room. Any second now my mom will come in, and she'll panic about why I've done what I've just done. So I force myself to get up, all energy zapped from my system. On hands and knees, I begin picking up the pieces of what used to be my phone. This doesn't look fixable. I can't even stand up, I'm so tired. I crawl into the kitchen, throw the fistful of phone into the trash, saving only my sim card. Then I crawl into the living room, climb back onto the sofa, breathe deeply, regain my breath, open the laptop next to me, and begin to order a new phone.

Chapter 16

Hannah, March

GEORGE AND I are in the garden one Sunday morning. It's time to introduce him to Joan. I feel about as nervous as I would be introducing him to my mum and dad, and I realize I see Joan as my London mum. It dawns on me that I haven't told Joan not to mention Davey, not to mention that he's been messaging but not sending. I don't know why, but I feel the subject of Davey should not be broached. I didn't remind Miranda not to do it yesterday, but I haven't told Miranda what I've seen Davey do. I haven't told her that I've messaged him, either.

Regardless, it's an unwritten rule between friends, isn't it?—don't mention other men who've once featured in your life. Unless they turned out to be bastards, which Davey . . . didn't. But Joan, is she up to speed on things like this? Maybe I'm overthinking it. I pull my phone out of my dressing-gown pocket, quickly type a little note to Joan—**Don't mention Davey**—and pocket my phone again. I lean over the fence a little way, see her in the kitchen, notice her glance at her phone as it lights up next to her on the countertop. OK, good, she's seen it. Joan shakes her head a little, throwing off confusion, and now I feel a little bit stupid. Of course she wasn't going to mention Davey. Why would she?

Next to me, George glances at his watch.

"You OK?" I ask.

"Yeah," he says, planting a kiss on my cheek.

"I still don't know why you have to do this in your dressing gown?" he asks.

"It's just . . . our thing. It's what Joan and I have always done."

George refused to borrow a spare dressing gown from me, and instead practically begged that I wait before telling Joan we were ready, as he changed his mind, ran into the shower, brushed his teeth, got dressed in his jeans and a sweater, and then declared himself fit.

I'm now gagging for a coffee, he's taken so long. He does look good, though. His sweaters are always that right side of "tarty man" and hug his biceps in a way that makes me want to reach out and stroke him as if he's a cat. I, however, look like crap in the mornings and am utterly at ease with it. But only for him. And only for Joan. And, once upon a time, for Davey.

I've not worked out how I feel about Davey's disappearing act online the other day. I left *A Room with a View* on pause for so long, staring, waiting for him to come back online, that I eventually went to bed without realizing I'd left the film on pause on the screen. George found it on in the morning, asked what it was, and, on finding out it was my favorite film, asked if we could watch it together some time. I think I might have stiffened. I can't be unwilling to share my favorite film with him. That's not a fair way to treat someone. I have to be willing to make it all work, and so I stood still, silently having an existential crisis, wondering whether, if I wasn't willing to share my favorite film with George, I was flat out admitting to myself that I saw this going nowhere. And that's the worst way to start what could be the beginnings of a great relationship. So I agreed, smiled, planned to buy popcorn later today, make an event of it—let George in even further.

Joan arrives, a tray of coffees in her hands, gives George a good once-over and beams a smile at him and then at me. George looks nervous, bless him, but smiles in return.

"He really is as gorgeous as you've made him sound," Joan teases. "Eleven adult sleepovers . . . yes, I can see that," she rounds off with a giggle.

I can sense George going through the mental equivalent of puffing out his chest at this, while I die on the inside. He introduces himself and I can see his charm level increasing.

We talk about her cruise, which is all Joan can think about, and I confess I'm going to miss her when she goes away tomorrow. She's been packed for ages, which is a trait I admit we share, and she says, "Oh yes, Thailand. And you, all heartbroken and probably not going to go."

Bloody hell, Joan. You had one job. "I mean . . ." I start. "Not heartbroken, just—"

Joan looks embarrassed, gives me an apologetic smile, and, to glaze over it, says, "India with Robusta Monsoon. Intensity eleven."

"Huh?" George queries.

"The coffee," I murmur and stare into my cup, appalled at how this morning has fallen flat so suddenly, as Joan talks for far too long about the woody flavor and how months of monsoons affect the taste of what's in our cup. George looks confused, as if she might be having some kind of stroke. I've told him we stand in the garden and grade coffee, but he's obviously forgotten this.

"I'm going to be generous," Joan says. "Five out of five."

I notice she hasn't even sipped her drink, but I sip mine and nod agreement. "George?" I ask tentatively.

George sips his. "Er, I dunno. Four. I guess?"

"Great," I say. Now that's dealt with, I want to disappear inside again.

"What are you crazy kids planning on doing today?" Joan asks.

George and I hadn't discussed what we might do today. I look at him. I'm guessing we're spending the day together.

"We're watching *A Room with a View* tonight," I say halfheartedly.

Joan nods. "And for the rest of the day?"

I'm not sure what else to do today. "I think sitting around feels like a waste of time on one of our precious few days together."

"Time you enjoy wasting isn't wasted," Joan chirps. "John Lennon," she says, referring to her idol. Lennon gets quoted at me fairly regularly.

George looks baffled at this, puffs air out of his cheeks, and says, "Do you want to head into town?"

"Sure," I say. "Shopping or . . . ?"

"No. You can do that online. Why don't we be tourists for the day?"

"O . . . K . . ."

"You don't want to?" he asks.

"No, yeah, let's do it."

I can see Joan's gaze flicking between us as she watches our verbal tennis.

"What do you want to do?" I ask.

"Let's get a bus tour of London," George says suddenly. "You know, one of those hideous red bus tours where you see everything in a matter of hours and someone shouts information at you."

I swallow my coffee. "No, thanks, I don't fancy that." I'd planned to do that with Davey, and I'm annoyed with myself that I don't want to do it with anyone *but* Davey. Although that is never going to happen now. I gulp at that. I should change my mind, say yes to George.

"OK . . ." he says, looking down. "What's easy to get to from here? The Tower of London?"

I look at him. He's just naming things that Davey and I were going to do together, and I swear if he suggests the National Portrait Gallery next, I'm going to scream.

"Is there anything new on?" I ask. "Some kind of exhibition maybe."

"Yes, there's a James Bond—"

"Sounds great. Let's do that."

"You've not even heard what I was going to say," he says with a laugh. "It's cars. You OK with cars?"

"I'm fine with cars," I say. I hate cars. "I'm sure it will be fascinating." But this is better than doing any of the other absurd things I had planned to do with Davey. I can't do them absurdly with George. Not so soon. I tell myself I just need a few more months and then I'll be fine. And as I say this to myself, I realize that means I'm probably *not* fine now. But I will be. And that's the main thing.

We say goodbye to Joan and I know I'm going to miss her over the next month as she weaves her way across the seas, eating pancakes, ice-skating, and discovering new things with Geoff.

That's what relationships are, in part: discovering new things about each other, with each other; discovering the world around you . . . together.

George closes the kitchen door behind us and laughs. "That was hilarious," he says. "She's a one-off."

"What?" I say, stunned.

"Cuckoo, totally bonkers," he clarifies.

"Yeah, I know what you mean, but she's not," I say, my hackles rising.

"'Course she is. All that five-out-of-five nonsense. For coffee? And she does this every week to you? That's ridiculous. And pretending you were heartbroken."

I'm quiet.

"I know you weren't going to come away to Thailand," he says, moving the subject on. "But you weren't . . . heartbroken, were you?"

Now that I think about it, it's kind of strange that George knew I was sad about Davey, knew that I didn't want to go on holiday, and then came knocking at my door, convincing me to go anyway.

And then, throughout all of Thailand, we never spoke about Davey, we just got on with our holiday; and we got on so well together, we simply kind of . . . happened. Discussions never extended to Davey, and I was happy with that. A subject I didn't want to discuss, for so many reasons.

But now it's probably unavoidable.

"You guys were just video-dating or . . . whatever, no?"

And this is why it's hard to discuss.

"Yep." I nod. "No. Not heartbroken. Yes, just video-dating."

"OK, phew," he says. "Because if I'm expected to match up to someone who broke your heart, who you'd never even fucking met, then . . . I am screwed."

"No," I say, moving toward him. I am determined. "You're not screwed. You're great."

At the James Bond car exhibition I am bored rigid and trying not to be. I read a few posters covering the age of the car and how many times they pretended to blow it up in such-and-such film. I think ahead to the gift shop and hope it's not made up entirely of James Bond artifice.

My mind wanders toward work, which is a tragic thing to think about at a weekend, especially when I'm supposed to be enjoying myself with George. But I can't help thinking that the more I carry on drifting through my job, the less happy I am and the more stagnant I'm becoming. I think I've been so distracted recently with Davey that I've only just started to realize I'm drifting, purposeless. I've been given more responsibility, but I sense that's because my boss Craig wants his workload down even further and shoved it onto my desk, rather than actually wanting me to develop. But I do want to develop—I do. I stare at another vehicle. Until Craig shuffles off to pastures new, I'm merely waiting to move up the ranks. But to what end, I'm not sure.

George is in his element, and I watch him as he reads every

single plaque, takes in every single detail of every single vehicle, and after a while his hand detaches from mine and he wanders off to look at a scale prototype of a helicopter used in *GoldenEye*. I feign interest because that is what couples do, isn't it? Support their other half in their interests, go to exhibitions they're not interested in, just so they can spend time together. This is what normal women do. And so that's what I'll do.

"Oh, Hannah," he says, and his hand finds mine again. "A Eurocopter . . ." And I nod, smile, ask something about the engine size, to which I receive an incomprehensible answer and we move on to the next vehicle. George is happy and that makes me happy, although I am now quite eager to get to the end and have a nose around in the gift shop.

Out of the corner of my eye I see a movement next to me, and I turn to see the back of a tall blond man adjusting his rucksack. I stare at him and, for the briefest of heart-stopping seconds, I think it's Davey. I inhale, too loudly, and the man turns, looks at me, sees me staring, and gives me a smile before turning away.

"Oh my God," I mutter. What is wrong with me? Of course Davey's not going to be here. Here is the absolute last place Davey would ever be. He's probably hooked up to drugs, lying in a hospital bed in Texas. But this doesn't stop me thinking I see him. In the queue in Tesco the other day I did the same thing to a tall blond guy stacking the shelves. I'm only serving to hurt myself, imagining him here. I must be losing my mind, always wrong about seeing Davey.

I am right about the gift shop, though. It *is* all James Bond items for sale. And books. A lot of books. About James Bond.

"What were you expecting?" George laughs.

"Homewares, soaps—the usual gift-shop finds," I confess.

"I'll take you shopping after. We'll get you something girly, if you like. My treat."

I incline my head and kiss him. And then George spies a hardback book—a signed limited edition that costs about £100—and my eyes nearly fall out of my head.

"You can't spend a hundred pounds on a book," I say, horrified.

"Why not? My money," he says as he finishes looking through the book and goes to stand in line to pay.

"It's a hundred pounds," I say again, as if he's misread the tag.

"I know. It's signed. Limited edition. And I want it."

"OK," I say, unsure where I thought mentioning it was going to get me. "Will you even read it more than once?"

"Yeah, it's got good pictures—look."

"OK," I say again.

Why am I fighting with George about this? It's his cash. When we're outside the shop we head for a late lunch. We've not booked anywhere, and I love that aimlessness of wandering around, looking for somewhere that ticks all the boxes. George and I both agree that we love a mix of achingly cool, somewhere that avoids tourists and is not too pricey. That triumvirate is hard to find and so we grab a bus, head over the river toward the South Bank, to the food stands that often litter the patch of ground spanning the Royal Festival Hall and past Tate Modern. We start walking the line of food vendors, discussing the array of cuisines and cultures on offer.

We go slowly, hand in hand. "George?" I ask.

"Mmm," he says, craning his neck to look over the heads of tourists and Londoners to see the prices. He frowns and I think: I'll buy him lunch. He's just spent all his money on that book. "Where did you grow up? Where are you from?"

"Dagenham," he says after a while. "Why?"

I shrug. "We spent ten blissful days together in Thailand and I know practically nothing about you. Did you grow up there?"

He nods. "Yeah."

"Do you have any brothers or sisters?"

"A sister. You?"

"No." I shake my head as we keep walking alongside the river. "What's her name?" I ask.

"Amanda."

The conversation stills, so I continue. "How old is she?"

"What is this, Gallagher: Twenty Questions?"

I laugh. "No, just making conversation."

I drop it and then something else dawns on me. "George? Where do you live?"

He laughs. "What?"

"Where do you live?" I repeat.

"Not far from you," he says. "About ten minutes away."

"Where?"

"You want to come to my flat one night?" he asks. "For a—what is it you and Joan call them—adult sleepovers? You want to come to my flat and have an adult sleepover?" he teases.

I giggle. "Sure," I say, nudging him in the ribs.

We pause by a pancake vendor and decide to get savory crêpes. "Here we go, Gallagher, your favorite thing. I'll treat you."

"No, I'll get these. You've made the effort to find something for us to do today. And also"—I can't resist—"you've spent all your money on that book."

George smiles, but it's a thin smile, and I wonder what on earth possessed me to bring it up again. I thought he might laugh. I misread that. And then he freezes, looks down at his hands. "The book. Where's the book?" he asks, as if I've taken it.

I look at his hands. He's no longer holding the carrier bag from the gift shop. "Where . . . ?" I start, about to repeat his own question. "Did you leave it on the bus?"

I can't tell if he's about to explode or cry. His jaw stiffens and he just nods. "Fuck," he mutters under his breath.

I don't know what to say. We get closer to the front of the queue. I order my crêpe, stroke his arm softly, his biceps flexing automatically under his jacket, but it's a twitch, as if to get me off him, rather than show me how built he is. I take the hint, remove my hand. He orders so quietly the vendor has to ask him to repeat it, and George replies through gritted teeth. After that, our walk along the river takes an awkward, stiff turn. I don't speak. I'm waiting for him to speak, to change the subject. But he's dwelling on the missing book, and I daren't speak now. So we eat as we walk, and a while later his hand slips back into mine after we bin our rubbish.

He smiles down at me. "Sorry," he says after a while.

"It's all right. I'll buy you another one," I find myself saying.

"Really? Oh, Hannah, you don't have to do that."

"I know. But you're clearly upset. You really wanted it."

"I said I'd buy *you* something," George teases, recovering himself. "So we're doing it. Come on," he says.

Our walk has taken us along the river and we can see the Tower of London on the other side. We walk across Tower Bridge, its ornate Gothic towers flanking us and the cars and buses that trundle along it as we walk across, hand in hand. For a minute I think we're heading for a bus home, but when we walk past the Tower of London, George spies the oversized gift shop, designed to sell royal tat to customers who didn't spend quite enough at the castle itself.

"Come on," he says. "Let's go in."

"In there? In the Tower of London gift shop?"

"Yeah, I'll buy you a present."

"In there?" I ask again.

"Come on," he says, dragging me in. "Want a pen with a crown on it?" he asks as he nods toward the spinning stand.

"Yeah, go on." I just want to leave. I'm sure this is supposed to be cute. But I'm cringing.

"Or a . . . coaster?"

"A coaster?" I echo. "No, the pen looks nice."

"Yeah? You don't sound very enthusiastic," he says.

The hint of grumpiness is coming back in his voice, so I smile broadly. "I am one hundred percent certain I want the pen with the crown on the top."

"Bloody hell, Gallagher, it's sixteen quid."

I stare at him and then I say gently, "Put it back, George. Honestly, it's fine."

"But I want you to have this," he says, looking genuinely concerned that I'm missing out.

"Then I'll buy it," I say.

He sighs, hands me the pen, and I stand in the queue to pay.

By the time we got home the last thing I wanted to do was prep for film night. I made an excuse that we didn't have any popcorn and I was tired from all the walking. And just when we agreed to call it a day, and I decided to file it away under "worst date ever"— blowing *La La Land* singing man entirely out of the water— George turns to me at my front door, apologizes so hard that he's been a total idiot, says that he really likes me and knows he's making a complete mess of this.

"I don't know what happened today, Gallagher. I mean, I really have no idea how I ended up going from hero to zero. Total twat. I'm so sorry."

I smile. "It's OK." I'm neither confirming nor denying his total-twat behavior. "I was a bit off, as well. I was a bit ungrateful in that gift shop." Although I realize I was ungrateful about a pen I didn't want, and that he didn't actually want to buy me. I can't work that one out now.

"It was the book," he said. "I was angry that I left it on the bus. Angry with myself. I took it out on you. I'm still pissed off. But I shouldn't have been such an idiot about it."

"It's fine, really. I'd be pissed off if I lost a hundred pounds as well."

"Yeah, all right," he says, inching toward me with a grin. "Don't go on about it."

"Ha!" I reply.

George leans forward, nuzzles my neck. "Can I make it up to you?"

"Yes," I reply, immediately caving in like some kind of harlot as his lips brush their way up my neck. We fall inside my flat, and George does that thing that makes my knees go weak, when he kicks the door shut behind him purposefully. He pulls my jacket off, drops it to the floor, picks me up and carries me toward the bedroom.

Afterward he goes to the kitchen in just his boxer shorts. I love watching him walk around the kitchen, half-naked, sourcing all manner of boring-looking ingredients from my fridge and beginning to turn them into something marvelous. I linger in the kitchen, wearing his T-shirt and a pair of knickers, because I've got some level of modesty, preparing to be a sous chef, but he doesn't need me.

"You got a food processor?" he asks, casting around for a kitchen gadget that I don't own. He begins opening cupboards.

"No, sorry."

"Aha," he says, pulling out a food processor I've never seen before.

"I think Miranda must have left that behind when she moved out," I say, moving to the cupboard. "What else is in there? Oh, there's a steamer too."

"Not one for healthy eating, are you, Gallagher?"

"In moderation," I tease as I move to the fridge, pull out a bottle of wine. "Want a glass?"

"No. I thought I'd go for a run when my dinner's gone down. Join me?"

"Maybe," I say, cracking open the wine.

George frowns, shakes his head, and moves back to the task in hand.

"What are you making?"

"Spinach pesto."

I nod. I didn't know you could make pesto with spinach. He spies some chicken in the fridge, sniffs it, decides it's worth pursuing, and chucks it into another pan, where it sizzles gently.

"You're worth your weight in gold, aren't you?" I suggest.

"You'd better believe it, baby," he replies, lifting me onto the kitchen counter, raising his head to kiss me. He moves away, throws things into the food processor and starts blitzing various green ingredients.

I watch him as I sip my wine—George stirring, throwing pine nuts into the processor, me on the kitchen counter. This is nice. This is what I wanted. I'm happy. Right now I'm happy. We should never have gone out today. We should simply have stayed in, had a lot of sex, cooked food. I will go for a run with him in a bit. I am obviously going to drink this glass of wine first, though.

Chapter 17

Davey, April

I'M WAITING TO see my oncologist again. I've gone into his office solo today. Mom's in the hospital restaurant, begging me to let her know how the second round has gone, what my results are: whether the treatment has worked so far. Two chemo rounds done. One to go. And I'm thinking about this a lot. This last round.

The most awful thing about this is that my body is now a wasteland. It's amazing how quickly friends abandon you when you're out-of-control sick. Those who did come over didn't know how to look me in the eye, couldn't take their eyes off the bumps where my eyebrows used to be, off my weight gain (thanks, steroids) and the clear lack of my usual blond hair. It was awkward for everyone involved.

I'm thinking about this too much. I'm thinking about everything too much. Dark thoughts enter my head about what happens at the end, if the chemo doesn't work. I've already asked this question of my oncologist, Dr. Khader. He looked serious. He must spend all day looking serious. Who the hell wants that job?

"Good news," Dr. Khader tells me the moment I enter his consultancy room. "Your tumor markers are . . ." He quotes a decimal number at me that means absolutely nothing, and I tell him that. I've gotten so snappy. I'm snappy all the time now.

Dr. Khader smiles kindly. He's obviously used to telling patients information they don't understand, and being called on it. He's ready to go into some level of detail and I listen as he tells me my markers are low—that this is good, that the chemo is doing its job, that everything is going according to plan. Then he asks how I've been. He always used to ask how I was first, and in the end I got so pissy because no one wants to go see an oncologist and have small talk about life, love, and everything in between and then get told how well the treatment's working or not. So now he bursts into details, clipboard in hand, gives me the tumor-marker lowdown, explains what the hell it all means, and then I allow him the proverbial chat that I'm pretty sure he could also do without, but is obliged to have for the sake of his bedside-manner reputation.

"I'm OK," I tell him. It's my default answer now. I am obviously not OK. I'm weak, tired, everything hurts, I feel sick all the time, I'm angry, but I sound like a broken record and so "I'm OK," I repeat when he looks at me, knowing I'm lying.

He nods. "Let me check you over," he says. We go through this rigmarole too, which seems crazy. They took the testicle away and put a false one in at the same time, which sits a little strangely, so God knows what he's looking for; but there must be boxes to check off on that clipboard, and so I lie back on the exam table, pants down, arms behind my head, while my downstairs gets more action and I'm moved around, wincing uncomfortably while he does it.

"OK?" he asks. "It hurts still—this long after surgery?"

"No, man, it's that you're manhandling my balls. Ball," I correct myself with a frown. "And you didn't even buy me dinner first."

He laughs, but it's polite, not real. He must have heard that one a million times.

"You can get dressed now. Everything's as expected. Scar's

healing nicely—nothing out of the ordinary." Other than the fact that half of me is missing, down there.

He moves away, washes his hands, and then says, "How are you? How are you really? You're on your own today?" He glances around his office as if I might have hidden my mom behind one of his plastic chairs.

"Sure am." I stand up, pull on my joggers, and move back to the chair.

"You got enough support through all of this?"

"I do. Mom, Dad, best friend."

He nods, looking at me distrustfully . . . waiting for me to open up.

"Good," he says finally. "Anything else on your mind? Any questions about your third cycle?" I notice he doesn't call it my last cycle. He's keeping that door propped wide open. Just in case.

"Yeah," I say, leaning forward. "I do actually. What happens if I don't do it?"

He gives me a startled look, a mix of *What the hell?* and *I'm sure I misheard you.*

"What happens if you don't do what?" he asks slowly.

"If I don't go through with it. This last cycle." I'm going to call it the last one. Because I can. I've earned it.

Dr. Khader sits back, folds his arms. "Are you asking me what will happen to you if you choose to reject the entire course of treatment? If you stop now, after your second cycle?"

"Yes." I want to congratulate him for getting there and then I realize I am being an ass, even though I didn't say it out loud.

I can tell he's thinking about how to phrase his response. "It's not really an option," he says.

"Why not?" I am genuinely curious. "My markers are low. You said so yourself. The cancer has all but gone."

"Yes," he nods. "All but gone."

As if in silent exchange, it's his turn to wait for me to get there, but I won't. "It really hurts," I tell him and I can feel something close to tears at the back of my eyes. I blink them away. "It really hurts," I repeat, quieter now. "I don't think I can do it again. I don't *want* to do it again."

Perhaps I've finally asked him a question no one's ever asked him before, because he's watching me, blinking unbelievably slowly, and he's not speaking.

"Do you have a counselor or a therapist?" he asks me eventually and it's my turn to be stunned.

"No."

"You don't want one?"

"No. But I'd like an answer to my question, please. If that's OK?" The old, polite me has returned temporarily.

He rubs his jaw and I envy him that slight dash of stubble that I haven't had in forever. I kind of miss shaving regularly; it's one chore I took for granted.

"I don't think it will work," he says. "That's why we do three rounds."

"You don't *think* it will work or you *know* it won't work?"

Dr. Khader shifts on his seat, distinctly uncomfortable.

"Three rounds," he says. "We do three rounds of this BEP chemo, spaced apart at certain intervals. Tried, tested doses. If we could stop you at two, we would."

I nod. "OK," I say. I don't want to do it, but there's no point going around and around on this again. I stand to leave.

"OK, you're going to do it, or OK, you just want to get out of here and stop talking to me?" he says with a smile, but I can see he's got a faint glimmer of worry behind that expression.

I simply smile in return. I need to think. I hold out my hand to shake his and Dr. Khader takes it.

"You have the clinic number. You call me whenever you need.

If I'm with a patient, I'll call you right back, if you want to talk it through again."

"I don't think I'll need to," I say, not sure at all.

I can see he's reluctant to let me leave like this, but we've reached a stalemate and so he releases my hand. I can feel him watch me as I walk down the corridor toward the reception desk to sign out. It's only after I've turned the corner that I hear him call the next poor guy into his office to read him his results.

I'm silent in the car on the drive home, after updating my mom and trying to remember word for word what Dr. Khader said about how encouraging it is, how the cancer has *all but gone.* And then I clam up because I need to think, to work out what to do next.

My life has been put on hold for most of this year. I don't know how April has arrived. I wonder what I would have been doing now if I hadn't been stuck here, blindsided like this. I'd be in London. I smile. I might have been doing something fun and stupid with Hannah. I still haven't replied to her message. I'm not going to, either. But I pull my new phone out every now and again, look over the messages Hannah and I sent to each other. I think about that first time I called her accidentally and how happy I felt in the weeks that followed—the video dates, the long talks, how I was so ready to meet her, get off that plane and start a new life in London. To say I am bitter is an understatement.

We pull up outside our house and my mom tries to talk to me. I just smile and nod. I have no idea what she's saying, something about making us both a sandwich. I go inside. I've only got a week or so of peace and then the chemo cycle starts again. My bag is packed and ready to go for it. Mom has been diligently washing my joggers and T-shirts, making sure I don't run out of toothpaste, and my bag sits there in between cycles, waiting to be dragged back to the hospital with me again.

The air-conditioning blows onto me as I watch TV, but I'm not really watching it, and then I see a familiar face enter the living room. My mom has let Grant in, given him her usual hug, asked after his mom, and he's now standing in the doorway—only he's wearing a baseball cap, which he never does.

I narrow my eyes at him. "What's up?" I ask.

"Nothing," he says in that strange mix of English with Texan thrown in for good measure. Our parents met through the British expat community when they all moved out here to work for BP. Although my parents came when I was tiny, Grant's came from England when he was thirteen, pulled him from his boarding school and brought him out here because they couldn't bear to leave him behind. And now his accent is all over the place. When he joined our school he hid his English accent, pretending to be American because he thought it made him sound cool. But when we grew up and he realized being English in America would get him laid way faster, he switched back—unsuccessfully—and now he sounds like a cross between Ray Winstone in a London gangland biopic and Dick Van Dyke in *Mary Poppins*: some sort of cockney Australian. He's constantly being asked where in Down Under he's from.

Grant bounces over to the couch, sinks into it forcefully, the way he has done since we were thirteen, and then gives me a knowing look. There's something different about him, other than the baseball cap, which is throwing me.

I turn, eye him next to me.

"What are we watching?" he asks.

I glance at the TV, now on mute. "*Grey's Anatomy.* Rerun."

"You not so sick to death of hospitals yet that you want to watch them on TV when you're not there?"

I laugh. "I hadn't even thought about that. It was just on."

"Count to three," he says suddenly.

I do as I'm told, and then on three he takes off his baseball cap.

My mouth drops. "What have you done?" I cry, sitting up straight.

"Shaved my head. In solidarity with you." He goes to fist-bump me, but I can't even move as I look at his head. I move my fist slowly to return the bump, but my wide eyes still betray my surprise.

His confidence wanes and he touches the stubble on the top of his head. "You don't like it? You're offended?"

I shake my head slowly and then say, "What have you done?" I ask again, which makes him laugh. "Why?" I ask. "I mean, it suits you. You look like a young Jason Statham. But . . . why?"

"For you, man. Solidarity. I don't know why it took me this long to think of it. I should have done it the same time we shaved your head."

"But you had good hair," I say.

"Thanks, man." He looks pleased. "So did you. Yours will grow back, and then so will mine. I'm going to keep shaving it down until you're over all this shit and yours starts coming back through."

I don't know whether to laugh or cry. I swallow down a telltale lump in my throat.

"Don't cry, man," Grant warns with a smile.

I have cried so many times these past few months, but never in front of anyone.

"OK, I won't," I reply. I take a deep breath and, after I exhale, "Thanks" is all I can say.

"You're welcome." And then he confesses, "Remember when we shaved yours? And when the clippers ran through that first wave, sinking your hair to the floor and you shouted, 'Fuck'?"

I nod.

"That is exactly what I did when I started on mine," Grant says. "What a shock!" Mine is soft, downy, like baby hair now. Grant reads my mind and says, "I'll shave yours again today if you want? Even it out?"

I nod again, make an appreciative noise, and we sit in silence.

"Thanks," I say. And it's both for him shaving my hair and for him shaving his. "You didn't need to."

"I know. So . . ." Grant starts. "How you doing? Really."

"Not great," I say, looking to the kitchen where my mom has retreated. I hope she can't hear this. "I don't think I'm going to do the last chemo round."

Grant freezes. For once he has no words, no string of expletives. And then, "What?"

"You heard me."

"Why not?" he asks.

"It hurts. It makes me want to die."

"OK," he says quietly. "I was in that first meeting with your oncologist when they told you what would happen at each stage."

"My markers are down," I say, ignoring the direction he's tried to take the conversation.

"I don't give a fuck. You're having that chemo."

"No, I'm not."

"Yes, you are."

"It hurts, Grant. It stings. It makes me feel more sick than I've ever felt in my life."

"All this effort," he counters. "And for what? To let the cancer take you just a few months later than planned."

"Fuck you!"

"No. Fuck you, Davey. I'm not on this shit journey with you so that you can call it a day halfway through, you lazy . . . prick."

I stand my ground. Quietly, I say, "Grant, I cannot tell you how much it hurts. I taste metal all the time. My ears ring with tinnitus. I can beat it. I can beat the cancer. Without chemo."

"By yourself? Without drugs? What are you, a fucking hippie? You have the chemo or . . . I'm telling your mum."

I laugh but it's bitter. "You're gonna tell my mom? Are we six? I'm gonna have to tell my mom anyway. What other threats have you got up your sleeve?"

Grant stands, looks down at me. His whole body is tense. He has no words. He merely stares, his jaw clenched. I can't tell if he's going to hit me or not. He looks like he wants to.

"Look," I say. "I know that isn't the plan. But, Grant . . . I cannot go through any more of this. I just can't. It's too hard. I want my life back. I want to go and . . . live—and do the things I've put on hold."

"I know it's hard," he says.

I'm exhausted, I know that now. Mentally, physically, I have nothing left. I look up at Grant. "I'm done," I say with a sigh, and I *feel* done. I let my shoulders dip. I'm not going to have that last round of chemo. The doctor said it's all but gone. I need to stop all of this now.

"But you have to keep going," he says in desperation.

I shake my head. "No. I don't."

Chapter 18

Davey

I'VE NEVER SEEN Grant this angry, this shocked and confused. The more I think about it, the more I know I'm making the right decision in not having the final round. I am done. I can start making plans now. Plans to live.

Before he leaves, Grant asks me if I genuinely mean it or if this is a cry for help and he's misreading the signs. I can't help but admire his tenacity, clinging on to the final threads of an argument, checking to make sure I haven't gone entirely insane. But I haven't. I tell him this isn't a cry for help.

"But this is suicide," he says. "You really can't see that? This is you . . . killing yourself . . . really fucking slowly."

"I'm not," I tell him, and now that I know I'm not doing the chemo, I feel lighter, brighter. I feel the way I felt the night before I was supposed to leave for England—like all this fresh possibility is within reach. I just have to grab it. I can start making plans. I have no idea what those plans will be. But I can finally start, hit play, begin again. When Grant's gone, I'm going to google flights to Rome, find a culinary school. Maybe I'll take a year and go traveling, forget that the last few months ever happened.

He doesn't know what to do, what to say. I can see that. And instead of feeling sorry for myself, which I have done a lot of, I now feel really sorry for Grant. It's the same helplessness my mom and dad have felt, and I owe them so much simply for being there. I need to cut everyone some slack. They would have let me get away with murder. But I just retreated into crashing waves of silence, sleep, lack of appetite, and then, when no one was looking, crying in my bedroom. But this is me, done, moving on from all of that.

In his confusion, Grant can't stop staring. He runs his hand through the place where his hair once sat, and confusion barrels into him again as he remembers he shaved it all off.

"You OK?" I ask him. It's only fair.

He comes to his senses. "You're a selfish prick," he says and leaves.

I sigh deeply. I know it's going to be like this, and I wonder if I can change my mind. But the thought of going to the hospital again, sitting in that chair, having them drip those drugs into my veins on and off over the next month . . . It brings a sudden bout of bile into my mouth and I use all the energy I have to get up from the couch, run to the bathroom, and vomit. I can't do it. I know I can't. I've come to the end.

Ordinarily I would have about a week-long break, but knowing at the end of that I don't have to go back to the hospital makes me smile all day, every day.

"You OK, sweetie?" my mom asks.

"Yeah," I say, turning to her, and I mean it. I really am. My energy returns in fits and starts and tonight I'm cooking dinner for the three of us. I don't think I'll be able to eat it. But I'll try. I can't really eat that much, but I'm making pasta carbonara, my favorite. I'm making the pasta from scratch and it's going a bit lumpy. I think again of that culinary course in Rome that I'm determined to find. I haven't told my parents yet that I'm dipping out of the last round of chemo, that I don't think I really need it. And it's clear Grant didn't make good on his threat to tell my family. I look at my mom's blissful ignorance and decide I just might not tell them. What they don't know can't hurt them. There's nothing they can do about my decision, so why rub in the fact that they're powerless in all of this? I walk over, kiss her on the cheek. Hold my egg-and-flour hands up as if I'm a surgeon. She looks older than ever and I guess that's my fault. Watching her only child go through this has dusted more sprinkles of gray into her hair.

"I love you, Mom."

She smiles. "I know." She tells me she loves me too and asks if she can do anything to help.

"Make a salad?" I suggest.

"I didn't mean with dinner."

I look at her, smile, shake my head. "I got everything covered."

I need to shut her down. She wants to pour her heart out to me and I know when she does that I'll break down, cry, tell her I can't go on like this. But instead I say, "Could you add some sun-dried tomatoes?"

I sense her turn, move away from me, hear her opening cabinets, and then we make dinner in silence, waiting for my dad to get home from work.

I'm in bed hours later, staring at my cellphone. I have gotten the strangest message from Charlotte, my ex. It's a real blast from the past. Although we ended things around eighteen months ago, so I suppose not that long ago really. We didn't end badly. In fact, I broke it off when it became apparent we wanted different things. But there was never any anger, hatred, or resentment from my side, and it's clear from her message that there's none on hers, either.

Davey, she writes. I just heard. I'm so sorry. Can I come see you? She goes on to tell me she had no idea—none at all—and she's "devastated" that: (1) I have cancer; and (2) I didn't tell her.

I stare at her message for quite some time before considering how to respond. I don't want to be rude, but I don't really owe her this kind of news. We aren't part of each other's lives now. But once we were. It's easy to remember how she was back then. She was a tornado. Everything was fast. I kinda liked that about her. Back then we worked together well, until we didn't. She shared my "do-or-die" attitude. Maybe a little too much. No hesitations—just make a decision and go with it. I think I'm still like that. I was like that about moving to London.

At the end I felt like we were on different paths, though there was no "one thing" that broke us up.

Maybe it would be nice to see Charlotte. I reply that she should come over tomorrow and that she can bring ice cream. Ice cream is the only thing I can eat that doesn't taste like metal. Even the carbonara I made—my favorite—might as well have been pasta coated in paint. I hit reply again and say **please,** because I don't want to turn into the kind of guy who has so much on his mind he's run out of room for manners. It's not OK to expect people will forgive me.

When Charlotte arrives the next day she looks completely different from when we dated. I'm kind of impressed. I look different too, though in the sense that I look like shit. Although I wasn't really expecting to blow Charlotte away with how good I look, I've put a baseball cap on to hide my hair, or lack thereof, but I'm in my uniform of jogging pants and T-shirt. They're clean but it's not a good look.

"Davey!" she cries and throws her arms around me, holding me close. There's no preamble. No awkwardness. She smells good. Like vanilla cupcakes.

"Hey," I say into her hair, waiting for her to break off. But she doesn't. She pulls back, her hands still on either side of my shoulders, scrutinizing my face. I wait and then look away from her gaze when it goes on a little too long.

"I'm sorry," she says, shaking her head and laughing that kind of tinkling giggle she has. I smile—I forgot about that. Is she apologizing for holding on to me for too long or because I have cancer?

"Davey, it's been so long."

I nod. "It has. How are you?"

She enters the house holding a brown paper bag. "I just stopped at the store to buy ice cream. As requested. Is pecan still your favorite?"

"Oh yeah."

"I remembered," she says smugly and produces it, along with two plastic spoons.

We sit at the kitchen table, the windows thrown open as the warm air surrounds us, immediately sharing the tub of ice cream as she lifts the lid, discards it next to us.

"So tell me everything," she says. "Tell me how you are. How your treatment is going—everything."

I clench my jaw. I really didn't know what to expect from seeing Charlotte again. I remember this . . . this force of nature now. "I don't really want to talk about it," I say.

"Oh, OK. Why?"

I laugh. Same old Charlotte. Although prettier. Actually much prettier. She's got some eyeliner flicky-thing going on that makes her eyes really pop. And . . . I can't work it out. "You did something to your hair."

"I got bangs, and I get it colored now."

"Yeah," I say slowly. "It's kinda red now. I like it."

"Thanks." She shrugs and then tries again. "Chemo that bad, huh? Seeing as you'd rather discuss my hair."

"It sucks. Big time," I reply, dipping my spoon into the tub. And because there's no getting around it—she'll work on me until I fess up, so I may as well get it over with—I tell her everything. She listens quietly, nodding in all the right places, and then when

I tell her, tentatively, that I'm not going to finish my final chemo, Charlotte doesn't even bat an eyelid. I wait for her to digest this fact alongside her ice cream, but she looks at me, expecting more. And when I don't speak she says, "Do what you need to do."

"Really?" I sound as though I'm asking permission from my ex-girlfriend, but I think I'm just stunned.

"Sure. You know your own body, right?"

"Yeah," I say.

"Good. Then don't do it. If it hurts and you hate it, and you feel as though you can't do any more, that you're done—"

"I do," I leap in. "I do. I'm done. I can't do this anymore."

"Then stop. Do what's right for you."

"Grant says I should keep going—" I start.

"Forget Grant. That guy's a dick."

I laugh. "He's my best friend."

"He's still a dick."

"Um, OK," I say uncertainly as we reach the halfway mark on the tub.

"I've missed this," she says quietly. "You and me. Like this."

I did not see that coming. "Really?"

She nods.

"Are you not seeing anyone?" I ask, because looking like that, how could she not be?

"No. You?"

Momentarily Hannah flits into my mind. "No. Not really. I mean, no, not at all. Look at me, Charlotte. I'm overweight from the steroids, and maybe because of the ice cream. I've lost all my hair, I have cancer, I have no job, and I live with my mom and dad. Who would want me?"

"I would," she says quietly and her hand reaches out to touch mine as I dive back into the ice cream.

"Charlotte," I say. "You don't mean it."

"I do. I'd still be with you now if you hadn't ended things

between us. I loved you. Love you," she corrects herself. "I still want you," she says, avoiding my gaze and dipping her spoon into the tub. She lifts it, places the ice cream onto her tongue, and does something to that spoon with her tongue that makes me suddenly hard.

"Jesus," I mutter and then look at her. "Um, OK," I say, not for the first time today.

"You don't want me?" she asks in a voice that indicates *she* wants *me*.

I am not sure if she's referring to sex or to us getting back together. I am also not sure what my answer to either of those would be. Is this for real? I've seen how I look. Has she gone blind in the last year and a half?

"My mom is home" is the only thing I can stutter out, *in case* she's talking about what I think she's talking about.

"Is that the only problem?" she asks and her voice has taken on a seductive tone.

"I guess," I say slowly, a smile creeping up the edges of my mouth. Am I misreading this?

"And she hasn't even come down to say hi to me?" Charlotte asks with a snide smile. My mother made no secret of the fact that she hated Charlotte. It was no surprise that when I told her Charlotte was coming over, my mom made herself scarce upstairs, muttering something about laundry.

"I don't live with *my* mom," Charlotte says and somehow she manages to make that innocuous sentence sound . . . suggestive.

"OK," I say again. And then because I've known Charlotte so long, and we had the kind of relationship where the sex was great but the conversation was . . . well . . . Anyway, I ask, "Just to be clear, you want to have sex with me?"

She laughs, puts her spoon in the tub. "Sure."

"Now?"

She nods. "My car's outside."

I open my eyes wide. "This is sympathy sex, right?" I suggest.

She laughs, stands up, and pulls her car keys from the pocket of her jeans. "You can call it sympathy sex. You can call it one for the road. You can call it whatever the hell you like, Davey Carew. But the fact of the matter is: you either want me to bang your brains out or you don't."

I stand up so fast the chair falls over behind me.

Chapter 19

I'M IN BED with Charlotte hours later. I forgot how *pink* her entire apartment is. It would seem I also forgot how to "do" sex, so Charlotte took control, as I'd kinda hoped she would, so all I really had to do was lie there. Which was good because my energy failed me the moment I got out of her car and let her lead me into her apartment, where she just launched herself at me. I was so stunned I simply let her "do" sex to me. It was good, but not as good as I remember. Either way, I now know women want to have sympathy sex with me. Maybe I should have posted a status update on social media months ago, after all—"Happy Sunday, everyone, I have cancer"—and waited for women to turn up at my door. Although there was only one woman I wanted to turn up, and I pushed her away. Besides, she's five thousand miles away, getting on with her life.

Charlotte lights a cigarette and I stare at her. "When did you start smoking?" I ask.

"About five minutes after you broke up with me."

I don't know what to make of this.

"Want one?" she asks.

I shake my head. "Um . . . I have cancer so . . . no, thank you."

She nods, rolls onto her side to look at me. I climb out of bed, open the window and stand near it, so I don't inhale the smoke.

"Sorry," she says. "I didn't think about it." She stabs the cigarette out in a vintage teacup sitting next to her side of the bed. I can't tell if that's the cutest ashtray I've ever seen or if she's got a leftover cup of something in there. I look back to her.

"Two and a half years, Davey," she says to me.

I nod, move away from the window and then, "What was?"

"Us, silly."

Was it? I thought it was less than that.

She nudges me in the ribs as I climb back into bed with her. "And you just threw us away."

I frown at this. It wasn't quite like that. It's like being in this apartment again has brought it all back to me. Charlotte had become strange, needy, pushy, but I overlooked it, thinking, "This is women, right? Is this *all* women?" My experience was limited to a lot of casual hookups during college and then only one serious relationship, which had fizzled out naturally. So when Charlotte came along—all glossy hair and a libido to rival Hugh Hefner's—I never really saw her coming. She'd recently started work as an assistant at a local news network and said she was going to be the main anchor in a few years. She's never been shy about getting what she wanted. She hasn't made anchor yet, but she probably will soon, if I know Charlotte. She liked that I was an architect, that I had my own apartment in a new building with a gym. She liked showing me off, describing us as a power couple, which I knew we weren't. Before all this, I wasn't that bad to look at, either, I think. I hope. She told me I looked hot. She looked hot. I'm remembering now why we fell apart so easily, but she's still looking at me with that post-coital expression, all full lips and big eyes.

"Charlotte, what do you want from me?" I ask. "I have nothing to offer you."

She kneels over me on the bed, naked, and I am only human, so my gaze wanders south, away from her face.

"Nothing," she says, placing her finger on my chin and tipping my head back so I'm forced to look into her eyes. "You," she says, rethinking her answer. "I want you. And if you don't want me—"

"I never said that," I reply quickly. I mean, I don't want to offend the girl. We did spend two and a half years together, apparently.

"If you don't want me," she repeats, "we can just do this from time to time."

I raise an almost hairless eyebrow. "This?"

"Friends with . . . benefits."

I raise both hairless eyebrows. This has to be a trick. This is the best offer I've had—ever.

"OK," I say uncertainly.

I lie there, thinking. Maybe Charlotte will be different this time. She's eager to get back with me, I believe. I can't tell. I'm so out of touch. I don't want to see what she sees when she looks at me. But she does look at me. And she wants me, sexually, while I look like *this*.

"So, baby," she says and I can't help flinching as she says "baby." She doesn't notice. Thank God. "Before, in your kitchen," she continues, "you were telling me about Grant, and I cruelly cut you off so I could bring you here and do all kinds of things to you." She gives me that tinkling laugh.

"I can't remember," I say honestly. "I think I was saying Grant and I had a fight. Because I won't do the last round of chemo."

"Well, I hate Grant," Charlotte says.

"Wow, that's strong," I say.

"But you should stop, baby. Stop if it's hurting you. Life doesn't have to be this hard," she soothes.

I close my eyes, nodding slowly as I drift off to sleep. Charlotte understands me. I'm so worn down. "I am going to stop the chemo," I say determinedly.

And then my eyes spring open as she moves down, her hair brushing my groin. "Then stop, baby," she says, before wrapping her mouth around me. And all thoughts of chemo disappear.

Chapter 20

Hannah, May

I'VE NOW BEEN dating George for longer than I was—whatever—with Davey. And subconsciously I'm becoming more invested in working on this relationship rather than hanging on to something that started slowly and ended fast. With George, we started fast and . . . no, no. I'm working at this.

I'll take my hat off to him, because George has gotten me thin—although he says that wasn't his design; he just wanted me to be healthier and have more energy. Mainlining Hobnobs and white bread on a near daily basis isn't the way to ward off heart disease in later years. Apparently. Health and fitness have been his sole mission, I think, over the past few weeks after I muttered something about how I love pancakes, but pancakes don't love me, over brunch one morning. We still go for drinks, but now it's all about gin and slimline tonics, which I'm slowly learning to love, and less about piña coladas, full of coconut rum and cream, which are apparently the Devil.

I've been going running with him, too. Getting fit. Eating less. Drinking less. I've kicked it up a notch at the gym, and I've joined this boot-camp thing that George has started leading, in prep for summer bikini bodies. I am very much a guinea pig in order to encourage more pancake-loving girls like me to get on board, and he keeps taking photos of me in gym gear and we track my losses religiously with a tape measure. "It's all about inches, Gallagher, not stones and pounds." This was news to me, and I'm encouraged to slide my electronic scale out of sight. I can't tell if this is a good thing or not.

On George's birthday at the end of the month I'm going to give him the James Bond book he was desperate for, all those weeks ago. It's still £100, signed. I've been waiting for the price to drop, but George warned me prices for this kind of thing don't drop—they increase—so I bit the bullet and bought it for him. It's not exactly a surprise, but I remember his sad face when he realized he'd left it on the bus. Actually I think it was more of an angry face. No matter. He really wanted it. I've also bought him a coaster from an online royal gift shop, in the hope he thinks it's funny. I think it's funny. Mildly funny. Not that funny actually. I might not give him the coaster.

I put it in my usual "present hiding spot," in the cupboard under the stairs that leads to the flat upstairs, and when I go to place it inside, something falls out and lands on my foot in the dark. I pull out the object and look at it. It's the London tour book that I bought for Davey. I put it away after he'd finished things between us. Out of sight, out of mind, and all that. I open it. I'd forgotten I'd put an inscription inside:

> *Davey,*
> *I can't wait to share all of this with you. By the time I give this*
> *to you, it won't be Christmas anymore, but . . .*
> > *Happy Christmas, love from Hannah xxx*

Christmas—flipping heck, that was ages ago. So much has happened since then and, amazingly for me, I haven't thought about Davey—really thought about him—in, oh, at least a week. That's good going for me. I saw something on TV that really made me laugh and it didn't make George laugh, but I thought: Davey would have found that funny. He'd probably find the coaster story funny too. Oh, for God's sake, what's wrong with me?

I put the book on my bookshelf. I think I might actually read it and do some touristy things. I might even be able to do one of those big red bus tours now, without it actually hurting. I could stand next to a Beefeater with George, without thinking that it's what Davey and I had planned to do. We had planned to do so much. I close the book—onward and upward.

Chapter 21

Davey

I FEEL EMBOLDENED. This is a new me. I have so much more energy now that I'm back together with Charlotte. It's like it was when we first met. She's in control and I am being carried on a wave in whatever direction she heads, swept up in her wake. I don't have to think. I don't have to react. I just have to go with it. God, this is easy. This is what I needed. Not only the sex, although obviously that's great. Charlotte gets me. She gets what I need. She doesn't see me how I am now. She sees me as I was—as I am going to be again, sooner rather than later. And this is because of the decision I've made, the decision that Charlotte understands perfectly. I think if we do this, Charlotte and I, if we really do this, then it's starting perfectly. It's more adult now. We've grown up since we ended things before. It's good, meeting again like this. Becoming a thing together, because of conversation and *life,* is how it should have been last time.

The first time we met we gravitated toward each other in the darkness of a bar, high on life and alcohol and opportunity. Charlotte simply kind of happened to me.

We walk through the mall together, hand in hand, enjoying each other's company. I've hardly been out since I was diagnosed. It was always too risky for my white blood-cell count to be near people who might pass on what, to them, is a mild illness. But we're headed out for ice cream and categorically no shopping. I don't have it in me to watch her try on fifty outfits that all look the same. I don't dare tell her that, but I've made it clear I'm too tired to shop. She suggests a movie at the theater next door. I can't do that, either. I might sleep my way through it. Charlotte gives me her tinkling laugh and then says she'll come back and watch the movie another time.

"Who with?" I ask a little sharply.

"People," she teases.

Other things I don't do with Charlotte include bringing her back to my mom and dad's. So we hang out at hers mostly. It's nice. I like it. I feel like a grown-up again—not being fussed over by my mom. Some women want to mother men. Charlotte is *not* one of them. She's happy to let me eat ice cream all day.

As we're walking back through the parking lot, I spy Grant. He's got his arm around a girl I don't know and I can hear him, from here, hamming up his not-quite-English accent for her benefit.

"Yeah, I *am* from Sydney. How did you guess?" I hear him lie as he approaches. If Grant can't be bothered to explain his English roots, then it's the unspoken call sign that this girl hasn't passed the test and he's only in it for the night. I smile. And then his face falls as he clocks me.

I glance down at Charlotte, whose teeth look on edge at the sight of him. I stop, ready to talk to Grant. But he nods at me, ignores Charlotte, and walks right past us. I turn, look at his retreating figure as he heads toward the movie theater. But he doesn't look back at me.

When he's out of earshot, Charlotte says, "You see? Grant is not nice."

I frown, watch as he enters through the automatic doors.

Charlotte is pulling me toward her car, but I keep watching. Just in case Grant turns around to look at me. He doesn't. The doors close behind him.

I'm determined to get past all this: lose the weight from the steroids, eat less ice cream and more vegetables. I've already looked up culinary courses. I can't wait to feel better, to book some flights. I wonder about Hannah from time to time, and now is one of those times. I feel guilty. I haven't had the guts lately to type a message to her, even when I know I won't send it. What if she's online again? What if I do something stupid like hit send, make contact. I've forced myself to forget her, or at least try to forget her. It hasn't worked. And the worst thing is that I want to talk to her so badly, and now I'm ridden with guilt because of Charlotte. Things with Hannah were so easy, so hopeful. But complicated, because of our distance and my cancer. That distance isn't shrinking, but at least the cancer is.

When I was fifteen I used to have the hots for a girl called Candice Williams. I used to ride past her house on my bike, multiple times. I used to go by on one side of the street and then back up the other. Over and over again.

I figure what I do with the messages is like that. I go online, see if Hannah's online. It's the transatlantic twentysomething equivalent of riding up and down someone's street, hoping they'll appear at their front door. Even though I feel guilty because of Charlotte, I still do it now—go online and see if Hannah's online. Annoyingly she isn't, and even more annoyingly she's too similar to me when it comes to social media. She doesn't post anything online. Ever. And either she's a hermit crab these days or her friends have the same view on social media that she does and they don't tag her in anything. I've even tried torturing myself by hoping that her new boyfriend, whoever he is, has tagged her in a photo of the two of them looking blissfully happy somewhere. I want to know what he looks like. I want to feel that pain. But instead I have nothing new to feed off—like a junkie who can't get their next fix.

The door to my room bursts open and I drop my phone. "Jesus!" I exclaim as Grant hurls himself into the space like a hurricane. "What the hell, Grant? I could have been doing *anything*," I practically shout. Shock at his sudden arrival has got the better of me. But then I smile, because he's here.

"Charlotte?" He basically shouts back at me. "Charlotte?"

I look around. "She's not here, man."

He closes his eyes as if I'm stupid, steels himself. "No, I know she's not here. I asked your dad. That's why I came up."

I sit up straight on the bed, making room for Grant. But he doesn't sit.

"What are you doing, Davey?" he asks with concern, all anger dropped from his voice. "What, in God's name, are you doing? First you quit chemo and then you start up with that girl again?"

"That girl?" I query. "She hates you too," I state.

"Good. She's a bitch."

"Grant," I warn. "We're kind of . . . together."

"No," he tells me. "No, you're not. End it."

"What?" I splutter.

"Why is Charlotte back?" he throws at me suddenly.

"She . . . wants me," I say and realize how stupid that sounds. "She's nice."

"She's not nice, she's a dick."

"Funnily enough, that's the exact same thing she said about you."

"Davey, she is. The way she flirted shamelessly with everyone when you guys were dating each other was disgusting."

"What? I didn't know that. Everyone? Who?"

"People. Me," Grant snaps.

"You?"

"While you were dating. And after you stopped dating."

I narrow my eyes. "Really?"

"That girl is bad for you. But she's determined. I could see that in her eyes from all the way across the parking lot. That fierce determination. You looked good together—just how she wanted. Her architect boyfriend with his own apartment."

He's repeating words I've told him, but I let Grant have that. "Now I have no job, just cancer, and I live with my parents. I'm not a catch she's trying to bag anymore. She's genuine."

"I doubt it. But, hey, you might as well bang her a few times until you get bored and remember why you dropped her the first time."

"Grant. What the fuck?"

"I really don't like her, mate." He's whining now. "She's toxic. If you do get with her, don't marry her. Jesus, don't bloody marry her. I won't come to that wedding."

"Thanks." And he has the audacity to call *her* toxic?

"I'm going to do two things for you today," Grant declares. "One is going to hurt like hell. The other . . ." He shrugs.

"Go on then," I say halfheartedly. I'm exhausted now.

"Here's the first one." He takes a deep breath, looks me in the eye. And then he can't look me in the eye anymore. "Charlotte and I . . . we—" He stops.

I've gone very still. "What? What did you do?"

"It was just after you broke up. I don't like her. I'll make that clear. I didn't like her when you dated. I don't like her now."

"What happened?" I ask. I want to know. And I don't want to know.

"I was out in a club with a couple of guys from work," he starts. "You'd finished things with her about a month earlier. She came up to me and ground herself into me. She wasn't even drinking. She was driving. I should have sensed that she was probably hurting from you. But I was too out of my head to know which way was up."

"O . . . K. Is that it?" I mean, so far it's not great, but . . .

He shakes his head. "No. We kissed. A lot. In the club. And then somehow we were kissing out in the parking lot. And then in her car. She made it clear we were going to her car for . . . reasons."

I stare at him. I don't know what I feel. Shock. I'm shocked. My best friend. And my girlfriend. Or ex, but . . . still. That's a violation of every code there's ever been.

Grant's not talking and so I do. "And so you slept with her?"

"No. We kind of fooled around a bit."

I wince. Look away.

"Her hands were just . . . everywhere, you know?" he continues.

I do know, but I'm not going to say it.

"And then we're in the back of her car. And we're kissing and—" He looks away again. "And we're doing . . . stuff . . . and I was trashed."

"Nice," I say, feeling very sick. I close my eyes. "And then what happened?" Why do I even want to know this?

"We would have"—he shrugs—"only . . . I threw up."

This surprises me. "Huh? You threw up? In her car?"

A tiny smile flickers at the edge of his mouth, and then Grant remembers we're in the middle of an almighty argument and he adopts a serious expression. "A little bit. Yeah. Actually quite a lot. Dealing with that cleanup was no more than she deserved, now that I think about it. Charlotte coming on to me like that: it was a revenge move. I was too drunk to see it then. But I worked it out pretty fast the next day. She homed in on me in that club—her ex-boyfriend's best friend. I was drunk. She was stone-cold sober. I shouldn't have kissed her, let her kiss me. I shouldn't have let her get so . . . handsy, but that girl is very persuasive. She is bad news. She is bad for you. I realize now that you will never be my friend again, but I don't want you anywhere near her. She was toxic then. She's toxic now. She's a grenade waiting to explode. She's—"

"I get it," I say. This conversation has exhausted me. I feel I could sleep for a hundred years. "I get it," I say listlessly.

"I'm sorry you're tired, man. But I have to keep going before you kick me out and it's game over for our friendship, which I suspect it is already, but anyway . . . You need to have that chemo," he says. "You need to think. This isn't about you."

"No? I kinda thought it was."

"No. It's about your parents. It's about me. What will I do without you? No one else will be my best friend," he says and I can't help but laugh.

"I won't die."

"You will," he says. "I've researched. You need three rounds of chemo. It's spread into your chest. It's traveling through your lymph nodes. Next stop, your brain, lungs, liver."

"Stop," I tell him.

"You think it's gone, with two rounds. It's not. It'll creep back in. You *have* to do this. You have to be a superhero."

"I'm not a superhero. I'm exhausted. I need you to go."

"Because of Charlotte."

For the first time in I don't know how long I shout. I roar at my friend. "This is not about Charlotte! I don't give a fuck about what you and Charlotte did. I don't have the energy to care. This isn't about you. Or my parents. This is about me wanting to get on with my life, to have control of it again!"

He stares at me. Nods. "Then I have no choice," he says cryptically, turns from the room. "I love you, man," he throws over his shoulder. "You'll thank me for this later."

"Thank you for what?" I shout after him.

"For the second thing I said I'd do." And then he's gone and I hear his tread on the staircase and the slam of the front door as Grant leaves.

Chapter 22

Hannah

GEORGE IS COMING around tonight. It's my turn to cook, which is a bit annoying for two reasons: (1) I have a huge presentation I'm meant to be prepping for; and (2) I'm crap at cooking.

Also he's trying to make sure that I "engage fully with healthy eating" when he's not around to advise on meal prep, and so we're going to make some kind of ornate salad that includes kale. I don't swear often when it comes to vegetables but, dear God, I bloody hate kale. No matter what you do to it, it still tastes like kale.

When George arrives, brandishing all the ingredients, he bounces in, back in his Duracell Bunny mode that I've been witnessing more of recently. He's been upping the ante on all the green vegetables he can get his hands on. He has really been led by my enthusiasm that I've lost a bit of weight and feel a little healthier now. The personal trainer in him doesn't want me to give up, especially because, as he says, "It takes a long time to build a healthy-eating habit."

Even so, I don't really want to eat what he's suggesting for dinner. There's a part of me that could murder some Nutella right now instead. Not even *on* anything. Just with a spoon. My eyes glaze over as I think about this, and then I'm reminded that it's my turn to cook and he holds out the bag of kale and I smile thinly.

"So what you want to do with the kale, Gallagher—"

"Is put it straight in the bin?" I suggest and then stop smiling as I see George roll his eyes, following the action up with a frown. He is trying, bless him, and making time for me—giving over a good proportion of his energy and spare time to being with me.

"No, we're going to salt it—not too much—and then . . ."

My mind goes elsewhere as George drones on. I thought it was my turn to cook, but he's practically doing it all for me.

After dinner, which I need a lot of water to wash down, we settle in to watch TV together, with strict instructions that when we're done we either engage in some next-level shagging so that we can work off some calories (from kale? I wonder) or we're going for a run. I opt for sex, obviously, because I am learning to hate running. As part of my plan to *Let George In*—to really be part of each other's lives and give a bit more of myself to him—we're finally going to watch *A Room with a View* together. I've summarized the plot, I've warned him it's old. He's in.

"If it's your favorite film, then I'm sure it will be good."

I am obviously dreading this. I dreaded it when Davey and I watched it, but he really enjoyed it. Even he was surprised, I think, but he kept pausing to ask questions; and unless he was lying, he loved the scenery, the characters, the time, the place.

We start the film and I find myself watching George rather than the film. His eyes are narrowed for a while. I remind myself it was his suggestion that we watch this. Not mine.

He turns his head to me. "They're in funny outfits."

Is he joking? "They're Edwardian."

He grimaces, then switches it to a smile. "Righty-ho."

"We don't have to watch—"

"No, no, I want to," he says.

We keep going and I become more engrossed in Helena Bonham Carter being scooped up in the hero's arms in an Italian piazza, because she's just witnessed a murder and fainted. It's so romantic, in a weird way, and I glance over at George, who is busy scrolling through his phone.

"You're not enjoying this?"

He drops his phone into his lap. "I am loving this."

I shuffle on the sofa. Now I just want the film to end, but there's ages to go yet. I pick up *my* phone because I can't concentrate. I need a distraction.

I'm drawn to all the social-media channels and find myself flicking to see if Davey's updated anything recently. He hasn't. He never has. What am I expecting? A smiling picture of him hooked up to his meds? I wish I didn't think about him so much. I wish I hadn't sent that message telling him that I could see him typing. That merely turned him cold. He's never been online since, as far as I can see. And he never replied. Maybe that was the time he *was* going to hit send and I put him off. I could kick myself. I often wonder what he was going to say. I'll never know.

The film ends, George is practically asleep, and I nudge him as the credits roll. "Not your cup of tea?" I offer.

"Not really," he says. "I'm glad it's yours, though," which is a statement that makes no sense but I go with it.

I'm not really in the mood for sex or running, and I suspect neither is George, but he stands, stretches, blinks a few times. "Shall we?" he asks. "The Flats?" he says, referring to the park near me.

"For sex or running?" I say provocatively.

"Running," he laughs.

"Sure." I am a tiny bit concerned that he'd prefer to run rather than have sex, but I go and pull my running gear on, lace my feet into my trainers, pocket my phone, and overcome my regret that I just shared a part of my soul with George and he couldn't have cared less.

He stretches, clicks the timer on his watch, and sets off at a pace the moment we leave my flat. I jog along behind him as the night settles into a light drizzle. I'm a fair-weather friend and really hate running in rain, but I keep going. George is a few paces ahead of me and the music on my earpods is interrupted by the sound of my ringtone. I stop, slide to answer my phone, but pause as I see it's a +1 number. My heart lurches. It's not Davey. It would say if it was Davey's mobile number, but it's a US number and I immediately think of Davey. I don't answer. I look up to tell George that I'm stopping for a sec, but he's long gone—no backward glance at me. I don't think he notices I've stopped.

The caller is going to ring off if I don't do something about this and so, reluctantly, my heart racing, I answer it.

"Hello?" In my heart of hearts, I really want this to be Davey. I know that now. I'm scared it *is* him. I'm scared it's not.

"Hey," someone with a faintly Australian accent says. "Hannah?"

"Yes. Who's this?"

"It's . . . Grant, Davey's friend, do you remember? I messaged you a while back when he came out of surgery and I've still got your number," he states, obviously.

"Yes, I do remember." I glance around to find a park bench and walk quickly over to one. I need to sit. Why is Grant phoning me? I hesitate, as cold fear rains down on me. The worst has happened and I don't want to ask the next question, but I do. "Davey's dead, isn't he?"

"What? No," Grant says.

Relief floods through me so fiercely that I make a strange noise in the back of my throat and feel tears form behind my eyes. "Oh God," I cry and the tears fall. "I'm so sorry," I say between tears. "I really thought . . . I thought that's why you were ringing me."

"No." His voice is soothing and kind. "No, he's not dead. But, Hannah, I think he is going to die and I don't know what to do. He doesn't want to go through with his final round of chemo. I've shouted, I've pleaded. I have nothing left. I don't know what to do," he says again and I can hear the despair in his voice. I'm quiet. I don't know what to say. I don't know what to do, either.

"Are you still there?" Grant asks me.

"Yes."

"If he doesn't go through with this, everything that he's just been through will be for nothing. Can you help?" Grant asks.

"How?"

"Can you . . . call him?"

I shake my head, although Grant can't see me. "He doesn't want that. He made it clear I wasn't to contact him again."

"He really liked you" is all Grant has to say about that.

"I don't think he likes me now" is my retort. "Or else he wouldn't have . . . gotten rid of me, told me not to contact him."

"Are you kidding?" Grant says. "He really liked you. He talked of nothing else but you. You and he would be curled up somewhere in London, freezing your asses off together right now, if it wasn't for . . ."

"The cancer," I finish for him.

"The cancer," he repeats. "Which is gonna kill him if he doesn't have that final treatment. Not today. Or tomorrow. But in a year, two years. I have to do something. This is the something I'm doing: I'm begging you. You are all I have left. You are all Davey has left to convince him. Even evil-fucking-Charlotte is on his side, feeding him the poison he wants to hear. Now you have to do something."

Who the hell is evil-fucking-Charlotte? "There have got to be other people more qualified to talk to him than me. Doctors? His parents even?"

"Please, Hannah," Grant pleads and I suspect he's crying. "He was my only friend when I moved over from England. We've been best friends ever since. I can't lose him, Hannah."

Davey will die. Even if we aren't together, a world without Davey in it strikes fear into me and I feel tears behind my eyes again.

"I'm not sure what I can do."

"You have to try. Please, Hannah, I'm begging you. For Davey."

I'm going to have to swallow any sense of pride I have left. I have to try. My stomach twists and I feel my kale dinner on its way back up again.

But first I need to call my dad. He's a GP. He'll know what to say. I glance up at the sky. The rain has stopped and I am quite damp now, but I hardly notice.

I ring my dad's mobile number and he answers distractedly. I can hear the news on in the background. "Hi," he says. "What can I do you for?"

"Dad—I need your help." I stumble straight in with what Grant's just told me, and my dad listens silently. I tell him there's a part of me that loves Davey and it's the first time I've ever said it. The first time I've ever admitted it to anyone, even myself. But I do. Even if we will never be together ever again, I love Davey. This man I've never met. This man who took a piece of my heart with him when he announced he was going to spare me and go it alone.

"I need to know what to do," I say. "I need to know what to tell him. Statistics and . . . stuff."

"Hannah," he says and I hear that loving warning tone in his voice and I know I'm not going to like the answer. "For one, I am not an oncologist," he says. "I am a GP."

"I know, I know," I say hastily. I stand up, begin walking back to my flat, all thoughts of George in the distance gone from my mind.

"Secondly," he says, "Hannah, this isn't your job. To save a man on the other side of the world."

"It is, Dad," I say determinedly. "It really bloody is. It's just a phone call. Is his friend correct? If Davey doesn't have this last chemo, will he die?"

My dad is quiet. And then he sighs. "Probably. Eventually, yes. Chemotherapy regimens are carefully dosed, carefully timed apart, for a reason and—"

"Thanks, Dad," I say quickly. That's all I need to hear. "I love you."

"Hannah," he says and I tell him I have to go. I need to work out what I'm going to say to Davey.

I hold my phone in my hand as I unlock my flat door. My hand fumbles at the lock and I drop my key, pick it up, try again, close the door behind me.

I sit down on my sofa, still staring at the phone. I don't know what to do, what to say. I'm scared stiff—too scared even to dial Davey's number. But I know I need to. I never thought the next time I spoke to him it would be like this.

I scroll down in my contacts list, find his number, hit the green button to phone him. The butterflies rise and fall in my stomach. *Please answer, please answer.*

But he doesn't. It goes to voicemail and I hear Davey's voice instructing me to leave a message. Simply hearing his voice, after all this time, hurts more than I thought it would, even if it's generic and instructional.

I look at my phone. That can't be it. That just can't be it.

I really am swallowing down all pride now. I take a deep breath, hit the call button, ring again. And then, this time, he answers.

Chapter 23

"HANNAH?" HE ASKS uncertainly and I feel all the breath leave my body. Sheer relief that he's picked up mixes with concern that he's going to hang up on me any second, out of some kind of protest.

"Davey," I say, and it's been so long I don't know how to act, how to behave with him. I'm at serious risk of crying. "Please don't hang up on me," I say more forcefully than I feel.

"I'm not going to," he says quietly.

"You didn't pick up the first time," I say.

"I thought you were calling by accident. I didn't want to pick up and end up embarrassing us both."

"It wasn't a mistake," I say.

"I know. You called back."

"I wanted . . ." I don't know how to finish that sentence. I can't lie. *I wanted to see how you are* is bullshit and I can't bring myself to say it. "I miss you," I say instead. "I really miss you."

He's quiet and I've blown it already. Not even a minute in.

"I miss you too," he says. Relief hits me like a wave.

"Davey," I say and he says my name in return. "I've tried to let go. It's too hard."

I hear him sigh and then eventually say, "Me too." I'm smiling and he speaks again. "I keep looking you up online, but no one posts anything about you. You don't post."

"Neither do you," I say.

"Not much to post at the moment."

"No. Oh, Davey."

"I know," he says, placatingly. "I know."

"You type messages to me. You don't send them."

I hear him swallow. "No."

"Why not?"

"It feels good to tell you things. And then . . ." He stops.

"And then not to tell me things?" I offer.

A pause. "Yeah. You probably think I'm weird now."

"You believe I'll think you're weird if you tell me how you're feeling?"

"Yeah."

"Do you really believe that?" I say. "That I'll judge you?"

"I don't know. I'm chicken. I don't have the guts to send them."

"What do you say in these messages?" I ask.

"Things."

"How many have you written? And then not sent?"

"How many have you seen me typing and not sending?" he replies.

"Two," I say.

"Then the answer is two."

"How many have you *really* written and not sent?"

He laughs. "Ten. Fifteen maybe. They're really long. And then . . ." He trails off.

"And then you don't send them," I finish, even though it's obvious.

"I don't send them. And after you called me on it, after you sent me that message . . ."

"'I see you typing,'" I remind him.

"Yeah," he says. "The *I see you typing* message . . . I stopped after that."

"Have you got anyone to talk to?" I ask, frightened that typing messages to me and then hitting delete has been his only outlet.

"Not really," he says. "Mom cries. Dad's too . . . male to deal with emotion. Grant's been good but he doesn't understand."

"Will I understand?" I ask.

"I doubt it."

"Try me. Tell me what's on your mind, other than the obvious."

"Too many things," he says. "Firstly, Hannah, are we friends?"

I sink into my sofa, curl my legs underneath me. "Of course."

"If I tell you I'm dating someone, is that weird?"

Yes, it bloody is. "No," I say, but my heart hurts more than it did five minutes ago. "Tell me. What's she like?"

"Um . . ." Davey starts. "It's my ex-girlfriend, Charlotte."

Evil-fucking-Charlotte, as Grant referred to her. I knew I remembered a Charlotte. "You're back with your ex?" I query. "How'd that happen?"

We're on opposite sides of the world. We can't be together. I know that now. It hits me like a train. But I stare straight ahead, listen to the man I love but can't ever have tell me about his new girlfriend.

"She's . . . Charlotte. She's just . . . here," he says and I can't read anything into this, but I do.

"Right place, right time," I suggest.

"Something like that," he says. "Are you still seeing the guy you told me about in your message?"

I cringe. "Yes, but I didn't send that message to rub it in. I wanted you to know I was your friend, that I meant well, that I was happy—like you told me to be."

Davey's quiet and I resist asking if he's still there.

"And are you?" he asks. "Happy?"

I think of George, running around Wanstead Flats on his own. He probably still hasn't turned around to see I'm not there. "Yes," I say and I leave it there.

"Good," he says.

This could so easily be the end of the call, but I have so much I want to say, so much I need to do before he finishes things. Again.

"Davey," I start.

"Yeah?" He sounds sad and I want to tell him I love him. I want to tell him yet again that I miss him. But that won't do us any good. Not now. It's too late. So I steel myself.

"How's the treatment going? Not long until the end and then you're free of it?"

"Yeah," he says noncommittally.

"When's the next one? Or the last one or . . . whatever?" I sound too pushy. I know that. I must rein it in, go in slowly.

"Tomorrow," he says.

This is the test. This is the test of how much he trusts me, how much he values whatever it was we had all those months ago. If he tells me. My heart sinks as we descend steadily into silence. He's not going to—

"I don't want to do it," he says.

I inhale slowly, exhale slowly. I feel I've duped him; that I've led him along a path he didn't know he was walking.

"Why?" I ask.

Silence again and then I hear it . . . I think he's crying. "It really hurts, Hannah."

Tears I've kept in abeyance fill my eyes. "I'm so sorry," I say. "I'm so sorry this happened to you."

"It's not your fault. We were supposed to be together," he says suddenly. "I ruined that."

"You didn't," I reply.

"I've been taken hostage by this horrible . . . thing. It's got me and it's not letting go. So I want to let go of it instead. I want to start my life. I want to move on and do . . . anything. I want to do anything that isn't sleeping, vomiting, or being pumped full of drugs."

"It is letting go of you," I tell him. "Isn't it? Isn't it working?" I ask in a panic. Maybe he's not been truthful with Grant.

He exhales. "It is working. I think it's worked and I don't want to do any more because I think it's worked enough so far. I don't think I need the last one. I can't do any more. It's relentless. It makes me sick just thinking about going. I want to curl myself up in my bed, pretend it's all gone away, then wake up and be anywhere other than here."

"Davey, how long?"

"What do you mean?" he asks.

"How long does it take? Each session? Each day?"

"Hours," he says. "Hours and hours and hours. All day for three solid days, and then a few more hours in another few weeks. But it's not only that. It makes me so weak. It's cruel. I feel OK today, but I'll feel sick tomorrow, during, after. I can't even move afterward. It's such an effort to get up and use the bathroom. It's such an effort to think."

I can hear him crying. "Davey," I soothe. "You have to go in tomorrow. You won't beat this if you sit at home wishing it away."

"I know. But I've had enough."

I'm going to regret doing this, but I say it anyway. "I can't imagine a world without you in it. If you don't fight . . ." I trail off. And then I become brutal. He'll never speak to me again. But I have to do this. "There are people who would kill for this chance to live. There are people out there every day begging for one more treatment. Begging for another drug that doesn't exist to save them from an illness they'll never survive. And you've been handed this . . . this combination of drugs that works. You're two-thirds of the way there. This last third—just do this last third. I want to ask you to do it for me. I want to ask you to do it for your mum and dad. I want to ask you to do it for Grant. But I want you to do it for *you* more than anything. Not for Davey in the now. For

Davey in the future. The one who will bounce back, having beaten it. Because you can. Because you have to."

He's stopped crying.

"Hello?" I ask.

"I'm still here," he says.

"Davey. Will you promise me you'll go in tomorrow? Promise me? Honestly, the next time I hear from you, I want it to be because you've been in, started this last round. You've got so much to live for. Don't give up. Don't give up now. Please. I am really begging you. I'm desperate." *I love you,* I think. *I love you. Even though you're with someone else. Even though I'm with someone else. I love you. I can't make it stop.*

"I have to go," he says.

"No, Davey, don't—"

But the line goes dead. I look at the screen. He's gone. My chest is tight, but my mind is numb. I don't know what to think. What to feel. It takes a few seconds and the tears that threatened to fall the entire way through the call burst forth and streak my face. If Davey doesn't attend his chemo appointment, I realize that now all I will do is wait—a year, two years—for the call from Grant telling me that the cancer took Davey, that Davey has died.

The thought of losing him, even though I know I already have, is so painful and I feel my chest crushing me from within. I can't do anything else. I gave it my all. But I don't have the power that Grant made me think I had.

The front doorbell sounds and I go toward it, wiping all trace of tears from my face. George is on the other side of the door.

"You're here," he says. "Where the hell did you go?"

I look around the hall. "Here," I say as if both of us can't see that I'm in the hall.

"You've been gone forever. I got worried. You weren't behind me."

"No," I say simply. "I don't feel well." I lie. "I'm exhausted. I need to sleep." This bit is true. I am drained.

"OK," he says, putting his hand to my forehead. "You don't feel warm. But you look awful. You been crying?"

I shake my head, rub my face, which must look blotchy.

"Want me to run you a bath?" he asks.

The last thing I want to do is wallow in hot liquid. "No. I just need to sleep."

"Want me to stay?"

"Weren't you going to stay?"

"Not tonight, no. I've got to be up early. Client at six A.M."

"OK," I say.

"OK to me staying, or OK to me going?" he asks.

"I don't mind. I just need to sleep."

"OK," he repeats. "I'll leave you to it then." He moves over to me, automatically kisses me. I kiss him back, watch as he picks his stuff up, moves to the door, closes it behind him.

I go to bed, not bothering to wash, brush my teeth, or put pajamas on. I collapse in a heap, my running gear firmly plastered to my overwrought body. I fall onto my bed and sleep the sleep of the dead. Dreams of Davey rush in and out of my mind and, even though I'm dreaming, I'm still dizzy.

Chapter 24

I'VE DONE EVERYTHING I can. It's not up to me, on this side of the world, to save a man on the other side. Part of me hates that responsibility and is so incredibly angry that Grant felt he had to turn to me, and that I was the final key to try in the lock of getting Davey into his last chemo. And the other part finds it incredible that, after all this time, Grant *did* feel he could call me and that I could make a difference. Davey and I haven't spoken in months. That Grant called, does that tell me things about how Davey feels about me? Has he spoken to Grant . . . has Davey been speaking to his best friend about me—still—after all this time? I push this thought aside. It helps no one, least of all me, going down this path. And the way I treated George yesterday was unforgivable. I left him on his own in the park.

I climb out of bed the next morning, renewed. I'm not at peace but I'm halfway there. I needed that, yesterday. I didn't realize it at the time because I was so desperate to talk to Davey. But actually yesterday's call didn't mark the beginning. It marked the end. I need to put Davey behind me. I thought when we next spoke it would be the beginning of something, a fire starting underneath us, reigniting us. But he's with someone. And I'm with someone.

It's over. Speaking to him was never going to be the precursor to something greater. I can see that now, in what I would like to say is the cold light of day. But the spring sunshine filters in through the windows, bringing with it that change in weather, that freshness where London hits the periphery of summer. Spring is making way for the trickle of brightness that brings with it something resembling heat. I leave my coat at home today. A light little white blazer hangs at the back of my wardrobe and I pair it with skinny jeans and some pointy flats. I never dress like this. I'm not exactly drab, but I'm not remarkable in my clothing choices for work, but today I up my game, just a smidge.

I didn't know I was half-waiting for this thing with Davey to really, finally end. And I breathe in the fresh air, or as fresh as it gets in London, as I walk toward the station, picking up a coffee en route. I don't get my usual order; instead I opt for a macchiato and—I will not tell George—a shot of vanilla syrup. I feel different. I will be different. I consider George for a moment. Perhaps I should tell him about the syrup, actually. Perhaps today is a good day to start being a bit more honest with him, to focus more fully on him, on us. Davey's gone. And George is here. Today could be a fresh start for everything.

This afternoon I have a presentation at work. We're pitching to run the marketing campaigns for a charity that focuses on prisoner rehabilitation. I actually play quite a major role in the whole pitch process. Because my boss, Craig, wants to bring out the big guns, all of us are involved in wooing a new client, telling them everything we have to offer, and, from a marketing point of view, I have to wow and amaze. For once I think I can wow and amaze. I could probably do this presentation in my sleep, actually, I've been doing the same job for so long, and so I spent extra time researching the various ways prisoners are rehabilitated. I don't want to overstep the mark, but I can see there are ways to market the charity in addition to what they already do: team up with big companies and get them involved in mentorship schemes. I've had loads of other ideas and have toyed with whether or not to mention them. But I can see there's probably a bit more input they could squeeze out of people without it costing the charity a single penny. It doesn't strictly fall under the remit of marketing, but it's all communications.

I'm diligent and have overprepared, as usual. I'm actually good at my job. This pitch is not the most challenging thing I've ever done with my life, which is probably why I've had time to put a bit more research into it. So today I feel confident. Life is beginning again for me. Today will cement that.

And so I'm shocked at myself when I'm standing in the ladies' bathroom, before the presentation is due to start, checking my makeup, and my phone beeps from a US number I haven't saved. It's Grant and my stomach tightens, as I dread what the message may contain. I open it: I don't know what you said to him, Hannah. But Davey just went in for his last chemo. Thank you. Grant x

I hold my phone to my chest, close my eyes, and thank whatever there is up above me—the gods, the Fates, whatever—for sending Davey in for his chemotherapy. There's no part of him that belongs to me now, but I am so overwhelmed that, stupidly, I let silent tears fall down my face. A woman comes out of a cubicle, hands me a tissue from one of the dispensers near the mirrors.

"Are you OK?" she asks.

I nod. "Thank you, yes." Although she can see I'm not, but the polite answer to that question is never "No," and then you sob your heart out. So I pull myself together.

"Can I help?" she asks.

I shake my head, and say, "No, thanks." And then, because I can't help myself, I smile meekly, roll my eyes at myself, and say, "Boy trouble."

"Ah," she says knowingly. "They can be shits, can't they? That's why I only date women," she says with a laugh.

Her comment raises a smile from me.

And then she says, "If he does *this* to you"—as she gestures to my blotchy face—"then he's probably not worth it."

"Ordinarily yes," I say. "But it's not like that. He's sick. Cancer. And so . . ." I trail off. Oh God, why am I talking? I should have just nodded in agreement, pretended I had a crap boyfriend.

Her face changes. "Oh, I'm so, so sorry."

"Not your fault," I say, trying to make lightness rise from the darkness. I realize this is what Davey said to me the moment I told him I was sorry he had cancer.

She rests herself against the sinks, pulls another wad of tissues from the dispenser, and hands them to me.

I look in the mirror and find my mascara has headed a centimeter south. "Oh Christ," I say, rubbing makeup off my face.

"My girlfriend had breast cancer," she says suddenly and I swivel to look at her. "Cruel illness," she says simply.

I nod in solemn agreement. "It really is. Is she . . . OK now?" I ask tentatively.

She nods her head. "Alive. Lucky to be so. It's aggressive. We're always on the lookout for signs it might return. We try not to let that dominate our lives, but we're careful."

"I feel so inexperienced in this. He lives in the US and I live here and so we aren't even seeing each other anymore—or whatever it was we were doing, being thousands of miles apart." I take a deep breath, spilling my guts to this poor woman I've just met, who had the misfortune to find me crying in the ladies' bathroom. "And I didn't see him because he wouldn't let me see him. He pushed me away. He lives so far away and he pushed me even further."

She gives me a kind smile. "Sometimes they push you away even when you're living in the same house. Part of them wants to deal with it themselves. Part of them wants to shield you from the ugliness."

I wipe the tears from my eyes, thank her for her kindness. My makeup is nonexistent now and we both turn to leave the bathroom at the same time, she holding the door open for me as she leads.

"Good luck. I know that's a strange thing to say," she says. "The trick is to try to continue your life at the same time. Don't put everything on hold. Be there for him. But the world keeps spinning. Don't give up on everything that makes you *you*."

"I woke up this morning with that exact feeling."

"Good."

"God, I'm so sorry, I just blathered away at you."

She laughs. "It's fine, honestly."

I walk along the corridor behind her as I head in the direction of the boardroom, where I've already placed all my papers and laptop. I glance at my watch. I'm that little bit late now, which is not the professional look I was aiming for. She turns into the room ahead of me and I pause, horror filling every part of me. Is she a senior member of my company from another floor that I've not met? But she sits on the other side of the table, where the potential client's team is gathered, and then looks up at me. A kind of surprise passes over her face as my boss says, "And this is Hannah Gallagher, our marketing manager." Introductions are made all around and it becomes apparent that the main person I am supposed to be impressing is the woman I've just cried in front of, in the toilets.

I am off my game now, thrown from capable to idiotic. I'm unsure of myself and, whatever I say, Craig gives a slight frown at me and, every now and again, a slight nod. I can't tell if I'm making a hash of this or excelling. I make eye contact with the woman from the toilets—Cindy, her name is—and with her colleagues and try to let the words flow, and the presentation of success stories I've completed for other companies and ideas for their charity merge together. And then it's my turn to let someone else take over. Strategy ideas loom across the table and my boss is being extra forceful, probably to make up for the piss-poor job I've done.

Cindy looks as if she's being shouted at, even though Craig is delivering his presentation calmly, if perhaps a little loudly—his eyes wide with enthusiasm. Between the two of us, we have messed this up good and proper. I let my mind drift to the movements of grays outside the windows, the clouds that scud across the London skyline, until the end of the meeting arrives suddenly, business cards are being exchanged, goodbyes said, and we're shaking hands.

My boss turns to me and the two others who pitched. "I think that went really well." No one says anything. No one's committing. Vague nods all around ensue. I need to get out of here. Today was supposed to be me hitting refresh on the frozen screen that had become my life. Day one, help ruin client meeting involving combined effort with my boss. That wasn't on the schedule for the day. But a giant drink in the pub with Clare afterward firmly is.

"He's such a twat," she says. "I don't know how he got that job." Clare really is the least discreet HR manager I've ever come across. "He's less qualified than you," she says pointedly.

"More experienced, though," I offer in Craig's defense.

Clare thinks. "Not really. No. One year, max."

"Oh."

"Got the job because he's forceful," Clare remarks, in answer to a question I haven't asked.

"Oh," I say, looking at my wineglass, wondering what to take from that.

"You're not forceful," Clare says, finishing her second glass of wine more quickly than me. It's my round next. I'll get up in a second. I'm also going to buy us some crisps, which I won't tell George about. I sense Clare needs some food. She's getting tipsy.

"What do you mean—I'm not forceful?" I ask, fumbling in my bag for my purse.

"Er . . . never mind," Clare says.

"No, go on. I'm a big girl. You can say it."

I can see the cogs turn in Clare's wine-addled mind. She's about to be massively indiscreet and I'm silently willing her along. "Do you remember when you came for your second interview?" she asks.

I think back, five years ago. "Yeah."

"Remember when Craig—who, by the way, had only been here a year at that point and had just been promoted up from the job you were being interviewed for . . ." She's gone a bit slurry now. "Remember when Craig asked you what kind of salary expectations you had?"

I do remember. I thought it was a trick question. The advert had said £30–35k. I nod.

"Do you remember what your answer was?"

"No," I say, thinking.

"I do," Clare says, leaning forward to take a sip from her empty glass and putting it back down on the table again, after peering in and finding no wine inside. "It was awful. You said, *Well, I'm happy with thirty grand because it's a bit more than I'm on now and I really want the job.*" She rolls her eyes and then mimics slamming her head onto the pub table.

"Right," I say.

She looks up at me. "Do you still not see what's wrong with that? Even now?"

"No."

"Honestly?" she squeals. "The problem with it, Hannah, is that you should have pushed for the higher end of the bracket. The job advert gave a five-grand window and you undervalued yourself and went for the lowest amount we were offering. We could afford the higher end—that's why we put it in the bloody advert. Why would you ask for the lower amount?"

"Um . . . I don't know. I just . . ."

"This is your problem. You aren't forceful enough. Do you know how much Craig was on when he did your job?"

"Er . . . I think you probably aren't allowed to tell me." I give her an out.

"Yeah, that's right," she says, shifting in her seat. "I'm not allowed to tell you. Let's say it was the higher end of that bracket. And let's say that he's only got one more year's experience than you and now, as marketing director, he's on practically double what you're on."

"What the fuck?" I say.

"Honestly, Hannah, I could have screamed at you when you said that in your interview. Trust me. I know how long it takes to claw even another thousand onto your pay packet in this bloody company. Craig's a forceful sod. The way you're going, it will be bloody years before you get a salary paying what you're worth."

I look into my glass. Day one of the new Hannah is going pretty swiftly downhill. "More wine," I say, getting up.

"Get a bottle," Clare orders. "No more of these tiny little glasses."

A few hours later Clare and I are hammered, staggering out of the pub and sharing an Uber home. I collapse into bed, drunk, the world spinning, determined that day two of the new Hannah is going to have to be the new day one.

On my way to work the next morning I check my email and there's a message from Cindy:

> Hannah, Lovely to meet you yesterday.
> Will you give me a ring on my mobile when you get a moment?
> Regards, Cindy.

Typed underneath is her mobile number.

I look at this cryptic message and can't work out if this is work-related or if she wants to impart more advice, which I have now decided I don't want to receive. I'm not supposed to be thinking about Davey anymore.

I wait until I've had a large coffee from the station, ridden the hell of the Underground toward Liverpool Street, and am walking to the office. I sense that if this is a private chat, then I don't want to be having it at my desk. I walk slowly.

"Hello," Cindy says as she picks up.

"Hi, it's Hannah Gallagher, from yesterday. I got your message."

"Hi, yes. Thanks for ringing. I wanted to have a quick word. We've decided not to go with your company's services."

"Oh." Deflation kicks in. Day two is going swimmingly.

"However, it wasn't anything to do with you."

"No?"

"No. Craig is a bit . . . Anyway," she says. "I liked what *you* had to say."

"Right," I reply.

"Hannah, it would be very unethical of me to offer you a job and what I'm doing is quite borderline, but I just want to point you in the direction of a job that we have available here. We're a small charity, but our marketing director is moving overseas with her husband. As such, we have an opening. If you'd like to be considered for it, details on how to apply are on our website."

I stop walking and someone behind me swears, swerves around me, gives me a look, continues.

"Oh. Right," I say again. "Thanks."

"Hannah," she says.

"Yes?"

"I very much think you should apply."

"Oh, thanks," I say. "I'll . . . take a look."

"Do that. And even if you don't apply—which I reiterate that I think you should—it was very nice to meet you yesterday."

"Thank you. Likewise. Thanks for the help. And the tissues."

Cindy chuckles. "My pleasure. Bye, Hannah."

"Bye."

I start walking again, and a smile drifts over my face. Day two just got better.

Chapter 25

June

I HAVE A spring in my step. Nothing can top this feeling. I've left the office, late at the end of my first week working with Cindy and her team. I've been eased in gently, but projects are landing on my desk that actually mean something to me. I'm in charge of one other person who has only just joined and together we're learning the ropes, alongside the incumbent marketing director, who's staying for a handover period. Cindy's a bit of a force to be reckoned with, but we're getting along well and the charity is having a low-key summer party this Saturday to say thank you to its most faithful donors. I'm enjoying being involved with this one charity, rather than being spread across ten or fifteen brands simultaneously, as I was at the agency. This gives me space to be inventive for one job at a time, and the thrill of being a fairly senior member of a team, who is listened to and who listens to others, fills me with joy every day I wake up. I didn't realize how stagnant and robotic I'd become at my last job. I didn't realize Craig didn't actually value me very much.

Craig was livid when he heard I was leaving and made a huge jokey show at my farewell party of telling me I'd learned everything from him, and not to "fuck it up" in my new job or it would reflect badly on him. I held my tongue, hugged him goodbye, and, over his shoulder, watched Clare stick both her middle fingers up at the back of his head. I'd miss her the most, but we've got a date on the calendar to meet in a few weeks.

At the weekend I put on a floaty dress and heels and head to the HAC gardens in the City for the company's summer party. My predecessor is working with me until the end of the month, when she finishes and hands over to me, so this party is her responsibility, her swan song, and I'm learning as much as I can from her before she leaves, including how to put on a fabulous summer party on a limited budget. Our donors and my colleagues are here with their partners and I have brought George, feeling proud and excited to show him off. He looks good in an open-necked crisp white shirt, tailored shorts, and deck shoes. We've seen so little of each other recently—we've both been working so late—and I'm genuinely excited to see him. I'm still riding the wave of starting a new job that I love, of being on month two of the new Hannah, of planning to go home to Whitstable with George next weekend, where I'm going to introduce him to my parents. I wasn't sure this was a big deal. It felt like a natural thing to do. But my mum's voice was tinged with real excitement when I asked what weekend would work for them to meet George. She pointed out that I'd never brought a man home to see them before and, although I knew that, being reminded of it makes me a bit nervous. "Meet the parents" sounds so . . . official. And then I realize: We're a couple. We've not labeled it as such yet, but we are.

George holds my hand as we walk through the grounds of the summer party, the wide green space hidden in the city, flanked by buildings. Entertainers have set up for children, and there are races for those who are willing to embrace the unofficial sports-day theme. After a few minutes of chatting to colleagues, being introduced to donors, I feel George's hand detach from mine. "Just going to grab a few drinks for us," he whispers and moves away.

I talk and am moved around, introduced seamlessly by Kate, the marketing director who is prepping to move overseas.

"This is Jonathan White," she says to me and I extend my hand to shake his. That name rings so many bells, yet I can't quite determine why. Kate gives snippets of detail as I shake his hand. He's an architect in the City, responsible for the latest mind-bending skyscraper going up in EC4. He's nice, jovial, incredibly posh, and, as he and Kate talk, nodding toward me to include me, I place his name, realizing suddenly why I know of this man. Weirdly, this was going to be Davey's boss. Once upon a time. I try to picture him interviewing Davey, offering a man he'd never met a job over the telephone. I can see it happening. This man is likable. Davey is likable. They'd have got on well. But there is no way I'm mentioning Davey to him; although the urge is there, I have to resist it. He's probably forgotten all about Davey and that he had to decline the job in the end. He probably never even batted an eyelid—had someone in HR open the job back up again, and everyone carried on with their day.

We talk for a few moments about the possibility of Jonathan offering a mentorship scheme as part of our work. He already donates quite heavily and, as I nod along to his informed comments about the work we do, I try to fathom how, in general, people can sometimes forget other people so easily. And how some of us can't, no matter how hard we try. Then Kate ushers me on, keen to have me meet as many influential people as possible, until it's time to head to the BBQ. But I sneak off for a few minutes in the direction of the bathroom, finding Cindy hiding around the corner. She's having a crafty cigarette.

"Shouldn't really," she says, indicating the item in her hand. "Especially given . . . you know," she says. "It's my one vice. One a day. Awful, I know, but I don't drink or do drugs, so don't judge."

"I wouldn't," I say. I just met her other half, Lynn, as she was on her way to the BBQ. She told me that she and George ran an egg-and-spoon race together with a couple of others while I was schmoozing donors. I tell Cindy that.

"Fiercely competitive is Lynn. Did she let George win?"

"Not sure," I laugh. "Wasn't really watching. Too busy talking."

"He seems very lovely," Cindy says.

I smile. "He is."

"Looks in peak health. You'd never know," she says.

I narrow my eyes in confusion and then it dawns on me. "Oh. Oh no . . . George isn't—he's not the one with . . . you know. It's not him."

"Oh, right."

"No," I say again. "It's someone else. Someone I'm not . . . with. I haven't been with him in ages. But George and I have been together since February and . . ." I'm not sure where I'm going with this, so I stop.

"So the guy who's sick is still in the US?"

I nod. "Yes. We're not together. Anymore."

She looks out past me to where George has just crossed the finishing line in a race. I turn and look where she does. I suspect this isn't the first race George has won, as there's halfhearted applause from the onlookers. I feel a bit sorry for him at their lack of enthusiasm. It's probably because he's trying too hard to win, to impress. The sun is beating down. I could really use a drink, and George never brought one back for me.

"The one that got away," Cindy says.

I spin back around to look at her. "Sorry?"

"The chap in the US. The one that got away?"

I give a nervous, embarrassed laugh that doesn't even sound like me. "Perhaps."

"Right," Cindy says, inhaling the last drag of her cigarette. She looks baffled, as if I've duped her on purpose. But she leaves it there, puts a motherly hand on my shoulder, heads back out into the fray.

Chapter 26

July

"It's so pretty here," George says as we walk through Whitstable high street toward the beach. His hand is in mine, as it always is when we walk anywhere together. The crowds of tourists have descended as the school summer holidays are in full force, and kids in swimsuits pick their way across the pebbles, climbing their way delicately toward the shoreline, buckets in hand, ready to carry towers of pebbles.

I smile, wonder slowly what's next for me; for George, for us. His grip tightens on mine as we walk. My parents have set up a picnic and some deck chairs and we're meeting them there. Our dog, Andrex, is at home in the shady garden and I can't wait to see him, throw a ball for him, watch as he skirmishes up and down the patio trying to smell its location.

"So this is where you grew up, Gallagher," he says. "Quaint."

"Mmm," I say. "I love it here. I'd love to move back one day," I say far too casually, waiting for a response I'm not sure I'm going to get.

But he surprises me by answering. "Here?"

"Yeah. You don't like it?"

"Only been off the train five minutes, Gallagher, give me a while to make up my mind. Want to move here with me?" he asks, but it's not a genuine question. He's teasing me.

"Maybe. You, me, our five kids," I tease back.

He avoids answering by saying, "Bit different from Dagenham, where I grew up."

"Yeah, probably is. You'll have to take me back to meet your parents soon," I say.

"Let's see how today goes first, shall we?" he suggests.

I laugh. "How would you meeting my parents affect me meeting yours?"

He shrugs. "Just would."

"Why?"

"Dunno. Just would."

I stare ahead. I see my folks and I wave at them. George tightens his grip. "Here we go," he says.

"You nervous?" I ask.

"Dads always hate me," he reminds me. "Your dad will hate me."

"Why?"

"Because I'm shagging his daughter."

I don't know whether to be stunned or to laugh at this comment.

Two hours later we're walking back from the beach, George having offered to carry everything heavy, which my father is immensely pleased about. The beach outing has been a success, and my mum and George are in front as he continues charming her.

My dad walks in silence as we share holding the now empty cooler between us.

"What do you think?" I ask nervously.

"He's very nice," Dad says.

"You like him then?"

"Yes. I do. He's very talkative. Likes his job. A lot."

"I think he was a bit nervous," I say in George's defense. "All dads hate him, apparently."

"*All* dads. How many girlfriends has he had?"

"Not many. But I think he's been a bit unlucky in love, so far."

"Like you?" my dad says with a smile.

"Hey! I'm just very choosy."

My dad looks ahead, at Mum and George chatting away, and then he looks back at me. "How's that other young man? The one you phoned me about?" Without giving me a chance to speak, he continues, "I've thought about that quite a lot since, you know. I worried about you."

"Me?"

"Of course. You were very upset."

I look away, out to sea, as we walk along by the old oyster sheds. "I was. I am still, I think. Don't tell Mum. Don't tell George, for God's sake."

"You didn't answer my question," my dad points out. "How is he? Did he go ahead with his treatment?"

"Yes, he did."

"Good," Dad says firmly. "Good."

He'll be finished with his chemo now. I wonder what Davey's doing these days? Going through billions of checkups, tests, CT scans. Every now and again I try to work out where he is on his regimen, what he'll be doing. I look at forums, trying to ascertain what other men in the same position are going through. So much for putting Davey out of my mind.

"What does George think about . . . what's his name?"

"Davey," I say. Even saying his name aloud feels like a betrayal of George. Talking about this with my dad feels wrong. I feel we should be talking about something else—anything else.

"I've not really . . . I've not really talked to George about Davey. I don't want to." Davey is private. He stays firmly tucked inside my mind, at the back. I don't bring what Davey and I almost were to each other out for discussion and general dissection. It's safer to leave it alone. I wish my dad would stop asking about him, but in a way I'm happy that he does, that he cares enough to ask.

My dad doesn't reply. I can tell he's thinking about this. Without speaking about Davey at length, my dad is going to dissect it anyway. "You don't check in with him from time to time, see if he's all right?"

"No," I reply firmly. "We don't talk. We won't talk again, I think."

He nods, adjusts his grip on the cooler handle. I look away. High tide has come and gone, taking the sea in another direction, the pebbles unraveling themselves from the swirl of the water. I can sense, rather than see, my dad looking at me.

At the house George says he needs to use the loo, "And then we'll set off, shall we, Han?"

"So soon?" my mum says.

"I'd like a few minutes with Andrex," I say. "Quick cup of tea and then we'll go?"

George looks put out, briefly, and then flashes his trademark smile. "Sure."

"Come play ball with him? Or sit with me while I do?" I suggest. I'm ready to say something about it only being a quick one in this weather, as it's not good for dogs to play for too long in the heat of the sun, but George makes a face.

"I don't really like dogs, Gallagher. You play. I'll help your mum make tea."

As George goes off upstairs to the bathroom, and my mum goes off to the kitchen at the back to flick the kettle on, my dad turns to me, deadpan. "He doesn't like dogs, Hannah. We must kill George immediately."

Chapter 27

August

"THIS ONE," I say to Paul as we're in Tiffany & Co. in Bond Street. "Or"—I reach and point to the tray at the back—"that one. Let's start with those. They're both perfect. And by perfect, I mean gorgeous, glittery, and staggeringly expensive."

"I know," Paul says, "but she's worth it."

"Do you know how hard it has been this past week," I say as the shop assistant readies the trays for me to try on rings, on Miranda's behalf. "Not telling Miranda that you're going to propose?" I take Paul by the shirt collar and shake him jovially. I repeat, "Do you know how hard it's been?"

He laughs. "You're a trooper, Hannah. Do you know how difficult it's been for me? Not to say, 'I'm going shopping for engagement rings with Hannah—could you just back off me about where I'm going today?' Miranda asked about five times. I don't know how guys do this alone? I don't know how they sneak out to do this, without being put through the Spanish Inquisition by their other halves. The only reason I got out alone today was because I said I'm buying her a birthday present. So we need to do that as well."

I wince for him as I put on the first ring, hold it out in front of me. "An engagement ring *and* a birthday present. Expensive day for you, pal."

"I know." He looks at my outstretched hand. "Wow, that's nice.

I'm not sure why we're in Tiffany's when there are much cheaper places selling similar items," Paul says indelicately in front of the shop assistant, who pretends not to hear.

"Because Miranda has always wanted an engagement ring from Tiffany," I tell him, looking at the ring on my hand. "God, engagement rings are nice, aren't they?"

Paul gives me a sad smile, as if I'm a poor spinster to be pitied. We'll have words about that when we're out of earshot of the shop assistant. I take the ring off and move to try the next one on; it's a little bigger and Paul engages in chat about clarity in diamonds, nodding along as the sales assistant talks. I am blinded by the sparkles coming off this ring. I'm so happy for my friends. They're so right for each other.

After ring shopping, Paul and I try very hard to find a decent old man pub near Bond Street and, after about half an hour of searching for somewhere with less eye-watering prices, we give up and head to a burger joint that has a decent cocktail menu.

"My treat," Paul says. "A thank-you for giving up your Sunday to help me choose a ring for my future wife."

"Thanks," I say, as I immediately stop being price-conscious about my food order. "Lobster burger, in that case."

"Ha, go for it!" he replies. "Champagne cocktails to wash it down?"

"Seriously? I've always liked you, Paul."

We laugh, say, "Cheers" when our drinks order arrives, and wait for our food.

"So hard," I say, "last night over dinner in the pub, pretending we're both doing different things today—not meeting like this to choose a ring."

"We've never done this before," he says. "Just you and me. It's always you, me, and Miranda."

I nod. "It's nice. Let's not make it a habit or Miranda will flip out."

"Not once I've given her this sparkler of a ring," he says, tapping the rucksack on the seat next to him, which contains the telltale turquoise Tiffany bag. "All bets are off then. Can do as I please, she'll be so chuffed."

"You'd better not," I warn.

"I wouldn't do anything to hurt that girl. I love her to distraction," he says seriously.

"You're so lucky," I tell him. "You've found your person. Hold on to her forever."

"I will," he says.

"So how are you going to do it, then? How are you going to propose?"

He tells me he's taking Miranda away on her birthday, to a little country hotel in the Cotswolds. They stopped in once for a drink on their way back from a weekend away, sat with their pints under a willow tree, a stream running through the grounds behind them. "I'm doing it there. In the spot we sat before, talking about life, love, us. Under that willow tree. No clichéd fanfare in a restaurant. Nothing. She won't see it coming."

"That's lovely," I say, picturing it in my head. I can also see Miranda screaming for joy in a very unladylike way, and jumping up and down with excitement in this delicate, nature-painted backdrop. She'll probably say, "Fuck." A lot. It makes me smile. "I'm so happy for you."

"Christ, she'd better say yes," he murmurs as our half a lobster and "the Big One" burgers arrive, along with truffle fries and another round of cocktails.

I decide it's best not to tell Paul that Miranda has already started secretly eyeing up wedding venues overseas and is biding her time until Paul proposes. She needs guaranteed sunshine on her big day, but hates beach weddings. Apparently this combo is a bit of a challenge, so she started looking ages ago. "She will say yes," I tell him. It's not in any doubt. I'd better start budgeting now for an overseas wedding. Excitement for my friends bubbles up inside me.

"Shall we get wasted?" he says, as he downs his drink and scouts around for the cocktail list.

"Absolutely," I reply.

An hour later I've had to leave half of my dinner on the plate, which is criminal, but I've gotten so small, thanks to George's mammoth efforts to get me healthy, that I've no longer got room in my stomach to house the portions I ordered.

"How's the new job going?" Paul asks.

"I love it. Love my boss. Love my co-workers. Love my pay packet."

"Good, you can get this then," he says with a sideways smile.

I throw a chip at him.

"I'm glad you went for that job. You never *go* for anything. So I'm pleased you went for that."

I pause, my mouth halfway to the straw of my drink. "What?" I ask and sit back up again.

"Oh, you know what I mean. You never push yourself. Never really fight for anything—fight for what you want." Paul slurps his drink noisily and I stare at him.

"Let me stop you right there. I just started a new job, remember," I remind him.

"Because someone phoned you and told you to apply."

Ouch! I pick my drink up, toy with the straw. Put the drink down again.

"What else don't I fight for then?" The moment I say it, I wish I hadn't.

"That American bloke. You didn't get on a plane to see him."

I feel my throat tighten. "He told me not to."

"Pft!" Paul replies. "You got on another flight, though. With another man." He wiggles his eyebrows.

"It was a pre-booked holiday. I didn't simply get on a flight to

Thailand. George and I had already planned it. And we went just as friends." Although we didn't come back just as friends, but I don't say that.

"I notice George no longer comes out for Thai pub Saturdays," Paul says, almost but not quite changing the subject.

"No, he's so busy at work," I say. "Summer's here. Last-minute holiday bikini panics do lead a lot of girls to his door."

We sip our drinks. These ones are practically milkshakes with copious amounts of Baileys dripped into them. Paul leans over, attacks the fries I've left in their little silver bowl, silently indicating to the waitress that she can leave my plate exactly where it remains as she helicopters past, attempting to take it. There's a blond man queuing at the door, waiting for a table, and I look over and rest my gaze on the back of his head. He turns. It's not Davey. Of course it's not. Why do I keep doing this to myself?

"Do you love him?" Paul asks with a mouthful of my fries.

"Sorry?" I've been blown off course. George. He's talking about George. "I'm not sure how to reply to that."

He stops chewing. "With the truth," he says, as if I'm simple.

I'm thinking and so I don't immediately answer.

"Han, that's a telling silence," he says when he's finished chewing.

"How does anyone really know if they're in love? I think . . . I think it's coming, gradually, y'know. I'm letting it grow, organically," I say. "I do like him."

Paul narrows his eyes, slurps his boozy milkshake slowly, the paper straw disintegrating into his drink.

"We've not said we love each other. We're still just . . . sort of . . . seeing each other," I clarify. Paul needs to talk now or I'm going to keep rambling.

"It's been how long?"

I calculate. "Six months."

"It's been six months and you're still just seeing each other? All that means is a code phrase enabling you both to shag other people."

"No," I protest. "That's not what we're doing."

"But you don't love him." It's a statement, not a question.

I think. "I'm not sure." I opt for honesty this time. "It still feels new, you know? As if I've not given it a chance yet—as if I've not given George and me together enough of a chance." This is true. I've broken up with men much sooner than this because I've *known* it wasn't right. With George, I don't have that feeling. We get on well, we communicate, I've been preoccupied with Davey and that hasn't been George's fault at all. I want to give this the chance it deserves.

"If you don't immediately know, then it means no."

I swallow. My blood pressure is on the up.

"I knew I loved Miranda pretty early on," Paul says before I can even reply to his last observation. "I knew I wasn't wasting my time," he says.

"Charming."

"You know what I mean," Paul replies, casting his eyes over the half of my burger that I've put to one side. I push the plate toward him. He continues, "I compared how I felt with Miranda to an ex-girlfriend, although I knew I didn't need to. Camilla."

"Posh name."

"Posh girl," he says. "Mucky posh, though, y'know. Drank Bollinger with her parents at the weekend and thought nothing of going down on me in a bus shelter at two A.M."

"Jesus!"

"I was twenty-two, horny as hell."

"No change, I reckon."

He sniggers. "Thought: this must be it. Camilla and I had been together for a few months. Assumed I was in love. Didn't say it 'cause I wasn't sure. I asked my mum how you know when you're in love. She said, 'If you have to ask, you probably aren't. Because you just know.' And I knew, deep down, I wasn't in love with Camilla. Nor was I likely to be."

I nod. "Wise words from your mum. So you broke up with Camilla?"

"Are you mad? Of course not. I was getting regular sex. Did I not mention I was a horny twenty-two-year-old?"

I laugh.

"But with Miranda, I just knew. She swept me away. I was— am—besotted. We're a team. We do so much for each other. We're each other's cheerleaders. We have time for each other and, when we don't, we make time. She's the first person I ring when something amazing happens, when something shit happens. Is George that person for you?" he asks.

I think, look down at a drop of spilled ketchup on the marble table. I shrug, quietly reply, "No." Then I find myself thinking: *Who do I tell?* When I was "with" Davey, I told him everything good, everything bad, so easily, and the conversation flowed. And then when the worst happened and I no longer had him to tell, I didn't even tell Miranda about Davey texting me. Miranda's my best friend, but I worried so much about judgment. I was judging me by my own standards, not giving Miranda a chance to have an opinion on the matter. But I opt for, "It's Joan next door or Miranda, depending on who I see first."

"Lucky Joan. As for Miranda, you'll have to get in line," he says.

"Let's see that ring again." I'm desperate to change the subject. Paul fishes in his bag and opens the box up, so that we watch the mood lighting in the restaurant sparkle from it. "Miranda's a lucky woman," I say.

"Damn right she is." He laughs. "Thanks for the help choosing the ring."

"Pleasure."

"Do you love him?" he asks me again, suddenly.

"How drunk *are* you? We've just gone over this."

"Not George," Paul says quietly. "The other one. The American one."

I look away. "Please don't. It's not worth it. He's with someone else. I'm with someone else."

"There's one person out there for everyone," he says, attempting to be wise. "And they're not always close to home."

"Paul?"

"Yeah?"

I lean forward, smile to diffuse what I'm about to say. "Shut up."

Chapter 28

Davey, September

IT'S BEEN A whole year since I started looking for jobs in London. At first it was half-assed. And then I got serious about it. I started making plans, updated my résumé, set up email alerts, registered with agencies in England, really started paying attention to the job market.

I don't even know what persuaded me to start looking there in the first place. I don't think it was restlessness. I think it was . . . change. Not change for change's sake. But . . . a need to experience something new. People do it all the time—relocate. The more I thought about it, the more I wanted it. And the more it made sense to go to London. My parents are English, and technically so am I. Although I've never really felt it, and so I wanted to see what I'd been missing.

It took a while to find the kind of thing I wanted, and the job with Jonathan White checked every box I had, and some boxes I hadn't even known I wanted checked. And when I was offered it in December, it was a mix of fear and dread with shock and a sense of "This is it. This is actually happening."

I think if I hadn't had Grant and . . . Hannah to tell, to encourage me that actually it was kinda cool, I wouldn't have gone through with it. And as excitement built, brick by brick and the day of departure (D-Day, Grant and I had nicknamed it) loomed,

I was so into this idea that I felt unstoppable. Isn't that so completely ironic? I felt unstoppable.

And then I got stopped. And man, oh man, didn't every part of that order to cease and desist suck. I'm now in an aftercare state, and part of that is being reminded tirelessly by people who love me: *You're one of the lucky ones.*

I nod mutely, and when I see Dr. Khader and he asks how I am as he glances down at my notes, I resist the urge to ask in all seriousness, "You tell *me.*"

"I'm great, man," I say instead, because it's hard for anyone to argue with a response like that.

There are things I haven't been able to do recently, things I've been meaning to do but have put off and, I'll be honest, not for an admirable reason. I kept Charlotte hanging on. Grant and I tried to examine the reason why I felt I *had* to call things off with Hannah, but couldn't bring myself to end it with Charlotte. Again. Grant decided it was because I had easy access to good sex with Charlotte, and she made most of the effort because I had no energy, and that did help; but it was other things with Charlotte that meant it was nice to keep seeing her. She listened to me, though I started to realize she only ever answered me with whatever I wanted to hear. I couldn't understand the agenda behind that, and maybe she didn't have one. But when I was at my worst—the absolute lowest I've ever been—she was there, making me feel normal, wanted. And I had to thank her for that because it was the biggest gift she could have given me.

I overlooked how much like hard work the relationship was becoming, how we drifted into our old ways of total incompatibility, how she'd started partying hard again on the nights when we didn't see each other, acting as if she was at least ten years younger.

I could see everything she did on social media and it looked . . .

exhausting, the way she lived now. And then at the back, or probably even at the front, of my mind was her going after Grant. I think Grant's right. It was some kind of petty revenge. I think that episode has scarred him for life. I never talked to Charlotte about it. I didn't see the point because I knew, deep down, that this wasn't forever and, like a coward, I let it ride its course because that was the easiest thing to do. And on the final day of my chemo, when I felt so ill and would have done anything to get some sleep to avoid the nausea, when I didn't want to keep buzzing the nurse for anti-sickness pills, Charlotte sat with me, playing on her cellphone. I broke it off with her, then and there in the hospital. I couldn't keep her hanging on, and I suspect the thrill of telling people the guy she was dating had cancer was starting to wear off for her. I know that sounds malicious of me, but she'd become less and less interested. This wasn't doing either of us any good. Surprisingly for Charlotte, whom my dad always politely called "highly strung," she didn't even shout at me. Just threw me one line as she stood: "Good luck finding another girl who'll put up with all this shit," she said as she gestured at the drips and cannulas.

I didn't like to jinx everything by pointing out that this shit wasn't lasting much longer—that this was the last cycle of chemo—because . . . what if it wasn't? What if it didn't work? What if my scan, my blood results come back with a red flag and I'd have to start new treatment all over again? The moment Charlotte left the room I threw up, just thinking about it.

And now I've been offered therapy. Again. The doctors can probably see I need it, and I kind of agree that it's better late than never, so I will see someone about the things I've lost because, as Grant points out, I'm like Harry Potter; I'm the boy who lived. But parts of me, mentally, have been taken in exchange. And I think it's time I recognize that. Time I pick myself up off the floor, dust myself off, get back to the old me, something resembling my old life.

Grant drives me to my first therapy session and, as we park, he tells me, "Even if you don't get anything useful discussed in there, agreeing to go is the big first step."

I want to tell him, "Don't be a dick, man," but I love him too much for that and this man is rarely serious. So I just say thank you and force him into an awkward bear hug across the front seats of his car.

I open the door and the cool of the air-conditioning disappears entirely in the ninety-degree heat and then I turn back, remembering something.

"Hey," I ask. "You told me you'd do two things for me? Do you remember?"

Grant looks blankly at me.

"When I wouldn't go in for my last cycle," I remind him.

Recognition and then a small smile. "Yeah, I remember."

"You told me the hard truth about Charlotte."

"Sorry about that," he says, embarrassment flitting across his face.

"What was the second thing?" I ask.

"It doesn't matter, does it? Not now. It worked. You went in to get your last chemo."

I run my hand over my head, nodding, digesting this. I'm pleasantly surprised to feel the beginnings of soft, downy hair. I smile. I climb out of the car. I'm ready to go in. And then he climbs out of the car and calls my name, and I can tell Grant is practically bursting to tell me. He says it.

"I told Hannah."

"You told Hannah?" I turn back, face him full-on. "You told Hannah what?"

"That you wouldn't have your last treatment. That basically, if you didn't, you'd probably die."

Grant waits for me to speak. My hands are in the pockets of my loosest jeans, which go on a little bit easier now that I'm not pumped full of "make you want to eat everything, even if it tastes like metal" steroids. If I keep going like this, I might be back in my old clothes in a month or two. I might feel a bit more normal. Not yet, though.

"I can't tell if you're gonna throw your cellphone at my head or thank me," he says.

"You asked Hannah to call me?"

"I didn't ask her. I *begged* her," Grant says simply.

"Why her?"

"I just . . . knew she could do it."

"How? You never met her. You'd never even spoken to her."

"I did," Grant defends. "I shouted hello at her on New Year's."

I smile, and then the smile fades as I realize I'm pissed off.

"But how did you know she would help?"

"I didn't. I had to hope. I had nothing left. I needed you to live. And Hannah . . . after the way you spoke about her. The way I knew you felt about her. She's nice, man, she was so nice. And . . ." he trails off. Starts up again. "What happened on that call?"

I shake my head. "I don't want to talk about it."

"Real mature, man. Do you still love her?"

"I never said I loved her." I'm quick on that reply.

Grant stills as the heat swirls around us. I'm being engulfed.

"You don't, then?"

"Leave it," I say. "She's with someone else."

"Maybe she's not, after all this time."

"Either way. I messed with her head. I messed with my own head. It's not fair to chase after her again."

"Yeah, man, she's nice—really liked you, went to look at apartments for you. She clearly wasn't into you at all. You should definitely never pursue that line again."

And then there's the rest. We watched films together, we slept next to each other. I didn't imagine those things. In my darkest hours, after vomiting into the hospital's disposable bowls, I thought of those nights. Hannah in her pajamas, hair piled up on top of her head, sleeping so soundly as I watched her, as I carried my phone around, muting myself so as not to disturb her, as I made dinner, as I worked into the night, as I slowly started packing things up to move. Hannah accidentally falling asleep . . . it was strangely addictive viewing. I could watch her sleep again. Why have I gone down memory lane? Now it just hurts.

Grant coughs. I kind of forgot he was there. "You should call her," he says.

"I should be angry with you for sticking your nose in my business" is my childish reply.

"You do that," Grant says. "Meanwhile, between Hannah and me, we got you back into chemo. We saved your life. At the very least, you owe us both a thank-you."

"I'll thank you now, from the bottom of my heart." I mean it, but I know my voice doesn't sound like I mean it.

"And Hannah?"

I look him in the eye. "I said I'd let her get on with her life. And I'm gonna do that. To show up now would be unfair."

Chapter 29

SO IT TURNS out I have a lot more issues than simply my beef with chemotherapy. I knew that was coming. Don't we all have "issues"? I'm still unsure how I feel about therapy, I only know that subtly—so subtly it took until I got home to work it out—the therapist is trying to open up the root cause of all my anger. The therapist did acknowledge that a huge part of me has been taken away. When I joked, "Sure, a testicle," it was met with a raised eyebrow and a slight smile. I triumphed at the smile.

But now I need to work on getting back the part of me that's missing mentally, the part of my life I had lined up, but had to hit pause on. I'm reminded it *is* just a pause, a delay. The plans I made got put on ice. But not forever. I kinda knew that. But it's the insecurity of the cancer returning that worries me the most, I think. That "not knowing." The waiting, the routine checks I'll have for the next few years. The word "remission" gets bandied around as if it's a shiny trophy. It's not. It's the bare minimum of what I want out of this.

Now I'm about to take my life off pause. I open up two windows on my laptop. Architect jobs in London. Culinary schools in Italy. I stare at both options. I can't choose which I want more. To go for it: Really take my career forward in a city in which I'd planned to live? Or to take a sabbatical from life? Learn to cook? Learn to enjoy my surroundings? Just to . . . be. I've taken involuntary time off from earning any money, so maybe I shouldn't do the latter. Maybe I should stay put here, find a new job or ask for my old one back? I definitely need to get a new apartment—I can't live with my parents for much longer.

There are only so many big decisions I can tackle in one day. But I know I have to work out what I want to do eventually. I need to make plans again. There are things I want to do. Dr. Khader tells me my records can be sent anywhere I need them to go. So if I choose to leave the US, or at least try to for a second time, then wherever I go, my records will follow me on; and Dr. Khader says he'll make sure I don't get lost in a system, that I'll get the checks I need, the blood tests I require. This moving on to somewhere else . . . this is a real possibility. I look over at my mom, next to me on the couch, staring at the TV but not really seeing it. I can tell what she's thinking as she glances over at my laptop screen. She almost lost me to a horrific disease. She doesn't want to lose me to another continent. But if I don't start again, carry on with . . . life, then hasn't fighting to survive been pointless?

Chapter 30

Hannah, October

MIRANDA AND PAUL are engaged. It happened just as Paul said it would, under the willow tree by a stream running through the secluded back garden of a hotel in the Cotswolds. I am so happy I could burst. It was hard keeping the secret for so long. Miranda called to tell me, screaming down the phone with excitement. And then she thanked me for choosing the world's best ring. "It's from Tiffany, Hannah, you clever thing!"

I didn't like to point out she'd told me over and over again that Tiffany & Co. was the direction in which I had to send Paul, the very moment it looked as if engagement was in the cards. I also suspect she'd informed Paul that he was to come straight to me for shopping advice, the very moment engagement looked to be a possibility.

And now we're planning wedding outfits. Hen parties. The works. I've been made chief bridesmaid. I've never been chief anything before, and the last time I was a bridesmaid was at my older cousin's wedding when I was seven years old. They're divorced now. I jog on quickly from that thought. I was cute as hell back then, but this time I'm going to have turned twenty-eight and be sexy as hell.

"What did you wear back then?" Miranda asks as we're sitting in the flat she shares with Paul, a half-eaten pizza in front of us. I won't tell George about this, I think, as I dunk the solid crust into the garlic-and-herb dip. I'm mainly using the crust as if it's a spoon for the dip. My God, it's good. For so many reasons, but mainly because it's not kale.

"Pink taffeta, obviously."

"Obviously," Miranda nods seriously.

"White lace gloves, like a Victorian."

Miranda thinks. "That could work," she jokes. "Cute on a seven-year-old. Slutty on a twentysomething."

I nod along. Other than the taffeta, I'm all right with lace gloves making an appearance. "There was even a parasol involved," I offer bravely.

"Oh my God, parasols," Miranda cries excitedly and googles wedding parasols.

"If I've got a parasol in my hand, how do I hold my bouquet and yours at the altar?"

"Good point." She backtracks on parasols.

"I'm so excited," I say.

"Me too." She stands up, brings a bunch of magazines over.

I feel my heart race, but in a good way. I've seen glossy wedding magazines on the shelves in the supermarket and never been brave enough to pick one up, look through, dream. And so I never have. But now Miranda has six glossy wedding magazines and I am going to devour all of them.

"Tonight we are going to tick everything off our list," she says.

I look up and stare at her. "Everything? What do you mean, everything?"

"Dresses—mine and yours; suit for Paul and his best man and the little pageboys; color scheme; and, most important, venue."

"Bloody hell," I say. "What's the rush? Are you pregnant?"

She glugs a giant mouthful of wine. "Christ, no. But we don't want to wait. So we're aiming for May. Abroad, obviously. Then we can combine our honeymoon while we're there." She looks smug about this, but it sounds exhausting, and then I think.

"May? That's . . ." I have to use my fingers to work this out. We're on our second bottle of wine, and our pizza was late arriving and it hasn't soaked up enough booze yet. Drunk wedding planning should not be allowed. "Seven months away. Don't most weddings take a year to—"

"Time is money, Hannah. Let's do this." She picks up a magazine, begins flicking, and, with a newfound fear and respect for my friend, so do I.

Chapter 31

November

I CAN HEAR Christmas music playing in the supermarket as George and I do the weekly shopping together. It's started already. Actually, I spotted Christmas crap in the shops in October but pretended I hadn't. To be honest, it does brighten the city up quite a bit and I've nothing against Christmas. I love it so much that Christmas lights stay up in my flat all year round. But I can't help thinking this year has whizzed by. At Christmastime last year a man on the other side of the world was accidentally phoning me. I smile at that. At the randomness of it. At how it turned into something so unexpected. How it almost turned into something so wonderful. And then it didn't.

And now I'm with George. And we shop for food together. I've let him into every facet of my life, and he's slowly following suit. We've both been very leisurely about letting each other in, both of us treading carefully after painful experiences in the past. Neither of us wants to get hurt, dumped, rush things. We're pacing it. We're getting there.

I'm meeting his mum in a few weekends' time. It's been a long time coming and George has taken some convincing, but it's the next natural step. He's still not sure if I should hang out with him and his mates yet. He's taking some convincing about this too. He thinks they might hit on me, or tell me stories about him that might put me off. We'll get the scarily titled "meet the parents" out of the way first, and then we'll work on the friends group.

I've also not been to his flat, because George says his flatmate treats their place like a dump and George prefers staying at mine, where it's just us in private, and where we can have sex without having to remember to be quiet. He also loves that my bathroom is clean. I don't like to point out that my flat is spotless because I clean it, and he could do the same to his flat. It'd be nice to see where he lives. Although maybe it's not that important anymore, because he sort of lives with me most of the week now.

He usually stays at mine about three or four nights every week, but has opted out of Saturdays in the pub with Miranda and Paul and seems to have managed to miss out on coffee with Joan weekend mornings, as he needs to be at work earlier and earlier as his client list grows.

We've gotten closer, sillier, happier, and we're planning another holiday. I yearn for the hedonistic version of us—that silly flirtiness that we invoked in Asia together. George and his guidebook, suntan lotion, and laughter as we compared bad dates and drank piña coladas with umbrellas in them. And if one of us wasn't pushing the shopping trolley around Tesco, I'm sure he'd have his hand in mine. To be honest, food shopping was a part of my life I didn't *actually* want to let him into. Everything on the shelves I reach for, he frowns at. I have such an urge to throw packs of Hobnobs in the trolley, just to watch that little muscle by the side of his right eye go bonkers as he calculates macros and calories. But I don't. Instead I pick them up on my way home from work. My excuse that I need biscuits for Joan wasn't up to scratch, so I sneak them in. I'll be hiding them in the toilet cistern next, like an addict.

We spend approximately 70 percent of our time in the fresh fruit-and-veg aisle. Which is a good thing. And George has learned the hard way not to even question how many five-liter bottles of wine go into my trolley. I yearn for a tub of Häagen-

Dazs but it's not worth the discussion, so we go past the freezer aisle, toward the checkout. It is totally worth the calories, though. Some things aren't. Häagen-Dazs is. But I have two wedding outfits that I need to fit into and the first one is next month, so I sigh as I pass the pralines and cream tubs and think of how good I'll look next month in my dress.

I hadn't expected *two* of my closest friends to declare they were getting hitched. But Joan surprised me last month by announcing that she and Geoff would be getting married just before Christmas. They've been together the same amount of time that George and I have, and when we stood over the garden fence, hugging as I congratulated her, I'll confess a part of me felt renewed on her behalf. She and Geoff are proof that old relationships and past loves don't define them and that they can move on, start again, fall in love.

Would I get married to George after knowing him the same length of time that she and Geoff have known each other? Probably not, no. And so I test the waters with my friend with a casual "Moving fast, Joan" on the Sunday morning she tells me. We stand in the bitter cold, dunking forbidden Hobnobs into our Nespresso Palermo Kazaar. It's about as bitter as the weather and we award it a four and a half, mainly because the coffee is warming us when nothing else is.

"Death moves fast, Hannah. We don't have the luxury of time, like you kids."

Death moves fast. I think about this a lot as I stand in the kitchen later on, watching George as he, in turn, watches Joe Wicks, on a YouTube video on his phone, doing something culinary with broccoli stalks I thought I'd put into the green waste a day or two ago.

"Do we have any almonds?" he chirrups.

I don't even know what I reply, or if I reply, as he begins ransacking cupboards. *Death moves fast.* Should I be accelerating

things with George? If I died tomorrow, would I have done everything I'd ever wanted to do? No, of course not. These are two
stupid things to think in quick succession. I think I'm happy with
where I am now, though. I stare out of the window. Behind me,
George has found a pack of out-of-date almonds, has resumed
watching his YouTube video and is furrowing his brow as he mutters something about tahini.

Outside it's snowing. It's been snowing for some time, because
the little patch of concrete outside my kitchen window is smoth-
ered in a blanket of thick, fluffy white. I put down my glass of
wine, open the back door, and watch it fall, uninterrupted, from
the sky to the ground.

"Brr, Hannah, flipping freezing. Shut the door."

"It's snowing," I point out as I watch it fall. My voice reverber-
ates around me as the thickness of the snow muffles all sound,
makes everything sound closer or further away . . . I can't tell
which—just different.

"So it is. Do we have any tahini?"

He knows the answer to this is no. "If you call secret Hobnobs
tahini, then sure, we've got plenty," I mutter, more to myself than
to him.

"What?" he asks distractedly and I hear him talking to himself
about alternatives.

The last time it snowed, a man thousands of miles away told
me I should go outside and make snow angels. I laugh at myself
for having done it then. And I'm going to do it now. Except that
I'm going to make George do it too.

"Come over here," I instruct in a sexy voice.

"Sex in the kitchen? Again, Gallagher? I can't keep up."

"Yes, you can," I reply. "But no. We're going to make snow
angels."

"Christ, no," he says, turning back to his phone and his broccoli stalk.

"Yes, we are," I say. "Live a little."

"Nope." He's insistent. "You'll get pneumonia."

"I won't," I say as I pull on my battered Uggs. "Come on."

"Well, you'll get wet then. Put a coat on."

"It's not very spontaneous if I go and put a coat on," I laugh.

He looks at my feet. "You had time to put those hideous slipper-boot things on."

I'm ignoring him now, half out of the door, half in. I move further into the garden, where I know the concrete has ended and given way underneath to patchy grass. It'll be softer for lying in. George is in the doorway, silently refusing to join me, but not quite willing to keep going on that cooking video for the moment. He's watching me now, his arms folded, with that bloody broccoli stalk still clutched in his palm.

I lie down, don't move for a while, watch the snow as it falls down onto me, let it land on my cheeks and forehead, into my eyelashes, and then I open my mouth, stick out my tongue, let the cool of the snow melt into my mouth, and then I laugh at myself. I make a snow angel, swiping my arms and legs up and down in the freshly falling powder until I'm sure I've made a me-shaped dent worthy of the Archangel Gabriel. I think of Davey, and the phrase "Death moves fast" travels all around my head, landing as thickly as the snow. And I stand up, soaked but smiling.

"You're mad," George mutters and I can't tell if it's an honest statement or if he means it affectionately.

Chapter 32

December

IT'S ONLY THE beginning of December, but I am *on it* when it comes to Christmas this year. My tree is up and once again I've bought new fairy lights. I count all the presents under the tree. Miranda and Paul are coming over for a mock-Christmas get-together on the twenty-third before we all flit off after work on Christmas Eve, scattering on trains like the rest of London, back to our family homes. George is going to be here too on the twenty-third and I'm now actually quite excited about this dinner, Christmas, and what next year will bring. I have survived my probation period at work and am now a fully fledged member of the team. Not that I wasn't considered such, but there's always something slightly bottom-clenching about a probation period, no matter how good at your job you are.

This year is rounding off quite nicely. It's our first Christmas together—well, mock-Christmas, as George is going to his parents for the big event and I'm heading to Whitstable to mine. But it's the same thing, he reassures me, and it's good enough for us, as neither of us is quite committing to go to the other's family for the day itself. Maybe next year.

I've bought George a whole box of goodies for his Christmas present. To say I put time and effort into it would be an under-

statement. Alongside some little stocking fillers and varying flavors of protein powders is the latest Joe Wicks cookbook, plus an
overnight voucher for a spa in the countryside in north Essex,
where the gym looks amazing and so do the pool, steam room,
and spa treatment menu, because I'd quite like to go too. I put
the finishing touches to the decoration on the box: red glittery
ribbon and some of that fun synthetic ribbon, which I run vigor-
ously across the open blades of a pair of scissors. I watched someone in a shop do it and it was a mind-blowing magic trick as the
ribbon looped and swirled. I really hope he likes all of this.

But before Christmas we're off to Joan and Geoff's wedding.
It's the last Saturday before Christmas. The nation must be out in
droves doing the last bit of high-street shopping, but I am smugly
complete in that respect. To celebrate the season I'm wearing a
red dress and faux-fur wrap, along with the tiniest red kitten
heels. The whole ensemble practically shouts, "I am going to a
Christmas wedding!" I've even gone down a dress size, which has
cheered me up no end, but I do wonder if it's simply that my
boobs seem to have shrunk a bit, when the rest of me seems
much the same.

George stayed over last night and we're getting ready together.
His patience is wearing that little bit thin, as I go over my hair
with the straighteners again.

"Looking good, Gallagher," he says, tapping his watch.

I turn to look at him in his dark-blue suit, his hair just that
right side of floppy. "So do you. You got a girlfriend?" I tease.

He laughs. "Not for much longer, if she makes us late. And
they're your friends."

"Charming! Geoff will be pleased to hear that. He likes you."

"Yeah, he's all right, I suppose. Be strange to see them full-
length. Only ever see their top halves over your garden fence
every now and again. Chop-chop, Gallagher, chop-chop."

He switches off my straighteners and bustles us both out of

the door. For a man who's eternally late, he's keen today. So am I. This is quite possibly the swankiest wedding I've ever been invited to. It is clear that Geoff is very, very loaded, judging by the location, the agenda, and the fact they've got more than a hundred people coming. Joan has made no secret of the fact that the cruise was no expenses spared, and he's booked Mauritius for the honeymoon. I still have no idea what he did before he retired but, whatever it was, Geoff was obviously very good at it and is reaping the rewards of retirement.

I read through the thick, embossed-card invitation again as George and I ride the Central line.

"We need to change to the District line in a bit," he says absentmindedly, adjusting his tie and cricking his neck.

"Mm-hmm," I say, looking at the order of events taking place in Kew Gardens. The civil ceremony is taking place in the Nash Conservatory, drinks in the Princess of Wales Conservatory, and the reception in the Orangery. That's a lot of conservatories. But I am so excited, for Joan and Geoff, but also because I've not been to Kew Gardens since I went on a school trip years ago. I've looked up winter weddings at Kew Gardens to whet my appetite. There are going to be fairy lights everywhere. And mulled wine. Thank God I'm wearing red. I am a not-so-secret spiller whenever red wine and I meet.

I can't wait to see Joan's dress, which she says is understated and elegant, but which she wouldn't allow anyone to see. I hold George's hand while we're on the Tube, let our hands rest together, entwined in the space between us.

I'm holding my small clutch bag and, because it's so small, I've loaded the pockets of George's trousers and his inside jacket pockets with all my belongings that don't fit, such as a natural rose-petal confetti box, lip gloss, bronzer, deodorant. In my bag are basically just my phone and tissues, because I know I'll cry when they say, "I do."

George looks down at me as if seeing me for the first time. "Damn, Gallagher, you look fit."

"Thanks," I murmur against his lips as he kisses me.

We stand and we prepare to go through the rigmarole of changing lines.

"Do you think she'll grade the after-dinner coffee?" he teases as we walk through the station, allowing the crowd to swallow us in its midst as we stride purposefully toward our line. Whenever George stayed over, he stopped coming to weekend chats over the fence with Joan, either heading off to work or appearing briefly for a wave, a hello, and then a retreat. I was glad. They were our thing anyway—mine and Joan's. "A four out of five," he mimics Joan as we arrive at our new platform. "But not as good as the Valpolicella capsule from last week."

I frown. "That's a wine. And don't be unkind."

And then it happens—the thing I'd wanted to happen for so long and then put out of my mind, as being about as likely as winning the lottery. I'm on the platform with George, waiting for the train.

And I see him. Davey.

From across the other side of the platform, waiting for a train heading in the opposite direction. Or at least, it looks sort of like him. I'd put Davey out of my mind, or at least attempted to, and I have been very good at not hallucinating him recently on any other train journey, and yet . . . now . . . there's a man standing on the other side of the platform waiting for a train and it looks like Davey. It looks so much like Davey that I stop speaking, stop listening to George as he continues berating Joan, making himself laugh.

George's hand is wrapped around mine and I'm convincing myself that I'm mental, that this isn't Davey, that this can't be Davey. But all the same I slowly extricate my hand from George's. He uses the moment to check his watch, and I was going to pretend I had a scratch but I don't even bother. I only ever saw Davey on our video calls and in the few photos he sent me, so I'm trying to compare this man standing in front of me—albeit across the platform—to the one in the photos from so many months ago. God, it really looks like him. His hair is so much shorter, like it's been shaved off and is just growing back a little wildly. He has two huge rucksacks next to him and is unscrewing the lid on a water bottle. He tips his head back to drink and then someone asks him the time and he smiles as they thank him and he mouths, "You're welcome" in that way only Americans seem to, and everything around me stills.

That smile. Dear God, I think it's actually him. I move, back away from George, and then, without really knowing what I'm doing, I run fast, barreling through people. Behind me I hear George cry my name, but I don't stop. I take the stairs two at a time, run through the passageway that divides the platforms, that divides us, slide through people as I get to the turn, begin the descent to the other platform.

People are coming up the stairs, which means only one thing—there's a train in the station and it's just let people out. I could scream. I run faster, through people heading toward me, begging them to move, and I land on the platform. He's gone. But the train is still in the station. I run along the platform to where he was standing about halfway down. I'm guessing now that he was standing right here. I start looking in the carriages. The doors are still open. I should get on, although it's madness . . . I should get on. But I don't. Instead I look further down the platform, where people are moving and . . . Maybe he's not on the train, maybe he's moved further along, waiting for the next one. I run toward the crowd, glancing around me for a tall blond man with two rucksacks. I strain my eyes to look inside as I'm almost running again. And the doors close. "No. Shit! No." Everything's happening so fast—too fast.

And then I see him. He's typing something on his phone. I stare. If I was clever, I'd bang on the window, but I'm not clever. I don't even move. I just watch him typing. I don't have any time left to pull my phone out of my little bag—to call him, text him, tell him to look up. So instead I stare at the man I never met, finally in front of me in the flesh. Because I am so entirely sure it's him. And sensing he's being watched . . . he looks up and directly at me.

His phone lowers and there's no recognition in his face, and I think, *It's not him. This is it, Hannah, you have lost the plot one hundred percent.* The train starts moving and the man stops looking through me, looks at me, smiles and then the lightning bolt of recognition hits him, he visibly inhales, the train moves, and then I watch him mouth, "Hannah," as his eyes widen in shock. And then he's gone, carried away into the tunnel.

I'm so in shock that I simply stare at the empty spot where he was, and I don't even have the time or the brainpower to wonder what he's doing here, why he hasn't messaged me or . . . anything. We left things so strangely before. Behind me I hear my name and I turn. I don't know why I expect it to be Davey when he's heading into the darkness of the Underground, but I do expect it to be him and I hate myself because of the disappointment that hits me when I see it's George.

"Hannah," he says again. "What the hell?"

"I . . . I thought. I thought we might be on the wrong platform."

He looks around, as if the platform might provide the answer to my madness.

"No. We were on the right platform." He stares at me.

I nod. "OK."

"You just left without me," he says. "Were you going to get on a train without me?"

"No," I say. "No, I wasn't getting on the train. I wouldn't have done that."

He looks hurt, disappointed, confused. "What's going on?"

"Nothing," I say, shock reverberating through my mind. I can't think of anything else to say, so I repeat my lie. "I thought we were on the wrong platform."

George opens his mouth to say something. Closes it. Shakes his head a bit. He goes to put his hands in his pockets as he assesses me, but he can't, as they're rammed with all my stuff. He lets his hands hang limply by his sides. He ran all the way over the bridge and down the platform and the man isn't even out of breath, hasn't even broken a sweat. "Shall we get back on the right platform?" he asks quietly.

"Yes." I nod. He reaches out for my hand. And I look one last time into the darkness of the tunnel that carried Davey out of reach. And then I take George's hand.

It takes me the entire length of the journey to Kew Gardens to get my thoughts together. In that time I don't speak to George, don't look at my phone. I just stare ahead as the train stops and starts at stations and carries on, shooting us through darkness and then light, darkness and then light, over and over until we arrive at Kew.

It's only as I'm sitting down watching the civil ceremony that I'm able to form coherent thoughts. Davey is well. He looked well. He looked a bit different, but he looked well. He had rucksacks. Does he live here? Has he just this second moved here? Has he been here a few weeks already and is now leaving—going back to the US? That thought hits me fast and furiously and if I hadn't already been sitting on a chair, I would have stumbled. What if it wasn't him? But it was. I'm sure it was. He said my name. *He said my name.*

Chapter 33

Davey

IT WAS HANNAH. It was actually Hannah. I'm so stunned I don't know what to do. Should I go back? I should go back. I should. But she'll be long gone by now. I missed my stop anyway and had to turn around a few stations up and double back until I found the right station. I stare, totally confused, at the Tube map up above me on the wall of the next train that I catch, seeing it, but not seeing it. The colored lines mean nothing to me and someone points me in the direction of where I'm headed, toward the Gatwick Express.

It's only as I'm sitting on the express train taking me toward the airport that I can finally pull myself together, try to work out what happened, *how* it happened. Hannah was on the Underground platform at the same time I was. Hannah was in front of the train window, in front of me for the few moments I was standing there . . . She was there too. I can't get my head around that. If I believed in fate, I'd say that was meant to happen. But if it was meant to happen, wouldn't she have gotten on the train, or wouldn't I have stood there longer, or wouldn't the train have been delayed—anything that enabled us to actually . . . meet?

I sit back. I can't close my eyes to sleep in case I miss the stop again, so I stare wildly around me. Exhaustion comes so much quicker these days.

I'm leaving already. My time in England was short and I managed to cram a lot in, even visiting Cornwall for a weekend. In a way I needed to prove to myself I could still do all the things I could have done before the chemo wiped me out. It still wipes me out, but I needed this. I've beaten cancer and I'm unstoppable. Until around 4 P.M., when I need to nap for twenty minutes. Not every day. Just some. And after that I'm unstoppable again.

Cornwall was a long way to travel for such a short time, but it was worth it. The turquoise of the sea in St. Ives blew me away. It's part of my roots, my DNA, but I don't have any living relatives there now, and I fought loneliness while eating Cornish pasties in Falmouth and ice cream on the harbor wall in Padstow.

And then I went up to Whitstable. I'd like to say it was for some real tourist reason, but I went because Hannah talked about it so much that I had to see what she saw, and where she grew up. I sat on the pebbles in that little coastal town and looked out across the end of the Thames where it fell away into the sea.

This is what she saw on New Year's Eve when I called her.

I ate fish and chips on the pebble beach, picked up a pebble and took it with me, slipping it into my pocket to look at every now and again. Just because. I walked through the town and fell in love with that little place that, until Hannah mentioned it to me, I'd never even heard of. And then London went by so fast. I never expected it to. I did all the things she said we'd do, in my few days here. I took a big red bus tour, went to the Tower of London. I was too embarrassed to take a selfie with the guys in the red outfits, but I said hey to them as I stood in line for about two hours to look at the Crown Jewels. I went to the National Portrait Gallery and found the picture of the Brontë sisters that Hannah once told me she liked so much. I sat in front of it for a while, taking in the brushstrokes and the invisible space where their brother once sat. There, but not there. A bit like how I felt. But not anymore. And then I went next door to the National Gal-

lery and got totally lost. She was right. The National Portrait Gallery *is* better.

And then today, on my last day, I woke up, packed my stuff
back into my rucksacks, paid my hotel bill, and, to save money,
decided to ride the Tube instead of getting a taxi to the station.
And that's when I saw her. I thought I was going mad. But it was
her. It was Hannah. She looked . . . amazing. Beautiful. That
dress. Her hair. All dolled up like that, she was nearly unrecogniz-
able and it took me so long—too long—for the pieces of her in my
mind to fit together and for me to realize . . . it was her, standing
right there, in front of me, staring at me as if she couldn't believe
I was there, either.

And now I pull out my paperback copy of *A Room with a View*,
which I bought on impulse in a bookstore near Covent Garden,
and stare at the cover, feeling nothing but regret that I'm leaving
London. Nothing but regret that I never got in contact with her
again. I was such a coward. Everything I did concerning Hannah
was cowardice, pure and simple. I never contacted her because
I'm the worst kind of quitter. I quit on Hannah. I quit on chemo,
until she and Grant collectively forced me back in. A man on a
mission, a path, but to what . . . ? I have no idea. A new path, one
where I don't know what's around the corner. One where I can
choose the direction, be in charge of my own life again. And I'm
sure it was the right thing to do, ending things with her. That was
confirmed when I saw that guy arrive behind her. His eyes moved
from the back of her head toward me. That look on his face. Pos-
sessive anger. He was one unhappy guy. But the look on hers:
shock, hurt, confusion. I did all that to her. I did that.

I told her to get on with her life, not waste her time on some
guy being pumped full of drugs thousands of miles away, some
guy trying not to give up on life, who then did give up on life. I did
the right thing, I'm sure of it. It had to have been the right thing.
I didn't want to mess with that girl's head any more than I'd

already done. Besides, I told her to be with someone else. And now I can see that she is with someone else.

I may be many things, but I am not the kind of guy who muscles in on someone else's girl, who breaks up couples, even if Hannah was once—in some loose definition of the word—mine.

Chapter 34

Hannah

I'M STILL IN shock. I nod, I smile. I watch Joan sweep down the aisle with a dainty tiara on her head and a dress that looks like gossamer silk clinging flatteringly to her small figure. And Geoff, who looks like a man so utterly in love as his bride-to-be moves toward him. But I can't think about any of it, can't process it. It's so far removed from me all of a sudden. Davey is here. Davey. Is. Here.

I'm silently glad it's a civil ceremony. No hymns. It makes the event go quicker, although the happy couple have chosen the Beatles' "When I'm Sixty-Four" for us all to sing. Which makes me smile, although I don't feel present enough to appreciate it. Joan giggles ironically throughout it all, because she and Geoff are now north of that august age.

Paul and Miranda have been invited. After all, Miranda used to live with me and sometimes partook in our over-the-fence chats before she moved out, when she wasn't mortifyingly hung-over.

The wedding is the very definition of beautiful. Christmas beautiful. But I move as if on autopilot toward our table. Paul and George chat together as we wait for the wedding breakfast to be served and I watch them, thinking they're getting on well—not friends as such, only chatting because they're forced into the same room together. Paul says something and George laughs and then gives me a look as if he's desperate to roll his eyes. I smile thinly and my expression drops a split second later when George looks away.

Miranda talks to me about her wedding. I'm sure she's saying something about getting married in a different country, something about how it always rains here but overseas weddings are different, allegedly, and I make the right noises at the right points in the one-sided conversation. I can't think and I can't talk. I certainly can't talk about Davey, about having seen him. I feel sick. I think I might throw up. Or scream. Or do both together, as if I'm that little girl from *The Exorcist*.

I stand up, push my chair back so suddenly that Miranda stops talking to me halfway through her sentence. I'm so rude. I don't mean to be, but I have to get out of here.

"Sorry," I announce to everyone and no one at our circular table. "Just need to . . ." I turn and hope they think I'm going to the loo. I half expect Miranda or George to follow me, but no one does and it's the first time I'm able to form a coherent thought since seeing Davey, so I'm glad no one has gotten up to trail me to the ladies' room. Inside I pull down a toilet seat and sit on top. And so I start. I make a decision. I'm going to delete Davey's number. If he'd wanted to talk to me, to be with me or to make contact, he would have done that by now. He never phoned me. He didn't tell me he was coming here. I phoned him, because Grant asked me to; begged me to. I feel like a fool now.

And if I'm not going to see him ever again, I have to accept that was it and I have to do something drastic, to admit to myself that it is all over and it will never be anything other than over. I pull my phone out of my bag. I open up the WhatsApp messages to and from Davey. I hit delete on all of them, and one by one they disappear as I move them to the side and hit the red trash-can icon. Afterward I don't feel cleansed of him. I feel like a piece of me has been ripped out. But I continue ripping out more pieces of me as I find the photos he sent me, look at his handsome face, his ridiculous pose making eyes at Kirstie and Phil. I only notice I'm crying when tears land on my phone screen, blurring the pixels.

My hand shakes, but I hover over the trash icon, tap it, hit yes to confirm I want to delete that photograph. And the first he sent: impromptu, his shirt off, tanned, muscular, traces of water on his skin from his shower. He looks so good. He was kind, funny, nice, and then ill, and now he's here, without a word. Delete. It has to go. I can't hang on to this any longer. I can't hang on to him.

And then—because if I don't do it now, right now, I know I'll cave—I pull up a message to Davey. I admit to him the thing I knew, but never told him. "I love you," it says. "I love you."

And then I do exactly what Davey did to me all those months ago. I hit backspace on the entire message, knowing I've said it, but not sent it. And then I find his number in my contacts list. "Delete contact?" I hit yes, and Davey disappears out of my phone and my life forever.

I walk back to the table after fixing my makeup with my fingers, to find Miranda putting a spare bread plate over my food to keep it warm. I shoot her a grateful look and she wipes a stray fleck of mascara from my cheek that I must have missed.

"You OK?" she asks.

I nod. "I am now."

She gives my leg a squeeze, a silent solidarity that doesn't need explanation.

George is watching me, but he's not smiling, not speaking, just watching me. I turn to him. Give him a false smile that sickens even me. He turns and carries on talking to Paul.

What have I done? What am I doing? I have no idea. I'm

exhausted, but Miranda tops up our wineglasses before the poor waiter even has a chance to notice she's downed hers.

"Come on, drink up. It's a wedding. This table's like a funeral."

I do as I'm told. It's easier than resisting. I knock back the glass of wine and can't work out if this is going to make me feel better or worse. I'll find out later.

"I got to you a few seconds before I called your name," George tells me, his hands thrust into his pockets, now that we're back at my flat and he's decanted all my bits and bobs from his attire.

"Sorry?" I ask. I'm trashed. I know this. The world isn't exactly spinning. If I wasn't feeling so . . . odd about today, I'd call myself merry. However, I am anything but.

"At the station, when you ran off. I got to you a few seconds before I called your name."

I turn and look at him. "I feel drunk," I say, because I don't exactly understand whether he's asking me a question that I need to contrive an answer for. Not yet.

"Kitchen," he barks. "Coffee."

He makes us some instant coffee and we sit at the little table that's pushed against the kitchen wall.

"Can I have some milk in it?" I ask hopefully as he presents strong black coffee. "It's a bit bitter."

"So am I," he startles me by saying.

I look at George as he sits down, ignoring my request for milk. I want to stand up and fetch some, but I don't. I'm unsure if that will help things right now.

"You were running after someone," he declares. It's not posed as a question. "I saw him look at you. I saw him say your name. Who was he?"

George saw it too. I don't know whether to be pleased or mortified. It means I didn't imagine it, at least.

"No one," I lie instinctively. I don't want to talk about it. It won't help us. It won't help me by talking about it. It will do no good whatsoever. "No one who means anything to me anymore." And I know this is also a lie, but in time I'm sure it won't be.

He holds the handle of his mug and I can see he's working out how to phrase the next thing he says.

"I didn't see your face. Just the back of your head. But I saw the speed at which you ran. I've never seen you run like that, Hannah."

I notice he's not calling me "Gallagher" anymore and I know this is a bad sign.

"I need to know who it was. I think you owe me an explanation as to why you ran away from me that fast—who you were running to."

I can't lie anymore. I don't have it in me and it's not fair to George. So I tell him. "Davey."

He looks confused. No idea what I'm talking about. "Who's that?"

"Davey. The American."

He still has no idea, and that's because those words are so entirely devoid of detail. But also I think this says everything about us. I know that I didn't exactly open up about Davey. But I was honest. I did tell him Davey had dumped me. I used his name. I even told George that we were seeing each other without actually being together. And that the reason Davey finished with me was because he wanted me to live my own life and not stick around while he battled cancer. And as I remind George of this, he starts laughing.

I stop. "Have I said something funny?" I ask quietly.

"Davey? *That* was Davey?"

"Yes."

And then he stops laughing. "Video Davey. Davey from thousands of miles away. Davey who you never even fucking met?

Davey who dumped you?" I can't get a word in and he continues. "You leave me standing on a train platform to run after a man you dated, who dumped you, who you never even met?"

I'm silent. It does sound bad.

He tips his head back, looks at the ceiling as if it contains all the answers.

"You ran away from me for a man you've never met," he says, but it's more to himself, to remind himself torturously.

"I didn't run away from you. I . . . acted on impulse. I just ran."

"That's not good enough, Hannah. This isn't good enough." He slumps in his seat. "This hasn't been good enough for ages."

I know this. I've known it for such a long time.

"Have I ever asked anything of you?" George demands.

"Not really."

"I only ever asked you to do *one* thing for me. Just one. I wanted you to go on the pill."

I blink in shock at this strange twist in the conversation.

"I told you I hate using condoms," he says as justification.

"I hate being on the pill," I counter. "I told you this. I've never found one that didn't make me ravenous and fat, that didn't reduce my libido to dust. I've got an appointment booked to get the coil and—"

"How long did that take to get sorted, though? I've mentioned it a few times. But still you made me use condoms. We've been together nearly a year. How long did you wait before you even phoned the GP?"

I wasn't about to go on the pill for someone I didn't even love, I want to shout at him, but I don't. It was only at the doctor's office that the nurse sat me down and politely informed me the world had moved on since I last tried long-term contraception, and she helped me decide on the coil.

I stand. I need to think. I need to work out what to do next. I leave my coffee on the table as I move toward the fridge for the little carton of milk, but it's behind a bottle of wine and I pull that out of the way.

"Haven't you drunk enough?" George says, clocking the wine. "For fuck's sake, you and your boring friends drank the open bar dry."

I stare at him. "We didn't. Miranda only drank a few, because she's dieting already for her wedding next year, and I only saw Paul with—"

"I'm going to go," George snaps.

I don't even think about stopping him. We've been so unfair to each other that it's only just dawning on me. I knew we weren't right together, but I kept thinking: This will get better. This will get better.

"Are you going to say anything?" he asks.

Shamefully I don't. I'm too busy thinking. This is the push I need, the push I didn't know I was waiting for. I don't think George and I should do this to each other anymore. This isn't how relationships are supposed to be. We want entirely different things, we're completely different people. It was good in the early days, but it's apparent we're not right for each other, not anymore. I let myself drift into this relationship and I ignored it when it turned sour. When I look back on this moment I know I'm not going to regret this decision, but I am going to regret any hurt I cause him. I get ready to speak, but he's there first.

"Hannah—I'm going to take my stuff. This is . . . it's not working for me anymore."

I inhale quickly. A mixture of emotions hits me. George and I, for once, are actually on the same page. It still stings, but only for a moment. After that, I'm grateful he got there before me.

"I don't think you've been into this for a while, actually," he says. "I think you've been going through the motions. Maybe we both have."

I can't argue with that. George never let me into his life. Always an excuse. Always a reason. But maybe I didn't let him fully into mine, either. He'd never said he loved me and I'd never said it, either. And the reason for that is blindingly obvious.

George gathers his things, moving around the flat quietly. I wait in the kitchen because I'm not going to trail him around. I shouldn't be shocked. I really shouldn't. But I sort of am. Do relationships always end so much more quickly than they start? After a few minutes he stands by the door. A part of him seems reluctant to leave. A part of me feels the same.

"I have a Christmas present for you," I say.

He laughs bitterly. "Keep it."

"No, I want you to have it." I move past him in the doorway and fetch his box from under the tree. "I put a lot of effort into it."

"Shame you didn't put more effort into our relationship."

I close my eyes, take a deep breath, don't respond. He wants the last word. I get that.

"Thanks," he mumbles as I hand it to him. "I haven't gotten you anything yet."

Christmas is merely days away. How long was he going to leave it before buying me something? *Was* he going to buy me something?

"It started so well," he says. "Us, I mean. Thailand was a blast, but we should probably have left it there, no?"

I agree with a smile that he half returns. Though I'm tempted to, I don't remind him that this was what I actually said at the time, and it was he who encouraged us onward. But I shouldn't have carried on. I could see him changing so rapidly. Ten months. We lasted ten months. We should only really have been together for those ten days. I'd put money on this all being my fault. Maybe I never really let George in mentally, only physically; never really gave him the chance he deserved. I can't tell now.

Paul was right: I am obviously easily led. I let Davey end things and I didn't fight it. I knew George and I shouldn't have gotten together, but I let it happen. I even quit my job and went for a new one because I was told to by Cindy. Thank God that worked out. If she'd known that's what I was like, would she have hired me? But this—this I know needs to happen, even though I didn't need to be the one who said it first. Point-scoring is not my style.

George surprises me by putting his Christmas box on the kitchen counter, stepping forward, and hugging me. "Ah well, Gallagher, we gave it our best shot."

I raise my eyes to him, smile. "We did." I'm grateful this is ending well, civilly.

"Listen, do me a favor, will you?" he says. "Cancel your gym membership. Find another gym."

"Oh. OK."

"I don't really want to see you ever again, if that's all right."

Oh, wow. So much for civil. I nod. "Sure, OK." I don't like to point out I get free gym membership at work now, thanks to one of our donors, and only went to George's gym to be near him because he worked so much that I hardly ever saw him otherwise. But his parting shot stings nonetheless.

"Bye, Hannah," he says, picking up his Christmas present. He mumbles an awkward-sounding, "Thanks for the present," fumbles for the door latch and leaves.

As I move to close the front door, the ice-cold December air penetrates the entrance hall and I step out onto the path to watch his retreating figure as he turns and leaves without a backward glance.

I stare up into the cold night sky. I can feel the chill wrapping around my legs. The clouds have parted and thousands of miles above me stars are twinkling brightly, the light traveling so far until it reaches me.

By the time I look back to the end of the street, George has already gone.

* * *

"You never let *him* in?" Miranda explodes at my own reasoning as to why George and I have finished, when she and Paul come over for fake Christmas. Hosting this was the very last thing I needed, and also the very best. "He never let *you* in! Did you ever see his flat? In nearly a year?"

"No. George said he didn't like it, didn't like his flatmates, my place was nicer."

"Do you even know where he lives?"

"About ten minutes from here."

"Ten minutes by car, on foot? What road?" Miranda pushes.

I rub my forehead. I've had a stress headache for a solid twenty-four hours and this isn't helping. "I'm sure he told me. I can't remember."

"And he met your parents. Did you ever meet his?"

"No. But I was going to."

"Why, in almost a year, has it taken until now for that to get planned?"

I try to think. "There wasn't a reason. It just never happened. Timing and work and . . ." This is a lame excuse that I was fed by George and so I drop it.

Paul chimes in. "He's done you a favor, getting in first. He's an idiot. An annoyingly good-looking idiot who, by all accounts, gave you some decent sex, but he's gone. And without too much of a fight, by the sound of it. George being gone is a good thing for you," Paul says.

I give him a well-earned smile and nod in agreement. It is a good thing for me. I know this.

Miranda dusts her hands together as if to say, "Case closed."

"Yeah, I'm not exactly crying. I'm OK. Really. I just need to go home, see Mum and Dad and, you know . . . Ugh!" I rub my hand over my forehead. I know that now is the time to tell my best friend the reason why George and I have finished. But how do I say it? I can't. It hurts too much to keep thinking about it. And I know I really am going to cry if I talk about Davey. So I'm not going to. I'm not going to tell them I saw Davey. In the spirit of self-preservation, I'm simply not going to.

"Yeah," Miranda says. "Good. Perfect, in fact. So no sad pep talks needed then?"

"No sad pep talks needed."

"Thank God." She pulls out a bundle of presents for me from a huge Selfridges shopping bag. "Can we do Christmas presents now then?"

Chapter 35

January

I'M STANDING IN sludge. The thick winter snow is melting beneath my boots, which are now even more battered than ever and stained with the wet marks of melting snow. I hand the plate of biscuits over the fence to Joan and she looks at it appreciatively as she zips up her winter coat. I note she's tucking into the biscuits with even more aplomb than usual, now she's not got a wedding dress to fit into. One friend is out of the wedding woods, while Miranda is skipping merrily toward hers. I should probably feel a bit left out of all the bridal shenanigans, but I'm actually deeply thankful that I'm young, free, and single.

"Hallelujah," Joan says when I tell her this.

She does that trick of dunking her Hobnob and saving it from drowning at the last second. So impressive. I've still not mastered it.

"And I notice you've put a bit of weight on," Joan says.

I pause, munching my biscuit. "What? But I'm going to the gym three times a week," I protest.

"In a good way," she says hurriedly. "In a good way. You were getting scrawny and unhealthy-looking. All that running."

"All that kale," I say. "I'm not missing that."

"Not missing *him* then?" she asks.

"George? No," I say emphatically.

"Of course George," Joan says. "Who did you think I meant?"

I can't tell if she's teasing me or testing me. I don't take the bait. Instead I stealthily change the subject. "So, tell me about the honeymoon."

I listen to Joan tell me about the beautiful old buildings of Mauritius, the national park, the snorkeling in crystal-clear waters, the sunbathing and reading novels, and then she shocks me by telling me she's leaving Wanstead.

My mouth drops. "Are you serious?"

She nods. "Geoff's home is in Hertfordshire, has a lot more green space, and we're married now."

Of course. It's so obvious that I don't know how I didn't work this out before.

"We thought about keeping this as our London crash pad, but the trains from Hertfordshire mean we can pop in and out of the city for the day when, and if, we want. I'll rent this place out. Geoff's been making all the effort, traveling here and . . . well, I don't think we'll be in Hertfordshire much anyway. Geoff loves to travel, and I must admit I could get quite used to the Upper Class cabin on Virgin Atlantic. They have a bar on board, Hannah."

I laugh and take hold of her cold hand, perched on top of the dividing fence. "I'm really pleased for you, Joan. Honestly. I'm so happy for you both."

"Thank you," she says, giving me a squeeze back.

A movement inside Joan's kitchen catches my eye and Geoff, resplendent in one of Joan's spare dressing gowns, looks out, giving me a wave and a warm smile. I reciprocate both readily.

I sigh. "I love it when love finds love."

Joan winks. "Me too. No word about your . . . um . . ." She blows out a puff of air.

I'm not used to Joan being stuck for words and I narrow my eyes, waiting.

"The American," she says eventually.

I inhale deeply. "Oh . . . no. No word." This is the truth. "Although . . . I saw him," I tell Joan.

She opens her mouth to speak and then closes it.

"On your wedding day, actually," I explain. "In real life. I saw him. Here. In London. On the train." I'm talking in clipped sentences, but every time I think about it, which is about every three minutes, clipped thoughts are all I can conjure.

"Did you speak to him?" she asks.

"No. He was on the Underground. Going the other way."

She nods and then, "Shit!"

I chuckle, hearing Joan swear. She usually only ever does this when she's drunk, which doesn't happen often. "Shit indeed. I ran. I ran to get to him. And he saw me. And I saw him. And George ran after me. But Davey had gone. The train doors closed and . . . well, that was it. He was gone. And we got through the whole of your wedding without George mentioning it. And then when we got home . . ." It's my turn to blow out a puff of air and then, because I don't know how to finish the sentence, I shrug. "And among many reasons why George and I weren't right for each other, that was the catalyst that brought it all to an end."

Joan has a look of concern about her now, but she's not speaking and, because I don't like an awkward silence, I continue.

"I'd pushed him to the back of my mind, you know?"

Joan nods.

"But every now and again he'd filter through to the front. And then he was there. Right there. And I didn't know whether to laugh, cry, stop breathing . . . but I knew I had to get to him."

"But you didn't get to speak to each other?"

I shake my head.

"And how did he look?"

"Joan, there's a torturous question. He looked hot."

"No," she says. "That's not what I mean. I mean . . . did he look annoyed, unhappy, overjoyed, surprised?"

I shrug again. "I have no idea. He looked through me, at first, and then he smiled and he said my name and then he was gone."

Joan's mouth has dropped open and she whispers, "Oh my God."

"He didn't call me," I say simply.

"When?" Joan leans forward over the fence.

"At any time. He didn't call me after he finished his treatment. I'm assuming he's finished. I have no clue. And he was in London and he never called me. So . . ." I let that hang there, hoping Joan's going to justify Davey's actions.

But she doesn't. "I don't know what to make of that," she says.

"Neither do I."

"Would you have run for George?" she surprises me by asking.

I narrow my eyes at her until she clarifies.

"Your situations with George and Davey weren't so completely different. Both men didn't last too long—"

"Thank you," I say pointedly.

"You know what I mean. But only one has had this effect on you. George isn't the one that got away. Davey is. You ran for him, despite the fact that he'd finished things with you. Did you love George?"

I go to speak but I can't. I just shake my head, look into my coffee cup.

"Did you love Davey?"

I sweep my eyes up from my empty cup to look at her. "I think . . ." And then I nod. "Yes, I think so. We had some connection. But I feel a fool for saying it."

"George was a classic rebound," Joan says knowingly.

I take a second and then, "I know. Long rebound, though."

"Wasn't it just. So what now?"

"Nothing," I say. "I'm done. I've deleted Davey from my phone." And then I trill out my favorite phrase. "Self-preservation."

She looks into her coffee cup as if there are tea leaves in there, telling her my future.

"A man isn't what I need," I say certainly. "I need to see friends, work hard at my job, which I love. I need to see my family as often as possible, give myself a few months away from bad dates with shit men. It's not healthy to lurch from one guy to the next, the way I've done. I'm going to enjoy myself. I'm going to cultivate a single life," I announce as if it's a mantra on a meme I read.

"Life is what happens to you when you're busy making other plans," Joan says. "John Lennon," she clarifies.

"You do love Lennon."

"I do. Man was a genius."

I clink my empty coffee cup against Joan's empty coffee cup. "Amen to that."

I can't help but google the Upper Class cabin when I get back indoors and this puts me on the path of googling holidays. I haven't been away properly since last February, when I went to Thailand with George. I cringe inwardly thinking about this, closing my eyes tightly to shut out the recent memory of where that all led to, and vow that this time I'm not going to go on holiday with anyone.

Solo holidays in February produce a multitude of results, but I'm strangely drawn to a skiing holiday. I've never been before. I don't know how to ski. But I feel that a fresh year should bring with it a challenge, and none more so than learning something new. I'm going to go away alone for the first time ever, and I'm going to learn to ski. I will probably break my arm while on a slope, and this is all completely out of my comfort zone, but it's different and I feel invigorated just thinking about booking it. I need to be out of my comfort zone for once.

I drop an email to HR asking for time off and then get a quote together for the dates I want to book. I am going to join a ski school, ski to my heart's content, eat tartiflette, drink red wine, make friends with strangers, join in all the activities they organize as part of the solo tour package, and I am going to let life and fate take hold of me for as long as they both want. No, I'm going to let life and fate take hold of me for as long as *I* want.

Chapter 36

February

I'VE COME TO a complete stop on the easiest of blue runs as I field a call from Miranda about her hen-do. I feel like a skiing wanker, poles gripped in my left hand, mobile phone clamped to my ear with my right, goggles positioned on my forehead. I want desperately to say, "Yah, yah" very loudly in response to whatever she says so that I feel properly ski-posh, but I resist. Just.

The wedding countdown is firmly on. Miranda is crossing days off her calendar as if she's a prison convict waiting to be released. I get a text every day with the new countdown, which unnerves me because I have spent the past few days necking so much yummy hot wine with the other solo travelers at lunch that I think I'm going to need yet another bridesmaid-dress fitting when I get home. I make a note that I will not order the cheese board for dessert for the third time in a row. I will not order a pudding, full stop. But I'm so ravenous after a day of gliding up and down the blue runs (I'm so nearly on reds, so nearly) that I need to eat everything on the menu for dinner.

Tonight's solo activity (I'm so glad they don't call it a "singles" holiday) is a quiz night, and the eight of us on the tour are automatically a team against all the other tables. In our hotel there are other couples and families who have blatantly pulled their children out of school, because it's not half-term, I checked. The prices are sky-high in half-term and I wasn't paying that.

I've made friends with one of the other solo skiers, a guy called John who's quite sweet, and we made plans to join each other in the afternoon twice to ski after ski school had finished for the morning. But I am now so averse to getting involved with men on holiday (I have previous form on this) that, after I sensed him getting a bit too flirty—not unpleasantly so, just a bit sure of himself— I made certain that I included a really quiet thirtysomething called Nicole, who seemed to be struggling to find her place in the group.

But for now I have Miranda in my ear, as Nicole tries not to listen while we watch some six-year-olds in ski school glide past us without the use of poles.

"Smug little fuckers," I hear not-so-quiet-Nicole say with a laugh and I know we're going to get on.

"They have a low center of gravity," I whisper to her while Miranda gives me the lowdown on the wedding, which she's practically hand-picked from the pages of all those bridal magazines.

"So," Miranda says, changing the subject, "is it like a real-life version of Tinder—this singles holiday? Like some kind of reality-TV show: lots of singles in a ski resort, let's see who shags who?"

"Miranda!" I chastise. "Of course not."

This actually was my main worry, that it would be a *singles hoping to mingle* kind of thing. My shutters would have come firmly down on that.

John is cute, funny, and we connected over the last few days. But I could sense the old Hannah coming back into play, and I put a stop to where things were going so fast that poor John looked a bit stunned. I watch him now, eyeing up one of the female ski instructors, and know he's moved on. Nicole and I have already made plans to go on a wine-tasting tour tomorrow to give the skiing a break, to give our feet a rest from the cumber-

some ski boots. It's nice, finding something in common with people, making new friends. I wish I'd done this in Thailand.

My dad often says the one thing we learn from history is that
we never learn anything from history. I'm feeling a heady mixture
of pride and contentment that I've not let that happen to me
again.

I come home renewed, invigorated, revived, ready for life, and
with a clutch of new friends. Nicole and I have agreed on a date
to meet up, and John asked if we could swap numbers, which I
could hardly say no to, but which came with the unsaid caveat
that we have friend-zoned each other.

I can't help remembering that this time last year Davey and I
were knee-deep in whatever it was we had together. He's not
going to call. I know that now. He didn't contact me after he saw
me on the platform. I'm not sure if he's still in London, if he's
moved here permanently, or if he was passing through and is now
back in Texas. But I hope, whatever he's doing, he's happy. I think
about that moment at the train station more often than I should.
If I allow myself to really analyze that day, that moment—what it
meant . . . what it didn't mean—I can't. I just can't. I hope he's
happy and healthy, wherever he is now.

Chapter 37

Davey, March

I'M MAKING PACCHERI with Sicilian red prawns and fresh arugula. When I say I'm making it, I'm really *making* it. From scratch. The paccheri pasta is wide and tubular, and chef Marco is teaching me how to roll and form the thick, fresh bands.

The trattoria is tiny, and the comforting smell of wood from the pizza oven emanates all day inside, while most of the seating is outside in the square, surrounded by the pale, sand-colored buildings of Montepulciano. The architect in me salivates over that square, the handmade uniformity of the medieval buildings that glow under the bright Italian spring sunshine. And in the distance, down the hill, tall cypress trees stretch all the way into the horizon. Although I don't see too much of the view, because I spend most of my days inside the tiny kitchen. I am in my element in here. I'm doing something I love.

"You're smiling," Marco says, leaning over my shoulder as I take the small roller and move it over the pasta ribbons, removing it gently and starting on the next. Something as simple as pasta is a real labor of love. How did I not see that before?

I'd been happy before. But it feels like a long time ago. Now that I'm happy again, putting aside thoughts of how sick I might get, whether the cancer may return, where it will strike when it does. If I get a headache for more than a day, does that mean it's returned and chosen my brain as its point of reentry? I know I will never stop looking for lumps that shouldn't be there or for any kind of sign—anything at all. But, honestly, I don't totally know where to look. So I'm going to be mindful, but I'm not going to let it dominate every waking moment the way it did before. I am lucky to still have waking moments, and I'm doing other things with them now. I no longer feel sorry for myself. I survived. I get to live.

I made friends with a woman from New York who began teaching me Italian. I met her on a little culinary course I found in Rome. Then we went traveling together. She was waiting for her boyfriend to join her later and we buddied up backpacking our way through Italy, saying goodbye when we reached Tuscany. I hadn't intended to continue through Italy. I don't really know how long I'm going to spend here. But I'm enjoying myself. I check in with my doctor every couple of months, and I know I have to get blood tests and a scan soon. I know Dr. Khader will tell me when. My newfound sense of adventure has been hard to ignore. *You've got to live, Davey—do something with that life now: something new, something different.*

I listen to Marco, the chef/owner of his tiny family-run trattoria, give me instructions in very slow Italian as I make another dish, whipping ricotta ready to go into the sweet, fried cannoli dough, and I no longer feel like a responsible adult, an architect. I feel younger again, like I'm fresh out of college and am traveling under my own steam, which is something I never actually did before.

Marco's being kind because he knows I'm excited to learn his craft. He also speaks incredibly good English and overheard me talking to Dr. Khader one day on the phone, so I sense he's put two and two together and knows something was once very amiss in my life. But we're persevering in slow Italian and then, when I give him a look that indicates I have no idea what he's just said, he switches to English. He's patient.

We met when he came outside his restaurant kitchen to smoke a cigarette. I was sitting on his terrace in the town square, treating myself to one of his dishes from the specials board, and enthused about how great it was. It was one of the most beautiful trofie pasta dishes I'd ever had, with chestnuts and Fontina cheese, finished with a hazelnut gratin. I joked that I'd wait tables and clean dishes if he'd teach me how to make it, and he took me seriously. When it was clear that my Italian wasn't quite up to waiter-level, Marco politely put me in the kitchen full-time, washing pans, chopping vegetables, prepping fruit, and learning. I'm going to stick it out for a few more months until summer, when my full-time culinary course starts and I have to leave Marco.

When we finish last service and I've stacked the chairs outside, Marco stands on the terrace overlooking the main square and hands me a beer, taking a sip of his own. Usually he hands me a coffee, but today he's chosen a Peroni for both of us. I haven't drunk anything in more than a year, not since New Year's Eve, when I was readying myself to go to London; to go to Hannah. I wonder what she's doing now. I try to shake her from my head. After that last night of partying, life went downhill. Since chemo I've found it difficult to drink alcohol. I wonder if I should drink this. I'm healthy now. In remission. I look at the Peroni as if it holds the answer.

"You have earned it," Marco says.

"Not talking to me in Italian tonight?" I ask.

"It has been a long day. I do not have the energy," he jokes.

We clink bottles and I take a sip from mine. It turns out I've missed beer. Marco pulls out two of the chairs I've just stacked and sits on one, pushing the other in my direction. His shirt's open at the neck and he looks cool, at ease with himself. Two young women look at him as they wander past and he calls something brazenly in their direction that I can't translate quickly enough. They laugh, despite themselves, one shaking her head. He raises his bottle in their direction.

Despite all of this, his first and only passion is his food. I tell him this and he shakes his head. "There is always time for women."

"I don't *see* you with any," I point out.

"I am discreet," he says with a smile. "Mamma would not approve of the kind of women I take home." He nods his head inside toward the bar, where his mother is cleaning the last of the glasses and readying herself to leave. "This is why I do not live at home anymore."

In his pocket his phone beeps. He pulls it out, types something quickly, and replaces it. It makes me smile. Marco has a good life.

"You've got a girlfriend now?" I inquire.

He leans forward conspiratorially. "I have three."

"What?" I splutter. "How? And also, might I add, how do you have the energy?"

He shrugs. "I just do."

"Do they know about each other?"

"No. Of course not. I am not stupid."

I now can't work out if Marco has a good life or a terrible one. Three women at once. That sounds like work. Hard work. Busy. Maybe also a bit lonely.

"And you?" he asks. "A string of women in the US? Their faces sad because you came to Italy? Hearts broken?"

"No." I shake my head slowly, offer no more. I think of Charlotte. Her heart anything but broken. If she was sad, she didn't show it. I think she was merely angry that I'd broken it off with her again. And then I think of Hannah. Hannah, who I let go.

"Davey has no time for women? Davey is a . . ." He clicks his fingers, thinking. "Not a nun—the other word . . ."

"A monk," I offer. "No, I'm not a monk."

"Hmm," Marco says, looking at me. If he's waiting for details, he's not going to get them.

Sensing this, he stands, downs half his beer in one fluid movement. "I have a date," he says with a wink. "I will see you tomorrow, my friend." He stacks his chair, fist-bumps me, grabs his things from inside.

I watch as he and his mother leave, lock up, exchange goodbyes. I lean back in the chair for a while watching the night's activities in the square, the streetlights, the people milling around. I sip my beer slowly, taking my time to enjoy the solitude.

I'm half a beer in and maybe because, to a man who's been sober for more than a year, half a beer feels like four beers . . . I'm feeling warm and a tinge of drunkenness filters into my bloodstream. I'm about to do something stupid. I open my phone, pull up Hannah's information, look over her old messages. I go right back to the start, follow our trail together, smile at the ones exchanged when I misdialed her, the ones arranging our first call, the ones arranging our next and then our next. I pull up the pictures I have of her. Every part of me tightens when I see her. And then I think of her on that platform, staring at me as if I was a ghost.

What is she doing now, right now? The sky is clear here tonight. Is it clear where she is now? Can she see the same stars I can? Is she looking up? Is she watching Netflix? Is she out with her friends? Is she with that guy? I want so much to know who he is. Is it the same guy she messaged me about before? The one she told me she was happy with? Or is she with someone new? I'm not sure which of these two options would hurt me more. Ah, fuck it. There is nothing I can do about any of this. I'm here. She's there. We're on the same continent finally. The distance between us has finally gotten smaller.

But right now she has never felt further away.

Chapter 38

Hannah, April

IT IS CLEAR that in my next life I am not coming back as a wedding planner. This is *hard*. But Miranda's all over it, loving every second. No bridezilla for her. A couple of months ago she found her wedding dress on a discount site, ordered it, tried it on, and invited me over to see. I was looking forward to an outing to a posh bridal store, a woman with a double-barreled last name who thought herself far superior to us, handing us a glass of champagne while we awaited a series of big dress reveals. What I got was actually better. Miranda didn't even wait for me to arrive. She opened her front door to me wearing the dress and demanded, "What do you think?"

I cried. She looked perfect. She even let me try it on. It drowned me, obviously, because I'm not five foot eleven thousand, like Miranda. But even I had to admit that wedding dresses get a good rep for a reason. And then afterward Miranda got her spreadsheet and ticked things off, highlighting columns, clicking and dragging.

In Paul and Miranda's flat, with only weeks to go before the big day, we have what Miranda thought was going to be an awkward conversation. I could see it in her face: that look of near-dread as she asked me if I *needed* a plus one.

Of course I didn't. Who would I take? And if it meant she could loosen up that hallowed place at the wedding breakfast for someone else, then I was more than happy to enable that. Besides, I'll have Joan and Geoff for company and, in my newfound state of making new friends everywhere I go, I'll enjoy doing just that. I'll dance with strangers and come home happily single.

"As long as you don't put me at the singles table," I say pointedly. "I need Joan and Geoff at the very least."

"We're not having a singles table," Miranda says and then she screws up her face. "Who even does that?"

We nod our agreement at the worst of all wedding horrors.

"Unless you've got fit men coming, of course," I say, but I'm unsure if I actually mean this or not. "I still don't want to date anyone, but I can always be swayed by a pilot in full outfit, obviously."

"No fit men." She casts her eyes over at Paul, who's staring unblinkingly at his PlayStation as he continues guiding little men playing football across the screen. "All Paul's single friends are unattractive," Miranda whispers.

I nod sagely and Paul glances over at us, smiles, looks back at his screen. "She's right, they are. Miranda bagged the best one of my group of mates."

Miranda looks at me. "Fact." And then she agrees to sit me with Joan and Geoff, filling it in on her sheet. "Done."

I am envious. I know it's terrible to admit it, but I am. I haven't even been yet, but I know it's going to be the wedding of the year. Weddings overseas are either the most exciting thing ever or a financial burden for guests. I've been invited to so many foreign weddings that, in the end, the combined cost of attending hen weekends, then airline tickets and hotels for the actual events themselves, was starting to bankrupt me. I had five in one summer once, dotted all across Europe. That's the summer my parents had to have a frank conversation with me about money. How to earn it. How *not* to spend it all in one go.

But this. This is different.

This wedding is in Italy.

Chapter 39

May

I'M DESPERATE TO see a Tuscan poppy field. It's the end of spring and the poppies are in full bloom. From my room at the top of one of the most beautiful sand-colored old hotel buildings I've got a great view over the rest of the hilltop town, which slopes gently downward toward the valleys and the vineyards beyond. I'm in the attic space and I have to duck to move around the low beams but, with the windows open, the sun streams in and lights up my room.

As I look out the window I can see a flash of scarlet from here and I know they're there, waiting for me. If I don't stand in a poppy field even for just a minute and let the sea of delicate red flowers surround me, I'm going to burst. I have no idea when I'm going to do that, though, because Miranda's schedule is frenzied.

Cobbled stone streets and cream brick walls give the town an air of calm. Before the big day itself, there's me, Miranda, Paul, and their respective close families. We're spending the days before the big event sightseeing and then the evenings eating at little trattorias all over town.

I've caved in and purchased a copy of E. M. Forster's *A Room with a View*. I'm so scared it's not going to be as good as the film, but I have at least purchased a copy of the novel. As yet I've not opened it. Just being here makes me feel like the heroine, Lucy

Honeychurch. I glance at it guiltily as Miranda knocks on my door, collecting me as we go sightseeing.

Over the course of the next few days we visit the Duomo—the cathedral—go wine tasting, and visit at least three churches. I'm reminded of being with George and the endless temples he wanted to explore. When Miranda's mum suggests our fourth church, I have to call time. I could do with a little bit of sitting in the sunshine, reading my book, drinking a large glass of local wine, and letting the world pass me by. As they decide to head off to a church at the bottom of the hill, I go to my room, retrieve my book, and wander into the main square, the Piazza Grande. The buildings on all four sides are low-level, a mix of reds and sand-colored fourteenth-century architecture, and in one corner of the square there's a trattoria with only a couple of empty tables outside. I have next to no Italian to hand, but I sit, convey myself well enough to the waiter, and, feeling hungry, decide to order something to eat. I don't remember the last time I ate alone in a proper restaurant. The Pret near Liverpool Street Station doesn't count.

I usually order lasagna, but today I get brave, look for something I'd never normally order (other than the wine, which of course I ordinarily order), and sit back, taking in the locals carrying their bags of fruit and vegetables home, their fresh bread. I watch the tourists, phones in hand, navigating the streets, reading about the buildings in front of them. When did guidebooks get replaced by phones?

I'm in heaven as I tuck into my little plate of appetizers: courgettes fried in a light batter and stuffed with mackerel, olives, cherry tomatoes, and capers. Next to it is a pile of fresh pink shrimp with burrata and then a heap of anchovies, fried in Parmesan, tomato, and pesto. I've opened my book, but am only one page in before I've eaten everything on my plate.

The waiter emerges to top up my water glass, spies my empty plate, and jokes, "You did not like it?"

I laugh. "It was heaven. Your menu is amazing."

"Yes, it is," he says proudly. "Would you like something else to eat? An entrée, if an appetizer was not enough?"

"It's probably enough for now," I say. I'm still not back to my usual weight, even all these months after George and I broke up. And I still can't eat as much as I would like to, which is a good thing, I'm sure. But now as I look over this divine menu, I think I'll come back to Italy. I'll try to come here again and take it at a slower pace. Maybe I'll start taking life at a slower pace more generally, make some time to eat out at restaurants on my own some nights. That said, I'm not going to slow down much more before tomorrow. Tomorrow is the wedding, and I have a bridesmaid's dress to fit into.

Chapter 40

Davey

IT'S TIME FOR me to leave. Marco's convinced me to stay around for an extra day to help with an event. He's been prepping for this for weeks and could really do with the extra pair of hands, so I decide to stick around for another twenty-four hours. And then I'm gone, off to my next adventure.

I've come to a realization. It has taken me a long time, a change of direction, a new hobby, and a different continent but, after my summer at culinary school, I will need to go home. The thing is, I don't know where home is. I don't have my apartment anymore or my old job. I can't live with my mom and dad again. Not at my age. I need to find a new place to exist. A new life to forge. I need to settle, to be present, to be more permanent.

I think I need to go and discover this about me—where I fit, where I should be. That's the next step in this adventure. I'm not sure I want to continue to be as nomadic as I have been. But I need to know where home will be.

Chapter 41

Hannah

MIRANDA AND PAUL marry in the town hall in the Piazza Grande. Kew Gardens was swanky, but it's got nothing on this Renaissance palazzo. I've just watched two of my favorite people say, "I do," and I confess my eyes wandered too much toward the grand, ornate furniture, antiques, and gilt-framed portraits held within.

While Paul and Miranda sign documents and the photographer takes their pictures, Joan, Geoff, and I sit in the second row of chairs, watching our friends look so contented and happy while a harpist plays a selection of pop songs melodically on her strings. This was Paul's concession to having a harpist at all—that there be no real classical music. It had to be recognizable. We're having fun trying to identify what we're listening to.

"It's 'Fix You' by Coldplay," I offer tentatively for the second time. I have no idea.

"It's 'Bitter Sweet Symphony' by the Verve," Geoff retorts knowledgeably as the harpist moves steadily into her second tune. Both Joan and I turn to him.

"Oh, you won't score coffee with us, but you'll play this game," Joan mutters.

"I understand this game," Geoff replies. "And I'm good at it." Joan and I have to nod our agreement reluctantly as, the very moment the next one starts, Geoff practically shouts with joy, "It's 'F.E.A.R.' by Ian Brown."

I give him a look. "Geoff," I whine, "you're not even giving us a chance to guess."

"You can guess the next one, as long as you don't say 'Fix You' by Coldplay for the third time."

As we file out into the gentle Tuscan spring sunshine and throw pale dried-petal confetti toward the bride and groom, I realize how lucky I actually am to have friends whom I count as family.

I look over to the restaurant in the corner of the piazza as we leave the ceremony. Miranda chose this restaurant to cater for the wedding after reading the Tripadvisor reviews. She'd approached them and negotiated directly with the owner/chef and said it was far cheaper than hiring a caterer. Sometimes she just knows what she wants and goes for it. I wish I was more like that. Although recently I think I'm not a million miles away from getting there. Making choices, decisions, powering under my own steam. It's led to me being genuinely happy.

Waiters and waitresses begin carrying trays over to us and we take glasses of Prosecco and little skewers of antipasti to nibble as we walk across the square toward the private enclave where we're going to eat, drink, and be merry for the next few hours.

I see the waiter who served me yesterday and smile at him. He doesn't recognize me, which is mildly disconcerting. I'm not wearing *that* much more makeup today compared to yesterday. Crikey, am I so forgettable? I neck my glass of Prosecco and make a beeline for a sleek-looking Italian waitress, who looks mildly alarmed at the number of us British people swooping in on her and her Prosecco tray. I'm no different, but I do at least give her a thank-you and a smile as I take the remaining three glasses for myself, Joan, and Geoff. They're only halfway through their first ones and look at me and my eagerness with curiosity.

We're led into a garden area, where in the distance six large circular tables have been set up with white linen tablecloths, napkins, and small jars of wild flowers. Other than the flowers and the glassware, everything is white. White fairy lights are draped around the cream brick walls, where hanging potted plants dot the masonry and tea lights flicker in the breezeless afternoon.

Miranda comes over to us and we hug her in turn and give her our congratulations.

"It looks like an Instagram picture," I squeal.

"I know!" she squeals back. "I'm supposed to be mingling, so obviously I'm starting with you three and I'm not moving until Paul gives me a look."

"You were right when you said no fit men," I say and give her a little elbow nudge for fun.

"I know—sorry. Still, a few of those waiters are quite good-looking."

"A few of those waiters look about nineteen," I chastise her.

"So?" remarks Joan seriously, and Geoff gives Miranda and me a "what the fuck?" look.

We settle in for the wedding breakfast. I've never understood why it's called a breakfast when it's always quite clearly lunch. The waiters wheel in wagons heaped with a colorful array of meats, cheeses, and breads for us to pick on, and we're encouraged to hover, plate up our own, and indulge until the main course arrives. Miranda confessed that the only bridezilla moment she was going to have was making sure that the food was mostly beige. With an ivory wedding dress, she wasn't taking any chances with marinara-sauce spillages, and so the main course is a trio of pastas that I hoover up readily, with my favorite being orecchiette in cream with crispy asparagus spears, toasted pine nuts, and burrata. I never thought it was possible to love pasta quite as much as this and, when it's gone, I look longingly around just in case there's more being offered out. There isn't.

And then I cry buckets when it's time for the speeches as I watch Miranda's dad give the loveliest speech about the day she was born. And to finish, the best man tells lots of jokes about blow-up dolls, and how Paul wrote all his French verbs up his arm and cheated his way to a B in his GCSE. We laugh. His mum's face falls slack in horror. Which makes us laugh even more.

After the speeches I'm polite enough to remember that I need to turn to the person on my other side and engage him in conversation too, as he's finished talking to the guest on his other side.

It's one of Paul's buddies called Jim, and we discuss holidays and Italy and Tuscany. We've neither of us been here before, but I've had the benefit of a few days here now and Jim's decided to stay on a bit longer, so we talk about where he could go. I pull my phone out, show him some pictures of the churches . . . oh, so many churches, galleries, museums, vineyards.

And then he tells me that all he's seen so far are the poppy fields, which are beautiful. That he borrowed a bike from his hotel and cycled there and back yesterday.

"How long to cycle?" I ask.

"About half an hour. They're beautiful."

I'm quiet, thinking about how I could achieve seeing a poppy field before I fly home tomorrow. I don't think it can be done. There's no time, with the wedding today and my silly-early flight tomorrow.

"If you want to borrow the hotel's bike, I'm sure I can wangle that," he volunteers. "The route's easy enough—simply follow the main road out of town and down the hill."

I think of those flashes of red I can just about see from my hotel window. I have to go. I have to see the poppies. Half an hour of cycling. Ten minutes standing in the field and then half an hour back. If I do this, I have to ask Miranda if I can sneak off in the middle of her wedding, whether she'll mind.

I tell Joan and Geoff what I'm planning to do, and Geoff says if I'm off to stare at a field, then he's going to sneak off for a nap, the way men of a certain age can get away with doing.

"Of course you guys go and chill for a while," Miranda volunteers. "They've opened the clock tower especially for us, if anyone wants to go up and look at the view. Some of the guests will go and do that. So there's a bit of downtime. We aren't cutting the cake until much later on. Just be back for eight o'clock, if that's OK? Until then we're sitting around, listening to a singer, soaking up the sun, drinking limoncello, and mingling."

Jim and I make a beeline for his hotel. He's going to borrow a bike for me and send me on my way down the road, and I promise to return it in an hour and a half or thereabouts, once I've whizzed down to the poppy fields and back. I am giddy with excitement. I don't think the poppy fields are going to be life-changing. But I know that I'm here, in Italy, and I have to get to them.

Chapter 42

Davey

MARCO SAUNTERS IN as I'm putting the finishing touches to the tiramisu. I've only been working with him for a few months and this is the busiest day we've had. Marco was thrilled to be offered this contract, thrilled by the money and by the kudos that the bride and groom chose his restaurant over all of the others in town. This tiramisu is the biggest dish I've ever worked on and I can't believe how trustworthy he's being, leaving me with it.

An opera singer starts up across the square, over in the gardens. I can hear her faintly. I've been in the kitchen all day and Marco tells me I need to get out, grab some fresh air. I spy one of our waiters looking totally zapped. He's carrying trays of empty coffee pots and waits for Marco's mom to refill. They look beat, so I volunteer for both roles, giving them five minutes to catch their breath. I refill two pots, grab fresh cups from the special china brought in for the event, and leave the trattoria, walking into the sunlight. It's so bright I need sunglasses, but I don't have any. My eyes adjust slowly. I think it's being stuck in the kitchen all day. I was happy in there. But now that I'm outside it's good to see the scenery.

I carry the coffee over to the garden, cast my eyes around for anyone who looks like they want any. I'm not a natural waiter, but given that Marco assures me the guests at this wedding are mostly English, I'm fairly sure there's no language barrier here.

A guy walks past me, heads to an older woman at a table, and sits near her. She turns in my direction, spies the coffee pots I'm carrying, and gestures for me to come over.

I give her a smile as she says, "Caffè, per favore." She turns to the young guy next to her. "I try. That's about as far as my Italian extends."

"Mine too," I say.

She looks up at me. "Well, *you're* not Italian. The blond hair should probably have given that away, shouldn't it?"

I smile, pour coffee for her, yawn, and then apologize. "Would you like some?" I offer the guy and he shakes his head.

"You look exhausted, mate," he says. "Do you want to take a seat?"

The opera singer is going full pelt and although it's not my kind of music, it adds something to this indulgent atmosphere. But I can't sit with the guests, surely? Isn't that a bit awkward?

"Nah, it's OK. I don't want to intrude. I'll watch her from over there," I offer, gesturing to one of the stone pillars by a portico, with fairy lights and white flowers wrapped around it.

"No, sit, please," the woman says. She glances around. "If you won't get into trouble, have a coffee, wake yourself up a bit."

It's not a bad idea and so I nod and take a seat next to her. The other seats are empty, the detritus of the food long since cleared away by my colleagues. There's a mobile phone on the table with a pink cover on it, in the empty place I'm sitting at, and I push it toward the woman, assuming it's hers.

"Oh, that's my friend's. I didn't realize she'd left it here."

The guy sitting with us barely acknowledges our conversation, and I wonder if these two actually know each other well or if they've just been seated together here, random guests, friends for a day and then . . .

That happens all too much in my life, I realize, especially now. Friends for a day. Or for a few months. And then, nothing. Gone.

Why do weddings make me morose? Why this one? I was better off in the kitchen. Marco's getting ready for the evening buffet. I can see the band assembling their instruments in the far corner. The atmosphere will change soon. I'll get up when the opera singer's finished, head back inside, out of sight of people.

The guy looks over. "She'll be back soon," he says to the woman. So he *was* listening. "I put her on a bike to the poppy fields. She won't be long. An hour maybe?"

I yawn again.

"Pour yourself a coffee," the woman instructs me and she lifts a cup from my tray, pours me a strong black coffee, inhales its aroma. "My husband's gone for a nap. I should have just told him to have one of these."

"Do you live here?" the guy asks me.

"Temporarily," I confess. "Learning how to cook with the chef."

"Well, the food is excellent," the guy remarks. "Truly. Brilliant. I stuffed my face."

The woman nods enthusiastically.

"I'll tell the chef. He'll be overjoyed." As am I, having helped to cook some of it.

They're intrigued that I'm an American in Italy, ask me about places to visit, where I recommend, how long I'm here for. The woman makes me laugh and punctuates her sentences with the odd swear word. I sense she's had a bit to drink. I like her immediately.

The guy gets up and takes his coffee with him, tells both me and the woman next to me, "Nice to meet you both. I'll keep an eye on the time and check your friend comes back safely," he tells her.

The woman picks up her friend's phone, slips it inside her own handbag for safekeeping, and tells the guy, "Thanks."

"Nice to meet you," I say in return. I wonder if that's my cue to go too, but I don't want to leave this woman by herself, so I don't. I stay awhile longer.

The singer moves into her next song and I'm strangely trans-fixed, calm. I have no idea what this song is, but the woman I'm sitting with hums along a little, takes a sip of her coffee. "Oh yes, this isn't Nespresso, is it?"

I laugh. "Lavazza."

She nods wisely. "This is, without question, a five out of five. And I hardly ever score a five."

I turn from the opera singer, give this woman my full attention while my mind processes what she's said. A pause, just for a beat, and then I ask, "Is grading coffee a British national pastime or something?"

The woman laughs and smiles awkwardly, a mix of proud and embarrassed. "No," she confesses. "It's a sport that I and my next-door neighbor indulge in. My husband thinks we're nutters, standing in the cold, rating Nespresso flavors out of five. He, not so secretly, thinks we should grade them out of ten, or at least create a more cohesive scoring system, rather than picking a number out of thin air."

I nod, take a sip of my coffee, but my brain has gone some-where else, back in time to a conversation I had long ago with someone else about grading coffee. "Your neighbor?" I ask.

"Yes, it's the only time I get to see her really, over the garden fence."

I think. My brain isn't catching up, not yet. Maybe because I'm so tired. And I don't want to ask the question. I don't want to mention her name, so I don't ask what her neighbor's called. Because it can't be Hannah. Her neighbor *can't* be Hannah. So I don't ask. I don't let myself think it.

They say each person is connected to everyone else in this world by only six other people. Six degrees of separation. Six people stand in the way between me and every other person on this planet. Allegedly. And I look at this woman to my right, this woman I've just met, and I dare so tentatively to think that she's not six people away from Hannah, she's so much closer to Hannah than that. And when my silence goes on too long and I can't hear the opera singer anymore, because all I can hear is the beat of my heart in my chest getting harder, faster, I turn to her, dare to ask . . . "Is your name Joan?"

She stares at me and I think the air just got sucked out of this garden as she replies, "How on earth did you know that?"

Ten minutes later, Joan's gripping my arm hard as she pulls me away from the table, toward the bride and groom. I can't speak, can't think. I'm barely walking. So Joan's doing it all for me, since we established that she is who she is and I am who I am.

The bride steps forward and accuses Joan of "bagging off with a fit waiter while Geoff sleeps off his lunch."

Joan shakes her head and, with wide eyes, she says to the bride, "I need to borrow you for five minutes."

Joan and this newly married woman move away from the small circle of friends we've interrupted and walk toward the portico. Then Joan looks at me, beckons me over.

The bride sweeps her eyes over me, once, twice. I feel self-conscious now, even more so than before.

And then Joan speaks. "Miranda, this is Davey."

Miranda smiles at me, extends her hand. "Hi, Davey. Are you one of Paul's friends?"

"No, I'm from the restaurant," I say automatically. I'm not here right now. Leave a message. This is *Miranda*. This is *Hannah's* Miranda.

"The food is great," Miranda says. "I can't wait for the cake," she goes on.

"Thank you. I'll pass on your compliments to the chef." I'm more than automatic now. I'm not even aware I'm speaking.

Joan cuts in. "Shut up about the food. This is Davey."

Miranda half laughs, half looks awkward. She speaks in an embarrassed sing-song voice. "So you said."

"Davey," Joan says again, more forcefully now. "As in *Hannah's* Davey."

Miranda looks from me to Joan and then back again. She tips her chin up. "What?" she asks slowly.

Joan nods. "Hannah's Davey," she repeats, and the three of us are standing in a strange triangle of total disbelief.

"Hannah's Davey?" Miranda says slowly. "Hannah's Davey. Is . . . here?"

I nod. There's very little else for me to do. Or say. I don't know what I can say that would sound even remotely normal.

"What are you doing here?" Miranda asks. Her voice is an octave higher than it was before. Incredulous.

"I work here. Or I did, for a while. I leave tomorrow."

Miranda's face goes slack and she blinks a few times. She looks like she wants to swear. "Fu-u-u-ck," she says eventually as she stares at me. "My God, you are like your pictures, now that I look at you."

She straightens, glances around. None of us speak until eventually the groom wanders over to us, looks at me.

"Hi," I say, because no one else is speaking.

"Hello, mate," he says a little tipsily. "I'll confess I've had a few beers and I know that I must know you, because you're at my wedding, but I'll be honest and say I can't remember where I know you from, or what the hell your name is."

Miranda and Joan look lost. I know I do too, but I extend my hand out of habit and say, "I'm Davey."

"Nice to meet you, Davey . . ." and he extends his hand, but stops halfway, steps closer, scrutinizes me. He looks at Miranda as if he wants to say something but doesn't know how.

"Davey?" he questions. "Not . . . ? Not . . . ?" He casts a look at me. "Er . . ."

"Yes," Joan chimes in. "He's *that* Davey."

"What. The. Fuck?" Paul replies. "For real? Did Hannah invite you?"

"Ssh for a second—I need to think," Miranda says. "Actually, where is Hannah? I don't think we should spring you on her, but I can't see her."

At this I straighten. "Hannah's *here*?"

Miranda nods.

Of *course* Hannah would be here. This is Miranda. This is Hannah's best friend. Of course she'd be at her best friend's wedding. Oh my God, Hannah is here. I don't know what to do. Other than that almost-time on the train, I've never met her in real life. I never got that chance. Fate or something resembling fate had other plans for me, made sure I never met her. And then *I* made sure I never met her, never called her.

And now . . . she's here. And I'm here. And I'm scared. What if she doesn't want to see me? What if she hates me? This is Hannah . . . who I liked, who I was falling for, and with whom I ended things. I refused to speak to her. I never thanked her for encouraging me to go in for my last round of chemo. Between her and Grant, they saved my poor excuse for a life. I didn't treat her the way I should have. I should leave this wedding now. I shouldn't be upending things for Hannah again, especially as she's with someone else now. I tell Joan I think this is going to do more harm than good.

"Don't talk rot," she commands. "They're not together anymore. He wasn't the one for her. That girl cared about you, worried about you, and I'm pretty bloody sure she loved you."

"Oh Jesus!" I rub my hand across my face. What the hell do I say to that? I can't tell her I felt the same. I can't tell Joan anything like this. But even if Hannah's not with that guy anymore, can I do this—can I just walk into her life as if nothing's happened?

Miranda chimes in, "If you think you're walking away again now, then I'm going to make Paul . . . no, I'm going to make Joan hold you down, while I work out what on earth to do next."

I look at Paul, who shrugs, sips his beer.

Miranda speaks. "Don't you fucking dare leave," she warns me. She's rummaging in Paul's trouser pocket for a mobile phone, taps urgently into it. Next to me, Joan's handbag rings, and Joan is forced to explain what's happened as Miranda hangs up after her fruitless dialing of Hannah's phone.

I have to do something. This isn't about them. This is about me. This is about Hannah. It's finally my turn to take action. "I'm going to go and find her," I say determinedly. And they all look at me as if they doubt my U-turn, as if they're still expecting me to run.

I know this is what I need to do. Whatever happens: Hannah and I, we *have* to meet. I don't know if we should be together. I don't know if she even wants me after all this time. But I do know that I have to find out. I have to look her in the eye and I have to apologize. I have to see her, in real life. I have to do at least these few things before we go our separate ways.

"She's in the poppy fields on the main route out of town," Joan says. She has a look of excitement about her.

I nod. "OK," I say quietly.

I turn and then Miranda calls me back. "I know you've had a rough time of it," she says. "And I can't imagine what you've been through. But if you find her, and if you break her heart a second time, I will track you down and I will gut you like a fish."

My mouth falls open. But I nod. "That sounds fair."

I move slowly, walking away from them all, out of the garden, across the square. I know they're behind me, watching me, but I don't look back. I stare down at each of the cobbles underfoot as I cross the square until they form a blur, as I'm running. I'm running faster than I have in such a long time. I'm gripped by this quest now, in a way I know I once was before, last year. But it's back: that need to see Hannah. It's an overwhelming rush of adrenaline that hits me.

I burst into the restaurant. "I need your motorcycle," I tell Marco. "I wouldn't ask if it wasn't important."

"Cosa intendi?" Marco looks up from stirring a sauce.

"It's a long story. I need to borrow your bike. There's someone I need to find."

"Vita o morte?"

Now is not the time for me to dig deep, talk slow, try to respond in Italian. So I stick with my default setting of half-and-half. "I'm not gonna lie. It's not life-or-death. This is about something else. *Amore.*"

"Amore." Marco nods, reaching into his jeans pocket for his motorcycle keys. "Say no more, my friend." He tosses the keys to me and then points to his motorcycle helmet. "Take that too."

"Grazie, Marco."

Marco let me ride up and down the street on his bike for fun one night, after we closed. I got the hang of it, but I didn't enjoy it. "Donor-cycles" my mom calls them. I've had enough brushes with death recently. But now thoughts of falling off this thing— killing myself in the need to see Hannah—kinda feel worth it. Around the back of the restaurant I mount the bike, twist the key in the ignition, pull on the helmet, and ride it out of town toward the poppy fields.

Chapter 43

Hannah

OUT HERE EVERYTHING is so still, except the flowers, the smudges of orange-red poppies littering the field, blowing so readily against the lush green landscape, like a painting full of primary color that's come alive just for me. I've caught them in their glory. In a few weeks the poppies will start to fade away as spring comes to an end, making way for a heady Italian summer. But now they're so blowsy, the petals so thin and delicate. A row of tall cypress trees line the pathway and I prop Jim's borrowed bike against one of them.

Behind me the sandy-colored buildings of Montepulciano, perched on a rock and dominated by its medieval citadel, look down at me. Above me the Tuscan sky is deep blue. I sigh audibly, but there's no one to hear. I'm truly alone for the first time in I don't know how long, and I wonder how it is that although I live by myself I'm always with someone, with people, seeking company and never really knowing what to do with myself unless I'm busy. I never stand in silence in my flat. I'm always occupied. Or watching TV. Always moving. And so I do it now. I should close my eyes, but the scene surrounding me is too glorious for that: simple flowers, blowing gently and stretching into the surrounding fields and valleys. I need to spend less time running through Wanstead Flats and more time actually looking at the clumps of wildflowers when they grow. I'm always running. Never pausing. Never appreciating the simpler things.

Now I've seen the poppies, I don't want to leave. Not yet. I told Jim I'd be ten minutes here and I don't want to worry Miranda on her wedding day. But the sun is high in the sky and the poppies are so abundant.

I don't feel like Lucy Honeychurch in *A Room with a View,* although I should—here, like this. I feel like me. And this makes me smile even more. Being me isn't actually that bad. Maybe I've been searching for something that I had all along. Good things come to those who wait. And so I've waited to find out if I like me, and I think: I do, actually.

The stillness surrounds me but doesn't engulf me. I start walking further into the field. Ten more minutes. I'll spend just ten more minutes here, because this day isn't about me. It's about Miranda and Paul, and I should get back. But I reach down and my fingers skim the poppies as I walk further into the field. I've snuck off for long enough. I'm going to go back soon. I will.

Everything around me is silent. Except for the dull roar of a motorcycle on the road behind me.

Chapter 44

Davey

I CAN SEE her. She's in a pale-pink dress. My stomach knots, even though I'm nowhere near her yet. This is happening. This is actually happening. I pause on the bike and, because I am not a pro, it wobbles underneath me. I kill the engine, wheel it over to the cypress trees, put the kickstand down, and position it near a push-bike that's been left there. Hannah's. I lift off my helmet and put it on the seat of Marco's bike and then I begin panicking afresh. What do I look like? Is my hair neat? I look tired. The guy at the table told me that much. Will Hannah even recognize me? Will she want to recognize me? What will she say? Whatever it is, I can take it.

I start clicking my fingers nervously and then run my hand through my hair, which has grown back a little darker blond than before. I can't stand here all day. It's now or it's never. I've come this far. It has to be now.

Chapter 45

Hannah

THE MOTORCYCLE NOISE has stopped, thank God. I look around and can't see it or the rider, so they must have carried on down the road. I turn back to spend a minute more here and then it really is time to go.

As I turn to work my way back through the sea of poppies toward my bike I see a man walking through the cypress trees and into the field.

I continue moving and half wonder if he's the rider, stopped because he's seen a lone woman in a field and now is a great time for him to stop and mug someone unsuspecting. He's still at a distance, but as he moves closer I can make out how tall he is. He lifts his head and looks directly at me. I can't make out his features, but something makes me stop and stare. I glance around and then slowly begin walking again, but this time I'm at half the pace I was before. We're the only two people here, so it would be rude—strange—if I didn't at least acknowledge another person as I pass him. So I'll do that. I'll say hello and then I'll keep going, begin the cycle ride back to the wedding.

He moves toward me and I move toward him until we're about a hundred feet from each other, but as I open my mouth to greet this stranger, no words come out. I just look at him. I didn't realize I'd stopped walking but he's continued, closing the distance between us. And then he's so close that if I stepped forward, two or maybe three paces, I could reach out and touch him.

I blink once, twice, but still no words come. Because the man standing in front of me cannot possibly be who I think it is. I used to see him everywhere. I used to think I saw him in the street or on the bus. I used to think that when I went to work I'd open the main door to the office and there he'd be, waiting for me. And then there was the time I'm *positive* it was actually him, on the train, silently saying my name, no longer divided by a continent and five thousand miles, but only by a centimeter of window glass . . . and so much more; so much that has been said—and so much that hasn't been.

And so this man, in front of me in a poppy field in Montepulciano, cannot possibly be Davey. Although all the evidence tells me it is. My teeth are ground together and it's only when the pain begins ricocheting through my jaw, and another kind of pain finds its way to my heart, that I dare to breathe, dare to speak.

Only he gets there first.

"Hannah," he says, and the accent is unmistakably Davey's. The slow smile that spreads over his face is his. The same as he had on all our video calls and the photos I deleted. And I can't say anything. I can only nod, and then every emotion I held on to throughout all this time—and some I hadn't—bubbles to the surface and I cry. He steps forward. "Hannah," he says again, softer now. "Don't cry."

"You're here" is all I can muster. Disbelief floods my synapses.

He nods and his eyes never leave mine. "So are you."

"Yes," I mouth, but I'm not sure the words are audible.

He moves forward and brushes a stray tear from my face. "I am so, so sorry," he says.

"What for?" I ask. *Davey is here.*

"Everything. Everything I did. Everything I said. Everything I didn't say. Disappearing. I thought it would be like a Band-Aid, I thought saying goodbye to you would be like ripping it off and then the pain would leave me. I think I only just realized the pain stayed behind. Only you weren't there. I'm sorry, because I pulled you into something that wasn't yours to suffer and then, when you tried to be there, I wouldn't let you. I was sure it was for the best."

"You hurt me," I say, because it's the truth and because I can't think what else to say. He's actually here, standing in front of me. I was right, I do have to look up to see him; he's so tall. And his hair isn't quite as blond as it used to be, and now I can see his blue eyes so clearly that I notice little dashes of yellow almost forming a halo around both his irises. "I didn't know what to do. I wanted to help. You pushed me away."

"I know." He takes one of my hands and I can't believe how good it feels that, after all this time, he's touching me. His hands are bigger than I imagined they'd be. They engulf mine, and it's as if all the electricity in the world is coursing through us. "Your hands are really soft," he says. And there's a shocked laugh as if he can't quite believe I'm really here, what I feel like.

I can't believe he's really here, either, and I tell him as much.

But Davey has something he clearly needs to say and he steams onward. "Misdialing you . . . I don't know if that was fate. I'm not sure I believe in that. But finding you here—now—and this time you're actually in front of me. There's no denying that you and I are supposed to be here, in this field, and I'm supposed to tell you I'm sorry and I'm supposed to say thank you. And after that . . . Jesus, I have no idea what happens after that."

I clutch his hand in return now, my fingers folding around his tanned ones, because I don't know what he means by what he says, and because he's here and we might not have this chance again. I might not have this opportunity to hold his hand again, to touch him again. He might make another ridiculously noble gesture and cut me out of his life once more. I clutch his hand tighter. "Why are you saying thank you?" I ask.

"You saved my life."

I know I look puzzled. "How?"

"You called me and unequivocally demanded that I go in for my last round of chemo."

"You'd have done it without me."

"I'm not actually sure I would have. As Grant said, I was being a selfish prick. I did it because of what you said—about others killing for the chance to have the treatment I was on. The chance to live."

"How are you now?" I whisper. I hope beyond hope that the chemo has done what it was supposed to. The odds of him surviving only five years without it don't bear thinking about. I couldn't bear the thought of a world without Davey in it, even if he's in this world and not with me.

"I'm good. I think. My blood results have been good. I'm alive. I'm a little messed up in the head now," he says with a sideways smile. "But I'm here."

I look up at him. I want to smile along with him, but instead I whisper, "What now?"

He smiles even wider. "I don't know, Hannah."

"I kept seeing you everywhere. And you weren't there. And then you were. On the platform and then in the Tube carriage. It *was* you, wasn't it?"

He nods. "Yeah. It was."

"Where were you *going*?"

"Nowhere. Everywhere. I know I'm gonna sound like a dick if I say I went to find myself, especially when it didn't work. I didn't find myself. And so I went to find you, without finding you. I went to Whitstable."

My mouth opens. "Really?"

"I sat on that pebble beach looking out across the sea. I wanted to look at what you saw when we spoke that New Year's. I wanted to see the town you grew up in. I wanted to feel you there. And I did, to some extent. But I was too chicken to call you . . . The way we left things, the way I behaved, I genuinely thought you were better off without me."

I nod and then I shake my head. "Cutting me off, when all I wanted to do was be there for you . . . it was so hard. But I understand why you did it."

"I didn't want you to be a part of my illness. I didn't want the association you and I had to be because cancer pulled us together."

"That wasn't what pulled us together," I say. "I was already too far in by the time you got ill. But you let being ill drive us apart."

He takes a deep breath. "I know that now. I didn't have any energy to work out what was best for us. I didn't even know if we were going to be an *us*. I knew I liked you, and instead I thought I'd worked out what was best for you and that was to let you go. And through it all, I missed you. I missed you so much, and losing you hurt so much, and I couldn't tell anyone. I couldn't even tell you."

He takes my other hand in his and we're standing there, just the two of us in a field of scarlet poppies, our fingers entwined, when, a year and a half after he first misdialed me, I never thought anything like this would happen.

"I don't know what to do now," he confesses.

"Me neither." And then I do know what to do. I let go of one of his hands, let one of mine touch his face, run across his cheek. Finally I can feel him beneath my fingers, this man who's real, who's here, who's no longer so far away from me, who missed me, who I missed, and who I want to spend every day from here on getting to know, getting to touch, getting to kiss, getting to be with. And so I grow brave and I tell him. I tell him how much I want to know him, how much I want to be with him. And I try not to cry as he tells me he wants the same, how lucky we are that, after everything that's happened, we've been handed this second chance. Then he dips his head, puts his arms around me, pulls me so willingly against his chest, and every part of me comes alive as Davey kisses me in a poppy field in Tuscany. And it's everything I'd wanted it to be. And so much more.

Chapter 46

October

I'M AT THE airport waiting for Davey. I've been at this airport almost every weekend since we found each other in Italy. I've flown out of here, and I've waited for him to arrive here, more times than I can count after we stood in that field, our fingers entwined, and made plans. We agreed that he'd still start cookery school in Florence and that we'd fly to see each other in London and Italy on rotation, knowing it was only for the summer. I don't think I'd have cared if it had been forever. Home is a person, not a place.

But now it's different. We agreed to take one day at a time, and those days have merged into months and now we make plans for years to come, about when we'll fly to the US together for me to meet his parents. We make plans about where he's going to live in London. Or, rather, we don't make plans about that. I don't know if it's because he's going to stay with me for a while or if he's going to find somewhere close by. We still have so much to discover about each other and, luckily, so much time to discover it in.

I have flashbacks to that time I was here nearly two years ago, holding a banner, deliberating over whether I should ditch it in favor of buying a coffee for Davey. I was waiting for a man I'd never met, a man who never arrived. Only this time, here, now, it's different. This time he's actually coming. He messaged me, multiple times, before he boarded his flight from Italy. And again once he landed, so I know he's actually here, in this airport some- where. I'm waiting for him. He's waiting for me.

The summer's over, and Davey's finished his course at cookery school. The autumn chill has extended its way into the depths of the Arrivals hall. I pull my jacket around myself as people bustle past me, meeting old friends, loved ones. There's Christmas stuff in the shops in the airport already. I've always loved this time of year. Another new set of fairy lights has worked its way into my flat, this time snaking its way joyfully around the cupboards in my kitchen. And it's not even midway through October. I'm ready for Christmas. I'm ready for Davey. I'm ready for everything.

I receive a photo message from Davey as he's collecting his luggage. Two rucksacks, with his movable life inside. In the photo message at the conveyor belt his eyes look tired after his flight, but he's smiling conspiratorially and he's pointing at someone else in the photo behind him, who's also standing there. It's one of the presenters from a property show we've been watching simultane- ously some evenings, him in Italy, me in London.

And then, a few moments later, I look at the automatic doors as a six-foot-two blond American man walks toward me, carrying his bags. He approaches me and we hold each other tightly.

I stand on tiptoes to kiss him.

And then I take him home.

Author's Note

YOU MIGHT BE wondering why, when I sat down to write a love story, I chose to include a cancer diagnosis. And I'm here to tell you that it's because my love story also had one.

In the first few months of 2013, my husband, Steve, and I were just your average young married couple trying to plan our littler girl's second birthday party, wondering why she wouldn't sleep, why she ate like there was no tomorrow, and how we were going to manage childcare with both of us running our own businesses. I was running a PR company and hardly ever in the UK, and Steve was managing building sites in the southeast of England. We thought that life couldn't get much tougher.

And then Steve—young (only thirty-one), fit, healthy, non-smoker, not a heavy drinker, and very much an all-around active kind of guy—started feeling unwell. Not massively sick, just sick enough to lay in bed for a few days and complain of feeling so tired he couldn't move, saying that he just needed a rest. But by day three, even my unflappable husband was a bit unnerved.

And then came the fateful words: "One of my testicles looks a bit odd."

"How odd?"

"It's swollen to the size of an orange."

"And the other one?"

"Not the size of an orange."

Having read this book, I'm sure you can see where this is

going. And I could cut a long story short here, but I won't—because if you've got men in your life or if you're a guy reading this, I know a little information goes a long way, and that this is the kind of information that might just save your life or the life of someone you love one day. But Steve, unlike Davey, wasn't diagnosed right away. So strap in—we're going on a cancer misdiagnosis journey and you don't want to miss this.

I didn't rush to summon the doctor. I didn't think it was anything other than a blip, and neither did Steve. Instead I called my mum. Collectively, we had a little google (do *not* do this) and we diagnosed Steve with mumps even though he was "pretty sure I've been vaccinated against that."

But because our little girl hadn't yet been vaccinated, I whisked her off to my mum's to stay there while Steve recovered. The recovery for mumps is basically "ride it out," so that's what Steve did. Until two days later, when enough was enough and he got even sicker.

Madly enough, we look back at this time and realize that our dog knew something was seriously amiss even when we didn't. Dogs have a tremendous sense of smell and often have an intuition that we do not. Socks, our sensitive, clever little dog, took a big sniff of Steve and then curled up next to him in bed, whimpering and basically refusing to move from his side.

I booked an appointment with our doctor. We got a newly qualified doctor who had perhaps a little more enthusiasm than actual knowledge and who sent Steve home, agreeing with our self-diagnosis that he had mumps.

Another few days passed when we were told to wait for a blood test form that never came, while my husband was still in bed and turning grayer every day.

Cue some further phoning on my part as I became increasingly worried.

We finally managed to see a senior doctor who looked very

serious, and he organized to send Steve up the system to a specialist. We waited until finally Steve was summoned to have an ultrasound that, according to the sonographer, showed nothing.

"Does it hurt?"

"No." (By the way, it turns out that this is a massive red flag.)

"It doesn't hurt at all?"

"No."

"You're probably fine. It's probably an infection."

Sixth sense is a funny old beast. Steve was ecstatic at the news and smiled with triumph, even though he still looked (and felt) like shit. I, however, felt sick with worry and knew that something was so incredibly wrong. At home, Steve went back to bed and took more paracetamol, and I walked Socks after coercing him off Steve. Halfway around our usual walk, I pulled out my phone and gave my uncle—who worked at a private hospital—a call and said "Do you know any good urologists? I think Steve has cancer."

Enter the life-saving Henry Lewi, a man who by this time had already worked out years prior that sometimes seemingly innocuous things could possibly be contributing factors to testicular cancer—from sports injuries to police gear rubbing certain areas the wrong way. These particulars didn't relate to Steve but just go to show that Mr. Lewi had enough experience to know that this kind of cancer didn't spare men just because they seemed young and healthy.

He immediately sent Steve in for another ultrasound. I watched the specialist as she scanned over Steve's proverbial parts and then moved into his lower abdomen, before scanning his upper organs, then moving into his chest and up toward his neck. I remember thinking, *Oh my God, she's chasing something up.*

And she was. She'd found the tumor that wound its way from Steve's testicles into his chest. Steve had a blood test processed in record time, and we saw Mr. Lewi, to be told there was both good news and bad.

Spoiler alert: The bad news was that it was cancer.

This was a Wednesday, and Mr. Lewi's surgery list was full for the following Saturday, but he told us he'd spoken with his surgical team and they'd all agreed to come in and open the operating theater early because they needed to move fast.

When a private surgeon tells you on a Wednesday he can remove a tumor on Saturday, then believe me, you too will dig deep, hand him thousands of pounds you don't actually have, and pray it saves the one you love.

Of course, surgery wasn't the end of the journey. While the tumor had been removed, the cancer had already spread all over his body—meaning Steve also needed to undergo a serious chemo regimen. At that point, we had to leave the marvelous hands of Henry Lewi in the private sector and go back to the National Health Service (for any non-Brits reading this, that's our state-funded national healthcare system in the UK).

I have such deep respect for healthcare associates and nurses. They worked around the clock to keep Steve comfortable and to deliver his carefully spaced, carefully timed, and expertly dispensed chemo regimen, always doing so with smiles on their faces and a joke to keep his spirits up—even though he only smiled back every now and again in between bouts of throwing up and begging for it to stop, eventually asking to end the chemo regime after only two thirds of his treatment.

I wasn't as kind as Hannah is to Davey when Steve and I had that near-same conversation about stopping treatment with many of the same words. Our conversation was shorter, louder, and swearier. I won. And as a result, I'm writing this nearly ten years later while on vacation, watching Steve play in the pool with the kids.

After that final round of chemo, we felt like we were getting our lives back. We waited the required amount of time to start trying for another baby (chemo hangs around in the body for a long time, so Steve was too toxic to father a child for a while). We knew that the chances of getting pregnant again would be low, and we'd already decided not to risk tearing ourselves apart with IVF given Steve's, as he put it, "only-enough-for-one-shot jar offering."

And then, after a few months, amazingly, we naturally got pregnant with our second daughter. And after everything Steve had gone through, and after being told not to get our hopes up, she was born in 2015.

We've told our daughters what happened to Steve (leaving out some of the more graphic details), and once or twice we've jokingly called our second little girl a miracle baby. Because it is a bit of a miracle that we got pregnant at all after all of that. Steve's rightly very proud that even "firing on one cylinder," we still got our second child.

So now, because she misheard us the first time we told her, our miracle baby calls herself the "America baby." We don't correct her—it's funnier this way. And if she tells people that and they say "er what?" Steve and I just look at each other and knowingly say, "Don't worry. It's a long story."

So Steve and I got our happy ending, just like Hannah and Davey. And I hope our story—Steve's story—can help others find and keep their happy endings as well.

Acknowledgments

THIS BOOK WAS written through those long series of lockdowns when the seasons changed from spring to summer, to winter, and then back to spring again in the UK. *The Man I Never Met* is very different from the historical fiction I usually write under my real name, Lorna Cook. Potentially it's different *because* of those lockdowns. Not being able to spend time with friends or family gave me plenty of hours (once the horror of homeschooling was done!) to think about and to develop the idea for this book. I felt it was madness to write it, for two reasons. First, I'd never written in this genre. It turns out I do now and can't wait for you to read my second book as Elle Cook. But second, I felt this story wasn't mine to tell.

If you've read my Author's Note, you know this story is really my husband's story. And while I am not Hannah and Steve is not Davey, there were parts of his cancer diagnosis and treatment that I drew upon when writing it. The subject was incredibly personal to us both, but more so to him, and so I thank Steve here, over and over again, for letting me write part of his story into that of Hannah and Davey's.

When I tentatively asked Steve what he thought of the idea, he genuinely had to sit and think for a while. Eventually his words were, "If this encourages at least one of your readers to tell the men in their lives to check their downstairs regions regularly for any changes, irregularities, lumps, or bumps, then it's fine by me. So please do that."

Steve is always going to be my hero.

Likewise, I also dedicate this book to, and thank wholeheartedly, Mr. Henry Lewi, who we saw "just in case," but who identified immediately what was going on. There is no doubt whatsoever that Henry Lewi saved my husband's life.

That was ten years ago, and there are people I've met since then who I have to thank with bells on for bringing this book into the world. My agent extraordinaire, Becky Ritchie, believed in it enough to call it "really really special" (yes, Becky, I've kept that email in a little folder) when I submitted it after telling her I'd written something a bit different. The poor woman gets next to zero notice when I go off and do these things. Thank you for your amazing support and for guiding me through the fast-paced and heady pre-empt process along with everything you do behind the scenes. I'm grateful every day for everything you and the team at A.M Heath do.

To my wonderful editor, Emily Griffin, and her team, thank you for arriving at breakneck speed, making the editing process totally painless, and loving Hannah and Davey as much as I do. Likewise, to my lovely US editor, Caroline Weishuhn, thank you for jumping onboard and being a champion for the novel. And thank you to the brilliant Laurie Ip Fung Chun for your painstaking skills in taking the book toward the editorial finishing line.

Writing acknowledgments for a book that won't be out for a while means I'm invariably not going to know everyone who's been involved in the long process of bringing *The Man I Never Met* into the world. So to designers, proofreaders, copy editors, sales teams, marketers . . . those of you who've been involved with any and all stages of bringing Hannah and Davey to bookish life . . . thank you.

As ever, huge thanks to the Romantic Novelist's Association and my local Chelmsford chapter for gossip and lunches.

Write Club, our breakaway unit, is a thing of wonder, and I'm so grateful for encouragement and well-honed advice from Peter, Sue, Tracy, Nic, Karen, and Snoopy. What would I do without you all?

And to the Savvies on Facebook. You almighty team of incredible authors: always knowledgeable, ever sharing.

Thanks to Steve, Mum, Dad, Emily, Alice, Luke, Cassie, Natalie, Sarah, and Nicky for your unending support and for always showing how proud you are of me.

Authors would be nothing without their readers. So to you, lovely reader, thank you so much for buying this book, listening to it on audio, or borrowing it from the library. If you enjoyed it, it would be so wonderful if you could leave a review on Amazon or Goodreads. Reviews are everything. They feed me more than chocolate and wine could ever do (and more important, help readers find new books to read). And if you've been in touch to say hello, share pictures of reading my books in sunny locations or to say how much you enjoy them—I know how privileged I am that you take the time to do that. I've been very lucky to have so many of you on the journey with Lorna Cook, and if you've come on this next step with Elle as well, then I thank you from the bottom of my heart.

Come and find me on social media where I chat all things books, recommend reads from authors I love, share pictures of sunsets, beaches, books, wine, cake . . . and will happily chat away for hours on end.

With love, Lorna/Elle

About the Author

ELLE COOK worked as a journalist and in PR before becoming a full-time novelist. *The Man I Never Met* is her first contemporary novel. She is also the author of three historical time-slip novels under her real name, Lorna Cook. *The Forgotten Village*, *The Forbidden Promise*, and *The Girl from the Island* have sold over 200,000 copies combined. She lives in coastal Essex with her husband and two daughters.

www.lornacookauthor.com
Facebook: LornaCookWriter
Instagram: LornaCookAuthor
Twitter: LornaCookAuthor